Francisco Goya

Francisco Goya

EVAN S. CONNELL

COUNTERPOINT
A Member of the Perseus Books Group
New York

Frontispiece: *Portrait of Maria Theresa, Countess of Chinchon*, wife of the Spanish Prime Minister, Manuel de Godoy (1767–1851) by Francisco Jose de Goya y Lucientes (1746–1828). CREDIT: Private Collection/ Bridgeman Art Library.

Counterpoint books are available at special discounts for bulk purchases in the United States by corporations, institutions, and other organizations. For more information, please contact the Special Markets Department at the Perseus Books Group, 11 Cambridge Center, Cambridge MA 02142, or call (617) 252-5298, (800) 255-1514 or email specialmarkets@perseusbooks.com

Library of Congress Cataloging-in-Publication Data
Connell, Evan S., 1924–
    Francisco Goya / Evan S. Connell.
        p.   cm.
    Includes bibliographical references.
    ISBN 1-58243-307-0 (hardcover)
    1. Goya, Francisco, 1746–1828.   2. Goya, Francisco,
1746–1828—Criticism and interpretation.   3. Artists—Spain—
Biography.   I. Title.
N7113.G68C647   2004
759.6—dc22

                                                    2003015679

COUNTERPOINT
387 Park Avenue South
New York, NY 10016–8810

Counterpoint is a member of the Perseus Books Group.

10 9 8 7 6 5 4 3 2 1

To James and Jana Hamilton

As in all the turbulent periods which have foreshadowed crucial and violent phases in the history of mankind, many writers and artists tended to translate into their own idiom the repugnance they felt for an established but tottering order from which they wanted to dissociate themselves at all costs.

JEAN-FRANÇOIS CHABRUN

I

Doña María Teresa Cayetana de Silva, thirteenth Duchess of Alba, was by every account a mankiller. We are told that when she rode through the streets of Madrid citizens peered from their windows, children paused at their games. A French tourist, Marquis Fleuriot de Langle, obviously numbed by what he saw, wrote that every hair of her head incites desire. Nor was Doña María Teresa Cayetana unaware of her crowning glory; she disliked wearing a wig, although she was not above using kohl, rouge, and eyebrow pencil.

Again, again, and again we are told of abundant black hair, sparkling eyes, provocative little mouth, tiny waist. If we believe Marquis Fleuriot, she is impossible to surpass, nothing on earth could be more lovely. Lady Elizabeth Holland, who visited Spain in 1802, mentions her beauty, grace, popularity, wealth, and exalted rank. Moreover, Lady Holland remarks that she did not wantonly violate public standards, either in conversation or deportment. Her wealth was immeasurable—seventeen palaces or mansions and such tracts of land that people thought she could walk the length of Spain without stepping off her estates.

As good students of female nature may have guessed by now, the Duchess was cruel, an essential trait of mankillers rich or poor. Certain biographers assert the opposite, that she was kindness itself. No doubt this could be just as true; after all, a woman isn't a bolt of cloth, identical in texture from thread to thread.

She loved, or seemed to love, earth's disinherited. In the Alba entourage she kept a stuttering old monk named Basil, not too bright, incapable of doing much. She provided him with a mule so that he might accompany the party when she and her friends went riding, which was considerate, yet they enjoyed playing tricks on Brother Basil. In those days, of course, the nobility maintained fools, dwarfs, midgets, parrots, monkeys, hunchbacks, etc. for amusement. Cynics might observe that nothing has changed. Anyway, during one of these excursions Brother Basil slipped off his mule, or was thrown off, and ended up in a ditch. When he climbed out, or was helped out, the Duchess smothered him with kisses.

I understand him, she told her husband. I knew from the beginning that he had a soul like mine.

And there was young Lusito, Luis Berganza, whose father supervised the Alba estates. Lusito's job was to carry perfume and cosmetics. He probably couldn't read but once in a while the Duchess sent him a letter, calling him her own dear son.

And the black-skinned child, María de la Luz. Album A of Goya's Sanlúcar drawings includes an India ink sketch of the Duchess holding La Negrita on her lap, affectionately cradling the child's head in one hand. Goya with his acute sensibility to fraud perceived nothing but tenderness, and nowhere in letters to his friend Zapater does he imply anything else. Still, one scholar remarked that La Negrita was treated like an exotic pet.

Consider the young seminarian: picked up, tantalized, mocked, discarded. A member of the Somoza family told historian Joaquín del Bayo that one day when the Duchess went for a stroll near her Madrid palace she was approached by a theological student who had no idea who she was. She suggested that while getting acquainted they might have a little snack. And once settled in a cafe she ordered expensive pastries, custards, ices. What happened next could have been lifted from an eighteenth-century farce. The seminarian couldn't pay the bill so the cafe owner, acting upon her private instructions, insisted that he leave his trousers for security. You might think this humiliation would be enough. Not at all. When she invited him to visit her the following night he accepted, visions of paradise skipping through his head. One of her maids came to fetch him. And he, perhaps thinking the beautiful stranger must be another maid, followed his guide to the palace. There the Duchess received him in grand style before an assembly of guests, all of whom knew about him losing his trousers. The story may have been embellished over two centuries, but there's no doubt that she took what pleased or amused her, discarding it the instant her fancy turned. She loved to flirt, loved the game of seduction, which doesn't quite coincide with Lady Holland's remark about patrician deportment.

In those days Spain overflowed with women named María Teresa, just as today, and because we will meet a few the Duchess will be identified as María Cayetana—or La Alba, as Goya once called her in a letter to Martín Zapater.

Her father, Don Francisco, womanizer and gambler, died when she was seven.

Her mother, Doña Mariana de Silva y Sarmiento, Duchess of Huéscar, had a certain reputation as a painter and poet. Indeed, she had talent enough to be named honorary member of the Royal Academy of Fine Arts, although the fact that she was who she was probably influenced the selection committee. A 1774 portrait by Anton Mengs shows a not unattractive woman, blondish, pleasant, with an expression that might be construed as melancholy. She is said to have been quite fond of "gilded Bohemianism, unfaithful lovers and French Encyclopaedists." One might assume, therefore, that she would know how to control a Bohemian daughter. Apparently not.

She was left mostly in the care of her grandfather, twelfth Duke of Alba, a famous art collector and music lover who had built a palace on the ruins of a medieval castle near Ávila. This stately aristocrat had been at one time Spanish ambassador to the court of France and he went about preceded by the dwarf Benito who wore his medals. He was known to alternate between fits of rage and refined urbanity, between pride in the splendor of his name and terror at the thought that the great name of Alba might die with him. Painting, sculpture, music, books, such were his passions. It's doubtful that his library—the walls lined with silk—held a single page of trash. Montesquieu, St. Augustine, St. Teresa, Fray Luis de Granada, Molière, Calderón, Racine, and Maestro Juan de Ávila stood shoulder to shoulder. He admired Jean-Jacques Rousseau. He visited the celebrated Frenchman in Geneva and later requested his complete works, hang the expense. He especially liked *Émile* and brought up his willful granddaughter more or less according to the precepts of Rousseau. Mr. Wyndham Lewis refers to *Émile* as "a work of advanced lunacy," but goes on to say that such an education seems to have done the child no harm.

The elderly Duke was, of course, shocked and horrified by his son's premature death. It seemed imperative to get the little girl married and in a family way as soon as possible. Not only was the Alba name endangered, the Alba fortune approximated that of several European dynasties, including the Spanish Bourbons.

The designated husband, Don José Alvarez de Toledo Osorio Pérez de Guzman el Bueno, didn't object. Or if so, he didn't put up much of a fight. Goya painted him in 1795. He is not what we expect. Here is no Spanish gallant in rainbow uniform, sword unsheathed, galloping insanely toward a bank of enemy troops. No, he leans against a clavichord, in his graceful hands a score by Joseph Haydn, with whom he corresponded. From bottom to top he wears knee-length black boots, turquoise breeches, white waistcoat, and a swallowtail burgundy coat resembling a bathrobe. He enjoyed collecting clocks and he liked to play the knee-fiddle. He looks thoughtful, intelligent, exhausted. But of course Goya painted him after twenty years of marriage to María Cayetana. Now and again this must have been a picnic, at other times a fandango in hell.

She was not quite thirteen when they married. The ceremony was blessed by Father Ramón Pignatelli, canon of the Saragossa cathedral, and we will meet Father Pignatelli again.

As for her husband Don José, instead of retaining his title by inheritance, Marquis of Villafranca, he became Duke of Alba because the child bride demanded that he assume her name. Maybe so, but the imperious features of Grandfather Alba are visible just off stage. Everything considered, we should not be surprised if Don José looks tired.

Goya painted María Cayetana for the first time in 1795. Most likely he got to know her during the previous year. He first mentions her in a letter to his friend Zapater, and there are at least a couple of very odd things about it. The letter is dated Londres 2 de Agosto 1800. Goya never in his life got to London and scholars have determined that it must have been written between July 1794 and August 1795. What's going on? Nobody knows, though biographers have been speculating since 1868 when much of the correspondence was published by Zapater's nephew.

Así estoy.

Here I am, Goya scribbled at the end of this cryptic letter, followed by a string of dots leading to a caricature of himself, jaw and lips grossly protruding. He resembles a crescent moon.

He wrote that the great lady thrust herself into his studio, or charged into the studio, although one translator merely states that she came to the studio. By this time he was rather famous. He knew María Cayetana's good friend and rival, the Duchess of Osuna. He knew the lecherous prime minister, Godoy. He knew the royal family.

It had been a long, dusty, bumpy road from the village of Fuendetodos where he was born. His parents moved there from Saragossa because one of his mother's relatives owned a house. Not much of a house. Roughly made of stone, thick walls for protection against blistering summer heat and brutal winters. Huge fireplace with stone benches to either side, stone-walled kitchen. Smoky, shadowy rooms. An alcove where sausages hung from a sloping roof. One visitor half a century ago said the house smelled of old wood and stored linen.

Fuendetodos, meaning the fountain that belongs to everybody, wasn't a place where you would care to spend your vacation. Rocky land, little water. The one attraction might be crumbling Roman and Moorish forts surmounting nearby hills. What money the villagers earned went mostly to priests and to the landlord, El Conde de Fuentes. Very few coaches lurched and swayed down the winding road from Saragossa six leagues north. An English traveler who visited Fuendetodos less than a century after Goya died described it as a straggling hamlet with a few hundred people at the edge of a sluggish stream. Mountainsides black with pine trees poking through tangled underbrush. At times a breeze would bring the sound of church bells from Saragossa.

Goya's mother, Gracia Lucientes, claimed nobility of a sort. Her family was entitled to a coat-of-arms and this heraldic device clung to various doorways, but meant nothing. Spain was awash in titles. Spaniards joked about it. Anybody with a little extra cash might become an hidalgo—hijo de algo—the son of something or someone who lived not by the sweat of his body but thanks to income from property. In Goya's day, half a million low-level aristocrats, 5 percent of the population, strutted through villages cooked dry as bricks by the sun, each man pretending to live in the glorious past.

Goya's father had married above himself, though he too claimed distinction from days gone by. José Goya's ancestors lived at Cerain, near Cegama, deep in Basque territory. His boast wasn't unique. Just about everybody in Basque country claimed noble rank. However, nobility is unequal; a titled grandee would ignore a Fuendetodos hidalgo.

Consider this. The great Dukes of Alba and Infantado shared northern Andalusia. Southern Andalusia belonged to the Dukes of Alba, Medinaceli, Medina Sidonia, Arcos, and Osuna. J. F. Bourgoing, secretary to the French embassy at Madrid in those days, wrote that for ten leagues he crossed the Duchy of Medina Sidonia, which consisted entirely of pastures and cornfields. Not one orchard, garden, ditch, or tile. No vestige of human habitation. According to M. Bourgoing, the Duke reigned over this expanse like a lion of the forest and by his roaring drove away those who might approach. Eight million reales annually went into his pocket. How you equate that with today's money is academic; it amounted to wealth beyond understanding.

And how was life at the grubby end of the street? Beggars everywhere. During the late eighteenth century, nearly one fifth of the people in Madrid were maintained by charity. According to Martin Hume, Spaniards had succumbed to sloth and had grown to like it. The monarchy didn't help, imposing a 14 percent tax on merchandise of any sort whenever said merchandise changed hands. There were seventeen universities in Spain, all of them open to poor students, nine-tenths of whom registered as a mask for idleness, "living on the doles of food at the monastery gates—for which purpose they carried in their hat-brims the traditional wooden spoon—begging at the street corners on the pretence of a need to buy books. . . ."

The sixteenth-century Council of Trent, along with denouncing the Reformation, stressed the importance of mendicancy. In other words, those who were sick or starving ought to beg in public so that Christians might enjoy the privilege of giving. By Goya's time, mendicancy was a business. Aragón had a blind-beggars' guild, its statutes defining in fifty-three articles the rights of members and of novices.

What degree of prominence José Goya asserted for himself isn't known. Perhaps a Basque noble by heritage, he worked as a gilder, which rings of the Middle Ages: wheelwrights, tinkers, lackeys, minstrels, jousting. Francisco later would try to document his noble ancestry, not unlike Cervantes and Shakespeare. He even tried to reconstruct the ancient coat-of-arms.

One day after his birth he was taken to the parish church and the baptism carefully noted, which indicates that his parents were substantial members of the community.

On the 31st day of March, 1746, I, the subscribing vicar, baptized a child born on the day immediately preceding, the legitimate son of Joséph Goya and of Gracia Lucientes, legally married, inhabitants of this parish, in the district of Zaragoza. He was named Francisco Joséph Goya, his god-mother being Francisca de Grasa, of this parish, single, daughter of Miguel Lucientes and of Gracia María Salvador to whom I made known the spiritual kinship which she had contracted toward the baptized and the obligation to teach him the Christian doctrine should his parents fail to do so. By virtue of which, I have drawn up and signed this document, in Fuendetodos, on the date, month and year herein above mentioned.

Lic. Joseph Ximeno, Vicar.

Who first realized that the child was unusual? A priest carrying a sack of wheat to the mill happened to notice him drawing a picture on a wall with a burnt stick. The boy was drawing a pig. Ah, very good! said the priest. Who taught you to draw? Nobody, said Goya. You have no teacher? No, Father. And so, thanks to the priest, Francisco went to drawing school in Saragossa. It sounds familiar. Cimabue was traveling from Florence to Vespignano when he chanced upon a young shepherd drawing a picture on a rock with a pointed stone. The boy was drawing a sheep. Cimabue stopped to watch, asked if the boy would like to come and live with him. The boy said yes, if his father would agree. And so, thanks to Cimabue, Giotto began to study art in Florence.

Similar stories have been told of other juvenile masters.

It is said, also, that the Count of Fuentes noticed Goya's talent and arranged for him to study in Saragossa, which sounds a bit more plausible. Or it may be that José Goya, being a gilder, a decorator, would naturally encourage his son to draw. Old people many years later would insist that they remembered him sketching all around town. Perhaps. More likely they wanted to touch the hem of the famous man's cloak.

An early biographer wrote that while other children played games, young Goya was covering the walls of his home with pictures. He listened to village elders reminisce: "These strange tales sank into the child's subconscious mind and, in later years, were to find an outlet in the fantastic dreams and visions. . . ." Goya's mature work does show traces of that bleak village and the Aragón landscape, but there's no proof that he drew on the walls.

Not much, if anything, can be found of his early work. Charles Poore states that while visiting Fuendetodos just before the Spanish civil war he saw a cabinet of relics in the parish church. The Virgin of Pilar had been painted on the retablo, and to each side were painted curtains. If he had seen this anywhere but in Goya's native village, he says, he would not have believed it was done by Goya. He calls the work extraordinarily inert and uninspired. In 1936 during the war this reliquary cabinet was burned or shot to pieces; nothing of it remains but photographs. The doors swung apart to show a Madonna and Child on the left, Saint Francisco de Paula on the right. Two cherubs appear to be holding the painted curtains aside.

Exactly when he painted this cabinet has not been determined. José Gudiol, Director of the Instituto Amattler de Arte Hispanico in Barcelona, dates it circa 1763, when Goya was about seventeen. Although stiff and uninspired, it does show a degree of technical skill that he could not have acquired much earlier. The use of light and shade, for instance, repeats the pictorial formula employed by a Saragossa painter of religious themes, José Luzán. Connoisseurs of Goya would be able to pick out several characteristic traits, but to the uninitiated what seems most obvious is one angelic face near the bottom; here one sees dark rolling eyes upturned, the whites exaggerated, a mannerism he called upon decades later to express lunacy. You see it in the witches' sabbat, the madhouse, the San Isidro pilgrims.

Goya himself looked around Fuendetodos in 1808 during the Napoleonic war and disavowed the retablo, exclaiming that he could not have done such a thing. What he seems to have meant is that it was dreadful. Some collectors have paintings which they believe he did in his adolescence; but if so, as one critic remarked, their only value would be that of relics.

Eugenio d'Ors spent quite a while in Fuendetodos before starting work on his biography of the artist and must have spent hours in the Goya house, which he compared to an Eskimo igloo. The kitchen had no window. The chimney didn't work very well because burning wood dispersed not only heat but a substantial cloud of smoke that hung from the low ceiling, as well as what d'Ors called the delightful odor of evaporating resin. He thought the kitchen had been hewn out of a cave. "If fat melts in the hearth it impregnates stone, brick, furniture. . . ."

Laurent Mathéron, a nineteenth-century biographer who never visited the place, seems to have raided encyclopedias for local color. He writes that the little river Huerva flows past Fuendetodos, pine-covered mountains surround it, the skyline is magnificent, remnants of a Moorish castle add a touch of historic richness. Well, not quite. Francisco Zapater y Gómez was the nephew of Goya's best friend; he knew Fuendetodos and didn't think much of Mathéron's purple description. Anybody familiar with the village could tell you there's no river, no valley, no pine-clad hills, no bewitching shepherdess to soothe a weary traveler's brow. The economy depended upon agriculture and a small industry of wells for storing ice. The village takes on a yellowish hue at harvest time because of dust from threshed wheat. That must have been the place Goya knew, that and a house like a smoky igloo.

Because his uncle never married, Zapater y Gómez inherited—along with half a million pesetas and two Goya portraits of his affluent uncle—132 letters. He published excerpts from these letters in 1868. Romantic writers of that time presented the famous artist in their own image, or at least an image they projected of themselves: misfit, lecher, brawler, enemy of sanctimonious priests, victim of the Inquisition, friend of actresses and matadors. Zapater y Gómez did the same, except that he was a conservative gentleman. Thus, through selective editing, like a chicken plucking grains of corn from gravel, he showed us the good Catholic who began each letter with a cross, frequently invoked La Virgen del Pilar, and painted devotional scenes.

Casanova, perched on a mule, crossed the Pyrenees followed by his equipage on another mule. At Pampeluna, as he spells it, he obtained a coach and employed a guide. Whenever they met a priest carrying the viaticum, his guide would insist that he get out of the coach and kneel. There was no help for it, Casanova explains rather defensively. He spent a fortnight in Saragossa, amazed by the homage paid to Our Lady of the Pillar: "I have seen processions going along the streets in which wooden statues of gigantic proportions were carried. . . ." He observes that the Church of Nuestra Señora was built on the city's ramparts to protect Saragossa. No army could break through, so the people believed. We will come back to that.

At the close of the twentieth century an English novelist, Julia Blackburn, set out to visit Goya's home town. At a nearby village she found several thousand Aragonese crowding into the plaza. Nearly all of them carried drums and they were dressed in purple robes, prepared to celebrate the beginning of Easter week. At midnight on the Thursday before Good Friday a barrage of pounding drums opened the festival known as Tamboradas. Everything answered the drums. "The pillar against which my hand was leaning, pulsated. The door behind me trembled. . . ." Many of the drums had been decorated: bleeding heart, crown of thorns with bloody spikes, Christ weeping. In another town she saw a little girl dressed as Salome carrying the severed head of John the Baptist, a mongoloid man wiping away tears while fiercely pounding a drum, children eating ice cream while wearing Inquisition costumes.

Bartolomé de las Casas, Bishop of Chiapas during the sixteenth century, knew the famous conquistadors: Pizarro, Alvarado, Pedrarias, and Cortez, among others. These Spaniards, he wrote, would string up their victims on gallows in lots of thirteen to glorify Our Redeemer and His twelve apostles. Las Casas saw half a dozen Indian nobles tied to grids, burning, whose cries so disturbed the captain's sleep that he ordered them strangled; but a constable, choosing to disobey this order, gagged the victims with sticks to keep them quiet, "and he stirred up the fire, but not too much, so that they roasted slowly, as he liked. I saw all these things. . . ."

On March 12, 1781, when Goya was thirty-four years old, Spaniards marched out of Cuzco to exterminate Peruvian Indians. The Inca, Tupuc Amaru, after seeing his wife, son, uncle, brother-in-law, and cousins executed, had his tongue torn out. Four horses pulled his body apart. Spaniards burned his corpse on the summit of Machu Picchu.

It might be noted that King Charles III didn't order such atrocities; in fact, he had little idea what his subjects in the New World were doing. Nevertheless, conquistadors were extensions of Spain, exemplars of zealous Christianity. Goya's subjects would be the degenerate inheritors of that murderous imperialism.

All nations have their barbarous times, wrote the eighteenth-century philosopher Jean François Marmontel. In our time, Hans Magnus Enzenberger wrote that Las Casas' book "has a penetratingly contemporaneous smell." Anyway, Blackburn went for a walk in the hills near Fuendetodos. She noticed the old mule track leading to Saragossa, signs of wild pig, a beautiful hoopoe with a powder pink face and a crest like a lady's fan. Overhead, solitary eagles circling and a crowd of vultures.

Just when the family returned to Saragossa is disputed. Scholarly guesses range from 1749 to 1759, so Francisco was anywhere from three to thirteen—a bit young to draw an excellent pig with a burnt stick, much less the Holy Virgin.

2

Saragossa has been around quite a while, nobody is sure just how long. Emperor Augustus named it for himself, Caesarea Augustus, now corrupted to Zaragoza or Saragossa. Goths took it during the fifth century. Three centuries later the Moors captured it, so it became Sarakostah. Charlemagne wanted it, but Moorish armies drove him back. And we might note that for a while Spain's great champion, El Cid, served the Moorish ruler. Alfonso I of Aragón seized control during the twelfth century and made it his capital. One historian states with considerable panache that in Aragón a dagger is always close at hand because the people do not forget that long ago their province was an independent kingdom. They boast that in their veins flows the blood of ancient Iberians, Berbers, and Goths.

José Goya enrolled his son at the Escuela Pía, a school for the poor directed by Father Joaquín. In those days Spain lagged a century behind the rest of Europe. Most of the teachers were monks who dispensed knowledge handed down by their predecessors, nothing new. Harsh punishment for recalcitrant students. What did Goya learn? Fragments of Latin, several of which became captions for drawings. Some light acquaintance with Virgil's poetry. And ever afterward, as long as he lived, he would trace the sign of the cross at the beginning of his letters.

Age fourteen, we find him enrolled at the Luzán academy, a fact well established by an 1828 catalogue of the Prado:

> He was a pupil of Don José Luzán in Saragossa, from whom he learnt the principles of Draughtmanship, who made him copy the best prints that he possessed; he was with him for four years and began to paint from his own imagination.

Spanish art of this period, according to one critic, was at best mediocre, and Luzán contributed to the mediocrity. Another observed that he worked in a debased Neapolitan manner. European engravings were plentiful in Spain and he ordered his students to copy them. Day after day, week after week, month after month, they hunched over Italian, French, and Flemish engravings before being allowed to draw from plaster casts, before being allowed to draw from life. Every art student who has been instructed to make charcoal drawings of Greek and Roman sculpture will recognize the Luzán method. Is it beneficial or stifling? Goya declared years later that he learned nothing. One last fact about Luzán: The Inquisition made use of his piety and skill, employing him to censor works that if left untouched would corrupt public morals—here and there a leaf, a garment, a shadow. While enrolled at this academy Goya met the brothers Bayeu. Francisco, the elder, was a graduate who had just returned from additional study in Madrid.

Saragossa, capital of Aragón, basking in the glow of miraculous relics, looked incomparably better than Fuendetodos. The crypt of Santa Engracia held the bones of numerous martyrs. Silver lamps burning night and day strangely failed to blacken the low ceiling, nor would the smoke blacken a sheet of white paper. And one might visit the Church of La Virgen del Pilar and La Séo—Chair of the Savior—which had been an early Christian church, then a mosque, bursting with gold chalices, jeweled monstrances, Chinese porcelain, paintings by Ribera, Andrea del Sarto. Quite obviously Saragossa had more to offer than Fuentetodos, all the same it was not Madrid. Madrid was where things happened, where a man could make a name for himself.

Fictioneers give a tumultuous account of his departure from Saragossa. Various religious brotherhoods marched through the streets during festivals, demonstrations that could become bloody confrontations. Parishioners from Nuestra Señora del Pilar often clashed with parishioners of San Luis, and Goya—champion of El Pilar—would lead the attack. One night three men were stabbed. The Grand Inquisitor obtained a list of those responsible. At the head of that list a notorious ringleader, Goya. Just in time did he learn that the Inquisition was after him, therefore "the turbulent youth resolved on flight."

What actually happened is less dramatic. Francisco Bayeu moved from Saragossa to Madrid in 1763. Bayeu knew important people in Madrid. Goya followed him.

Now, having reached the heart of the universe, he decided to apply for a scholarship. Every three years the San Fernando Royal Academy of Fine Arts staged a competition. Goya's assignment was to copy a plaster cast of the fat drunken satyr, Silenius. Goya received a scholarship, of course. After all, he had been drilled at this sort of thing by Luzán. Wrong. Nobody voted for his copy of the ancient masterpiece, which means he came in last, or tied for last. Three years later, age twenty, he tried again. We will get back to Goya's second attempt.

The director of the Royal Academy in 1766 was Antonio or Anton Raphael Mengs, a devout neoclassicist who insisted upon being called Raphael. Mengs is worth noticing. His father Ismail, a Danish painter of miniatures, is said to have been a man whose personality was stronger and his aspirations loftier than his ability to express them. He therefore resolved that his son should equal or surpass the great masters. And to make certain that the boy understood his destiny, Ismail named him not only Raphael but Anton in homage to Antonio Correggio. And because there was no sense wasting time, Ismail gave his son paper and pencil instead of toys. That was it. Nothing else. When the boy was twelve years old Ismail took him to Rome, parked him in the Vatican galleries with a hunk of bread and a bottle of water and told him to start copying.

There sat young Anton week after week, immured in the Vatican, at a time of life when other boys his age were kicking soccer balls or whatever boys did in those days. There, nipping at bread and water, he copied the works of his godfather Raphael, he copied the Belvedere collection of antique statuary, he copied the ceiling of the Sistine Chapel. You might think he would turn into an ax murderer but the program worked, at least to his father's satisfaction.

Later he studied Greek and Roman art with the great panjandrum of that era, Johann Winckelmann. Together they became convinced that no living artist could hope to excel the long-gone masters.

Who is to say they were wrong? Vasari tells us that the origin of art is nature itself, which nobody would dispute, the first image or model being the beautiful fabric of our world; and we were taught by that divine light infused in us by special grace, which has made us superior not only to animals but similar to God Himself. Accordingly, the first men were more perfect than we, endowed with higher intelligence, because they lived nearer the time of Creation with nature as their guide: "So is there not every reason for believing that they originated these noble arts and that from modest beginnings, improving them little by little, they finally perfected them?"

Artists long ago knew nothing of color but worked exclusively with lines. According to Pliny, Gyges the Lydian saw his own shadow cast by firelight and forthwith seized a bit of charcoal to draw the outline of himself on a wall. Cleophantes of Corinth introduced color. Apollodorus was first to employ a brush. So the majestic art of painting evolved. Now here we are, for better or worse.

Some years after his medieval apprenticeship Mengs was appointed director of the Vatican's painting school. He taught aesthetics, published *Thoughts on Beauty and Taste in Painting*. His friend Winckelmann described him as the greatest painter of his era. Spain's ambassador to the Vatican wrote a biography, calling him better than Raphael, praising him as a philosopher who painted for philosophers.

Word reached the King of Naples, who would become Charles III of Spain, that Anton Mengs was the genius of the century.

Subsequent critics have been less impressed. *An Illustrated Manual of Art Throughout the Ages,* published in 1904, stated that Mengs had been misled "by the fatal seductions of eclecticism, which knows beauty only at second hand."

No more did Charles succeed to the Spanish throne than he set about luring this genius of the century to Madrid. Mengs, awash in honors, understood his value and his service did not come cheaply. Two thousand doubloons per annum, a house, a coach. Charles didn't flinch. In 1761 he dispatched a ship to bring Anton Mengs to Spain "with all the consideration due a sovereign."

Goya, meanwhile, was bent over Flemish engravings in provincial Saragossa.

Charles imported the pedantic, opinionated Mengs because he wanted Spain brought up to date artistically, socially, and economically. For this reason he also imported a team of Italian experts, among them a treasurer named Squillace, Francesco Sabatini who was an architect, and—one year after Mengs—the old Venetian master Tiepolo. With Tiepolo came his two painterly sons, Giandomenico and Lorenzo. King Charles had no great enthusiasm for the arts so why did he send for Tiepolo? This may have less to do with the King's taste than with the completion of a new royal palace, thirty years in construction, a colossus described as a postmaster's dream: hundreds of rooms, Trojan walls, lofty ceilings. Whatever his logic, Charles authorized Mengs to take charge of embellishing the palace.

Casanova had known Mengs in Rome. They were friendly enough, and in Madrid he stayed a while as Mengs's houseguest, but the friendship soured. Years later, Casanova had little good to say about him. Mengs had invited him merely to gratify his own vanity. Mengs was overwhelmingly ambitious, jealous, hated other painters. As an artist, excellent color and design, no imagination. An ignoramus pretending to be a scholar, lustful, ill tempered, envious, miserly. Casanova is just getting started. The painter spoke four languages, all badly. He beat his children with a stick, saying that was how his father made him a great artist. He thought the antediluvian Tower of Babel still existed, which Casanova scornfully calls a double piece of folly because in the first place there are no such remains, and in the second place the tower was postdiluvian. One begins to feel sorry for Mengs. Evidently he wasn't very smart and Casanova didn't tolerate fools. Seldom does he credit the painter with anything beyond good color and design.

However, Mengs did paint a Magdalen that Casanova liked and he asked why the artist continued working on it day after day while insisting that it was almost finished. Ninety-nine out of a hundred connoisseurs would have said it was finished long ago, Mengs replied, but I want the approval of the hundredth man. He added that nothing ever is finished until you stop working on it, and even then it's relative. Not one of Petrarch's sonnets is finished, he said, nor the sonnets of any man. Casanova was impressed. "I told him that I warmly admired the excellence with which he spoke."

Although the King appointed Mengs to decorate the palace he entrusted the ceiling of the saleta to that grand old master, Tiepolo. Mengs was offended. The artists couldn't have been more different. Mengs, who thought natural imperfections ought to be corrected, might have stood for Grant Wood's farmer with a pitchfork. Tiepolo reveled in color, motion, anything exuberant, and what he did to the ceiling was predictable: winged cupids, Mercury bearing the Spanish crown, Mars in golden armor, Venus clasping Eros to her bosom, Neptune out of his element, a castellated tower, a chariot, a couple of white doves yoked together, blackamoors, some sort of griffin or humanoid lion, assorted cherubs, pneumatic clouds, flags, swirling draperies, mirrors, on and on. Charles liked it.

Tiepolo also painted seven altarpieces for a church near the Aranjuez palace, but here the exuberant Venetian ran afoul of the King's confessor who denounced them as coarse and pagan. They were replaced by the work of more suitable artists, notably Mengs, whose neoclassic formality didn't upset anybody. As a result of this clash Tiepolo found himself more or less out of a job. He died soon afterward.

What of Mengs? These early days at the Vatican paid off. Tedious apprentice work abetted by Winckelmann's knowledge produced a first-rate journeyman, precise, deft, cautious. He died at fifty-one, hugely successful, and was buried in the Pantheon in Rome at the feet of his god Raphael. He couldn't have hoped for anything more.

1766. The Royal Academy announced its triennial competition. Each applicant for a scholarship to submit one painting, oil on canvas, six feet by four and one-half feet, the subject taken from Fr. Mariana's history of Spain:

> Martha, Empress of Constantinople, presents herself to King Alfonso the Wise in Burgos, to ask him for a third of the sum with which she has agreed to ransom her husband, the Emperor Valduino, from the Sultan of Egypt; and the King of Spain commands that she be given the whole sum.

After that, a test of the candidate's ability to paint impromptu for two hours and thirty minutes on a subject to be disclosed at the time. How many eager candidates submitted to this ordeal isn't known, but they assembled on July 15, 8:30 A.M. Various subjects were dropped into a hat. What was plucked from the hat?

Juan de Urbina and Diego de Paredes, in Italy, upon seeing the Spanish army, discuss to which of the two the arms of the Marqués de Pescara should be given. The prize, along with a scholarship, was a three-ounce gold medal. At 11:45 A.M., the judges announced their decision. One of the judges was Francisco Bayeu. The scholarship and medal went to his little brother Ramón. The country boy from Fuendetodos didn't get any votes.

Critics these days seldom exclaim over the Bayeu brothers. Ramón's work is "prettily colored, but very affected and devoid of artistic genius." Francisco gets higher marks. There is a portrait of his daughter that has been attributed to Goya, but may in fact have been painted by Francisco Bayeu. And to his credit it should be noted that after a while he stopped promoting Ramón.

Goya's second failure evidently persuaded him that if he wanted royal patronage he had better learn to paint like a neoclassicist; he therefore apprenticed himself to Francisco Bayeu. And during this period he noticed Bayeu's young sister, Josefa.

Wrapped to the eyeballs in a black cloak, face hidden beneath a slouch hat, Goya prowled the streets of Madrid, Cyrano in search of adventure: "Often he dallied beneath the balconies of the fair sex, singing pretty coplas to the accompaniment of his guitar." For amusement he painted a street sign. He attacked a water carrier who mistreated a hunchback. He caroused with a one-eyed pharmacist, consorted with jugglers, varlets, merryandrews, and gypsies, this outrageous rustic who moved at ease through the imperial court of Spain. If he appeared at Catalina Square, rendezvous of fencing experts, the circle opened to admit him and those who crossed swords would respectfully present their foils, "receiving mock knighthood at his hands."

Why such stories about an almost unknown young artist circulated through Madrid is difficult to explain. No doubt some were invented after he became famous and were conveniently backdated. But there are men and women whose presence inexplicably creates tension. It's said that people could sense the arrival of Theodore Roosevelt before they saw him. If you look at Picasso's burning eyes you know he announced himself without a word. Goya may have been like that.

He went to Italy. This much we know, although the reason is unclear, except that he wasn't getting much attention at home. He had studied Titian, Velázquez, Rembrandt, Murillo, Ribera, and had listened more or less patiently to Bayeu, with very little result; so we come to the shopworn fiction that he left Madrid because the Inquisition was after him and one morning he woke up with a dagger in his back. A dagger in the back might convince anybody to leave town but doesn't explain why he went to Italy.

How he got from Madrid to Rome hasn't been learned. Bayeu might have helped, if only to rid himself of Goya, who was no daffodil. He might have worked his way through Spain as part of a bullfighter's cuadrilla. We have no proof that he did, but later he would speak of his days in the ring and he signed one letter Francisco de los Toros. Another letter, not by Goya, states that when he was eighty years old he reminisced about fighting bulls, sword in hand. Most likely he worked at his trade, cranking out portraits of shopkeepers, village altarpieces, this or that, whatever would buy a hunk of bread and some cheese.

He traveled through France, meaning that he didn't catch a ship from Barcelona or another Spanish port. Almost nothing about his journey can be documented, but he may have spent a while in France because he copied the *Pietà* of Simon Vouet and made sketches of two works by Poussin: the *Last Supper* and *Virgin of the Pillar Appearing to St. James the Apostle.* From southern France he may have gone by ship to Italy.

For all that has been learned about his Roman sojourn he might as well have wandered the streets wrapped to the eyeballs in a cloak. Nevertheless it produced a fresh crop of stories. He earned his daily bread as an acrobat. Madly in love with a nun, he attempted to climb the convent wall, another Filippo Lippi hot on the trail of Lucrezia Buti, saved from the gallows only because the Spanish ambassador intervened. Catherine the Great's ambassador offered him a job as court painter in St. Petersburg. He clambered around the tomb of Cecilia Metalla in order to carve his name above that of Vanloo, court painter to Philip V. Students at the French school showed new arrivals some letters on one of the most inaccessible points of the dome of St. Peter's: Goya's signature. No mention is made of a telescope, so how did they know it was Goya's signature? And he met Jacques Louis David and later these two corresponded and David's revolutionary fervor excited Goya. Not plausible because they weren't in Rome at the same time.

It does appear that he got in some sort of trouble. José Nicolás de Azara probably interceded on his behalf. Azara is identified as "Agent of Prayers" and procurator to the papal court. Not only was he Spanish, he came from Aragón. He has been described as a closet radical who criticized certain Church practices. Did he feed Goya tidbits of anticlerical propaganda? This is speculative but among other interests Azara collected antique sculpture, meaning that he was less than rigidly orthodox. He had a brother, Félix, a naturalist, who sat for a Goya portrait some thirty-five years after this Roman holiday.

How long did our man putter about Rome? Nobody knows. The city attracted a great many art students from other countries who behaved much as expatriate students behave these days—arguing theory in coffee houses, issuing manifestos that interest no one, cultivating wispy beards, denouncing the bourgeoisie. Goya seems to have avoided or ignored such entertainment. Where he lived is a mystery. He might have stayed with a Polish-German artist, Taddeo or Tadeusz Kuntze. If so, he probably had a letter of introduction from Bayeu's father-in-law, who was German. The connection is tenuous. Nor do we know which Italian masters influenced him. He copied the so-called Farnese Hercules at least four times, he drew the Belvedere Torso three times, and it is obvious from *Desastres de la Guerra*—see the armless man impaled on a tree limb—that he remembered those muscular torsos. Unquestionably he studied the Vatican paintings of Raphael and Michelangelo, although his subsequent work reveals no influence. There are traces of Correggio whose brilliant frescoes could be seen at Parma.

While in Rome he learned that the Academy of Fine Arts at Parma had invited submissions on that popular theme: Hannibal crossing the Alps. Annibale vincitore che rimira, la prime volte dalle Alpi, l'Italia. This was unusual for the Academy. Subjects ordinarily were chosen from classic sources. The explanation is that Abbé Frugoni, the Academy secretary, had just died and members decided to honor him by selecting a theme from one of his sonnets. The prize: a five-ounce gold medal.

Because of archaeological work at Herculaneum and Pompeii, and because of Winckelmann, neoclassicism was de rigueur in the late eighteenth century. Voltaire's body was carted to the neoclassic Pantheon in an ersatz Roman sarcophagus. George Washington, unlike that grim Gilbert Stuart president who floats into view when his name is mentioned, sometimes was depicted as a Roman general. Canova sculpted Washington in marble, complete with toga, thoughtfully studying a marble tablet.

April 20, 1771. Goya wrote a letter from Rome "in correct Italian" to the new secretary, Count Rezzonico, declaring his intention to compete for the medal. His Spanish grammar was less than perfect, so he couldn't have written perfect Italian. That helpful Agent of Prayers and fellow Aragonese, Don José Nicolás de Azara, almost certainly dictated the letter.

Goya shipped his canvas to Parma instead of delivering it because the rules stipulated that foreign artists must submit their work to an Academy delegate in the city or town where they lived, and Goya was a long way from Madrid. He sidestepped this rule by signing his work as an Italian would sign it—Goja—and said he was Roman, a pupil of Vajeu—Bayeu—court painter to the King of Spain. And having thought about it, or perhaps at the suggestion of Azara, he included a line from Virgil: Jam tandem Italiae fugientes prendimus oras. Which is to say, we in flight at length touch Italian shores. This odd fabrication, and the fact that his painting already was en route to Parma, might have baffled Count Rezzonico. Whatever the case, his entry was accepted.

This time he did better. On June 27, 1771, the Academy notified him that he had received six votes. Good enough for second prize, according to some scholars. Not true, according to biographer Sánchez Cantón, who argues that the Academy report has been misconstrued and there was no second prize. Anyway, Paolo Borroni, just about forgotten these days, carried off the medal. Jurors praised Borroni's delicate and harmonious coloring. As for Goya, the brushwork was excellent and "a warmth of expression in Hannibal's eyes" pleased the judges, as well as a quality of grandeur in Hannibal's attitude. If Goya had displayed less eccentricity in composition, they said, and if his colors had been more faithful to nature, he would have won. The judges also remarked on a touch of levity in his work, which annoyed them.

For a long time this painting was thought to be lost. Now it belongs to the Fundación Selgas-Fagalda and most viewers today would agree with that 1771 verdict. The work is preposterous. Hannibal, stripped from shoulders almost to the loins, melodramatically shades his eyes while peering toward Italy. Blue predominates. Mountains near and far, Hannibal's muscular torso, a celestial goddess rolling toward him in what looks like a blue wheelchair, an angel with cerulean wings who might be adjusting his baby pink cloak, or perhaps congratulates Hannibal for having traveled this far. What was Goya thinking?

One critic notes that Hannibal resembles a figure of Mars by the Venetian painter Jacopo Amigoni. The general's helmet sports a winged dragon, a motif copied from ancient shields and breastplates. In the foreground Goya painted an ox-headed deity, symbolizing the river Po. And he signed his magnum opus: Goja. How desperately he must have wanted that medal. The doors of Madrid surely would open if he returned with such a prestigious award.

During this Italian visit he may have produced some erotic work, no surprise if one considers his youth and the liberal atmosphere, altogether different from that of Spain. These diversions, if they exist, must be little treasures in private collections.

No first prize, no five-ounce trophy to illuminate his return, but things were looking up. How much time he spent abroad is uncertain, perhaps two years: 1769–71.

Parma was more or less on the way home, so he might have stopped there, hence the influence of Correggio. Again, we have no evidence. What route he took has not been learned. First prize would have sent him flying straight to Madrid, Caesar with a paintbrush, but also-rans don't get much respect. He decided he might do better in Saragossa where he understood the people. There, instead of knocking hopefully at doors to the imperial court, he might build a reputation and earn a few pesetas before renewing his attack on the capital. He took an apartment on the Street of Noah's Ark, which doesn't mean a thing but is somehow engaging.

The most noticeable effect of his Italian trip is that he gave up the struggle to paint like a neoclassicist.

3

Not long after his return to Saragossa in late summer or early autumn of 1771 he was commissioned to do a series of wall paintings in Sobradiel Palace, owned by the Counts of Gabarda. He recreated three biblical episodes derived from Italian and French sources. The Aragonese nobles approved.

In October he was asked to submit sketches for a fresco in the shrine of La Virgen del Pilar. He delivered the sketches in three weeks. Such enthusiasm pleased the committee members, who were further gratified to learn that he would do the job for 10,000 reales less than the next lowest bidder—Antonio González Velázquez, who was experienced and highly regarded. Goya, being almost unknown, was asked to provide an example of his work in this difficult medium. Again the judges were pleased. Goya completed the fresco in six months. Choirs of angels, billowy clouds, a golden triangle to symbolize the Trinity.

He did eleven oil paintings in the church of the Carthusian Monastery of Aula Dei. Only seven remain and these are in bad shape, damaged by time, weather, war, and the twentieth-century restorative efforts of the

Buffet brothers—French artists whose work brings to mind Puvis de Chavannes.

His reputation grew quickly. According to the tax rolls, by 1774 Goya had become Saragossa's most prosperous artist. He was earning more than his old teacher José Luzan, which must have been satisfying, and more than the region's premier painter, Juan Andrés Mercklein.

While busily illustrating biblical scenes and celestial paradise he was considering earthly matters because in the summer of 1773 he went to Madrid where he married Josefa Bayeu.

How much he loved Josefa has been questioned. Enough that he married her, but if obliged to choose between Josefa and his work, would he have kept his wife or his brushes? Anybody who follows Goya from Fuendetodos to exile and death in Bordeaux knows quite well what he would have done. Ernest Renan, meditating on the life of Christ, wrote that like all men preoccupied by an idea, He sometimes ignored family requirements.

During their life together Josefa was pregnant more often than not, which indicates that they got along pretty well. Thirty-nine years of married life; nobody is quite sure how many births. Just one child survived to maturity. Old biographies state that Josefa may have had twenty children, but Madrid parish registers show the baptismal records of five. The first child, Vicente Anatasio, was born in Madrid, January 21, 1777. Or maybe August 25, 1775. It depends on your scholar. The child soon died. A daughter, María del Pilar Dionisia, was born in 1779. Another son, Francisco de Paula, 1780. A second daughter, Hermengilda, 1782. All died young. Goya inscribed the names of some of his children and the dates of birth in a notebook, but he did not report any deaths. In those days fifteen or twenty pregnancies wasn't unusual. The idea was to have a great many children in the hope that two or three would survive pneumonia, fevers, smallpox, tuberculosis, and nobody knew what else.

Finally, in 1784, Francisco Xavier—or Javier—Pedro was born, described by Goya as the most beautiful sight to be seen in Madrid.

Jacqueline Hara, who translated Goya's letters to Martín Zapater, remarks that when he mentions his wife she is usually bleeding in bed. She lay in bed if he needed her. When not confined or ill she did what was expected, running errands, making soup, whatever. She was useful, available. Goya wanted to be a father and seems to have been frustrated by his wife's miscarriages. In letters she is La Pepa, the diminutive of Josefa, which sounds mildly affectionate. Not much is known about her. Evidently she was a simple woman who made few demands, although she did enjoy dressing up. Goya once wrote to Zapater that Josefa had been sick from a miscarriage nine days previous, but as soon as she felt well enough she meant to visit the English tailor. Excepting this lust for plumage she seems to have been a tranquil woman, content to exist in the shade of her husband. She referred to domestic life as the tomb of women, la sepultura de las mujeres. She resented it but there was no escape. Year after year she did what was expected. She seems to have felt passionately about nothing except clothes.

When I was a child our family employed a housekeeper like Josefa: a placid, expressionless, devout, overweight farm girl. Not once did I see her angry, excited, depressed, or amused. Day after day, month after month, heavy on her feet, she cleaned house, prepared meals. Sunday morning she dressed up to attend church. Wednesday night she attended Bible class. Life being what it was, she acquiesced.

Goya did one or two portraits of his wife. Laboratory technicians sooner or later will develop a method for dating pictures exactly; at the moment it depends upon whatever fingerprints show up, documentation, analysis of technique, and so forth. In other words, circumstantial evidence, together with a little help from the lab.

Portrait of the Painter's Wife, Doña Josefa Bayeu, was bought by the Museo de Trinidad in 1866, and has been dated anywhere from 1790 to 1812. The museum bought it from somebody who bought it from Goya's descendants, but there weren't any documents, only a statement by the first buyer. Also, the woman appears to be in her thirties, though her dress and coiffure date from the time of the French Restoration—1814—when the Bourbon monarchy returned to power under Louis XVIII. Josefa died in 1812. Had she lived until 1814 she would have been sixty-seven. Furthermore, X-rays show a different face behind this one. Which is to say, Goya used an old canvas, suggesting that the model was someone close to him. *The Painter's Wife*, therefore, might not be Josefa but Leocadia Weiss with whom he spent his final years. And yet what we have is the face of a patient woman, temperamentally unlike Leocadia. This painter's wife is not going to throw a fit, brain her impetuous, erratic, infuriating spouse with a soup ladle. From two centuries ago she gazes at us, large soft eyes a trifle apprehensive and sad like those of a household animal afraid of predators, the mouth compressed, remembering. Large hands in gray gloves, working hands, rest on her knees. A transparent scarf around her shoulders could as easily be a woolen shawl. It isn't a big picture. Goya often painted the aristocrats life-size or larger, but this Josefa might be the wife of a shopkeeper who couldn't afford the artist's usual price.

The second portrait, dated 1805, shows a woman in middle age, visibly battered by life. At that time Josefa had been living with the artist for thirty-two years, long enough to test the stamina of any woman. Most scholars believe this drawing in pen and black chalk is the artist's wife. If we exclude the questionable oil portrait, this seems to be the only picture of Josefa: one little drawing on paper, 4½" by 3¼ inches.

Josefa's brother evidently didn't object to her marrying his erstwhile assistant. Francisco Bayeu was now a man of stature, court painter to His Majesty Charles III, and he petitioned the King for a raise on the grounds that his sister was getting married. As for Goya, he knew quite well that his former teacher had emerged as one of the most distinguished painters in Spain. Marriage to Josefa would bring not only a pliable and subservient wife but entrance to court.

July 25, 1773. Goya and Josefa Bayeu were married.

About a year later, King Charles decided to rejuvenate the imperial tapestry manufactory whose products were something of a national embarrassment compared to the Gobelin tapestries of France. This meant drawing sketches for the weavers, steady work for quite a while and good pay. Mengs would be in charge, Bayeu his assistant. And who deserved a share of this lucrative work if not Bayeu's little brother Ramón? Nor did Bayeu forget his new brother-in-law. Goya and La Pepa moved to Madrid.

Director Mengs thought it prudent to switch from biblical and mythological subjects to the sort of thing King Charles liked—views of country life, picnics, excursions, scenes more or less derived from Boucher's *Arcadia*. Mengs probably disapproved, this being a sharp turn from the neoclassicism he favored, but he had a good job and the wise employee doesn't irritate his employer. Goya's first assignment was a sequence of hunting and fishing scenes, so inert, predictable, and lifeless that for a long time they weren't attributed to Goya. Landscape bored him. Nor could he draw animals very well, except bulls. Nobody knows why. He had seen animals from the day he was born and he loved to hunt. One biographer remarked that he cared about nothing that wasn't human, which perhaps explains it.

Each September these tapestries hung in the Escorial, a monumental construction as sinister as an American prison. Charles stayed at the Escorial during hunting season and quite possibly the first time he became aware of Goya was when he looked at the tapestries. Records show that each December they were transferred to the Pardo Palace north of Madrid; more interesting is that twice a year they were taken to the river and washed, which was thought to discourage moths.

Goya's commonplace designs were obviously nationalistic and for that reason Spaniards approved. He got more assignments, more artistic latitude, and a salary increase to 8,000 reales. So far so good. He began doing the street people he instinctively understood; vain majos wearing tight breeches with a knife concealed in the sash, saucy majas. The men worked at jobs demanding more muscle than brains. The women might be household servants or street vendors peddling whatever was seasonally in demand—oranges, roasted chestnuts, ribbons, picnic fare. The word probably derives from maya, the prettiest girl of a district who reigned as queen of May Day festivities. The relationship of these young bloods has been described as "ritualistically stormy. Her desire, presumably, was marriage; his was to keep her faithful without resorting to such a disastrous expedient." And because the maja often carried a dagger beneath her skirt their arguments might end sooner than expected.

For a reason yet to be explained, Goya's sketches ended up in a garret, forgotten until 1869. Today, as everybody knows, even the roughest sketch of a celebrated work is worth a modest fortune.

Early in 1797 he was introduced to the royal family. He wrote to Zapater that he kissed the royal hands, showed four paintings, and never in
his life had felt so fortunate. In that same letter he mentioned that he was
acquiring enemies.

Not long after this social triumph he applied for a job as Painter to the
Court, no doubt anticipating further happy encounters with royalty.
Mengs had just died so there was a vacancy and surely the King would tell
Bayeu whom to appoint. Don Manuel de Roda, an Aragonese of some influence, urged that Goya's petition be granted. The Duke of Losada
replied on behalf of the court that although Goya was industrious and
promising there seemed no great insistence to the matter nor any dearth
of capable painters and Goya had best continue at the factory. A friend
of Bayeu got the job.

One year later the wheel of fortune stopped at Goya's number: He was
elected to membership in the Royal Academy of San Fernando. Those who
mattered were indeed beginning to appreciate him, but Goya had tinkered
with the wheel. He now understood that success depended not only upon
vision and skill; one must take into account one's superiors. He therefore
accompanied his petition with a work the academics would like. *Christ on the
Cross*. It wasn't original. He repeated a Bayeu study of the Crucifixion that
Bayeu had copied from Mengs. It was somber, as befitted the subject, yet
not disturbing. The Royal Academy liked it. Things were looking up.

Bayeu, meanwhile, was haggling with the Saragossa Council of Works
about frescoes for the cathedral. Six years earlier, with brother Ramón
and Goya assisting, he had painted one of the cupolas. Now he submitted ideas for completing the work. The council approved. Goya and Josefa
moved back to Saragossa.

If Goya collaborated on a project it very often did not go according to
the script. Bayeu, successor to Mengs, not unreasonably considered himself the boss. Goya thought otherwise. After all, he was himself a Fellow
of the Royal Academy and therefore Bayeu's equal; it was insulting to have
the older man tell him what to do. Bayeu was in charge, true, but that
didn't mean his ideas were better. Bayeu objected to some of Goya's colors; Goya refused to change them. Bayeu informed the Council of Works

that he would not endorse what Goya had in mind. If they, the council members, thought Goya's plan was acceptable he would say no more, but he disliked what he had seen.

Goya was subpoenaed by the Junta del Fábrica del Pilar, which is to say the council, and the cathedral's canon, Matías Allué. Explain yourself, they said. Explain this insubordination, is what they meant. Goya furiously denied the charge of arrogance. He called upon his friend Zapater, who was an attorney. With Zapater's help he drew up a lengthy appeal. The council was not impressed. Goya, further inflamed, decided to pack up his brushes and return to Madrid. Then he heard from a Carthusian friar, Félix Salcedo, whom he had met years before while painting at the monastery. Father Salcedo had been called in to referee the squabble. He advised Goya that nothing could be more Christian than to humble oneself when common sense and the law of God requested it. In other words, Father Salcedo went on, adjusting his tone, you should consider that Bayeu is more esteemed by the council and may very soon be appointed First Painter to the King, whereas you—although the greater artist—have yet to achieve such distinction. Therefore, with generosity and Christian charity you should subject yourself to his judgment.

Goya accepted Father Salcedo's good words, albeit with no indication of Christian humility. He was exasperated. By early summer of 1781 he had finished the job: luminous clouds, cavorting angels, Roman soldiers, the Holy Virgin portrayed as Queen of Martyrs, St. Sebastián transfixed by arrows, John the Baptist carrying his head in his hands.

So it was done, not the way he imagined it. He demanded payment at once because he wanted to get back to Madrid where, given a bit of luck, he might obtain royal patronage. His demand irritated the Saragossa Council of Works.

Canon Allué authorized payment, but felt insulted by the artist's behavior and the councilors made it clear that he would not be decorating anything else in their cathedral. They presented all three Bayeus—Director Francisco, brother Ramón, sister Josefa—with silver medals. Josefa had nothing to do with decorating the cathedral but she got a medal. Goya did not get a medal.

1783. He was commissioned to paint the Count of Floridablanca, next to King Charles the most powerful man in Spain. Although Floridablanca charged him to say nothing, Goya wrote to Zapater that he wanted to share this important news. Josefa knew about it, he said, and he wanted his best friend to know. "When His Lordship came to have lunch in Madrid this afternoon I was with him for two hours. . . ."

Floridablanca stands confidently, resplendent in a red satin suit, peacock-blue sash draped across his right shoulder, starburst medal on his breast, gold-buckled shoes. Somewhat awkwardly he holds a pair of spectacles away from his body, a gesture that draws attention to them. In the eighteenth century, spectacles represented intelligence or heightened sensibility or acute perception, just as a dog in Flemish paintings symbolized fidelity. Goya therefore shows us a Prime Minister who is intellectual and discriminating. Floridablanca gazes beyond us while he contemplates the destiny of Spain; or, as one critic meanly remarked, he gazes toward the footlights. Spread out on a table are plans for a canal. Behind the plans, discreetly in shadow, sits the apprehensive architect, usually identified as Francisco Sabatini, who was imported by Charles III along with Squillace, Mengs, Tiepolo, et al. Goya presumptuously included himself, although clearly subordinate to the Prime Minister, which tells us something about the wrestling match in his head. He displays a picture for approval; Count Floridablanca, preoccupied with affairs of state, ignores it.

According to the journal of an English traveler, Floridablanca was "little" and felt sensitive about this. Goya was a sturdy man of average height so Floridablanca came up to his ears, maybe his chin. In the portrait, however, he represents himself as being smaller than the Prime Minister, which was at once tactful and obsequious.

Three years earlier while walking by himself through the summer palace at Aranjuez, Count Floridablanca had been stabbed in the back. The would-be assassin was a French citizen, a longtime resident of Spain, who was heard to shout "Muera este pícaro!" Death to this rogue! Just why he hated Floridablanca could not be determined, although it was learned that he had petitioned the government about something and never got a response. He was executed with unusual ceremony, not for attempted murder but for being French. In other words, a liberal atheist.

As to the portrait, critics treat it roughly. One said that Goya collected in it everything meretricious he had learned from Mengs and Bayeu: "The full force of eighteenth century pretentiousness is gathered there."

Another said it was painted with unforgivable clumsiness. "In all this mismanaged composition a single detail catches our eye today: the figure of Goya himself. . . ." Not so. Floridablanca's tomato-red suit splashes the middle of the canvas. What you see next is the apprehensive architect. Goya, a shadowy midget, ranks third, just ahead of an ornamental bronze clock on the table.

On April 26 he wrote to Zapater that he had finished the head of Señor Moñino, that it had turned out to be a very good likeness and Moñino was pleased. This is odd. The Count of Floridablanca's name was José Moñino. He came from an undistinguished family in Murcia, his father a notary, and was wholly conscious that now he stood beside King Charles. Goya's allusion to his background would not have pleased him.

Months went by. No payment. We'll clear up the business one of these days, said Floridablanca.

On January 3 the following year Goya wrote to Zapater: "I won't disturb him. . . ."

March 3: "Thus far I've had very little luck. Everyone is astonished that nothing comes from the Minister of State. . . ."

Eventually he got 6,000 reales. Not enough.

In April of 1785, along with two colleagues who had been shortchanged, Goya presented a joint petition, stiffly worded. And so the Prime Minister, weary of battling this obstinate serf, coughed up another 4,000 reales. Meager payment, but that was all.

In France at just about this time Jacques Louis David was getting rich. So was Sir Joshua Reynolds in England. However, the life of a successful artist in Spain during the eighteenth century wasn't bad, not if compared to an artist's life in previous centuries. Velázquez became court painter to Philip IV at the age of twenty-five and held that position until he died.

He got a studio in the palace, which must have been nice, but he was paid no more than a barber.

Michelangelo asked Pope Julius for leave to visit Florence on the day of St. John. When are you going to complete this chapel? His Holiness asked. When I can, said Michelangelo. The Pope hit him with a staff.

Uccello was given plenty of cheese but little else while painting the cloister of San Miniato. When he didn't show up for work one day the abbot dispatched some friars to look for him. What's wrong? they asked. It's the fault of your abbot, Uccello said. He stuffed me so full of cheese I'm afraid they'll use me to make glue.

Composers were no better off. Haydn and Mozart ate with the servants.

Once upon a time things were different. When General Marcellus looted Syracuse he gave orders to burn the city—excepting the district where a famous painting was housed. He did, naturally, carry the painting off to Rome. Nicomedes, King of Lycia, nearly bankrupted his country in order to buy a statue by Praxiteles.

Anyway, Floridablanca regarded Goya as a semiskilled laborer, coarse, difficult. When Goya had trouble getting paid for a job at the Church of San Francisco el Grande, he again petitioned the minister. His plea was seconded by an official of the San Fernando Academy. Floridablanca grudgingly acquiesced, noting in the margin that he didn't think much of the work.

By all accounts he was an effective deputy, although rigid and imperious. It's said that he let a Russian ambassador wait several weeks before granting audience. He sent money to American revolutionaries, which we don't expect, but England was Spain's traditional enemy and those uncouth provincials were giving England a headache. He tried to carry out the moderately humane reforms proposed by Charles, at least for a while, but progressive French ideas troubled him. In April of 1791 he issued a decree suppressing every newspaper except the official *Gaceta* and *Mercurio de España*. Strict watch was kept at the frontier. No French propaganda. Voltaire? No. Montesquieu? No. Rousseau? No. Edward Gibbon? Certainly not. Foreigners entering Spain must swear allegiance to King

Charles and to the Catholic religion. Further, each must "renounce all claim or right of appeal for protection to his own nationality. . . ."

Alas, the infernal malice of Frenchmen would not be denied. Revolutionary propaganda slipped through. A Parisian haberdasher secreted pages from liberal tracts in the lining of hats bound for Cádiz. At the Bilbao fair a Frenchman from Pau was caught with paper fans depicting Louis XVI, Lafayette, and the fall of the Bastille. French ships dumped revolutionary material in Spanish harbors "in sealed metal boxes which accomplices from the shore could later pull up by means of a string left attached to a floating piece of cork." Floridablanca must have been enraged. At Logroño the Holy Office collected evidence and by the end of 1791 could point to 429 incriminating items. Copies of *Assemblée nationale* somehow got through the minister's net, as did *Le Bulletin et Journal des Journaux* and *La Feuille villageoise.* Well, how does one proceed against envoys from Satan?

The Holy Office resolved to make an example of a prominent scholar, Bernardo María de Calzada, responsible for translating *La logique* of Condillac, *Le fils naturel* of Diderot, Voltaire's *Alzire,* and a biography of Frederick II. Calzada held the rank of lieutenant colonel in the Queen's cavalry regiment and he had served in the Ministry of War, but it wasn't enough. The Inquisition jailed him, condemned him to abjure de levi—meaning he was suspected of heresy, and banished him from Madrid. A relatively light sentence, perhaps, but he was professionally destroyed, an unmistakable warning to others.

Goya surely hoped and perhaps expected that knowing Floridablanca would lead to further commissions. The great man remained chilly, unapproachable. However, during those sittings Goya had become acquainted with the Infante Don Luis de Bourbon, His Majesty's younger brother.

4

Don Luis de Bourbon had been ordained a cardinal at the age of nine. Not sixty, fifty, or fifteen. He was not quite ten years old when they settled a red hat on his childish head, a prize that most ecclesiastics would kill for. Along with the hat he got the Archbishopric of Toledo. These plums together ensured him a fortune since they included revenue not only from Spain but from Mexico. In short, Don Luis, being the King's brother, could look forward to a life of luxury and respect. Don Luis renounced it. Why? As he himself put the matter, he was an ordinary sensual man. The idea of an empty bed night after night, decade after decade, was appalling. He knew—everybody in Spain knew—that he could take a mistress, as ecclesiastics have done since time began. But this meant duplicity and Don Luis was not up to it. Indeed, judging from Goya's portrait of him surrounded by family, Don Luis might not have been up to much of anything more strenuous than a wife and children. He looks amiable, feckless, with a bulging pink nose. He could be your indolent neighbor.

That might have been true enough when Goya painted the aging Infante, but some decades earlier he was a different case. One fine day while amusing himself in the forest he succumbed to salacious misconduct, from the Latin salax, also known by a four-letter word: rape. He then found himself attempting to explain the regrettable situation to his brother. King Charles probably considered having Luis garotted but that would be awkward. And he must have thought the church's insistence on celibacy contributed to his brother's ungovernable lust because he sanctioned marriage for princes of the blood. The church did not object. Charles then suggested that Luis marry his daughter, Princess María Josefa. In other words, Luis should marry his own niece. María Josefa threw a fit. Not only was Don Luis her uncle, he was a rake, a scoundrel, a lecher. She wanted nothing to do with him.

Goya painted María Josefa when she was an old maid—deformed, goggle-eyed, cursed with that unmistakable Bourbon nose. She had been young at the time her father suggested marriage, true, but Don Luis might not have been disappointed when she rejected him. Although her deformity isn't apparent in the family portrait, Goya caught the features of an ugly, shriveled, and possibly crazed spinster.

At any rate, having again consulted the church, Charles gave Luis permission to marry whomever he wished.

So, having discarded the red hat of a cardinal, Don Luis at age thirty-five looked around. He was interested in botany, butterfly catching, and similar pursuits; and while on a butterfly expedition, or perhaps during a conversation about butterflies, he was stricken to the loins by a young lady from Aragón. Her name was María Teresa de Vallabriga y Rozas, sometimes given as Vallabriga y Drummond, low-level nobility related to the English Stuarts. Her father was a cavalry captain.

Don Luis married her. He could not marry the daughter of another king, or the daughter of a grandee; Charles forbade this, probably to keep his brother's children from asserting a claim to the throne.

This morganatic marriage disgusted Charles who thought the lower orders ought to be kept in place. Now his brother had married some Aragonese woman. It was a bit much. Luis had no sense of protocol. What should be done? He contemplated shipping his black sheep brother and the Aragonese woman to Mexico, naming his brother Viceroy to the New World, but that would endow Luis with considerable status. What he did, finally, was exile Luis from court. He gave his brother a less than exalted title, Count of Chinchón, and suggested that Luis occupy himself on the provincial estate of Arenas de San Pedro some leagues west of Madrid. Enjoy yourself, said Charles, and try to keep your nose clean.

Once in a while, for the sake of appearance, his presence would be required at court. A royal carriage would be dispatched to pick him up, not at his estate but a few miles from wherever Charles happened to be presiding. Don Luis would arrive in a plain coach drawn by mules: coche de colleras. Valets-de-chambre would fit him with a suit appropriate for the occasion and away he went to visit the King. Charles would greet him cordially. They would chat like brothers on the best of terms. Once the affair ended, Don Luis Cinderella would be stripped of his costume and sent back to the provinces in a mule-drawn coach.

He might have challenged his brother's right to the crown because of a 1713 law that excluded princes not born in Spain. Charles was born in Naples. Don Luis was a Madrileño and must have known he could assert his right under the provision of that law. Should the wind blow favorably, he might dethrone his brother and have himself crowned King of Spain. He didn't try because he found life at Arenas de San Pedro quite agreeable. Day after day he could shoot partridge, chase butterflies, listen to music. He loved music. He patronized and enjoyed the respectful friendship of Boccherini, Scarlatti, and Padre Antonio Soler. He lived on a beautiful country estate with an attractive young wife, a bucket of servants, no mortgage payments. Being non grata at court didn't upset him very much. Biographer Vallentin remarks that he exhaled the contentment of a human being who had at last got rid of the constraints imposed upon him at birth.

If he went traveling he took along a picture of the Holy Virgin painted by Mengs. Holy Mary is seated on the grass, legs crossed, bare to the knees. Don Luis probably imagined that he was adoring the Mother of Christ. Maybe, maybe not. Casanova says that Don Luis was a true Spaniard, interpreting his passion in the most favorable sense.

Another artist favored by the Infante was Luis Paret y Alcázar. Paret had been doing quite nicely, climbing the ladder, winning a prize for his neoclassic version of Hannibal paying homage to the Temple of Hercules. But then, justly or unjustly, he was suspected of having pimped for the Infante. Off went the disgraced artist to Puerto Rico, exiled, his burgeoning career in ashes. He painted himself amongst the ruins of a classical building—miserable, hungry, a barefoot peasant with a machete. In fact, things weren't so bad; he had been making a fair living with his brush instead of harvesting bananas. Anyway, he sent the picture to King Charles. You might not expect this strange appeal to have much effect, but Charles modified the sentence, allowing Paret to settle in Bilbao, not Spain's loveliest city. Myself, I'd choose Puerto Rico. It's a sad story without a moral.

What happened may not have been Paret's fault; he was a craftsman equivalent to a wheelwright, a goldsmith, a boot maker, crushed by imperial forces. Whose fault was it that his dream of glory faded? The Infante, of course, or the Infante's unruly gonads.

Goya visited Arenas de San Pedro in August of 1783 and had a fine time, if we judge from a boastful letter to Zapater: "They gave me one thousand duros and gave my wife a silver and gold dress worth thirty thousand reales. . . . They regretted my departure enormously and insisted that I come back every year. . . ." He knew the value of the dress because he asked the Infante's wardrobe servants what it was worth.

Goya also mentioned that he and Don Luis went rabbit hunting. The Infante complimented him on his marksmanship. After a second visit, the Infante ordered a coach for his return to Madrid. Why shouldn't Goya boast? On the horizon lay Fuendetodos and his father's poverty. José Goya didn't bother to make a will because he had nothing to leave: No testó porque no tenía de que.

Those visits sound pleasant but Don Luis had not invited Goya to hunt rabbits as he might invite, say, the Duke of Saragossa. The artist dutifully painted his genial host and employer. He painted an equestrian portrait of Doña María Teresa and two of their three children. Two because the youngest was a baby. He also did an exquisite study of María

Teresa in profile. There used to be a label on the back stating that he executed this work between 11:00 and 12:00 in the morning, August 27, 1783. Why would he note the time? Perhaps because her milk-white face against a dark background suggests that it was done at night. Perhaps, again, he was boasting, proud that he could do such beautifully finished work in one hour.

Another portrait of the Infante's wife is almost Japanese. María Teresa stands beside a chair. Arched eyebrows, ivory skin, black hair. She might have been lifted from a woodblock print, though her gown with fringed sleeves is unmistakably Spanish.

And while visiting Arenas de San Pedro he did the mysterious family portrait. Don Luis sits at a green table on which there is a pack of cards and a burning candle. He looks dazed, befuddled, glassy-eyed. He resembles George Washington except for the nose, the grotesque Bourbon nose, swollen, possibly discolored by too many goblets of wine. Americans call this a whisky nose and since he was Don Luis de Bourbon they wonder if there might be a connection. No. That whisky is distilled from corn, which Europeans regard as inappropriate for anything except pig feed, and takes its name from a county in Kentucky where it was first produced.

Major William Dalrymple saw Don Luis in 1774 when he was Cardinal Archbishop of Seville and Toledo—before that infamous assault in the forest, before he was ostracized. Major Dalrymple found him to be of a most humane disposition and universally esteemed, albeit "the strangest-looking mortal that ever appeared." Dalrymple might not have seen Charles III who, if we judge from extant portraits, was at least as strange looking as his brother.

The Infante's wife, Doña María Teresa, seated on the far side of the table, is having her hair dressed. She appears to be taller than her husband. Then you notice the reason. All the surrounding family members, including María Teresa, and Goya himself, have been disposed to focus your gaze on the Infante. Diagonal lines converge on His Highness. Here and there, each carefully placed, other members of the establishment, among them a man with a bandaged head who grins at us quite stupidly. The effect is disconcerting. Three decades later when Goya painted the execution of Madrileños by Napoleon's troops he made a similar esthetic mistake. We will get back to that.

The wife of Don Luis also looks at us. Her white gown centers the picture and she is seated next to her husband. A nurse holds their infant daughter while the older child watches Goya at work. All in all, a puzzling composition, not only for pictorial reasons. It is, in fact, not comprehensible until one has been initiated, just as paintings of Dutch and Flemish masters cannot be understood without a knowledge of symbols: rings, mirrors, dogs. Thus the candle, Don Luis in profile, and so forth, are more than they seem. Members of the family have been scattered horizontally, yet the artist is shown working on a vertical canvas. What's it all about?

As to the candle and cards, scholars aren't sure what game Don Luis is playing; but divination by cards, cartomancy, was a popular diversion. He might be telling the future. There is less doubt about the candle, which shows the influence of Johann Lavater and silhouette making. Lavater was a Swiss pastor, champion of the art, who invented a device called "Reliable and Convenient Machine for Drawing Silhouettes." It is illustrated in his *Essai sur la physiognomie.* We have a lady seated on a chair. To her left is a candle on an ornamental stand so it is about the height of her head. Immediately to her right, a screen. On the far side of the screen a silhouette artist traces her shadow. The apparatus is reminiscent of those eighteenth-century reliable and convenient machines employed by debauched gentlemen who enjoyed trussing up young ladies for one purpose or another.

Dr. Lavater's essay on physiognomy came out in four volumes published between 1775 and 1778 beneath a thunderous German title: *Physiognomische Fragmente zur Beförderung der Menschenkenntnis and Menschenliebe.* Goya didn't read German. However, a French translation appeared not long before he went to work on the Infante's family, and he did understand a little French. Some historians/biographers claim he knew not a word. Indeed, that's what his close friend Moratín wrote many years later when Goya fled to Bordeaux. Moratín exaggerated.

Anyway, evidence suggests that he saw Lavater's ponderous volumes and was fascinated by the illustrations. He could have found someone to explain the text. We know, too, from caricatures and grotesque faces that physiognomy interested him. While working on the *Caprichos* he drew sixteen half-human half-animal heads on one sheet of paper. Somebody, not Goya, wrote his name at the bottom and dated it 1798. He probably made these drawings at the salon of the Marquis of Santa Cruz, maybe to entertain guests. As Frederick Licht points out, these bestial faces are reminiscent of animal heads discussed by Lavater:

> Here a man exhibits a nose similar in outline to the bill of a cassowary, in which Lavater saw an expression of weakness blended with presumption; two other noses are shaped like the bills of birds of prey; a human profile has a rodent-like appearance, expressive of lasciviousness and stupid gluttony . . . the head of the sheep, well rounded on top and lacking in lively or penetrating expression, finds its counterpoint in another of the human heads.

Nothing new about Goya's idiosyncratic doodling. See Leonardo's red-chalk drawing of a leonine man. And of course the belief that a man who resembles a beast probably shares the beast's nature might be traced to Ice Age drawings.

Dr. Lavater instructs us with Swiss exactitude. One's features are affected by one's moral state. All right. The town drunk, for instance, is easy to identify. Dr. Lavater goes further. The soul reveals itself in the face, which the artist must understand if he wishes to delineate the soul of his subject. True. And the most direct reading may be found by examining the profile. What next? Physiognomists therefore look to the silhouette which, in the lower half of the profile, reveals nobility, and to the nose we look for poetic sensibility. It's worth considering. The Infante collected butterflies. He loved music. Look at his nose.

Goya probably studied Lavater's magnum opus. We have an otherwise inexplicable candle and we have the vertical canvas Goya set up for a horizontal group portrait, which makes no sense except that its dimensions approximate those of the vertical screen in Lavater's extraordinary apparatus. If this much is correct, Goya may have had a difficult time explaining why he wanted Don Luis in profile. Royalty wasn't painted in profile, nobody was painted in profile. The idea would have been startling. Silhouettes were in vogue but they weren't serious art. One toyed with silhouettes for amusement. Now, along with butterflies, musicians, and similar novelties, the Infante collected coins. Coins often immortalized the profile of a conquering general or an emperor. So, it has been argued, Goya might justify his unusual idea.

Across the table from Don Luis stands a confident young man with arms folded, Luigi Boccherini, musician to the Court of Arenas. To his right, plump and solemn, the Infante's secretary, Manuel Moderna. To his right, a nurse holding the baby. Just behind the Infante's wife, a celebrated hairdresser, Santos García, attending to María Teresa's famously beautiful hair. Behind Don Luis, his son, at that time six years old, who appears to be studying Moderna's paunch. Behind the boy stands his little sister, who would become the Countess of Chinchón. She leans forward to watch the artist. Goya painted this child at least three times. Seventeen years after the group portrait he painted her alone, voluminously clothed in white, her eyes timid and sad. The Countess wears her prettiest gown, a high-waisted chemise, a spray of wheat in her reddish curls to represent forthcoming motherhood. She had been forced to marry Prime Minister Godoy. The position of her hands may indicate that she is trying to hide her pregnancy. However, the arrangement is natural. Goya probably suggested it because the acute angle of her left arm solidifies a composition that otherwise would dissolve.

That her husband was a sluggish lout and a grasping lecher seems indisputable. Finally she couldn't stand it but when Goya painted this picture she may have been in love, never mind the apparent sadness. On her right hand she wears an oval portrait ring in which can be seen a man's face. And who would this be, if not her husband? During the war with France they separated. She fled to Cádiz with other refugee aristocrats and was observed on a balcony singing a patriotic song that wished Napoleon the utmost in bad luck: *Muera Napoleón!*

Excluding a couple of female attendants, this leaves two figures in the group. Behind Luigi Boccherini stands the grinning fool, Francisco del Campo, an insignificant member of the household staff. Either he waits to be fitted with a new wig and the bandage is a necessary preparation or his wig is "under powder."

The last is Alejandro de la Cruz, former painter to the Infante's court. He lost his job. Now he stands at the edge of the picture, nine-tenths hidden, an unhappy man peeping around Francisco del Campo.

September 23, 1783. Goya wrote to Zapater that he had just returned from Arenas and was exhausted: "His Highness honored me a thousand times. I have painted his portrait, along with his wife and son and daughter, and received praise beyond my expectation since others have gone there and failed. Twice I went hunting with His Majesty. . . ."

The family of the Infante Don Luis de Bourbon isn't Goya at his best, although it brought one commission after another. The celebrated architect Don Ventura Rodríguez sat for a portrait. The University of Salamanca needed something. The Duke of Hijar wanted paintings for a church in Teruel. Everybody knew Goya was the man.

To Zapater he wrote: "You would kiss my butt at least seven times if you knew how happy I am to be living here."

5

Javier was born in 1784. None of Goya's other children lived very long.

He painted Javier at twenty: a slender cherubic sport, quite Byronic, walking stick, high boots, striped trousers, ruffled shirt, hair styled to give him the look of a Roman emperor, one hand thrust into his waistcoat. At his feet a crabby little dog of the sort favored by imperious ladies. It's been said that Javier projects a swaying indecisive delicacy unlike his father's sensual bulk, as though what remained of Goya had been diluted.

In 1805 he married María Gumersinda Goicoechea, daughter of a wealthy merchant. Goya wangled a government job for him as well as a royal pension. If the Duchess of Alba met Javier isn't known; she might only have heard Goya talk about him, but she left him an annuity. So, having totted up those doubloons, expecting thousands more when the old man died, Javier chucked his government job and spent the next half century loitering. Goya drew him in 1823, not yet forty although he looks older, a commonplace man aging rapidly.

By the time of his son's marriage Goya had become Director of Painting at the Royal Academy. This brought more honor than profit, he remarked to Zapater, and explains why he had not escaped the tapestry factory. Nevertheless he was edging closer to the throne. The Duke of Medinaceli, chief steward to the King, commissioned a large Annunciation.

He consulted his friend on how to invest: "You know all about money." He wondered if he ought to buy government bonds or bank shares. Perhaps a higher rate of return might be obtained elsewhere? Zapater's advice has been lost, but Goya bought twenty-five shares of the Banco de San Carlos. And like a good capitalist he attended at least one shareholder's meeting: February 24, 1788.

A tapestry cartoon, *The Blind Guitarist*, was rejected by weavers who thought it would be too difficult. Goya was exasperated. Although he simplified the design, he refused to change the blind man's anguished face. Street musicians, acrobats, itinerant entertainers of one stripe or another had long been favorite Spanish themes, but Goya had studied blind musicians and saw more than his contemporaries. Charles III, for whatever reason, liked it. So did the future Charles IV and his licentious wife María Luisa.

Among his last cartoons was a festival or picnic on the banks of the Manzanares honoring St. Isidro. This, too, was rejected. If his guitar player with not many figures had seemed intricate, what was happening beside the Manzanares must have dismayed the weavers. Madrid stretches along the horizon in addition to countless picnickers, horses, parasols, vehicles, and what-not. The day looks pleasant, the Manzanares flows smoothly as it should. All was right with the world in that reasonably tranquil year of 1788 and anybody looking at Goya's sketch, noting from the ladies' parasols that it must be a warm afternoon, would consider going for a swim.

Half a century later when Théophile Gautier arrived from Paris, the Manzanares was just about hors de combat. Gautier blames the Madrileños whose thirst was prodigious: "All the waters of the fountains and all the snows of the Guadarrama Mountains would not be sufficient to slake it." He tells us that in Madrid exists a trade unknown in Paris, aguadores or aguadoras, water sellers, whose stock consists of a cantaro of white earthenware, a little basket of reeds in which may be seen two or three glasses, a few sticks of caramel, maybe a couple of oranges or limes.

"Water! Water!" they cry from five in the morning till ten at night. "Who wants water? Iced water, cool as snow!"

Gautier sympathizes with the Manzanares, prey to such a thirst. The river has been drunk dry because these water sellers hunt for anything liquid between its banks and carry it off in their cantaros. Thus, washerwomen are obliged to wash clothes with sand, while in the middle of the river there isn't enough water for a Mohammedan to perform his ablutions.

Hugh Stokes early in the twentieth century reported that Madrid has few natural advantages. As for the Manzanares, it requires a careful voyage of discovery. Sometimes it might be in flood, yes, but all he saw was a trickle. Madrileños are called Ballenatos, whaling men, because once upon a time they noticed a saddle floating downstream and mistook it for a whale.

Gautier and Stokes sound like a couple of comedians.

Another step in Goya's career was his introduction to the immensely rich Duke and Duchess of Osuna, patrons of art, acting, playwriting, and bullfighting. They were among the most powerful figures in Spain. They happened to be first cousins but that was irrelevant. Not only did they marry, they had four children. The Duchess claimed a sheaf of titles even before marrying the Duke: Countess of Benavente, Countess of Mayorga, Duchess of Bejar, of Gandía, of Arcos de la Frontera, Marchioness of Lombay and Jabalquinto, Princess of Anglona, Princess of Esquilache, and more.

Goya painted the family in 1788. The Duke appears soft, tentative, unassuming, gentle, a considerate man tilted slightly aside in deference to his wife. He wasn't too bright. The Duchess, however, was something else. She feared nobody, nothing on earth, whether it walked on two feet or four feet. Lady Elizabeth Holland, who came visiting, described her as the most distinguished woman in Madrid. Lady Holland's diary, not published until 1910, goes on at length. The Duchess has a taste for French luxuries. She is hospitable and lively, albeit her wit disguises an utter lack of refinement. In figure, light and airy. Peña, her favorite cortejo, has been attached for quite a few years.

Cortejo has no English equivalent, though it approximates "suitor," or possibly "escort," and a lady might enjoy the attentions of more than one. The husband didn't object; at least, he was supposed to pretend that he didn't mind. A British traveler, Joseph Townsend, was fascinated by this custom, summarizing it in a two-volume memoir briskly titled: *A Journey through Spain in the years 1786 and 1787 with Particular Attention to the Agriculture, Manufactures, Commerce, Population, Taxes, and Revenue of that Country* . . . and so on. He informs us that no sooner does a lady marry than she is surrounded by young men eager to become the cortejo. They don't give up until she has selected one. He is then privileged to escort her to concerts, parties, the theater. In return, he is expected to buy or somehow obtain whatever she wants. The relationship might or might not be limited to social displays. Circumstances varied.

Lady Holland doesn't give much information about Peña. We do learn that the Duchess commanded her family, a statement verified by her dominant bearing in Goya's portrait. Her income exceeded that of the Duke, whose own revenue was vast. As for this diffident husband, he loved to read. He got the King's permission to import from other countries any books he wanted, even those prohibited by the Holy Office. He built an excellent library of classics, travel, history, and science. He wanted to open his library to the public, but King Charles denied this request. Too liberal.

A few leagues south of Madrid stood the Osunas' favorite retreat, La Alameda, literally the poplar grove, or park, an oasis flourishing on the desolate plains of Castille. It seems to have been inspired by English country estates because in 1787 the Duchess bought several prints of English mansions with "irregular" gardens, and work on La Alameda began not long afterward. In the argot of those days it was known as El Capricho, a sovereign folly, a monumental caprice, acres of land devoted to vineyards, greenhouses, gardens, thickets, ponds—"arrogant and egregious luxury" in the words of Vallentin, who describes La Alameda as a taste for the grandiose symbolized by the palace where immense granite steps, inviting a slow and majestic gait, led to the entrance. Round about loomed artificial hillocks surmounted by colonnaded temples, waterfalls, a hermitage occupied by replicas of hermits for authenticity, a miniature fortress whose silent cannons threatened occasional birds, "the relish of mystery in an existence of dulled sensations." Here lived the Duke and Duchess of Osuna in Asiatic splendor, festooned with titles accumulated through generations of intermarriage among Spain's noblest families. Each marriage delivered more titles, more doubloons, more estates. Here congregated Madrid intellectuals: Ramón de la Cruz, Leandro Moratín, and others of that fraternity who must have thought La Alameda a taste of paradise on earth.

It was here that Goya recorded the Osunas. We see them closely grouped. One critic thinks the composition stilted, satirical, family members anemic. The youngest child, who pulls a toy coach, might be a china doll. Another critic thinks it an affectionate family portrait.

The lean and stiff Duchess looks proud, unyielding, a woman without beauty or feminine grace. One biographer compares the elongated head to that of an Egyptian pharaoh. There can be no question about her intelligence; you mark it in the scant smile, the calculating eyes.

La Duquesa María Josefa Pimentel Tellez Giror y Borjia.

Three years earlier, in 1785, Goya had painted this unlovely woman standing alone. Her gown is French blue, styled à l'Anglaise, bodice fastened in front, huge pink bow at the waist. Her flat hips are padded, the artificial curve emphasized with ribbons and roses. The immense hat sprouts ostrich feathers. According to Sarah Symmons, she displayed her taste for modern fashion by adding ringleted curls to the outline of her hair, a detail she plucked from an important fashion periodical: *Cabinet des Modes.* Every woman in Madrid who cared about style knew she was the one to watch.

In those days no more than a hundred Spaniards were entitled to harness four mules to their carriages, to be escorted by four torch bearers, to wear a hat in the King's presence. His Majesty addressed these few as Cousin. The Osunas, naturally, belonged to this privileged group.

She considered herself an actress. Occasionally she would go on stage at La Alameda where she and the Duke kept a poet on the payroll, Tomás de Yriarte, regarded these days as a clever versifier, who could write skits and otherwise entertain guests. She understood the new science of economics well enough that she gave lectures and was elected president of the Women's Section of the Economic Society. She didn't trust clerks to keep track of the Osuna holdings but went over the books herself. She was, of course, a splendid horsewoman; she enjoyed galloping around the estates and would sleep wherever she happened to be, oblivious to storms and to the possibility of meeting human riffraff. She accompanied her husband on the conquest of Minorca, disguised as a sailor. We might assume she could handle the stiletto and sword.

If displeased, she could respond harshly. The author of a song alluding to her rivalry with the Duchess of Alba spent a year in jail. When Goya's friendship with La Alba became a subject of gossip she didn't turn against him as might be expected. She and the Duke remained loyal, generous patrons. Her taste in graphic art ran to macabre spectacles—witches and the like. If her husband shared this taste, we don't know; it's doubtful that he stood up to his wife. When a quarrel developed he probably retreated to his library or listened to music.

The Osuna line was most distinguished. Her ancestors included a couple of princes, half a dozen dukes, and Francisco Borgia, who became St. Francis. We don't think of the Borgia as saints.

First, a little background music. The most notorious member of this family was Lucrezia who spun her web in Italy, so we regard the Borgia as Italian. In fact, they came from Aragón. When the cardinal-archbishop of Valencia, Alfonso de Borja, became Pope Calixtus III he moved to Rome and various relatives followed. His nephew Rodrigo would become Pope Alexander VI. Rodrigo, before attaining the pontificate, had four children by a Roman woman named Vannozza. Two of these children have become nearly synonymous with evil: Cesare and Lucrezia.

Cesare, although tangential to our story, deserves a moment because it's hard to imagine anybody worse, excepting a few politicians. His father obtained a cardinal's hat for him at the age of seventeen but Cesare resigned the office when his elder brother was murdered. Why? Cesare probably had something to do with killing his brother. And there is little doubt that he arranged the murder of Lucrezia's second husband, Alfonso of Aragón. What next? Cesare gained control of Piombino, Elba, Camerino, and the Duchy of Urbino. After inviting his enemies to Sinigaglia castle, presumably to negotiate an end to hostilities, he had them strangled. But the good times were almost over. A new pontiff, Julius II, ordered his arrest. Cesare escaped to Naples, thence to Spain where he was sheltered by the King of Navarre. We are told that this cruel and treacherous man, unscrupulous to the ultimate degree, was a fairly common sort. It's worth thinking about. Machiavelli, having thought about it, used him as a model for *Il Principe*.

Concerning his sister Lucrezia, that illustrious poisoner, Lucrezia is the stuff of grand opera. See Donizetti, who took the story from Victor Hugo's drama. Lucrezia's first marriage was annulled. Her second husband, as has been noted, egregiously annoyed Cesare. The next husband, Alfonso d'Este, became Duke of Ferrara and scholars believe that as Duchess of Ferrara she escaped the influence of depraved relatives. In other words, Lucrezia's bad press is undeserved. Her brilliant court attracted artists and poets such as Ariosto. Her beauty, piety, and kindness won universal esteem. Rumors of participation in malignant plots, of incest with father and brother, of extravagant vices—all disproved. Maybe. Maybe she did get a bad press, but a nice woman doesn't make good opera.

More interesting is the fact that she had a son named Gennaro who was raised by a Neapolitan fisherman. Gennaro grew up to be a soldier and a bit of a prig who publicly denounced Lucrezia, not knowing she was his mother. He once attacked the Ferrara escutcheon, whacking off a B so that Borgia became orgia, which requires no translation. Lucrezia demanded that Gennaro be poisoned but rescinded the order when she learned that he was her son.

We now return to the good Borgia, Francisco, great-grandson of Alexander VI. He was born in Gandía south of Valencia and was expected to become a member of the imperial court. At nineteen he married Eleanor de Castra and they had eight children. When his father died he became Duke of Gandía. Eleanor died in 1546 and Francisco thereafter devoted himself to the Church. After being ordained he traveled through Portugal and Spain where his sermons drew enormous crowds. In 1564 he was summoned to Rome and a few years later became father-general of the Jesuits. During the plague of 1566 he raised money and organized his priests to help the victims. He died after what has been described as an exhilarating but exhausting tour of France and the Iberian peninsula. In 1671 he was canonized.

The legend of his epiphany makes better reading. It's a tale gruesome enough to scare naughty children. Emperor Charles V directed him to escort the casket of Empress Isabel—known as The Three Graces because of her marvelous beauty—to Seville. En route there was an accident, the casket broke apart, and Isabel's decomposed remains spilled out. Francisco saw what was left of the famously beautiful empress. The sight terrified him. How futile our existence. Vanitas vanitatum. He renounced family, estate, everything material, and turned to God.

The Osunas were proud of having a saint in the family. Who wouldn't be? They built a chapel to him at Valencia and sent for Goya.

Connoisseurs dismiss Goya's first attempt as uninspired pathos: Francisco Borgia tells his family goodbye.

The second attempt is better. St. Francis exorcises a dying man who lies stiffly on his bed, mouth agape, skin greenish-white. It brings to mind Holbein's *Dead Christ.* Goya might have seen a print of this painting. Beside the demon-infested man three monsters hunch in the flames of hell, fangs exposed, staring greedily at their prey. Blood spurts from a crucifix that St. Francis holds up while entreating the accursed soul to repent. Some historians believe Goya painted the dying man naked. This offended the Church; an unknown artist therefore was commissioned to paint a shroud over his genitals. They argue that the folds of cloth are depicted clumsily, whereas Goya would have rendered them with a few deft strokes. However, Goya's preliminary sketch, now in a private collection, doesn't show exposed genitals.

In 1786 he was appointed Painter to the King, a position worth 15,000 reales: "I thanked the King, the Prince, the other directors, and Bayeu who said he had urged Maella to select me."

Life was good. He ordered boots from England. He took French lessons. He complained that days weren't long enough; he painted himself wearing a plug hat fitted with metal candle holders to show that he worked at night, and here we catch a whiff of humbug. He seems to be addressing his public. I work very late, you understand, because I am such a popular artist. He might have stolen this idea from Michelangelo who is known to have worked at night with a large candle burning on his hat. Vasari saw the hat several times and observed that Michelangelo didn't use ordinary wax but pure goat tallow.

Goya indeed was popular. Within a few years he cranked out three hundred portraits and customers were delighted, never mind slovenly composition or anything else. Ah! Look there! He got my sash just right!

One dour critic wrote that his work during this period resembled American primitives or the portraits on tavern signs.

He bought an expensive house with a garden and a view of the river. He admitted that he was spending more than a few reales but explained that his position demanded it.

Why not a carriage? Perhaps a barouche, something stately, dignified, four wheels, four seats inside with an outside seat for the driver. Or something sporty. A two-wheeled cabriolet might be fun. Cabriolet derives from the Latin capreolus, wild goat. He told Zapater that it had been made in England, a la ynglesa, very light, a jewel, gold-painted. Marvelous. And he bought a ten-year-old horse from a Neapolitan. He and the Neapolitan went for a spin. They were rocking along in fine style outside city traffic when Goya speeded up. The passenger asked if he would like to see a Neapolitan turn. Of course, Goya said, and handed over the reins. According to his letter, the road wasn't wide enough. The wild goat crashed. Goya and the Neapolitan went flying, bum over head. Thank God, he wrote, the damage was light. He himself got the worst of it and had been laid up since St. James' Day. He was expecting a visit from the royal doctor to find out if he might have permission to walk. His right ankle was hurting, although he didn't think it was broken.

He had the cabriolet fixed and drove it a while longer, but for several months he limped and must have concluded that he wasn't so young and sprightly as he thought. He traded the goat for a dignified four-wheeled barouche drawn by two dependable Aragonese mules. He was forty years old.

In that same letter to Zapater, dated August 1, 1786, he remarked that no more did he wait in antechambers. No indeed, people must come to him. And unless it was a friend, or somebody important, he let the client wait.

His work during this period is inconsistent. He had outgrown the rigid world of tapestries but didn't quite trust his instinct. He failed most obviously when he tried to serve popular taste, although he was good with children. Don Manuel Osorio de Zuñiga. A fairy tale little prince dazzled by the splendor of his clothes, lace collar emphasizing the delicate childish flesh, eyes somewhat bewildered. Don Manuel has a pet magpie tethered by a string. Three murderous Goya cats—gray cat, black cat, brindled assassin—crouch together, focused on the magpie. They know they dare not pounce. The magpie understands. All's well.

Biographer Symmons looked at this picture differently. The child's stunted body places him in the role of a Velázquez dwarf: "Manuel Osorio's father was himself of dwarfish stature, and his son's large head, small body and tiny hands may have prompted Goya to remember." Six years earlier Goya had copied the Velázquez portrait of a deformed, fiercely mustachioed homunculus named Sebastián de Morra who amused the court of Philip IV.

He also copied a Velázquez portrait of Innocent X, doing his best to capture the Pope's fanatic resolve. Velázquez isn't credited with insight so much as technical brilliance, but he nailed Innocent. Goya never saw this autocrat alive on the papal throne; he depended upon Velázquez. He almost succeeded. But the man Goya sketched is somebody who might forgive. The man Velázquez painted will excuse nothing. In that face is no vestige of compassion.

King Charles III, a decent and likeable elf, may or may not have stood for a portrait. Goya doesn't mention painting him, which is curious. And there is an almost identical portrait by Mengs, dated 1761. Goya's monarch, circa 1787, has accumulated some wrinkles and he wears hunting clothes instead of armor. The stance is the same: right hand grasping a baton in Mengs, clutching a white glove in Goya. Mengs showed part of the King's thumb behind his baton; Goya eliminated that. And in both portraits the left arm is extended at the same angle. With Mengs, the King appears to be gesturing or pointing. Goya equipped him with a flintlock. The backgrounds are different, but that would be easy to fake. Goya settled a rakish tricorn hat on his head. That, too, would be no problem. Beneath the hat we glimpse part of a white wig. Below the wig, a glimpse of the King's dark hair. Mengs painted the same thing nineteen years earlier. So we don't know. Charles might have stood for Goya, although side-by-side comparison does suggest imitation.

However it came about, Goya shows him properly dressed for hunting—except the imperial blue sash and Maltese Cross. Curled up at his feet, a white hound. If we exclude those grotesques spawned by inbred royalty, Charles must be one of the oddest-looking sovereigns on record. Major Dalrymple said he had a mahogany complexion and a most peculiar appearance and described him as diminutive, a man who had not been measured for a coat in thirty years, "so that it fits upon him like a sack; his waistcoat and breeches are generally leather, with a pair of cloth spatterdashes on his legs."

Mr. Henry Swineburne, ancestor of the poet, visited Spain. His description adds a few details. Charles usually wore a long hat, gray Segovian frock, buff waistcoat, black breeches, worsted stockings. His pockets were stuffed with knives, gloves, and shooting tackle. He carried a small dagger. "On gala days, a fine suit is hung upon his shoulders, but as he has an eye to his afternoon sport, and is a great economist of his time, the black breeches are worn to all coats." Neither storm nor heat nor cold prevented him from hunting. If he heard about a wolf he would drive half across the kingdom to shoot it. Near the end of his reign he totted up the numbers in his game book: 539 wolves, 5,235 foxes. His passion for hunting must have been the subject of gossip because he mentioned that all those foxes and wolves would have killed a great many farm animals.

Although Charles was phenomenally ugly, the gods are just. To compensate for nonexistent shoulders and that Bourbon nose they awarded him good health and considerable intelligence. This might sound like an unfair exchange after you have looked at the wrinkled triangular face, but of course he was a monarch with everything that implies. He is said to have been entirely honest in his purpose, dedicated to equality as he saw it. He once rebuked the president of the Council of Castile for "pretty conversation." He wanted governmental business handled without delay, no dawdling: "I also wish that if it is possible to bend justice that the poor get preference."

His mother was Italian, Isabel Farnese, second wife of Philip V, a scheming, abusive vixen who thought her sons ought to govern Italy. This involved quite a lot of manipulation resulting in soldiers killed, maimed, collateral damage and all that, but it concluded as she wished. Spain acquired Naples and various Italian duchies.

Therefore, at age sixteen, Prince Charles sailed away to Naples and didn't return for twenty-seven years. His mother is remembered primarily as a termagent, but it might be noted that she had a world-class collection of fans; almost certainly Philip's wife could boast of more fans than any woman in Spain: 1,626.

Charles governed happily enough as King of Naples until the death of his half-brother, Ferdinand VI, whereupon he inherited the Spanish crown. Antonio Joli painted a graceful view of his departure in 1759. He embarked for Spain escorted by thirteen battleships and two frigates, crowds lining the harbor, Vesuvius lazily smoking in the background.

He liked exotic birds in gilded cages and musical clocks. He had no time for stage plays or dancing or music and he disliked bullfighting, but hunting he most dearly loved: "He goes out a-sporting every day of the year, rain or blow, whilst at Madrid." And being who he was, he enjoyed his own preserve, fenced to keep the quarry within, poachers without. This verdant enclave would have sustained hundreds of peasants, but that meant little to Spanish monarchs.

Charles died just before a cataclysmic outburst of rage in France and when the first thoughts about human equality seeped through the Pyrenees he did what he could to suppress them. Still, he is regarded as the best of the Spanish Bourbons, qualified praise in the light of what came after. We are told that if compared to his ministers, Charles seemed ordinary; if compared to his son Charles IV and to his grandson Ferdinand VII, he was brushed with genius. One chronicler of those days remarked that a fool succeeded him and a knave succeeded the fool. By eighteenth-century standards he was humane, yet he felt more strongly about animals than about humans. Stories were told of his indifference when a relative suffered or died. Now he stands as Goya perceived him: antique flintlock nearly five feet long, tricorn hat resembling a strange black kite or a stealth bomber, high-button boots, blue sash. He looks friendly and satisfied, as well he should because in those days the empire wasn't threatened. There might be discontent in France, but for those born to noble households in Spain life was secure and agreeable.

As to the portraits, he thought Mengs did better than Goya; he sent replicas of Mengs' painting to several European monarchs.

Not long after all those battleships escorted him across the Mediterranean he realized that his new kingdom had not kept up with the rest of Europe. What to do? He imported Italian experts: the old Venetian master Tiepolo, architect Francisco Sabatini, Leopoldo Squillace to serve as royal treasurer. These and others, although unfamiliar with Spanish attitudes, morals, and customs, offered plenty of advice. Encourage farming. Expand industrial production. Limit the authority of the Church. Create government offices where promotion depended upon merit. This last idea peeved Spanish aristocrats. Treasurer Squillace exasperated everybody when he set the price of corn: This was government interference.

Charles thought Sabatini would know how to clean up Madrid, famous as the most stinking city in Europe, maybe the filthiest on earth. Sabatini had grown rich constructing sewers and drains and he married by proxy the daughter of a Neapolitan architect without seeing her. She was eighteen, quite beautiful. When she arrived in Madrid and laid eyes on the groom, who was neither young nor handsome, she declared that she would not be his wife. Sabatini gave her a choice: him or a nunnery. She resigned herself to being Señora Sabatini. Casanova tells us that the sewer expert was affectionate and easygoing and gave her whatever she wanted, so things weren't altogether bad. "I sighed and burned for her in silence. . . ."

Sabatini went to work. Roads were paved, drainage improved, street lamps installed. Street lamps. What next? They are like children, Charles said of his subjects, grumbling and crying when you try to wash them.

Squillace decided to revise the tax code, expand trade, build more factories. All of which sounds commendable but Spaniards resented his ideas, perhaps because he was Italian.

King Charles made another mistake. Spanish men wore long black cloaks and broad-brimmed slouch hats, making them look sinister, therefore masculine. The hat shielded them from direct sunlight, true, but they liked the hat mostly because it was traditional. They liked the cloak, where a knife might be concealed. Charles, with an eye on masculine fashion elsewhere and no doubt troubled by numerous stabbings, cited an old law forbidding such attire on grounds that criminals might be able to hide their faces. Henceforth, young gentlemen should wear a tricorn hat or a hat with a narrow brim. As for long capes, out. Tailors equipped with shears were posted in doorways around the city, accompanied by police whose job was to prevent the tailors from being killed. It was a good plan, thoughtfully devised, foolproof; but as kings, advisors, chancellors, and presidents learn every so often to their astonishment, foolproof plans don't necessarily work. Having one's cape shortened by a tailor with a cop at his side was an unforgivable insult.

Palm Sunday. March 23, 1766. Several arrogant young bloods in slouch hats and forbidden cloaks swaggered past a military barracks. This enraged the soldiers. Scuffling, whistles, jeers, taunts, and here came a mob of citizens. Down went those street lamps. Why? Because a foreigner had put them up. Squillace was out of town, otherwise he might have been killed. The mob gutted his house. When he learned of the riot he "made a rapid circuit of the city" to reach the palace. He had no idea why Spaniards hated him; he told Charles that he deserved a statue. Next day brought more trouble. Citizens threw rocks at a detachment of Walloon guards. They had been recruited in Flanders, hence they were foreign soldiers, logical targets. The Walloons answered rocks with bullets, and what had been a disturbance became insurrection. Madrileños killed some of the guards, tore out their tongues and eyes and displayed the bloody heads on poles, each sporting a jaunty Spanish hat.

Government officials tried to pacify the mob by giving speeches. This didn't help. Charles finally appeared on the palace balcony and nodded assent while a friar with uplifted crucifix read out successive pledges to fire Squillace, to reduce the price of bread, oil, soap, bacon, to revoke the dress edict, to pardon insurgents. Charles then thought it might be a good idea to spend a few months at his summer palace near Aranjuez. Give his excitable subjects time enough to pick the burrs out of their breeches. He left at midnight.

He was an intelligent monarch, as monarchs go, and the riot taught him a few things. He replaced his Italian advisors with Spaniards, the most notable being an Aragonese soldier and diplomat, Pedro Pablo Abarca de Bolea, Count Aranda. Charles appointed him president of the Council of Castille.

That ingratiating gossip, traveler, scoundrel, philosophist, entrepreneur, spy, daredevil, jack-of-most-trades, director of the Paris lottery, and international lover Casanova, equipped with a letter of introduction from one Princess Lubomirska, announced himself to Count Aranda.

"This hideous personage, who squinted disagreeably, received me with coldness."

In difficult situations Casanova seems to have exuded charm, but Aranda was a tough nut. Why, Aranda demanded, have you come to Spain?

"To instruct myself by observing the manners and customs of an esteemed nation, and at the same time to put my poor talents to account. . . ." Blah blah. What Casanova had in mind is not clear, perhaps a job with the Spanish government. He himself may not have known, so long as there were opportunities. What might happen? Who could say? That's what made life exhilarating. His vocation could be the requirement of the moment. His avocation, naturally, the pursuit of women.

This affable rogue, first name Giacomo, was a Venetian who studied to become a priest but was expelled from school because of immorality. Somewhere along the road he thought to present himself as more or less French, Jacques Casanova de Seingalt. How often he came within an ace of being skewered by a jealous husband's rapier, he probably couldn't say. What difference did it make? Life was meant to be explored. He lasted longer than you might expect, dying in Bohemia at the age of seventy-three. The last fourteen years he spent rather idly, librarian to Count Waldenstein; and during this time, more to amuse himself than with any thought of publication, he wrote those memoirs. Had he not done so he would be as forgotten as the Count of Aranda. And because he considered himself at least half-French, he wrote in French, not very good French. Twelve volumes. His title, not a good title: *The Story of My Life to the Year 1797.*

He salvaged a potpourri of detail that otherwise would be lost. He thought King Charles less powerful than Aranda, a man so bitterly hated by Spanish people that he went everywhere escorted by twelve guardsmen, an epicure who permitted himself luxuries he denied others, bête noir of a nation. Still, Casanova recognized what was important, never mind the squint and frigid welcome. Aranda was a "profound politician."

Not only was Aranda deft at politics, he was clever enough to solve the cape-and-hat problem. Henceforth, he announced, the royal executioner would wear that costume. Some scholars think the slouch hat and cape rapidly went out of style because of this decree. Who wants to be mistaken for an executioner? But Goya's tapestry cartoons suggest that for a while the cape and hat remained popular.

Aranda supported currency reform and public education. Next he moved against the Church, specifically the Jesuits. This annoyed and threatened the upper class, which viscerally detests whatever might disrupt the status quo. And the Inquisition should restrict itself to matters of heresy and apostasy, no more meddling in secular affairs. Then there was trouble with England about the Falkland Islands. Aranda favored military action. This worried Charles, who wasn't belligerent; he decided to get Aranda out of the country by appointing him ambassador to France.

Next came Floridablanca, followed by Gaspar Melchor de Jovellanos who was not only an attorney but a poet, playwright, and economist. These and other progressives resolved to shake up the lethargic, oppressive Spanish bureaucracy.

Jovellanos is worth a moment. Member of the Academy of History and the Academy of San Fernando, focal point of Madrid soirées, he must have been a rare specimen in that ossified government. He has been described as a politician who strayed into literature, but that could be turned around. He sounds like Franklin or Jefferson. He translated Rousseau's *Le Contrat Social,* remarked the degradation of high society, and published satires on educating the nobility. Losing causes, every one. His big mistake was to challenge the Inquisition. This formidable clique operated through sixteen provincial tribunals. Its property was worth at least 170 million reales. It collected taxes at every port. Jovellanos asked the bishops to propose ways and means for ending abuses committed by the Holy Office. From that day on, the Inquisition lay in wait.

A French diplomat saw the Holy Office at work. Outside the door of a Dominican church a beggar was selling powder, supposedly aphrodisiac. He was denounced. A crowd of spectators gathered. Mass was celebrated, interrupted by the formal accusation. At the end of Mass the beggar and two female accomplices were sentenced. All three, dressed in the yellow garment of condemnation embellished with devils and other symbolic figures, wearing the pyramidal cap of the doomed, were mounted on donkeys. People watched from windows. "From time to time the hangman would brush the beggar's shoulders lightly with some strokes of the whip." The hangman didn't flog his prey. No, he brushed the victim gently like a cat stroking a captive mouse.

The Holy Office searched high and low. St. Ignatius of Loyola and St. Theresa of Ávila were investigated. Beggars, Jews, Moors, naturally.

In 1778 a man was condemned for having corresponded with Voltaire and Rousseau. "A royal councilor who witnessed the proceedings broke down and confessed himself to being familiar with the works of the two mentioned, as well as those of Spinoza and Diderot. To gain pardon, he had to expose others." How familiar it sounds.

In 1780 an old woman was convicted of witchcraft, burnt at the stake for having intercourse with the Devil. Eggs decorated with mysterious symbols had been found in her possession.

An English visitor reported the trial of a nun who liked to fling herself from a window and go sailing over the orange grove, which sounds like innocent pleasure, but the tribunal scowled: "Depositions were taken from various witnesses."

During the reign of Charles III and of his son, according to Canon Llorente who documented the Madrid tribunal, ten people met the stake.

People want the Inquisition, Charles explained.

That the Evil One existed, nobody could deny. His presence had tortured Spain for centuries. In 1610 at Logroño the Holy Office condemned a diabolic assembly in a meadow where the Devil held court disguised as a goat. More than once Goya painted this creature, obscenely upright, horns draped with foliage, hooves extended in a parody of benediction. Demonology experts who study his work are able to deduce that he came from Aragón. Naïve faith kept the dread of hell alive. Everything incomprehensible or inexplicable was embodied in superstition bequeathed from generation to generation. Spain during the late eighteenth century had about 10 million people, including 68,000 monks, 33,000 nuns, and 88,000 secular clergymen. Eternal wealth bathed the Church, much of it through mortemain—this being perpetual ownership of land and property, inalienable possession; from the medieval Latin mortua manus, dead hand.

Look at Spain, Thomas Craven wrote. Look closely

in the time of its most fruitful expansion or at any moment in its stagnant complacency, and you will find therein no love of nature, nor of art, nor of humanity. The great wave of Renaissance humanism could not sweeten its brackish hatreds, fertilize its harsh vitality or modify its intolerance. In the blood of Spain flow the perverse cruelty and savage contempt for life born of the deadly mixture of the old Roman and African strains.

6

Bumptious Spaniards joked about conservatism: When Jesus Christ requested admittance to the Order of St. James he was refused. Why? His mother was a seamstress, his father a carpenter.

Ministers Floridablanca and Jovellanos, ahead of their time, declared that workmen should be eligible for government positions. Butcher, baker, candlestick maker, tinsmith, anybody was entitled to a government job. Later, during the reign of Charles IV, this policy would be quashed: "There never has been a question of promoting manual laborers. . . ."

Cádiz and Seville dominated trade with the Americas. Floridablanca and Jovellanos destroyed this monopoly. They attacked a sheep monopoly, the Mesta, whose sheep had for centuries cropped the earth without restriction. Both ministers recognized the damage and understood the cause. Although they failed to break up the Mesta they did limit its authority, infuriating sheep owners. They tried to dismember vast estates, infuriating the nobility.

How much they had to do with enticing foreign peasants to colonize the Sierra Morena is unclear. The plan evidently was drawn up by a certain

Don Pablo de Olavides who might have gone traveling with Sancho Panza and his befuddled master. However it came about, the Spanish government persuaded a thousand Swiss Catholic families to settle in this pleasant, fertile, almost deserted region. The government paid moving expenses and did everything possible to accommodate the Swiss, even constructing a bull ring which Spaniards regard as necessary, which the Swiss did not patronize.

Casanova attended a dinner at which this project had been discussed. He tells us that he listened to the arguments, sensible and otherwise, and finally gave his opinion, as modestly as he could, that in a few years the colony would vanish like smoke. He explained that the Swiss were peculiar; if transplanted, they languish and die. If a Switzer begins to sicken, the only thing you can do is return him to the mountain or lake or valley where he was born. Casanova also pointed out that the project would fail unless the Swiss were guaranteed immunity from the Inquisition. He had seen enough of Spain to feel the warm breath of that vigilant fraternity. In places where he slept, the chamber door had a latch inside, bolts outside. Why? The Holy Office must have liberty to inspect the rooms of foreigners. What did the Holy Office wish to know? Everything. Everything. Men and women who sleep together, are they married? If not, both will be imprisoned.

He enjoyed the theater but was puzzled by how the boxes were constructed, not boarded up in front like theater boxes elsewhere. These were set on little columns, the front exposed. Why? So that amorous couples would behave. To make sure of it, Inquisitors watched. Casanova was watching the watchful Inquisitors when a sentinel at the door cried aloud: "Dios!" Everybody, actors on stage included, dropped to their knees and remained kneeling until the sound of a bell in the street could no longer be heard. A priest had gone by carrying the viaticum.

The King of Spain, should he chance to meet a priest with the viaticum, must offer his carriage to the priest.

J. F. Bourgoing served as secretary to the French embassy from 1777 until 1785. Later he returned to Madrid as ambassador. His memoir, *Nouveau Voyage en Espagne,* was published in 1788. He observed that confession and communion were rigidly enforced. Those who fulfilled their obligations received certificates; those who could not produce a certificate, especially at Easter time, were in trouble. The result was a black market. Bourgoing noted that Madrid whores went to communion as often as possible during Lent so they could fill their purses with certificates.

A vigilant Church didn't bother Spaniards; they loved ceremony, they loved processions. During Holy Week one could watch penitents flogging themselves along the street. To experience greater suffering, penitents often attached shards of broken glass to the whips. Nothing could be more gallant than to splash the dress of one's mistress with blood.

Casanova recorded not only what he observed but a number of things he could not possibly have seen, which doesn't mean they are untrue. He got a look at Charles and thought His Majesty resembled a sheep. The resemblance went deeper, he says, because sheep have no comprehension of sound. An Italian comic opera was just then amusing everybody at court, except His Majesty who chose to go hunting.

His Queen, María Amalia, died on September 27, 1760, a few months after arriving from Italy. She was sickly, the Spanish climate troubled her, and falling off a horse contributed to her death. Not much about Spain pleased María Amalia; she couldn't get strawberries as fresh as those in Italy and she thought Spanish women the most ignorant things on earth.

They had eight children, four of whom quickly died.

Her eldest son, Félipe, was imbecilic and therefore excluded from succeeding to the throne. Félipe died in September, 1777, perhaps from smallpox, although physicians weren't sure, perhaps "a malignant fever causing skin eruptions." He had been supervised night and day because it was impossible to guess what he might do. Particular care was taken to keep him away from women, but several times he managed to escape his keepers, found women in palace apartments and attacked them. What pleased Félipe most was a strange ritual: He would lift one hand while gloves were fitted upon it, glove after glove after glove, each larger than the one before, until he was wearing fifteen or sixteen gloves. At his death King Charles refused to allow public mourning.

Charles thought about marrying again, but when Princess Adélaïde of France saw his portrait she grew quite agitated and rejected him. This humiliated him so much that he gave up the idea. If a courtier suggested that he take a mistress he became angry. At night he sometimes walked through the apartments barefoot in a desperate attempt to avoid thinking about women.

Punctuality he considered a virtue, a requirement of kings. The clock regulated his life. He got up at seven—a quarter to six, according to some historians. He dressed, a valet combed his hair. He took a cup of chocolate, heard Mass, enjoyed a huge pinch of snuff "over which his big nose ruminates for some minutes." He then worked on papers, consulted with ministers and foreign ambassadors. He took lunch by himself, unless we count a swarm of attendants, after which a carriage drove him to the hunting grounds. Early in the evening he had a bite to eat. His meals were identical. He drank one glass of Canary at noon, another in the evening. He exhausted himself deliberately; he might be so tired that he would fall asleep before getting undressed.

He moved from palace to palace in accordance with the seasons. In January to the Pardo. Aranjuez at Easter. La Granja in July. The Escorial in October. Madrid in December.

Now we see Charles as Mengs and Goya saw him, this ascetic mahogany-colored leprechaun who preferred the forest to a dreary consultation with bureaucrats or silly Italian opera. His remarkable face suggests that life in Spain with a tolerant genial monarch wasn't bad. There might be rumbling beyond the Pyrenees, but France was a long way off. Attend the opera if you like. Go shooting in the forest.

Goya pointed the Marquesa de Pontejos, sister-in-law of Prime Minister Floridablanca, in 1785 or 1786. She holds a limp carnation as though Goya sensed the future. Hugh Stokes, fascinated by this portrait, called her a personification of the grande dame who endeavored to be fashionable in the lowering days when Rousseau preached a return to nature and Marie Antoinette played at rusticity in the Trianon gardens. How elegant, how poised, "fluttering with furbelows, frills, and ribbons, a mass of vapid but engaging extravagance. . . ." One tiny pointed foot advanced as though the Marquesa were about to dance. Not a Castilian dance, no, no. The minuet à la Versailles.

Aristocratic Spanish ladies looked to France for guidance. According to Symmons, a dress known as the Polonaise transformed their wardrobes, the name derived from a Polish fashion for a tight-fitting bodice and full skirt. "Goya's earliest depiction of such a dress is in the portrait he painted to celebrate the marriage of the young Marquesa de Pontejos. This harmonious picture with its silver-grey and rose tonality . . . "

Three years later the Bastille would fall.

Whatever disagreements the Spanish people had with Charles, whatever complaints, soon enough they would regret his absence. Just before daybreak on December 14, 1788, this phenomenally ugly little monarch died. He ate and drank no more than a hermit, and such moderation along with those hunting expeditions probably strengthened a naturally resilient body. Not once, not until the end, did he fall sick. But with the approach of winter he caught a chill. For the first time since arriving from Naples in 1759 he took to his bed. Now and again he rallied, although it became evident that he was dying. He is said to have remained singularly composed. As his will was being read aloud, Floridablanca started to break down.

Charles looked at him and said: "Did you think I would live forever?"

The bishop asked if he had pardoned his enemies.

Charles answered: "How should I wait for this pass before pardoning them?" He then added: "They were forgiven the moment after the offence."

All of which sounds very fine, if not quite true. Thirty years earlier, for example, he noticed an officer shielding himself from the sun with a parasol and ever afterward when the list of officers nominated for promotion was shown to him he would delete that man's name. He died insane, Casanova tells us, adding that the Queen of Portugal was mad. Likewise the King of England, which should not be surprising. Kings must almost invariably be condemned to madness by the enormity of their task.

A few weeks earlier his favorite son, Gabriel, had died of smallpox and Charles was heard to murmur that he no longer wanted to live.

Among the latest news I have something to tell:
the Infante named don Gabriel
has ascended into Heaven to look for his mate;
but there're so many up there, you can't elucidate . . .

This doggerel has been attributed to Goya and the verse is addressed to "Pablo," presumably Zapater, but scholars don't think the handwriting is Goya's. Who wrote it? Why?

The King's funeral was no less exact than his daily regimen. As church bells tolled he was ceremonially dressed, laid in a wooden coffin, and carried to the Hall of the Ambassadors where Madrileños might have a last look. Next day he was borne to the Escorial. The captain of the imperial guard broke the King's staff of office and his body was deposited in the so-called "rotting room" for five years, after which he would join his ancestors in the pantheon of Spanish monarchs.

Church, mausoleum, college, monastery, library, palace. Such is the Escorial, a sinister granite construction ordered by Philip II to celebrate a victory over the French at St. Quentin in 1557, and as fulfillment of a vow he made when obliged to bombard the Church of St. Lawrence. He vowed to build a finer church than the one he was destroying.

Escorial means dumping ground, dump, heap of slag. The architectural plan represents a gridiron honoring the martyrdom of St. Lawrence. Four towers symbolize the feet of the grid; connecting buildings symbolize the frame; palace and church make up the handle; transverse buildings represent bars; and so on. This idea, Gautier tells us, which must have been a great hindrance to the architect, is not easily grasped at a glance, though clear enough on the plan. "I do not blame this childish symbolism, which was in the taste of the time; for I am convinced that laying down limits, far from injuring an artist of genius, is a help to him, increases his strength, and enables him to find resources of which he would not have dreamed; but it seems to me that they might have been turned to a much better purpose."

The Escorial he compared to an ocherous yellow hospital with "crushed-looking" windows that gave it the appearance of a beehive.

Never, he says, did an ambitious monk consult with a suspicious tyrant to devise a gloomier monument for the mortification of their fellow men. In the vast courtyard, "an indefinable odour, icy and sickly, of holy water and sepulchral vaults, from which blows a draught laden with pleurisy and catarrh." Overhead, wheeling swarms of martins and swallows uttered sharp cries as though terrified by the silence.

Just inside the church he saw a Spanish woman kneeling on the pavement, beating her breast with one hand while fanning herself with the other. The woman's aquamarine fan somehow alarmed him and made him shiver all down his back when he thought of it.

His tour surpasses anything in a guidebook, which is to be expected. During the nineteenth century he ranked among France's most important writers, praised by contemporaries, known for immaculate prose and jeweled poems. Baudelaire said his ability to convey impressions derived from a concept of order regulating each stroke, every touch, and from an understanding of language that enabled him to select the perfect word. His meticulous style is apparent in notes he must have taken while being led around by a guide named Cornelio who was blind. Cornelio would stop exactly in front of a painting, correctly identifying the subject and artist. Gautier was entranced.

After a circuit of the church they descended to the Pantheon, the vault where Spanish kings are laid, an octagonal chamber thirty-six feet across. Niches had been hollowed out of the walls. The light of Cornelio's torch flickered on polished marble which sent back reflections as though water streamed over it. And to Gautier those dead Spanish kings seemed deader than others; it was difficult to believe they would rise again.

That should be the end. No. His party climbed to the dome. He saw a stork with three baby storks in a big nest of straw like an inverted turban atop one of the chimneys. He calls it the oddest silhouette you could imagine. In the middle of this turban stood the mother on one leg while her babies asked for something to eat, stretching out long beaks and necks. Gautier hoped to witness one of those sentimental scenes from a natural history book where the pelican draws blood from its side to nourish its brood. Alas, unmoved by this demonstration of hunger, the Spanish stork ignored her chicks, standing motionless as a bird in a woodcut, her neck sunk between her shoulders and her beak resting majestically on her breast like a philosopher in meditation.

At last the tour concludes. He sounds exhausted. He left the Escorial with an extraordinary sense of relief:

I felt as if I were being reborn, and might once again be young and rejoice in God's creation . . . when we returned to Madrid there was a stir of pleased surprise among our friends, who were glad to see us still alive. Few people come back from the Escorial; they die of consumption in two or three days, or if by chance they are English, they blow their brains out.

7

While Charles III lay in the rotting room here came his portly son with a nymphomaniac wife, María Luisa.

Henry Swineburne had met this couple some years earlier: "The Prince of Asturias is of an athletic make, his countenance rather severe, and his voice harsh. He seemed in a great hurry to get away from us, but the Princess stayed chatting a great while. She is not handsome, being very sickly, but seems lively and genteelly shaped, with a very fine hand and arm. If she lives to be queen, I dare say she will render the court a gay one. . . ."

Madrileños preparing for the coronation worked themselves into a frenzy. The Place de l'Arméria became a garden with triumphal arches, illuminated at night by thousands of candles. Glass lanterns, torches, candles everywhere. The Ministry of the Gobernación called upon Goya for pictures. The Duke of Hijar commissioned Goya portraits of the royal couple. The Osunas wanted individual portraits to be displayed in oval frames outside the Osuna palace. Guests at their party would dance all night in the Temple of Minerva, which is to say, their salon. Guests of the

Duke and Duchess of Alba didn't stop at dawn; they continued dancing while the sun rose, thereby scoring a point on the Osunas.

Goya was so busy that his studio has been likened to a factory or a printing shop where images of Charles IV and María Luisa were pulled out like pages still damp from the press.

July 14, 1789. French revolutionaries took the Bastille. Spaniards didn't get excited. Everybody knew the French cared about little except dressmaking and pastry.

On the night of September 21, young Charles and his Queen ceremoniously entered Madrid. After settling himself on the throne he restored bullfighting, which Spaniards interpreted as a good sign, and he appointed Goya Pintor de Camara, Painter to the Chamber. This brought a salary increase and fringe benefits such as a more intimate relationship with His Majesty. While sitting for a portrait Charles inquired about Goya's birthplace, sought his opinion of the political climate in Aragón, chatted amiably. When he saw the finished work he placed both hands on the artist's shoulders and they half-embraced.

"I am delighted to please him so much. . . . You can imagine the importance of this."

The College of Calatrava in Salamanca ordered some religious paintings, which netted 408 doubloons and a complimentary letter from Jovellanos, who lightly addressed him as Señor Francisco de Goya. That wisp of levity from such an important man started a brush fire in his heart. For a long time he had nourished the idea that his ancestors belonged to the upper class. He asked Zapater to investigate. He, himself, may have poked through the archives. He knew that his mother was descended from minor nobility and now he learned that once upon a time his father's people had been landowners. Not much else turned up and the search was costing money so he quit. However, he liked the sound of de Goya. He began to sign his name that way, not always, once in a while, then more often, with greater assurance. Years later he would mock such presumption with an etching of an ass trying to establish its ancestry.

His wife Josefa was in poor health and doctors advised her to get away from Madrid for a while. Goya took her to Valencia where they spent two months. He seems to have enjoyed himself; he went duck hunting and made a few drawings. Local artists gave a picnic in his honor. They elected him to membership in the Valencia Academy.

In Valencia he began a portrait of Doña Joaquína Candado, alleged to have been his housekeeper, alleged to have been his mistress, alleged to have been the model for *Maja Desnuda*. That beady-eyed sleuth, Sánchez Cantón, will have none of it. How curious, during a respite from work and surrounded by colleagues who would gossip—how curious that Goya would spend time with a housekeeper. But why is this remarkable? From toes to fingertips he was an artist. What else mattered? Something about the woman made him want to paint her.

His one surviving child, Javier, wasn't very strong. Several times he mentioned this to Zapater. "Thank God he is now better. . . ." Then the child contracted what Goya calls a pox, maybe nothing more than chicken pox. He told King Charles, "and he shook me by the hand and began to play on his violin." Shaking hands with a commoner had particular significance. People believed the King's touch could heal various diseases such as scrofula or the pox, a belief that survives in one form or another to this day. It was Javier, not Goya, who was sick, but the King's gesture signified more than friendship or affection.

Charles wanted amusing tapestries and one should accommodate the King. Still, Goya felt that he had produced more than enough cartoons, and before long he was confronted by the director of the tapestry works, Livonio Stuyck Vandergoten. Look here, Goya, said Vandergoten, you must pull your weight. And he pointed out that if Goya failed to deliver his assignments a good many weavers would lose their jobs.

No other artists of the King's Chamber have to do cartoons, Goya said, and besides, I've done quite a few, and besides, I'm working on important commissions.

This response seeped upward, irritating various functionaries including the Minister of Finance. Bayeu managed to smooth ruffled feathers after Goya wrote a letter promising to complete his assignment.

The Mannequin, or *The Dummy*, his final cartoon—known sotto voce as the dance of prime ministers—shows four girls tossing a straw man on a blanket and is regarded as an allegory of political upheavals. It also looks very like Goya's comment on the war between the sexes.

For a number of years he had suffered occasional blackouts, and as he contemplated himself in the mirror he saw himself aging. Self-portraits from 1781 to 1814 are painfully honest. At thirty-five he is alert, confident, fleshily handsome. A couple of decades later, missing some hair, he peers over the top of his spectacles. University students have listened to this man lecture on everything from the glory of Rome to business administration. Another year or two slips past. Goya affects a high silk hat, a plug hat. Now we have a dandy. He doesn't look pleased with what is going on. Fifteen years whistle by. His expression is not easy to interpret; he seems to be inviting dialogue. Jean-François Guillou notes that an artist who paints himself as a young man is a pianist running scales, skimming across a form that is nothing but surface, painting an identity that continues to gestate, registering an image that has not given time a hold on it. We read the future in lines of the hand; in lines of the face we read the past.

Now, face and body eroding, Goya writes to Zapater that he has stopped listening to popular music because it isn't dignified.

Blackouts recurred. He saw ghosts, assassins, monstrosities, skeletons.

Sebastián Martínez, a friend who lived in Cádiz, invited him to visit. Martínez, too, had escaped a wretched village in northern Spain marked by harsh winters and summers. He settled on the temperate southern coast. Goya's 1792 portrait shows a man in late middle age with a face not unlike that of Thomas Jefferson. He wears tight gold trousers that nobody could wear these days without being assaulted, if one excepts electric-guitar players and movie icons, but it was appropriate for a Spanish gentleman of the late eighteenth century. He sports a double-breasted coat, probably silk, with blue and gold stripes and gigantic buttons. We don't know what Martínez wanted to do when he was young; he might have wanted to become an artist, but as things turned out he got very rich in the wine trade and collected art. He seems to have had excellent taste and beyond doubt he was rich; he bought antique sculpture as well as paintings by Velázquez, Mengs, Titian, Rubens, and so on. His collection is said to have been one of the finest private assemblies in Spain. He especially liked hunting scenes, landscapes, battles, and provocative images of women. He owned several drawings of nudes, later impounded by the ever vigilant Holy Office. He commissioned Goya to enhance some wood panels of his home with pictures of sleeping women. One might, therefore, argue about his taste. Still, he commissioned Goya, not the local pornographer.

We must assume that Goya accepted this job happily enough; he liked to draw and paint sleeping women. Besides, he could visit his friend in Cádiz.

En route he got sick, although we have a pedagogic dispute. He might have gotten sick after visiting Martínez and not feeling well enough to go any further he returned to Cádiz.

Martínez wrote to an acquaintance in Madrid: "My friend, Don Francisco de Goya, left the Court, as you know, with the intention of seeing this city. . . . he arrived at my house in a deplorable condition, in which he remains, having been unable to go out of the house. . . ."

Soon afterward Martínez wrote to Zapater: "I have confidence in the spa and feel certain that when he takes the waters at Trillo he will get better. The noises in his head and the deafness have not improved, but he is seeing more clearly and is not so confused as he was when he lost his sense of balance. He can go up and down the stairs. . . ." Trillo was a popular spa on the Tagus southwest of Madrid, renowned for mineral springs.

Goya was not stoic, not a man to understate the case. If he got sick, he got sick dramatically. Years later after another illness he painted himself clutching the bed sheet while Dr. Arrieta offers him something to drink and nowhere in the history of painting do we find a more miserable patient. It's been said that he got into his own face the anguish he could never get into the Crucifixion.

This unlucky trip to Cádiz has baffled historians. He obtained permission to visit Andalusia, but no dates were specified and he may have received permission after the fact, when he was already in Cádiz. If true, this is hard to explain. He might have been working with the Spanish government in a cloak-and-dagger attempt to extricate Louis XVI. This project had been entrusted to the brilliant, manipulative financier Francisco Cabarrús. Several coincidences link Goya to the attempt. Quite a few years afterward his grandson Mariano told a fantastic story about Goya's participation, which included a flight through the Sierra Morena. Nothing definite has been established.

Almost every biographer is preoccupied with that illness. What, exactly, was it? What caused it?

A professor at the University of Saragossa, Dr. Roya Villanova, ascribed it to rheumatism and hardening of the arteries, stating further that Goya's deafness resulted from mumps contracted when he was a child.

Dr. Sánchez Rivera thought he had syphilis, which would explain the deaths of so many children.

Dr. Blanco Soler in 1946 did not think he was syphilitic, but maintained that he was schizophrenic and that his deafness created paranoid obsessions.

It has been proposed that he had Vogt-Koyanagi syndrome which results from an eye infection, or neurolabyrinthitis—inflammation of the inner ear.

Botulism has been suggested.

Typhoid fever.

Perhaps he suffered from an occupational disease: lead poisoning. Exposure to white lead is now a recognized danger; indeed, as early as 1839 it was called encephalopathia saturnina. Before that, a 1762 Italian treatise on painting warned against using vermilion and ceruse, this latter being white lead.

According to Priscilla Muller, Charles IV brought a certain Joseph Louis Proust to the Spanish court during the 1760s and this man's research on metals and pigments warned of possible danger in everyday elements such as lead and tin. An English traveler named Southey expressed concern about the lead in Spanish cooking pots. A Madrid journal reported that copper utensils in which the tin lining had worn thin could be poisonous. What did Goya know about this and when did he learn it? If he did know, did he care? The library of his brother-in-law

Francisco Bayeu indicates that Bayeu was alert to recent medical discoveries, so the two of them might have discussed cooking pots as well as vermilion and ceruse.

Records show that Goya ordered enormous amounts of white lead during the eighteen years he worked on tapestry cartoons. Muller comments that no artist would require, as he did, more than a hundred pounds of lead white each year. This was not used in painting but in preparing canvas: "Successive layers of white-lead and linseed oil priming were applied to the large canvases and each layer was ground to a fineness that would produce a satisfactorily smooth painting surface. Any physical handling of the lead white, or, even worse, inhaling its dust, could suffice to induce lead encephalopathy."

Male sperm count is thought to be affected in direct proportion to the amount of lead in the blood. That is, lead may cause infertility and birth defects. Goya's inability to father more than one surviving child might therefore be attributed not to venereal disease but to eighteen years of preparing canvas. At any rate he recovered enough to continue drawing. But again he collapsed and lay in bed for several months, half paralyzed, deafened, at times delirious.

Once more on his feet, without much confidence, he returned to Madrid. The paralysis was temporary, deafness permanent. For the rest of his life he could hear only a buzzing noise.

Goya's illness occurred during tumultuous days in France and reverberations could be heard south of the Pyrenees. Even so, what happened in France didn't happen in Spain. Quite the opposite. Charles IV, rather than interpret the hideous song of the guillotine, decided that tightening the screws was the best way to crush dangerous ideas. New censorship regulations were drawn up. Printed material of any sort alluding to France must go directly from customs to the Secretary of State. Nonresidents must leave Madrid.

Among the distinguished illustrados, enlightened ones, who opposed the medieval logic of Charles, were financier Cabarrús, attorney Pedro Rodríguez de Campomanes, Floridablanca, and Jovellanos. Cabarrús, along with Floridablanca, founded the National Bank of San Carlos, now called Banco de España. Goya deposited money and bought shares. Money is quite often mentioned in letters to Zapater whose judgment he trusted. Would it be smart to buy additional bank shares? What about investing in guilds? Royal promissory notes yielded 4 percent. How about that?

Cabarrús was arrested, left to meditate upon his crimes in solitary confinement at the distant port of La Coruña. The immediate cause seems to have been his *Elogio de Carlos III,* denounced by enemies at court as liberal propaganda, but María Luisa detested him which probably had something to do with it.

Jovellanos tried to help.

Four days later Jovellanos was told to draw up a report on coal mining in Asturias, which is to say he was banished.

A contemporary wrote: "Everyone loved him . . . a glance of approbation, a smile from Jovellanos was the best reward that talent and toil could receive." This sort of adulation did not please Manuel Godoy, whom King Charles had appointed Prime Minister.

On one occasion Godoy invited Jovellanos to lunch. He was already seated when Jovellanos arrived. His wife, Countess of Chinchón, at his right. His mistress, Pepita Tudó—daughter of a concierge—at his left.

"There's no solution . . ." Jovellanos later wrote.

In 1801 Jovellanos was imprisoned on the island of Mallorca. Godoy's hatred is described as so virulent that "little or no hope remains either of his deliverance or diminution of his captivity."

At first he had been sent to the Carthusian monastery where he was allowed to walk in the garden, if accompanied by a friar, and could use the library. But he addressed a letter to King Charles. This angered Godoy, who had him transferred to the fortress. There he was confined to one room with a grated window. A guard stood outside the window, another at the door. He could not go outside for a walk. He could not write anything because the Governor denied him pen and ink. This sedentary life weakened him and his legs began to swell. He asked to see a physician. Three months later a physician who examined him prescribed fresh air and bathing. After another long delay he was authorized to visit the beach accompanied by the Governor, the physician, and the captain on guard, escorted by twenty dragoons. Jovellanos rejected these terms, saying he didn't think the life of an old man worth so much trouble. He was fifty-two. He asked permission to retire to his home town. Request denied. A number of prominent citizens offered themselves as security if Godoy would allow him to retire. No.

8

Manuel y Alvarez de Faria Godoy. Spaniards called him among other things el choricero, the sausage maker, because he was born in Estremadura where a great many pigs are raised. Historians describe him as libidinous, sordid, despicable, loathsome, indolent, gluttonous, arrogant, greedy, etc. Although it is true that one discerned "a not unpleasant vulgarity." Another points out that Godoy muzzled the Inquisition, founded medical and veterinary colleges, improved highroads, lightened censorship, encouraged the arts, and stripped ranking clergymen of what might be called pork barrel benefits. All in all, though, not good press.

According to the Count of Toreno, no more did Godoy befriend superior men than he felt obliged to humiliate them. He allowed the Marquis of Caballero to distort and misinterpret the law. He sold office, dignities, and magistrates as though at auction, either for his own benefit or to gratify his mistresses. His vanity, said Lady Holland, was immeasurable.

Goya liked him, which is surprising. And the Prime Minister liked Goya.

Lord Holland noted another aspect of this contradictory outrageous sausage maker. Godoy's manner, however indolent, or as the French might express it, nonchalant, was engaging and graceful. "In spite of his education, which I presume was provincial and none of the best, his language appeared to me elegant. . . . Indeed, his whole demeanour announced, more than that of any untravelled Spaniard I have ever met with, a mixture of dignity and politeness. . . ."

Although his parents were third-class aristocrats, their influence probably enabled him to become a Gentleman of the Bodyguard at age seventeen. Just how he caught María Luisa's eye is still disputed. He contrived to fall off a horse while his troops filed past her window. He dropped a statue he was supposed to carry in a procession. He beguiled her with his guitar. Anyway, he had an older brother named Luis, also a guardsman, reputed to be the Queen's lover. And when Luis was assigned to another post, who should deliver his letters to the Queen?

Five years later Manuel was Duke of Alcudia and belonged to the Council of State. All of us have known Godoy—shifty, unscrupulous, ingratiating, haughty, obsequious, charming if it seems advisable, subordinate to the prevailing breeze.

When the French monarchy collapsed Louis XVI appealed to cousin Charles for help, requesting asylum in Spain. Too late. At Varennes the Republicans caught Louis trying to escape. Nobody could guess what might happen next. How best to calm the Spanish people? Prime Minister Floridablanca lost his job in February of 1792, replaced by the old Count of Aranda, replaced by Godoy. Why should the youthful, unqualified Godoy be appointed Prime Minister? Queen María Luisa. However shrewd and calculating she may have been, she lost her wits over this fleshy young bodyguard: "Your fame and memory will end only when the world is burnt to ashes, and they will after that be rewarded in glory."

King Charles appointed him in November of 1792, charging him to prevent the execution of Louis. Nobody on earth could have accomplished that. Imperial presumption had gone too far.

A wave of horror swept Europe when the head of Louis XVI thumped into a basket. And it may be apropos to remark that France's most celebrated painter, Jacques Louis David, voted to guillotine the monarch. So much for artistic sensitivity.

Louis XVI became a martyr in Spain because he had been Catholic and no people in Europe were more Catholic than Spaniards. A French immigrant, Le Duc d'Havre, conducted a memorial service in Madrid. Priests throughout Spain vilified the godless French. Mobs ransacked the homes of French people living in Valencia, attacked the homes of Spaniards who employed French servants. Spanish women who dressed à la Française and chose to wear the new Liberty caps, or who adopted French coiffures, were publicly insulted.

Godoy's attempt to save King Louis failed because it couldn't be done, although this had no effect on his standing at Court; by this time he was the Queen's lover. It's said that Charles refused to believe rumors of his wife's affair. It's also said that he knew but didn't mind. Other cuckoos had visited the nest, quite a few. Her Majesty's appetite could not be satisfied, one courtier observed, nor could passing years slake her lust.

First, Don Eugenio Eulalio Palafox, Conde de Teba. María Luisa was eighteen.

After him, Don Augustín Lancaster who was older and didn't last long.

Next, Don Juan Pignatelli, son of El Conde de Fuentes who owned the village of Fuendetodos.

El Conde de Fuentes had a brother, Ramón, who became chief of the Saragossa Inquisition and canon of the Saragossa cathedral—the same Father Ramón Pignatelli who blessed the marriage of María Cayetana. Most interesting about this eminent churchman is that every night he slept with a different girl. Casanova tells us that he would get up in the morning exhausted by pleasure; the young lady would be driven away, the procuress jailed. "He then dressed, confessed, said mass and, after an excellent breakfast with plenty of good wine, he would send out for another girl. . . ." The people of Saragossa held him in great respect. After all, he was a canon of the Church, a monk, an Inquisitor.

Following Don Juan Pignatelli to María Luisa's boudoir was Luis Godoy, Manuel's elder brother. As noted, both were members of the imperial guard. This elite corps became known as Los Chocolateros, Chocolate Boys, whose duty, aside from guarding the royal family was to provide recruits for the Queen's bedchamber. Charles was a large, strong, virile man, but she wore him out. That devout moralist Floridablanca thought the King ought to know what his consort was up to, for which he spent a while in prison.

"Never has the power of the Queen been so manifest."

Let it be said on behalf of María Luisa that she fought the relentless battle of age with fierce determination. Rouges from Paris. Correctives. Nostrums. Elixirs. Tonics. Jellies. Sirups. Oils and unguents from the royal pharmacy. Who shall cast the first stone?

Inside and outside the palace so much hanky-panky was going on that you begin to wonder how they found time for anything else. A British visitor in 1775 left a dour account of Spanish morality. With grim piety he writes of privileged young women who, as soon as they escape the convent, before they have fixed upon a lover, rise late and squander the remains of the morning or wear it out at church in a long bead-roll of meaningless prayers. Nowhere else did he observe such debauchery, such bare-faced amours.

Now, after Luis Godoy here came little brother Manuel who must have stroked Her Majesty in all the right places because her jealousy approached madness. She ordered two priests to keep track of him, posting one in an alcove of his bedroom. This wild surveillance explains a comment by another ambassador to the Spanish court: "Everyone is acquainted with her intrigues, down to the most intimate details."

Godoy is described as rather phlegmatic, unimaginative, solidly built. So he appears in Goya's portrait. Historians don't grant him much intelligence, though he was smart enough to learn French and Italian from other guardsmen. The most unusual thing about him was his lack of respect for the Queen; he treated her like a woman picked up on the street. He must have known that she spied on him but there is no evidence that he complained. What did exasperate him was gossip that he had won María Luisa's heart by playing the guitar. This, he felt, cast a slur upon his personal charm.

He arranged for his mother to become lady-in-waiting to the court. He tried to have his father appointed Minister of Finance, although this didn't work out because Floridablanca, in power at the time, objected to working with an unqualified provincial. Godoy neither forgot nor forgave the insult.

Next to visit the insatiable Queen's bedroom, Don Luis de Urquija.

After him, General Antonio Cornel y Ferraz.

Then another guardsman, Don Manuel Mallo.

It was public knowledge that Mallo seemed uncommonly rich. One day King Charles, María Luisa, and Godoy were standing on a balcony when the guardsman rode by in a splendid barouche. King Charles admired the horses and wondered how a guardsman could afford better horses than his own. I'm told his fortune comes from the Indies, said María Luisa. That's not what I hear, said Godoy. And what have you heard? asked the King. I am told, Godoy replied, that he is kept by a rich and ugly old woman whose name I don't recall. This is hard to believe. If Godoy did make such a gross and insolent remark, he must have felt that he had María Luisa tucked securely in his pocket.

Charles III wasn't deceived by his sensual daughter-in-law. On one occasion he and his son were overheard discussing morals when the younger man said it was difficult for aristocratic women to commit adultery because there were so few men of equal rank.

You are an ass, his father said, a blind ass.

In July of 1776 he wrote to his son: "Women are by nature weak, fickle, ill-informed and superficial, too easily beguiled by designing and ambitious flatterers."

Now, with a blind ass on the throne, with the loathsome Godoy at his right hand, Spain began a sickening descent. How much of it was their fault? How do six blind men describe the elephant? In any case, Charles and his advisers had been unable to save Louis XVI, nor could they placate the new French Republic.

March, 1793. France declared war on Spain, avowing its determination to liberate oppressed Spaniards. Spain announced that it would defend the principles of monarchy against Republicanism. Spain won a few battles in Catalonia but overwhelming victory seemed out of the question.

Charles decided to negotiate, anything to get rid of the French. So there went half of an exotic Caribbean island called Santo Domingo—today known as Haiti and the Dominican Republic—where French is spoken at the west end, Spanish at the east end. However, things could have been worse, such was the prevailing sentiment. The abominable French went home and Charles pinned another title on Godoy: Prince of the Peace.

Six years later Prince of the Peace Godoy commanded Spanish forces during the slightly comic War of the Oranges. What was it all about? England and Portugal were in business together because Englishmen had grown very fond of Portuguese wine. This irritated Spain, which at the time was allied with Napoleon. However, Spain didn't want Napoleon to cross the Pyrenees because—well, who could be sure what Napoleon might do? And a daughter of Charles and María Luisa had married the King of Portugal, which meant they would be attacking their own child. You see the possibilities.

England didn't want to get mixed up in it, so Portugal sued for peace a couple of weeks after Spanish troops crossed the border. Their Majesties Charles and María Luisa attended a festival in Badajoz where the victorious Prince of Peace again was honored. He, in return, handed María Luisa an orange branch liberated during the siege of a provincial town called Yelvas.

In his memoirs Godoy asserted that he had no wish to lead the Spanish forces, but felt obligated. The hand of Destiny, he wrote, had caught him in her nets. Not ambition but love of country motivated him. To María Luisa he wrote: "The devil with files of paper when I am on the point of making the enemy listen to reason at the cannon's mouth. . . . May Your Majesty deign to let me serve her with the sword for no shorter time than I have served her with the pen!"

Goya painted him in 1801, thirty-four years old, beefily handsome in a bespangled uniform. He loiters on an ersatz battlefield, one arm resting on what might possibly be a sofa in Goya's studio while he reads a military despatch. Plumed hat on the ground. Saber at his side. The saber was a gift from Charles, which Godoy would lose some years later during his flight to Aranjuez. The overcast sky is murkily blue. Day is ending, the battle won. Or perhaps it's dawn. Spanish troops in the background prepare themselves. No matter. Goya didn't include an orange branch but did show a couple of Portuguese flags, which Godoy would add to his coat of arms.

Between his meaty thighs a walking stick with a knobby handle stands erect.

Janis Tomlinson commented that although the walking stick between his legs "invites an interpretation not at all in keeping with the official nature of the portrait, it might also be approached from a purely formal vantage point." It interrupts his line of sight, thus calling attention to the despatch in his hand, "which implicitly mitigates Godoy's hubris by referring to his role as minister of the king's will."

Myself, I think Goya had a different idea.

A British tourist who met him about this time described him as large, coarse, with ruddy skin and "a heavy, sleepy voluptuous eye, not unlike Ld. Amherst."

What is unmistakable from looking at this large coarse man with a voluptuous eye is that he enjoyed women. One biographer remarked that he could be generous with his affections, dividing them among María Luisa, by whom he had royal infantes; his wife, the Countess of Chinchón, by whom he hoped to have nobles; and his longtime mistress, Pepita Tudó, by whom he had bastards. Undeniably a lecher. Overweight, true, but if he spent a few months at the gym he would be in good shape. It's no surprise that he attracted women. There on the faux battlefield he looks relaxed, amiable, good company at the local cantina. He is said to have behaved almost deferentially toward Goya. He learned to communicate with the deaf artist through sign language, which is unexpected. At times, at least, he must have been a sympathetic, sensitive man.

Connoisseurs sniff at Goya's work. A few offer qualified praise. The art historian José Gudiol, for one, speaks of a full composition richly surrounding the subject, correct and natural lighting, beautifully rendered sky within limited contrasts of tone, and so on. Complimentary, if less than enthusiastic.

A sleek, vulpine Godoy "at the commencement of his ministry" is presented by the engraver Carmona. You get a feeling that Carmona's Godoy smelled of pomade, talcum powder, and urine. He has a long, fox-like nose, swollen red lips, and the eyes of a used-car salesman.

We might ask what he saw in the Queen. Baron Wilhelm von Humboldt, brother of the famous explorer, traveled through Spain in those days. Humboldt described her as frightful. By another account, the hideousness of her face could be matched only by the vulgarity of her gowns. An elaborately costumed monstrosity, a thing of monumental ugliness, eyes brimming with arrogance, ruthlessness, and deceit, belly deformed by countless pregnancies. Repeated births, illness, and perhaps a touch of hereditary disease had annihilated her beauty, said a charitable Russian diplomat. Well, then, it's reasonable to ask how Godoy choked down the aversion he must have felt. What did he see beyond a tilt on the royal bed? Power, of course. Power and unlimited wealth, aphrodisiacs both.

The Queen liked Goya. Sometimes she invited him to breakfast. This was flattering. Anybody would be flattered. Otherwise we don't know if he enjoyed the hospitality. Letters to Zapater don't reveal much.

His portrait of Charles, María Luisa, their children, and relatives is immense: nine feet high, eleven feet across. Did he or didn't he caricature his subjects? It depends upon the viewer. It also depends upon the age in which we live. To us, the affected nonchalance of nineteenth-century group photographs is ludicrous. Those people didn't see it that way.

Some critics think Goya never meant to satirize King Charles and his family. Look, we are told, at this pictorial symphony of orange, blue, yellow, gray-gold, silver, and white. And would Goya, however temperamental, risk angering his patrons?

These thirteen arresting disquieting figures have been called insects pinned to a background. Elie Faure, whose ponderous *History of Art* appeared in 1924, saw a collection of vipers brutalized by devout practices, by accumulated imperfections, furtive orgies, fear. Of all the great Spaniards who were subtle and savage, he remarks, Goya was the most subtle, the most savage. María Luisa dominates, on that ravaged face a look of gastric malevolence. Goya painted this corpulent, scheming, lascivious woman larger than life. In fact, she was small, with very short legs. Her parted lips pretend to smile but who is persuaded? That smile could erupt into a barnyard cackle. She had lost all her teeth and was fitted with plates by three dentists who served the court. The plates didn't function very well; she disliked people glancing at her while she ate. She watches us through the meaningless brown eyes of a horse, in her stylish coiffure a jeweled arrow. Goya subsequently painted two hags, one of them with María Luisa's arrow, admiring themselves in a mirror. Que tal? he painted on the back of the mirror. What's going on?

To the Queen's left, a little boy thought to be Godoy's child, Francisco de Paula.

To her right, María Isabella, who may also have been Godoy's child.

In the background—next to Goya himself—with a black stain on her temple and a demented expression, stands the spinster sister of Charles, Doña María Josefa, who would die before the painting was finished. You might think a vandal struck the canvas but the stain is deliberate, a lunar, which the French call a mouche, a cosmetic device intended to emphasize by contrast the woman's white skin, a descendant of the mole which fashionable ladies have employed for a long time. A black dot came to seem inadequate so it grew into a manufactured patch that could be applied to the face here or there, as the lady chose. In 1800 when Goya did this huge painting the lunar was going out of style. The Queen doesn't have one. Her face is turned slightly aside, perhaps because Goya thought it strengthened the composition. Or maybe the Queen wanted to distinguish herself from her decrepit sister in law, a relic of days gone by.

Once upon a time the lunar connoted passion. Goya's portrait of the Duchess of Alba after her husband's death shows it on the right temple.

In front of Doña María Josefa, a voluptuous young creature whose face is turned fully aside: María Antonina, daughter of the Queen of Naples, betrothed to Ferdinand. Her face is averted because she doesn't yet belong to the imperial family. They might not have been affianceed; in other words, Ferdinand might marry somebody else, which explains why Goya painted an anonymous woman. Or perhaps everything had been settled but Goya didn't know what she looked like. In any event, two years would elapse before she reached Madrid, and her impression of Ferdinand is startling:

"I stepped down from the carriage and saw the Prince; I thought I was going to faint." She goes on to say that Ferdinand was nearly all body with the head of a dwarf and no legs. She had further unkind words: "He does not read, he does not write, he does not think; nothing; nothing. . . . The coarse and churlish things he does to people make me blush. . . ."

María Antonina's mother commented that he had a frightful face and a frightening voice, "a complete imbecile." Later, after getting to know Ferdinand, the Queen of Naples remarked that he was stupid, idle, lying, debased, sly, "and not even a man physically."

Queen María Luisa had something to say about the intended daughter-in-law, confiding to Godoy that the Neapolitan princess was a half-dead frog, her mother's spit, a diabolical serpent. However, María Luisa didn't think much of her own son, whom she called ugly and cowardly.

How long could any woman survive that kind of mother-in-law? María Antonina lasted five years. According to the Duchess d'Abrantes, she was pale and sickly when she arrived in Spain. During the winter of 1805–6 a mysterious illness weakened her. She died a few months later. Quite a few Spaniards thought Godoy poisoned her.

María Antonina's view of Ferdinand doesn't coincide with the young man Goya painted. He looks conceited, vain, selfish, whatever you like, but his head isn't abnormal and he does have legs. Thick, sturdy legs. Goya usually gave his men the legs of a football player, which is how he himself was proportioned. Ferdinand must have been short, perhaps several inches shorter than his fiancée, but in the painting he is almost as tall as his father.

Directly behind Charles stands the epileptic, feeble-minded brother, Don Antonio Pascual, gazing at nothing. Beside Don Antonio, the King's eldest daughter, Doña Carlota Joaquina, married to the King of Portugal, João VI. We see only her profile. She was deformed as the result of a hunting accident and has been called more licentious than her mother. At the extreme right, the Infanta María Luisa Josefina holding her baby. And if one notes a similarity throughout this gathering there's a reason. Span-

ish royalty intermarried—uncles, nieces, cousins—to make sure those titles, estates, and heaps of doubloons remained in the family vault.

At fourteen the future Queen María Luisa had been imported like any
other commodity because Charles III was determined to perpetuate his
line. Her intended groom, cousin Charles, had not yet reached puberty,
which annoyed his father and caused the wedding to be postponed. She
must have been appalled by Spain. Italy was more fun. In the palace she
could listen to music, which she loved, and occasionally there would be an
excursion. Not much else. Her tutor, Abbé de Condillac, evidently did a
good job because she grew up quite at ease and soon learned to manipu-
late the awkward lout she married. Cousin Charles, unlike his crafty over-
sexed wife, had trouble gluing his thoughts together; now and again he
teased her, saying she was an ugly creature growing old, not the mark of
an intelligent husband.

Goya shows us the raddled features of a dissolute harridan who could
never have been attractive. Still, Mengs painted her in 1768–9, when she
was seventeen or eighteen. Luminous eyes, porcelain complexion, Mona
Lisa smile. Mengs habitually flattered his subjects, nevertheless she must
have been catnip to prowling aristocrats.

Tomlinson thinks quite a few reports of María Luisa's early affairs
were fabricated: "No evidence for these accusations is offered by contemporary accounts. . . ."

Lady Holland tells us that the Queen's manner was gracious, that she
conversed readily and showed good taste in choosing her topics. Everything Her Majesty said was complimentary, obliging, well-expressed.
Lady Holland was invited to view the royal diamonds for which Her
Majesty "had a royal fondness." And this English lady who got along
nicely with the lecherous Spanish Queen described her as small, rather
pretty. María Luisa was proud of her arms, which seem to have held up
better than the rest, and liked to display them. You might think she would
avoid competing with ladies of the court, most of whom were younger.
Instead, she invited comparison by forbidding them to wear long gloves.
A French diplomat remarked that when she was fifty she exhibited pre-
tensions and coquetry barely forgivable in a young and beautiful woman.

She was middle-aged when Goya did the family gathering, but he had painted her eleven years earlier. At that time she was neither the attractive young woman Mengs had painted nor what she would become. Valentin eloquently summarized this grotesque yet strangely pathetic Queen. If she has forgotten her past loves, "if her mind, wholly intent upon the present, retained nothing of the past, her flesh remembered its dishonors and all its defeats."

Once upon a time, when she married Charles, in those days she must have oozed sensuality. And there stood a big strong husband. Indeed, we are told that Charles, robust as his father was slight, enjoyed wrestling with grooms in the stable. Old King Charles and the Spanish people were optimistic, anxious for them to produce an heir. But the Infante Carlo Eusebio didn't live very long. He died in 1783. Soon thereafter the Queen bore twins. Madrid erupted with joy. Triumphal chariots rolled around the city reminding citizens of legendary twins. On palatial pediments appeared representations of Castor and Pollux, Herakles and Iphiklos, Jacob and Esau, Romulus and Remus. María Luisa's twins died, one not long after the other, but at last she gave birth to Ferdinand. The people could scarcely express their happiness. They called him El Deseado. The Desired One. Ferdinand VII.

We think of this woman, assuming we do, as a creature with a stupefying sexual appetite who might be ranked alongside Messalina. Both women enjoyed, or suffered from, an affliction known clinically as furor uterinus.

Casanova, who understood the secret lives of women as well as any man could, saw the Duchess of Villadorias kneeling on the stone floor of a church in Madrid. He tells us that when the furor seized her nothing could hold her back, she would rush at the man who excited her and he had no choice but to satisfy her passion. "This had happened several times in public assemblies and had given rise to some extraordinary scenes." Casanova then digresses, as he very often does when pondering his favorite subject. He attended church with two women. After his companions prayed for half an hour they got up, all three left church and took a carriage. As they drove through the city he explained furor uterinus. This alarmed Doña Ignazia, who asked if he meant to visit the Duchess of Villadorias. He reassured her by saying he would not. He then embarks upon a soliloquy having to do with what he calls "the generative act." He concludes that women enjoy it more: "If woman had not more pleasure than man, she would not have more organs than he. The greater nervous power planted in the female organ is demonstrated by the andromania to which some women are subject and which makes them either Messalinas or martyrs." Inexplicably he says nothing further about the Duchess of Villadorias, leaving readers to imagine those extraordinary scenes.

What about Charles? Despite the imperial blue sash and a bank of medals on a sagging chest, King Charles played second violin to his wife. He resembles his uncle, the Infante Don Luis, a plump George Washington. He is said to have been rather sluggish, although now and again he would explode; if he happened to be thrown by a groom during those wrestling matches in the stable he might hit the man. Unlike his father who collected ornate clocks, Charles IV collected watches. And because he thought they should be kept warm in order to work properly, he assigned a valet to wear those he himself wasn't wearing. Years later this eccentricity would degenerate into obsession: His majordomo was instructed to carry six watches and must not announce supper until all six had chimed.

He shared his father's passion for hunting. Every day, winter and summer, he would shoot until noon. After lunch, shooting until dusk. As to Spain—ah, well, Godoy would look after it. He remarked to Napoleon: "Manuel told me how things were going. . . ."

On an everyday hunt a battalion of soldiers and servants accompanied him. Should it be a particular occasion there might be two thousand soldiers on the sidelines, muskets loaded, ready to annihilate whatever eluded His Majesty. He once ordered a herd of deer driven into a park and watched artillerymen blow them apart with cannons. At Aranjuez he built scaffolds in the garden for lackeys to stand upon and keep track of how many birds he killed. Above the fruit trees stretched an enormous green net. Why? So that finches unwisely seeking a juicy tidbit couldn't escape.

Dead horses, cattle, dogs, and other dead things were heaped together. Why? To attract vultures and crows, targets for His Majesty.

Aranjuez pleased him, as the Escorial did not. However, custom obliged him to spend two months each year at the Escorial where his ancestors lay in black and gold caskets: Spanish Hapsburgs beginning with Philip II, followed by Spanish Bourbons. Once a week he had to visit the gloomy octagonal Panthéon, walls lined with tombs thick as larvae in a beehive. After those visits you can hardly blame him for wanting to relax in the park and shoot something, anything.

He bought paintings, not what you expect of an oaf who would blast whatever came in range of his musket. But according to the inventory drawn up by a certain Julian Zarco, Charles either bought or owned 421 works of art, mostly canvases. He didn't buy junk. As Prince of Asturias before ascending the throne he bought Raphael's *Portrait of a Cardinal*, *Abraham's Sacrifice* by Andrea del Sarto, Ribera's *Apostles*, two panels by the Master of Flemalle, that sort of thing. When he lived in Italy as an old man, deprived of his throne, he went on collecting.

How ignorant was this man? He had been educated by German Jesuits and retained some knowledge of mathematics, a little geography, not much else. He didn't know the Americans were independent of England and as late as 1802—twenty-six years after the Declaration—he referred to the Minister of the United States as El Ministro de las Colonias, a degree of ignorance that may remind you of some recent American presidents.

Nobody ever called him handsome, although he is said to have had fairly regular features with only hints of the family inheritance in his long nose and protruding jaw. I'm not persuaded. Some years ago I bought two Spanish pieces-of-eight.

Around the rim of one coin: CAROLUS•IIII•DEI•GRATIA•1791.

Gradually it changed from silver to brass, but that's irrelevant. The profile must be accurate because it was copied from an authentic coin and there is more than a hint of his Bourbon inheritance. He has what we call a lantern jaw or a bulldog jaw and that nose almost hides his upper lip. Nevertheless he manages to look imperial.

The other coin is no fake. FERDIN•VII•DEI•GRATIA•1820.

Not much could be done with Ferdinand. His nose ends in a bulb. He lacks his father's gross jaw but it doesn't help. He resembles somebody's grandmother. The coin has been handled so much since 1820 that Ferdinand's features are nearly obliterated: which seems appropriate. This is a flyblown descendent of nobility.

Charles IV wasn't a complex man, not a subtle man, and he puzzled foreign dignitaries. A French ambassador reported that distinctions of birth meant nothing to him: "The Medinacelis, the Albuquerques, the Altamires, the Osimas, all these grandees who take such pride in their origins, mean no more to him than his grooms; he has the same way of speaking to anyone." He enjoyed painting, as did the Queen. We are told she wasn't bad, although her work has been lost or is secluded in private collections. Charles offered several of their paintings to the Academy. What the academicians said behind closed doors isn't known.

If Charles at the easel is unexpected, consider his passion for the violin. One biographer asserts that he handled it reasonably well. Nothing substantiates this. On the contrary, when he chose to join a quartet, as now and again he did, a court musician planted behind a screen drowned out the royal scraping. Charles must have assumed that he and the professional were rewarding the audience with a duet. Once he played for Goya, who mentioned this in a letter to Zapater, although without comment. Goya, of course, was deaf. The Marx brothers would have loved it.

In 1967 Goya's huge picture was cleaned. From the grime of almost two centuries emerged a painting of Lot with his daughters. Undoubtedly it hung on the wall behind the royal family in 1800; nevertheless, the King and Queen commissioned no more work from Goya. They may have disliked the implication.

Everybody wants to pass judgment on this painting.

The mystic poet Paul Claudel saw it in Geneva not long after the Spanish civil war and deplored Goya's focus on ugly realities. Claudel detested the "verminous" world of Bosch and Breughel, but thought Goya worse, more degenerate, "seeking to avoid the eyes and the image of God."

Novelist Hemingway called it a masterpiece of loathing.

Charles Poore in 1938 asked how Goya could paint them as he did and escape strangulation. The answer he provides is that Goya avoided the example of Velázquez "who gave all his Philips their look of poached nobility." It's a felicitous remark, but if Charles IV doesn't look poached, no Spanish sovereign ever did.

Anthony Hull saw the imminent decline of Spain mirrored in the static blue eyes of Charles, in the weak mouth, puffy cheeks, in the large fat body and torpid head.

Charles at fifty-three, sluggish, gaseous, jewels glittering on his chest like fireworks or the Great Square of Pegasus—brutally described by Gautier as a neighborhood baker who won the lottery. How did María Luisa with her foxy intellect overlook what we find so evident? Hugh Stokes, whose book appeared in 1914, offers this explanation: "It has often been said that Goya caricatured his sitters. On the contrary, he painted them according to the Spanish manner, which is disconcerting but truthful. The portraits of the sixteenth and seventeenth centuries are statement as matter-of-fact as a lawyer's bill."

Lady Holland moved through the highest circles of Madrid society and her diary brims with evocative notes.

June, 1803: "On ye 17th I was presented to the Queen and King. . . ." A private audience. The Queen did not insist that Lady Holland wear a hoop but did insist upon gloves. The sight of a gloveless female hand would cause Charles to become physically agitated. We aren't told just what he did, only that his response would be "sudden and violent." Lady Holland adds that white leather gloves would produce similar effects on quite a few members of the Spanish Bourbon family. She must not have inquired about this unique affliction because the diary proceeds as though everybody understood. She had no doubt that Prince Francisco de Paula was Godoy's child: "A pretty, lively boy, bearing a most indecent likeness to the P. of the Peace."

August 1: "Dined at the Bourkes. Present, Prince Masserano, St. Simon, Freire the Portuguese Minister, &c." Brisk appraisals of these guests. One is a most diligent courtier whose flattery of the court is so fulsome that refined ears would not endure it. The Portuguese Minister she calls a whispering civil man: "He was employed in England, and for his sins, he says, sent for 3 years to America!"

August 2: "Dined at home, only Mr. Vaughan." One gets the feeling that she is exhausted by upper-echelon affairs. But in Spain, as everyone knows, not much happens before midnight. Off to the Prado and Buen Retiro. Before this night ends she has met a certain M. de Betancourt, an authority on dams and waterworks, who is superintendent-general of something or other, a member of the family that discovered the Canary Isles. Next day she meets the King's librarian, Juan Antonio Pellicer, whose edition of *Don Quixote* was published in 1797.

So it goes. And because Lady Holland was perceptive, intelligent, and industrious enough to record the social minuet we have an exceptional documentary of Spanish administration in those exceptional times.

November 4. Remembering the previous day with Freire and Lambert. Painful memories of childhood, how she abhors birthdays. Dined at home, "had puppet shows, and a magic lantern, &c. Reports in the Puerta del Sol of the yellow fever being already in Madrid. . . ."

She is aware of turmoil in France: "Bonaparte's sisters hissed at theatre; called 'Princesses du Sang,' allusion to the murder of Enghien. Brunet, the actor, imprisoned for a joke."

July 9, 1804. American diplomat William Pinkney to supper. Spain quarreling with the United States about cession of Louisiana. "Pinkney has ordered his two black servants to announce thro' the town in all botillerias that he is to go home, and advertise his wine for sale."

July 11. Dined at "Freres"—presumably Freire, the Portuguese Minister. Among the guests, "M de Rouffignac, an old Frenchman, who leaves upon his cards, 'Le premier gentilhomme et chrétian du Limousin,' but compelled to fly his country many years ago for having killed his colonel in a duel."

July 18. Pinkney again. "In appearance, manner, and style of conversation very Yankee, but evidently skilful in making a bargain. Talks of the dispute between Spain and the U. States as he would of a difference between two of his neighbours. Talks with contempt of Spain. . . . Told us that he had charged 16 dollars for stationery in his acct. of extraordinary expenditure, whereupon, tho' the acct. was passed and paid, he received a private letter from Madison cautioning him agt. making such charges in future."

July 25. Lord and Lady Holland entertain Conde Fernan Nuñez, Academy member, patron of the arts, one of twelve gentlemen-in-waiting to the King. Goya had painted Fernan Nuñez a few months earlier. One of his duties included scratching the royal back while Charles lay in bed. Other guests: the Marqués de Santa Cruz, Marqués Penafiel, and so on, any of whom would have graced most dinner parties. "Much conversation about ye etiquette and ceremonial of the Sp. Court. King and Q., and even the little Infantes, served with drink by the gentlemen-in-waiting on their knees. Old custom retained of tasting what the King is to drink and eat. When the cup is carried through the apartments or corridors of the palace, every one by whom it passes must take off his hat. At the Escorial once lately an obstinate fellow refused. . . ." This impertinent Spaniard went to prison.

Such was life on the fringe of royalty for aristocratic tourists and such was life for Spaniards who objected to the status quo.

Agnostics, loudmouths, poets, philosophers, eccentrics, assassins, thieves, and similar undesirables had more than prison to worry about. French Republicans, as we know, punished enemies with that merciful device the guillotine. Americans have experimented with the noose, firing squad, electric chair, gas chamber, lethal injection. Spaniards in Goya's day employed "the fearful ceremony of garrotting." Firing squads might be used, but strangulation was favored. Those who had been condemned usually were drawn to the site of execution in a tumbril, that rickety wooden cart familiar to us from the French revolution—a two-wheeled farmer's cart used for carrying and disposing of animal dung, from the Old French tomberel, modern tomber, to fall. The condemned would be seated on a bench and shackled to an upright post with an iron collar. After a cord had been looped around his neck the executioner would tighten it by twisting the cord with a stick or by manipulating a lever behind the post. Justice could be administered quickly or slowly, depending on the crime. Goya made ink drawings of the garotte at work and from these drawings we know what he thought.

Lady Holland's occasional dinner guest, Charles Vaughan, watched an execution. What bothered him most wasn't the brutal death but the ceremony. Priests and monks holding up effigies of the Virgin and of Christ crucified walked alongside the wretched man. After he had been seated on a chair the rope that bound his arms was wrapped around his body. An old Capuchin then pressed a crucifix to his lips. Not many years earlier an English clergyman had inscribed on his tombstone: Ubi saeva indignatio ulterius cor lacerare nequit. In other words, here lies Jonathan Swift where savage indignation can no longer lacerate the heart. Mr. Vaughan, less corrosive, could do no more than call what he had witnessed "the most disgusting thing I ever saw." It brings to mind André Malraux's comment that the sacred and dreadful are powerfully united in Christians who for two thousand years have worshipped a man put to torture.

Excursions, new friends, dinner parties two centuries forgotten, such is the antique journal of a rich English lady visiting Spain. Pinkney squandering sixteen dollars on stationery. M. de Betancourt, authority on dams and waterworks just lately returned from Granada, "where he had been to confine the overflowing of the Xenil." Napoleon's sisters hissed. Count Fernan Nuñez scratching the meaty back of Charles IV. Marquis of this, Duchess of that. And she left thumbnail sketches of other notables.

El Conde Haro. A chattering coxcomb.

The Duke of Medinaceli. One of Spain's richest. A bigot, blind, imbecilic. The Duchess a clumsy, vulgar woman. Duke and Duchess both intolerant, illiterate, surrounded by monks and priests, served at table by gentlemen on bended knees. Lady Holland underlines "gentlemen" to indicate nobility. The Duke and Duchess think themselves rightful heirs to Castile and on the day the King is proclaimed they erect a gallows opposite Medinaceli palace to protest what they construe as the renunciation of their claim.

Duke of Aliaga, a heavy clumsy figure. "Two years ago he acted Cupid in one of his own plays."

Madame de Santiago. Profligate, loose in both manners and conversation, scarcely admitted to female society.

Madame de Xaruja. Extremely voluptuous, devoted to love. Was in England some years ago. Eldest daughter a magnificent glowing beauty, "offspring of the Sun."

Count Fuentes y Mora. "Came to England to marry Miss Beckford; checked by her refusal . . ."

So on and on. This was Goya's Spain, together with blind beggars, cripples, cutthroats, lunatics, swaggering majos, flirtatious majas, dwarfs, bullfights, carnivals, massacres, picnics beside the Manzanares, Inquisitors seeking the Devil. Much of it Goya saw through a glass darkly.

9

Goya may have been quite deaf in 1800 when he began work on the great family portrait of Charles IV, but his eyes weren't bad and surely he knew about the triangular cat fight at court: María Luisa, Duchess María Teresa Cayetana of Alba, Duchess María Josefa of Osuna. Everybody in Madrid knew about it, probably down to the last chestnut vendor. Poet-playwright Tomás de Yriarte, whom Duchess María Josefa kept on the payroll for entertainment, lamented that nothing else was to be heard from the time one gets up in the morning till one goes to bed.

Queen María Luisa held all the cards except youth and beauty. She might have been wealthier than her rivals. The Albas and Osunas both were stupendously rich although it would take an accountant to determine which ranked first. Not one of these three bothered to ask how much something would cost.

María Cayetana of Alba: second to Her Majesty, capricious, unruly, passionate, Spain's most glamorous butterfly.

María Joséfa of Osuna: dignified, angular, intelligent, patron of the arts.

One side of this triangle should include Don Juan Pignatelli. A 1793 pamphlet by Pierre Nicolas Chantreau describes the "amorous intrigues" of Queen María Luisa. We are told that Pignatelli was in love with the Duchess of Alba, who happened to be his stepsister. Because of this, we assume, she would have nothing to do with him. Not so the Queen. Not only did Her Majesty take Don Juan to bed, she gave him a little gold box encrusted with diamonds. You might think Pignatelli would be satisfied. No, he kept after the Duchess. And she, before submitting, demanded the little gold box in exchange for a ring. Pignatelli agreed. After all, who would prefer a jeweled trinket box to the most glamorous woman in Spain? That ought to conclude the story. But no, Her Majesty saw this ring on Pignatelli's finger and demanded it as a present, intending to wave it in María Cayetana's face at the next hand-kissing ceremony. Nor is that the end. María Cayetana gave the box to her hairdresser, who also served the Queen, instructing him to fill it with pomade and to make sure the Queen noticed. Beside this, what are the amorous intrigues of men?

Queen María Luisa ordered gowns from Paris. La Alba therefore dressed her maids in replicas and sent them promenading through Madrid.

She gave a party to celebrate the extension of her San Cristóbal palace. Charles and María Luisa were invited. Fireworks exploded in the evening sky. *C* to honor His Majesty. *L* for María Luisa. Then, to everyone's discomfort, *G* for Godoy. On two occasions fire broke out in the palace, which the Duchess thought no accident. Next time, she said, rather than give others the satisfaction of burning my house I shall set the blaze myself, with my own hand, por mi propia mano. Well, maybe. Picturesque anecdotes sprang up like dandelions around the Duchess.

These privileged women fought about music, one praising Lully, another praising Haydn. They fought about painters. They quarreled over the talent of actors and actresses. Who should play the leading role in a production of the Manuel Martínez company? The Duchess of Osuna favored Pepa Figeras. The Duchess of Alba favored María del Rosario Fernández. María del Rosario got the part. The Duchess of Alba, triumphant, presented some of her own gowns to the actress. María del Rosario's stage name was La Tirana and how she got this name has been argued. Probably she inherited it from her actor-husband, Francisco Castillo, who often played the tyrant. Francisco played this role off-stage at least once; crazed with jealousy, he stole his wife's costume. María del Rosario, the resourceful trouper, appeared on stage wearing one of La Alba's gowns. Like the Duchess, she was famously beautiful. In fact they resembled one another. Goya painted her twice and nobody has described the early portrait better than Antonina Vallentin who called it a regal silhouette, splendid, haughty:

> . . . that her kingdom is of the theatre is revealed only by the plebeian gesture of the arm resting against the hip . . . age had not yet touched her magnificent rounded arms, nor her sculptured throat with its reflections like satin; but the first tiny lines were already marking the corners of her mouth, the too-ardent eyes had worn a purple circle around the eyelids; the perfect oval of her face had only just begun to be hollowed a little, in the slight falling-in of the too-blooming flesh . . . her figure is streaked with pale gold, strangely pathetic: a column of light on the threshold of nightfall.

La Tirana aged rapidly. Goya painted her five years later, an undistinguished woman who is almost fat. She looks tired. Her mouth sags. The exquisite features have thickened. That was the year she left the stage, the artificial light, cheers of hundreds, mad applause. Three years later she returned to the theater, but not to perform. She accepted a job as cashier. Soon afterward she died of tuberculosis, a young woman not yet thirty.

They enjoyed arguing about matadors, these fabulously rich women. The Duchess of Alba championed Pedro Joaquín Rodríguez, aka Costillares, who invented the volapie and the veronica. Most of the Queen's sycophants favored José Delgado, aka Pepe-Hillo, renowned for his skill with ladies as well as for his style in the ring. All of Spain felt the blow when, in 1801, a bull named Barbudo hooked him. Goya memorialized Pepe-Hillo's death in the thirty-third plate of the *Tauromaquia* series.

We might not expect the great ducal houses of Alba and Osuna to be on good terms, but they remained quite close. María Cayetana stabled a donkey at La Alameda so that she might go riding with María Josefa.

In August of 1795 she came calling upon our man from Fuendetodos. She had not been invited. Goya wrote to Zapater that she wanted to have her face painted, "and she went out with it painted, which I definitely like better than painting on canvas." What, exactly, did he mean? He added that she would come around again because she wanted a full-length portrait. This implies that what resulted was *Maja Vestida* or the scandalous *Maja Desnuda*, if only because of the popular belief that she modeled for those paintings. In fact, the result of her second visit was a standing figure. She wears a long white gown with a red sash. Her lips are pursed. She points at the ground as though ordering a servant to kneel; you get the feeling she will stamp one tiny foot. Strangely, she took orders from Goya, even permitting him to touch her face with cosmetics. Queen María Luisa also behaved with the docility of a household pet. Years later Goya would encounter a more imperious subject: Wellington. The Iron Duke himself.

Historians as well as La Alba's contemporaries struggle to praise her beauty. She attracted men like ants to a honey pot. Jean-Marie Fleuriot, Marquis de Langle, lost his mind: Every hair of her head, etc. And yet, in both portraits by Goya what we see is not some unearthly beauty but an arrogant vixen. A pencil drawing by Mariano González de Sepúlveda, dated 1795, shows her with a double chin. Disorderly black hair tumbles to her waist, a waist noticeably thicker than that of the Goya woman. Fifteen more years and she will be stout, middle-aged. Marquis Fleuriot wouldn't give her a second look.

Now consider Doña Isabel Cobos de Pórcel, identified as such by a nineteenth-century inscription on the back of a canvas used to reline the portrait. That wasn't exactly her name. In 1980 this lining was removed. An earlier inscription was found, identifying her as *La Exma. Sra. Dna. Lobo de Pórcel, Pintado por Goya*. It's known that she was born in Ronda and married a counselor of Castile, Antonio Pórcel, who was a friend of that wretch Godoy. Just who bungled the transcription, turning Lobo into Cobos, is a mystery. But there's more. X-rays show an unknown man behind Isabel. Goya might have painted this man or he might have painted over a work by somebody else. Isabel's husband probably commissioned it. Why wouldn't Goya spend a few pesetas for new canvas? Anyway, the mysterious man's right eye can be found just beneath her chin, though it isn't obvious in reproductions.

The reason for mentioning this portrait is her voluptuous beauty. Women, most women, after one hostile glance say she's fat. Men who come upon Doña Isabel for the first time stop as though hit with a club. She's two centuries old. Nobody cares. Goya saw a radiant succulent woman who enjoyed being a woman who enjoyed men and that is what he painted. Two centuries from now Doña Isabel will stop traffic. This is no Duchess of Alba wound up like a mechanical dominatrix.

Why didn't Goya show us the fabulous mankiller?

When he mentions in a letter to Zapater that she came to his studio unannounced, it's ambiguous. Something unexpected and agreeable took place, but what? Or was he boasting?

His friendship with her might have developed slowly, perhaps cautiously, despite the implication of that letter. She may have encouraged it because he was a notable catch, even for a lady of her estate. He could not be called handsome. Twenty years earlier, if we accept his self-portrait, he was swarthy, intense, virile, growing bald yet not bad looking, physically powerful. Unlike King Charles who was strong beneath a good many kilos of blubber, Goya looks solid as a keg.

What might have attracted the Duchess was his deafness. Nature's disinherited excited this haughty noblewoman. The crippled, stupid, stuttering old priest, for instance. If members of her entourage joked about him she would exclaim that they were bad—everyone was bad except Brother Basil and herself. On one occasion, disgusted by the slavish manner of servants bringing food to the table, she cried that neither she, nor her husband, nor good Brother Basil ought to be served by such domestics: "What low rabble they are, capable of persuading us that we are better than they!" The moment is charming, eccentric, undeniably feminine because men don't behave like that, and it sounds calculated. When she ambushed the seminarian, gobbling up so much pastry that he had to leave his trousers at the cafe, she planned each move. These tiny dramas often seem premeditated. At her summer estate she was about to get dressed when a visitor walked in. "Amiguita de mi alma!" she exclaimed. Little friend of my soul! If it embarrasses you to see me naked I will cover myself with my hair! This story was told by a member of the Somoza family; he knew the Duchess and identifies the visitor as a woman who lived nearby. The scene is graphic, mildly shocking, but doesn't sound quite right. Visitors don't walk unannounced through a mansion staffed with servants.

Unlike the angular, stiff, intelligent Duchess of Osuna who concerned herself with the arts, economic problems, and government, María Cayetana delighted in flirtation, amusement, affairs of the moment, outrageous behavior, society gossip, ephemeral victories. She had a vast collection of shoes, as might be expected, and wore a different pair every day. Somoza wrote that she "received no education, heard no good precepts, read no good books . . ." This is curious. Somoza must have known about her privileged childhood—that monolithic grandfather with his library of classics, his art collection, his palace on the ruins of a medieval castle.

Goya painted a close friend of the Duchess, the Marquesa de la Solana, who died at thirty-three. The Marquesa understood that she didn't have much time and wanted to leave her daughter a portrait. Her crossed hands are pale. Her fan is closed. The face is sad yet resolute, almost masculine. Probably because she was dignified and unafraid she was delegated to scold the Duchess. In a letter dated September 11, 1785, her husband advised her against associating with the likes of María Cayetana: "Instead of considering what is proper and ought to be done, she idles away the time singing tiranas and envying the majas."

We are told of a certain Lord Beckford "trailing his British spleen across Europe" who wandered through a villa the Duchess had bought and was remodeling. Lord Beckford noticed magnificent frescoes on the walls and came upon a French artist, described as a painter of arabesques and love scenes, who was scrubbing the walls with pumice: "I saw lying on the floor some large flakes of marble-dust plaster that bore the touch of Rubens. . . ." Whether or not Rubens painted those frescoes isn't the point; whatever was scraped off the walls tells us that María Cayetana preferred frou-frou.

In 1796 her young husband's fragile health gave out. He may have loved the violin as much or more than he loved the Duchess, a love characterized as an exclusive interest that often is a form of resignation. It's said they respected each other but lived separately, husband and wife with acknowledged rights and duties. They had no children. She realized, of course, why her grandfather insisted upon marriage soon after her father's death; the ducal title had been in his family for generations.

Her husband, thirty-nine years old, died of "the malady" in Seville on the morning of June 9 and was embalmed quickly, a few hours later, because of the heat.

She retired to Sanlúcar de Barrameda for the traditional three years of mourning, one of the few traditions she chose to honor. Goya soon arrived. Whether she invited him or whether he came to pay his respects is a topic of scholarly dispute.

Thomas Craven's engaging survey of art and artists recycles the dramatic story of how they ended up à deux at Sanlúcar. The Duchess "comported herself so brazenly that she was obliged, at the Queen's suggestion, to retire temporarily to her estate in Andalusia." Goya applied for a leave of absence from court, which was granted. Away they went. On a mountain road the carriage sprung an axle. Goya kindled a fire and bent the steel back into shape. However, the exertion brought on a chill that affected his ears and eventually deafened him. Mercedes Barbarossa tells us that because of gossip about the Duchess and Goya, María Luisa "was only too glad to seize upon this pretext to secure her rival's disgrace and banishment from Court." Now we have two carriages, a solitary mountain pass, a cold dark night. "The painter has overtaken his Duchess, and the strong mules drawing the carriage are proceeding at a smart pace along the rough country roads, when the conveyance suddenly is brought to a standstill. . . ." After Goya bends the wheel into shape, "the voyage continues without further mishap."

What has been established by reliable historians is that Goya spent several weeks at Sanlúcar. They had plenty to talk about and he was busy sketching.

The so-called Album A, or Sanlúcar Album, contains sixteen drawings and five copies of lost originals. These five copies are thought to be the work of Goya's first biographer, Valentín Carderera. The drawings focus on "La de Alba" as he called her in a note to Zapater, and among these is a nude woman bathing at a fountain, girls walking or dancing, the Duchess arranging her hair, the Duchess cuddling her adopted black child María de la Luz—La Negrita. The atmosphere is light, casual, occasionally intimate. It's obvious that Goya felt at home and was free to sketch just about anything. No particular intensity suffuses these drawings; he might have been sipping lemonade while he worked. Here on a delightful country estate he worked not because he had been commissioned but because that was what he always did. Waldmann comments that these sketches are like a diary recounting moments and occurrences not in words but in the language of an artist.

Here in southern Spain a few weeks after her husband's death she and Goya became lovers, if ever they did. Perhaps at Sanlúcar, perhaps at the isolated country home known as El Rocío—which translates clumsily into English as something like Sprinkle or Shower or Dew.

In the Sanlúcar sketchbook a woman generally identified as María Cayetana wears a long dress. On the other side of the drawing that same woman hoists that same dress to display a voluptuous rump. Symmons, for one, doesn't think the smirking exhibitionist could be La Alba:

In other sketches she is shown nude, seated, masturbating . . . or as one of two women playing together on a bed. The sensuous display of erotic poses, from the elegant and elusive duchess to the lewd and available courtesan who trawls in the duchess's wake like a doppelganger, reveals not only Goya's interest in sexual imagery but also his fascination with opposites and reversals.

So, as with much of his work, we interpret it as we choose.

During this time he painted—or began—the second full-length portrait, similar to the first. Again she stands imperiously pointing downward, but now she points at two words traced in the sand: Solo Goya. That is, only Goya. From our point of view these words are upside down as if meant for the Duchess alone. Moreover, the portrait had been retouched soon after it was painted. The first word, Solo, had been painted out. This was not discovered for a century and a half when the painting was being restored. Goya himself obliterated the personal reference because analysis of pigment showed that the retouching and the original were contemporary.

María Cayetana married again. The name of her second husband has been forgotten, which is puzzling. He ought to be in the archives of this celebrated family. He is mentioned in a letter by the Countess of Montijo; she called him a good man but a man who was unhappy or sad, who comforted himself with philosophy and religion.

February 16, 1797. The Duchess composed her last will and testament. Nothing suggests premonition, merely concern for the House of Alba, for the administration and/or disposal of her vast estate: "I appoint as heirs . . . "

No relatives shared this fortune, not unless one counts a stepbrother who had been a friend since childhood. Otherwise, people she liked. Her chambermaid, Catalina Barajas. Catalina's three children. Benito, the court jester. A couple of physicians and their children. Tomás Berganza, administrator, and his son. La Negrita—María de la Luz—and the child's nurse, Trinidad. The Duchess included a list of poor people on the estate. Finally, Goya's son Javier, whom she may never have met. He was to receive ten reales a day as long as he lived. No mention of Javier's mother, Josefa, although there is a legend that the Duchess sent delicacies from her own table and instructed her footmen to leave the gold dishes.

Why and how the Sanlúcar interlude ended never has been learned. Maybe she tired of him. Maybe she guessed that he was in love with her and told him it wasn't appropriate.

On the way home he paused in Seville. His friend Céan Bermúdez reported that Goya entered a grotto to examine a famous statue of St.

Jerome by Torrigiano—not so well known for his sculpture as for the fact that he broke Michelangelo's nose. Goya spent an hour in the grotto and returned for a second look. He was at this time doing a portrait of Jerome for a church in Seville and evidently wanted to see how Torrigiano handled the subject. More than once he needed models for his religious work. In 1811 he and Josefa would dictate a joint will stating: "We firmly believe and confess the mystery . . ." Despite this avowed belief, his occasional reliance upon models implies doubt.

Instead of going directly to Madrid from Seville he went to Saragossa, possibly to visit Zapater. The long relationship between these two, dating back to Father Joaquín's school, had been disintegrating. Zapater's descendants would blame Goya, saying he had changed, had become too conscious of his good fortune. Maybe it was inevitable that they should drift apart. Goya, turbulent, obsessed with work, ambitious. Zapater, sedate, provincial, content to be a prominent attorney in Saragossa.

Home again, he found another patron. Godoy. Everybody in Madrid knew about Godoy's affair with María Luisa. Not only was the Prime Minister bedding Her Majesty right under the King's nose, there was the concierge's daughter, Josefa Tudó, whom he fondly called Pepita.

Godoy? Eh! He interviews pretty women in his palace late at night. You see them leave early in the morning, all ruffled.

Godoy's bad taste enraged the Queen; the problem was what to do about it. And this leads, however circuitously, to the French Revolution. El Choricero had traveled a long way from his childhood in Estremadura, home of innumerable pigs, but in his mind he had only begun to rise. He believed he could marry the granddaughter of Louis XVI. Why not? He was Manuel y Alvarez de Faria Godoy, Prime Minister of Spain, irresistible to women. Regrettably, King Louis lost his head and now the French were tearing their country apart. Who knew what might happen next? Godoy therefore lowered his aim. He decided to marry the sweet young Countess of Chinchón, daughter of the Infante Don Luis. She could not inherit the Spanish throne, but she belonged to the royal family. One step at a time.

María Luisa assented to this marriage. Nobody can be sure what went through the Queen's mind, but it is thought she reasoned as follows: If I permit Godoy to marry this child he will give up the concierge's daughter. Then, too, he will be part of our circle where I might be able to control him.

Godoy, a not unreasonable man, seems to have been rather pleased with the way things turned out. If he couldn't marry the granddaughter of Louis XVI, well, at least he would through marriage belong to Spanish royalty. He decided to refurbish one of his palaces in honor of his bride. And who should contribute to this? The most famous painter in Spain.

He commissioned a series of allegorical medallions. *Industry. Commerce. Agriculture.* Biographers argue about whether they hung on the staircase or in a salon. No matter. And for the library, a medallion representing that most esoteric art: *Poetry.* Allegories indicated rank, power, sensibility. Thus, in the lengthening shadow of France, Godoy commissioned the final emblems of eighteenth-century prestige.

Industry. The Prime Minister requested a circular painting, a tondo. Goya often seemed indifferent to composition but now he made an effort, perhaps because he liked Godoy. Women at machines. Wheels of industry. A splash of color to brighten the factory interior. Another circular form in the background, part of an arch admitting weak daylight—similar to *The Plague Hospital* and *The Madhouse* where yellowish light washes over men and women going through their days without hope.

Godoy wanted three more. *Truth. History. Time.* In this sort of work nudes were permissible, although displayed less publicly.

He may have commissioned the *Maja Vestida* and *Maja Desnuda* which are not the least allegorical. Connoisseurs don't look favorably upon these plump twins, not yesterday, not today, perhaps not tomorrow, although one can't be sure. During the late nineteenth century Burne-Jones was regarded more highly than Rembrandt. Pierre Gassier, after alluding to a thickset creature, observes that both majas betray a distinct slackness of touch. Further, he notes a disagreeable mawkishness and "boudoir realism of doubtful taste."

Anatomists complain that if such a woman could walk it would be a clumsy waddle. Short legs, we are told by Emilia Pardo Bazan, result from the cloistered, pent-up life of Spanish women.

Havelock Ellis found ethnic reasons for the waist and generous bosom; the chest of a Spanish woman is broad, hence she needs a different sort of corset, "while at the same time there is a greater amplitude and accentuation of the hips in relation to the figure generally. These characteristics of the Spanish women are well illustrated, it has been said, by a comparison between the statue which Falguiere modelled after Cleo de Merode and the distinctively national Spanish type represented in Goya's *Maja Desnuda.. . .*"

Chabrun, having declared that Goya felt most comfortable around women who appealed to him physically, described the model as "slightly stocky, slightly common and built for pleasure." True. Goya arranged that animal on the sofa, he enjoyed looking at her, and he enjoyed painting what he saw.

Julius Meier-Graefe was an influential critic during the early twentieth century. The more he saw of Goya's work the less he liked what he saw. After his first visit to the Prado he said Goya was worse than he suspected. Mengs had pointed out the road to beauty, but Goya refused to follow it. Meier-Graefe admitted that now and again Goya had a brilliant idea but everything was poorly executed. Goya didn't have a suitably analytical mind. Manet's *Olympia*, for instance, was superb, meeting the classical standard of emotion recollected in tranquility. Not so with Goya. "We are silent before the *Olympia*, whereas before the *Maja* we twitch and quiver."

Other critics say her face isn't attractive, pointing to the debauched expression of this undressed/half-dressed Messalina. Boudoir realism of doubtful taste.

Artists usually notice that the body and face don't quite fit together, which is suggestive. Prurient French esthetes during the late eighteenth century would sometimes replace the faces on erotic prints with the face of Marie Antoinette.

González de Sepúlveda, professor of engraving at the Royal Academy, saw the Prime Minister's collection on November 12, 1800, and later mentioned "the nude woman by Goya" that hung in a private chamber along with depictions of Venus by other artists. This is the earliest reference to *Maja Desnuda*. Sepúlveda evidently did not see the clothed figure, if it existed at that time. He didn't think the nude well drawn, nor did he think much of the color: "sin divujo ni gracia en colorido."

Godoy's estate was inventoried on January 1, 1808, by a French artist, Frédéric Quilliet, who had been appointed Curator of Works of Art by Joseph Bonaparte. This is the first reference to *Maja Vestida*. Quilliet listed the former as gypsy nude, the latter as gypsy clothed, both reclining—Gitana nue, Gitana habillée, toux deux couchées—because he could not imagine that any woman other than a gypsy would pose in such a compromising fashion. Charles III, celibate and miserable, no doubt would agree. However, the clothed model wears pointed shoes, a style favored by aristocrats. Lower orders preferred square-toed shoes with silver buckles. In any event, M. Quilliet assigned both works to his third category, meaning they had little esthetic value.

Now, as then, tourists jostle for position in front of Goya's saftig maja/majas while scholars dissect her.

Tomlinson: "Feet, thighs, pubis . . . the skin has no softness, the body does not sink into the couch . . . the breasts appear to be sculpted in marble. . . ."

Not every critic disapproves. Thomas Craven mentions an electric vitality that Goya's brush imparted to everything, "which distinguishes his naked *Maja* from Velásquez's corpse of Venus."

Gautier advised everyone visiting Madrid to see a sixteen-pound nugget of gold, Chinese gongs that sound like a copper stew pan when you kick it, three admirable paintings by Murillo, two or three splendid Riberas, a burial by El Greco, "and a charming woman in Spanish costume, lying on a divan, painted by good old Goya, the national painter above all others, who seems to have come into this world on purpose to collect the last traces of national customs which are about to disappear.

Francisco Goya y Lucientes is unmistakably the descendant of Velázquez. After him come Aparicio and Lopez—the decadence is complete, the cycle of art is closed."

Whoever presumes to evaluate Goya must confront that nude, which brings us to *Mlle. O'Murphy,* Boucher's little masterpiece of doubtful taste before which we twitch and quiver. Belly down, she sprawls on a velvet couch waiting—undeniably waiting. So does Goya's creature wait, although there's a difference. *Mlle. O'Murphy,* or *The Blond Odalisque,* is thought to be Louise O'Murphy who became Louis XV's mistress in 1753. She reappears as an aquatic nymph in *The Triumph of Venus,* still more noticeably in *Venus and Mercury Instructing Cupid.* Which is to say Boucher was stealing from himself, but that's often what artists do.

Frederick Licht proposes a simple experiment to show how differently these painters saw the nude. Imagine one or two babies around the Boucher woman. It would seem natural because she embodies love, fertility, motherhood, the appealing joy of sex. She might be considered an allegorical woman. If you try to visualize a couple of babies around Goya's maja the experiment becomes disgusting. This woman embodies sex, toujours sex, perhaps a commercial exchange. Licht mentions the taut, slightly arched body, the glacial challenge in a hostile face, the shabby couch where she waits, motionless and deadly as a spider.

However you appraise these twins, they shocked Western art. Goya demolished the honorable tradition of mythological goddesses. Almost. Not quite. Thomas Hart Benton in the American midwest continued stubbornly on his way. Benton took what he wanted from the past and ignored the rest. He updated *Susanna,* for example, elderly farmers peeping. Still, most artists felt obliged to redirect their course. Degas lamented that because of Goya he was condemned to painting a housewife in her bathtub.

On the basis of style or technique *La Maja Desnuda* is thought to have been painted around 1800, no earlier than 1795. The Duke of Alba died in June, 1796, and Goya arrived at Sanlúcar to visit the Duchess very soon afterward. The Duke and Duchess had a formidable art collection that included *Venus and Cupid* by Velázquez, aka the Rokeby Venus. Goya must have studied it; a drawing from the so-called Madrid album shows a nude woman in a similar pose who, like Venus, contemplates her image in a mirror. What seems fairly obvious is that Goya was measuring himself against Velázquez, wondering if he could equal a full-length nude by the seventeenth-century master.

Venus and Cupid caused a certain Miss Mary Richardson to take, as we say, violent exception. In 1914 she entered London's National Gallery, marched up to the painting and slashed Venus with a knife. Why? As Miss Richardson explained, she objected to the way men looked at her. Good students of the female psyche will have no trouble understanding this. For those who don't understand, the attack is worth consideration: Venus, photographed afterward, has become the victim of a sex murder.

Miss Richardson and Goya biographer Hugh Stokes were of the same vintage. Indeed, his book appeared during the year of her maniacal attack, which ought to be significant but probably isn't. Her feelings about Velázquez, or about what he had done, were unmistakable. Mr. Stokes, however, felt ambivalent. He commences by informing us that to some extent Goya founded his idea of portraiture upon those of his great predecessor. He then calls Velázquez "the uninspired man of genius." If that's not enough, "Dürer had more invention in his little finger than Velázquez possessed in his whole body." Nor is that all. The deficiencies of Velázquez cannot be better studied than at the Prado where he keeps company with Titian, Tintoretto, Van Dyck, and Rubens. Whereupon Mr. Stokes begins to sound as schizoid as Miss Richardson: "We can believe without question Rubens' legendary statement that Velázquez was the greatest painter in Europe."

Stokes then drifts afield. Velázquez went to Italy, where he awoke to the beauty of atmosphere. This leads to speculation. Among the first artists to go traveling in search of a subject was Turner, and what would Turner be had he not crossed the Alps to Italy? Ergo, what would result if Velázquez had gone north to paint misty Dutch canals? What if Rembrandt had one day packed up his brushes and caught the express to Madrid? How would Goya have been influenced by a visit to Hawaii or Japan?

Almost certainly he got the idea for a model nude and model clothed from two 1680 paintings by Juan Carreño de Miranda titled *La Monstrua*. This monstrous child, Eugenia Martínez Vallejo, was born somewhere near Burgos and was brought to the court of Charles II. She is said to have been sexually developed by the age of six and weighed as much as two grown women. Both paintings were in the royal collection where Goya would have seen them. The nude is presented as Bacchus, her pubic area hidden by a spray of grape leaves, although Miranda didn't attempt a symbolic face; this is a specific child with a distended body. The bloated, scaly right hand resembles a claw. She looks not quite at us but aside, frowning. In the other portrait she wears a decorative scarlet gown with puffed sleeves, the sort of thing you might see on the fat lady at a carnival. Now she looks toward us from a terrible distance, knowing she isn't human.

But what fascinates critics and public alike is the identity of Goya's model. La Alba? Some gypsy? A professional?

Could she have been Godoy's longtime mistress Pepita Tudó? Godoy obviously loved Pepita while remaining in love with his wife, which may be unusual but isn't impossible. Pepita allegedly had several children by him while he was married to the Countess. And the mistress, like the wife, had no illusions. Pepita noted in her diary that he was having an affair with the Duchess of Alba.

In 1800 the Prime Minister bought a house for Pepita on Desengaño Street—the very house where Goya had been living for twenty-two years. Why did Godoy want this particular house?

X-ray examination shows that the maja's face has been repainted. The model's features were scraped off and Goya substituted the generic face we now see. One authority thinks this occurred in 1797 when Godoy married the Countess. Off went Pepita's head. Another thinks *Vestida* and *Desnuda* both were painted at Moncloa, suburban home of the Duchess, and were intended for her private apartments. If that happens to be true, the model almost certainly was La Alba. Antonio J. Onieva, whose book *Spanish Painting in the Prado Gallery* was published in 1957, thinks she was indeed the model. Both paintings were displayed in her mansion on the

Calle del Barquillo, the nude hidden behind the clothed figure. At that time Parisian snuff boxes with a double enamel top were in vogue. The outer top showed a clothed woman, but slid aside to show the woman nude. This, Onieva says, is what she did to entertain friends: "When they had taken a look at the maja clothed, she drew the canvas aside and showed them the nude."

Stylistic differences indicate that *Vestida* was painted a few years after *Desnuda*, maybe as late as 1805.

Onieva dissents. He believes the clothed figure unquestionably was painted from life and Goya may well have used the Duchess, altering her features. "The glints on the cushion embroideries, the light that gently slides across the breast, belly and legs, cannot be, and had no reason to be, invented. . . ." The nude, in his opinion, was painted from memory or perhaps deduced from the clothed figure.

Curators at the Prado vehemently insist that María Cayetana was not the model: "Es indudable que la Duquesa de Alba no sirvio de modelo . . . "

Godoy owned both. Did he commission these erotic twins so that he could muse over them ensemble? Some scholars think they were meant to be viewed successively and his apartment might have contained a device that enabled him to gaze at them in sequence. M. Quilliet's inventory of the Prime Minister's collection lists no such apparatus. Tomás de Yriarte was told in 1867 by some old men—quelques vieillards—that the paintings hung back-to-back in the middle of a viewing chamber. Thus, the Prime Minister and his guests after contemplating one might walk around to contemplate the other. How did these old men know? They themselves had been invited to see the paintings. So said the vieillards.

Private viewing chambers weren't uncommon. Nudes could best be appreciated in darkened rooms, particularly if one chanced to be scopophilic. The Duchess of Alba's husband, for example, had his gabinete reservada.

González de Sepúlveda, who saw Godoy's collection in a private room, said it included *Venus and Cupid* by Velázquez. A few years earlier this famous nude had belonged to the Albas. How did Godoy obtain it? According to Sepúlveda, the Duchess gave it to him. If so, he and the

Duchess must have been very close. You don't give a present like that to just anyone. Later, when the affair ended, he confided to María Luisa that he was returning a letter the Duchess had sent him. He added that if she and all her sycophants could be buried in hell that would be fine with him.

Waldmann suspects that while they were intimate she might also have given him *Desnuda.* Why? La Alba lived for the moment, for an instant, a butterfly hesitating, fluttering away. Goya? Who is he?

Whenever the nude was painted, whoever she was, she's gone. Model and Venus, portrait and metaphor.

IO

Goya probably left Sanlúcar with a taste of wormwood in his mouth because not long after returning to Madrid he started work on another album, some two hundred sketches—his usual crowd of Spaniards laughing, flirting, strutting, dancing. But something else: demons, witches, animal-headed people. Most significant, *Sueño de la mentira y la inconstancia*, which is to say a dream of lies and inconstancy, a tangle of figures, Goya himself clutching the arm of a woman widely accepted as the Duchess. She has two faces. She looks at him but also at something or someone in the darkness. Butterfly wings sprout from the head of this two-faced woman. Now, the butterfly is a wanton creature, as everybody knows. And it settles on candles to extinguish their light. And once upon a time a butterfly emerging from its chrysalis represented the soul leaving the body after death.

Apparently he meant to include his dream of lies in that series of etchings titled *Caprichos*, but there exists only a preliminary sketch and one impression. Why he left it out is unknown, perhaps because the Duchess was recognizable. The artist himself could be recognized. And yet, both have been identified in other works. She reappears among four sinister majos, reappears as a flirtatious woman on a swing. Again, again, again. The faces imply obsession. Julia Blackburn wrote of "bitter sexual rage" roaring through these images. And did La Alba invite him "to listen to what her body had to say in the hot dark silence"?

During the summer of 1797 he rented a garret at the corner of San Bernardino street, constructed a table out of some boards and went to work on the *Caprichos*, although why he chose a garret rather than working in his studio is another little mystery. There he spent hours and days hunched over copper plates while images seeped from the depths. Woman: duplicitous, selfish, depraved. Early plates show her led to the whipping post, imprisoned, raped. So he revenged himself for whatever happened, boiling the past in imagination, isolated, deaf, scratching away, recalling and improvising.

Until Sanlúcar he had looked upon women as decorative shapes scattered along the banks of the Manzanares shaded by parasols, graceful creatures festooned with ribbons, untouchable delicacies, animated dolls on swings and balconies. Long afterward he would paint the Marquesa de Santa Cruz, Lorelei in a chemise. And very near the end he would paint that robust milkmaid of Bordeaux. He remembered how he had seen women and he could recapture his delight, but after visiting the Duchess he wasn't the same. His Madrid album is stamped like a visa with marks of passage. Jacqueline Hara comments that these etchings as well as the letters "express frustrated cravings and the degradation of voluptuous pleasure." More than once he would illustrate female depravity with animal-like masks. Hara believes he lacked confidence when representing women. His female subjects often stare at the viewer; we have no idea what they are thinking. The men, at least those he liked, seem comfortable and relaxed, willing to meet us.

That he paid little attention to nudes is surprising. Except for the famous maja, some lithographs, and a few sketches, nothing. You expect him to wallow pictorially in female flesh. Consider that devotee of the first rank, Boucher. Here, there, everywhere. Boucher was insatiable. Malraux thinks *Mlle O'Murphy* suggests nothing so much as complicity in rape. Goya, however, leaned a different direction: "His erotic fancy was happier with women in chains, or bound by some devil."

Rousseau admitted that secretaries, shop girls, and chambermaids never excited him; he felt hopelessly attracted to Ladies. What he couldn't resist was the air of elegance, lovely hands, tasteful dress, refined expression. Always, always that was what he sought. He admitted that his preference was ridiculous, "but my heart, in spite of myself, makes me entertain it." My heart, in spite of myself. That might be as close as we can get to understanding Goya.

About this time he met the Alcalophiles, lovers of ugliness, a society of disgruntled esthetes, writers, and artists who seem to have coalesced around ideas originating in France. Alcalophiles, too few and insignificant to create a political movement, had no doubt about their feeling for an established order. Disgust. Revulsion. They pretended an affection for whatever was hideous as a way of criticizing the status quo.

February 6, 1799. The *Caprichos* were announced, advertised in *Diario de Madrid*. They would go on sale February 20, a collection of prints on fanciful themes:

> The artist, being persuaded that human error and vice may be legitimate subjects for graphic art, just as they are subjects of oratory and poetry, has selected from innumerable follies common to mankind, as well as from those lies authorized by custom and ignorance, those that he considers appropriate to ridicule.

Those fanciful themes have been compared to grotesques in the mad world of Breughel and to the medieval vision of Dante. The Duchess of Alba soars heavenward, arms outstretched, supported by three men who are assumed to be matadors. Because the Duchess loved bullfights she flies to heaven with these men. She has lost her wits over them. Goya titled this etching *Volaverunt*, they have flown, everything is finished, the affair has ended. Inconstancy. Hypocrisy. Lies.

One man squashed beneath her skirt has been identified as the matador Romero José. Still, that rubber-lipped caricature looks very like a drawing Goya made of himself.

Waldmann shrewdly remarks that because he knew the Duchess so intimately he could acquaint himself with various feminine temperaments united in one woman. And because he had strength enough to disengage himself from personal anguish, supplanting it with sarcasm and irony, he found the source of artistic creation in private suffering. Thus we very often have a sense of encountering María Cayetana in *Los Caprichos*.

Baudelaire loved these ghoulish fancies, affectionately noting a trio of monks "with square murderous heads." And in 1857 he wrote for a French newspaper, *Le Présent*, concerning another plate, that all the vices imaginable were etched on those faces.

A caza de dientes. In this aquatint/etching a young woman shields her face from the stench of a hanged man's corpse while trying to pull out his teeth. Why does she want them? Everybody knew that the bodies of executed criminals worked magic. A year or so before Goya made this etching a number of spectators at Newgate, having watched an execution, scrambled up on the scaffold to touch the criminal's hands. And we are told that at another public hanging a woman exposed her breast for the dead man's touch because this was the way to cure breast cancer. It sounds like the Middle Ages.

Gautier remarked that before visiting Spain he thought the women Goya portrayed in the *Caprichos* must be nightmares, but changed his mind after touring the peninsula. As splenetic as Lord Beckford, infinitely more dexterous, he wrote that Old Castile was so named because it is home to innumerable hags, mouldy as hairy cheese, with mustaches like grenadiers. Macbeth's witches crossing the heath of Dunisnane to prepare that infernal stew were charming girls by comparison. Each of these frightful old shrews united in her person the ugliness of seven capital sins. Next to them, the Prince of Darkness was attractive.

Just fancy whole ditches and counterscarps of wrinkles; eyes like live coals that have been extinguished in blood; noses like the neck of an elembic covered with warts and other excrescences; nostrils like those of an hippopotamus rendered formidable by stiff bristles; whiskers like a tiger's; a mouth like a slit in the top of a money-box, contracted by a horrible and convulsive grin.

Only one thoughtful essay on the *Caprichos* appeared while Goya was alive, written not by an art critic but a scientist, Gregorio González Azaola. His article was published March 27, 1811, in the *Cádiz Semanario patriotico.*

Azaola is tangential to our story but deserves a moment because there aren't many such men. He was employed by the palace as chemistry professor to the royal pages, a quaint job, and it's believed that he knew Goya. He belonged to that subversive tribe of humanists who throughout history have collided with emperors, kings, generals, and popes. He translated Monsieur A. F. Fourcroy's *Systeme des connaissances chimiques.* He invented a double-barreled mortar. He was commissioned by the Spanish government to study iron smelting in Belgium. He wrote learned papers about grape sugar and vineyards and he worked on a plan to make the Guadalquivir navigable from Córdoba to the Atlantic. That ought to be enough, but Azaola was just getting started. Not only did he understand double-barreled mortars and smelting and chemistry and grapes and river bottoms, he got hold of Alexander Pope's *Essay on Man,* which he translated into Spanish. He got hold of a heterodox *Discourse* by the French attorney J. E. M. Portalis and meant to translate it. Portalis admitted the importance of religious belief but questioned papal infallibility. During the early nineteenth century you could get away with that in Paris, not in Madrid. The censor struck.

Azaola opened his discussion of the *Caprichos* by stating that although lovers of the Fine Arts might be familiar with Goya's portraits and Venuses and frescoed ceilings, not many would know these satirical prints. They were not absurd extravaganzas, he said; each one held some enigmatic message. He went on to call the series a didactic work of eighty engraved moral poems, a treatise on the prejudices and vices that afflict us. He thought no other nation could boast such satire. Only a man with a remarkable mind, who experienced life widely, could look so deeply into the human heart. The *Caprichos* reveal to us our vices and "fustigate our errors as they deserve."

This was not a majority opinion.

The Royal Academy professor, González de Sepúlveda, wrote in his diary that he had seen a book of witches by Goya and didn't like it. Very obscene. He was himself an engraver who ought to have been excited by this astonishing collection, but the subjects revolted him.

Count Joseph-Marie de Maistre wrote from Moscow to the Chevalier de Rossi in 1808 that a book of English-style caricatures on Spanish subjects had passed through his hands, published in Madrid about a year earlier. Eighty plates. "One ridicules the Queen in the most forceful manner possible, and the allegory is so transparent that even a child could see it." Count de Maistre liked things as they were. He did acknowledge various imperfections in the monarchy, changes could be justified, yes, but all in all monarchy wasn't bad. As to the Holy Office, he thought it appropriate and useful.

He may or may not have realized how closely Goya studied English-style caricatures. Various biographers have puzzled over the letter to Zapater dated Londres 2 de Agosto 1800, at the end of which he drew himself in profile as a crescent moon. Two years earlier, an English artist named Francis Grose had published *Rules for Drawing Caricatures*, which includes eight bizarre profiles, among them the crescent moon.

He might have studied *A Book of Caricatures, on 59 Copper Plates, with ye Principles of Designing, in that Droll & pleasing manner*, which appeared in 1762. The author, Mary Darly, included a concave face that resembles Goya even more closely. In brief, the face he drew on a letter to Zapater looks very much like two English caricatures and he alludes to England by pretending that he was writing from Londres.

When the Spanish playwright Moratín, a friend of Goya, visited England he noted shops overflowing with caricatures. Then, too, Hogarth's publisher distributed his work in France, equipped with French titles, and quite a few of these books had crossed the Pyrenees. Reva Wolf states that Goya's colleague Luis Paret and his longtime friend Sebastián Martínez both owned volumes of engravings by "Horgat"—Hogarth. Several plates in the *Caprichos* can be traced to Hogarth and to other English artists.

Similarity, yes. Influence, yes. Plagiarism?

One of Hogarth's most famous engravings is *A Midnight Modern Conversation*. We have a dozen bewigged, besotted Englishmen surrounding a punch bowl big enough for Pantagruel. Along came Elisha Kirkall, who reversed the image, added a few lines of verse, and produced a mezzotint. Otherwise, Hogarth redux. One year later along came a German engraver, Ernst Riepenhausen, who blatantly reproduced the original. Along came Vincenz Raimund Grüner who depended upon Riepenhausen who depended upon, etc. Copyright laws grew out of this.

Artists of every stripe analyze the work of predecessors, meaning you can always pick out similarities, influences. Goya's three gluttonous monks at table—the etching Baudelaire liked so much—could be descendants of Hogarth's drunken Englishmen. However, monks and their vices make natural targets. Daumier, for instance, half a century later.

Goya did steal, borrow, copy, or emulate an English mannerism which he would not likely have invented. That is, a cross-legged stance. The American painter Benjamin West lived in England where he became friendly with Sir Joshua Reynolds and served as historical painter to George III. We know him from *Penn's Treaty with the Indians* and *The Death of General Wolfe*. His canvases tended to be large. Copley described them as ten-acre pictures. Benjamin West painted his own family and there on the left stands his son Raphael nonchalantly cross-legged. Sebastián Martínez owned a print of this painting. Goya must have seen it and probably noted the casual stance in other English portraits. He painted the Duke of Alba leaning on a pianoforte almost exactly as young Raphael West leaned on the arm of his mother's chair. Influence, plagiarism, whatever.

Now, while standing beside a pianoforte the Duke wears riding boots, which seems odd, but Spaniards thought of horseback riding as characteristic of the English. Riding boots therefore identify the Spanish Duke as a gentleman in the English style. This kind of symbolism pervaded European art. A man who stood or sat with legs apart was drunk or sexually active. A woman who adjusted her stocking was a prostitute. There might be a painting of Cupid setting fire to a rocket, easily understood. There might be a fallen rocket, which the ladies no doubt thought hysterically funny.

In those days anything English was catnip to Spaniards. Books, clothing, attitudes. Richardson's *Clarissa* was reviewed by the Madrid *Gaceta* on February 17, 1795: "The best novel to be composed in any period, and in any language." Goya bought *Clarissa*, though we don't know his opinion. He bought fancy English boots. He bought a couple of English knives for Zapater.

What did the *Caprichos* illustrate? Dishonesty. Corruption. Avarice. Roguery. Disastrous marriages. Treachery. All had romped through the pages of Spanish novels, strutted across the stage, been sung up and down cobbled streets, but Goya was the first artist to unite realism, poetry, and satire.

Few of his contemporaries could see more than a generally offensive and puzzling exhibit. A certain Antonio Puigblanch, writing under the ludicrous pseudonym of Nataniel Jomtob, got the idea. He specifically mentioned two plates criticizing the Holy Office. Plate 23 shows the accused seated on a bench, wearing the requisite scapulary and pointed hat, while a secretary reads out his sentence. Plate 24 shows a woman stripped to the waist, riding a donkey to the place where she will be flogged or executed. She, too, wears that pyramidal cap, her head immobilized by a wooden brace like the head of a sheep or a goat in a slaughterhouse pen. Excited citizens accompany her. Jomtob/Puigblanch quotes from a manuscript commentary, not by Goya, which explains that she must die because she is poor and ugly, poverty and ugliness being infallible signs of witchcraft. Hence, no alternative to punishment. No remedy. Goya titled it *Nohubo remedio.* What seeps through this etching is not only his fury at the procedure, but disgust and contempt for the citizens.

Ya es hora. It's time.

Aguarda que te unten. Wait till you've been anointed.

No hay quien nos desate? Can nobody untie us?

Why did he compound these mysterious pictures with enigmatic titles? Fear of the Holy Office? Artistic perversity? In 1938 the Metropolitan Museum published a catalogue of fifty drawings from the *Madrazo Album.* A commentator wrote that Goya's drawings of prisoners were bloodcurdling in their realization of misery and the intent of a reformer could be deduced from his titles.

The Holy Office took a narrow look at what he was doing.

Canon Juan Antonio Llorente, who stood for a brilliant portrait by Goya, kept track of such business. Later, exiled to France, he gave his opinion. He thought several plates more subversive than the wretched heretic wearing a pointed hat or the woman riding a donkey. Plate 52, for instance, he judged to be a satire on monks who fake miracles, a serious charge.

The *Caprichos* stuck it to more than a doctrinaire Church. Goya went after His Majesty Charles IV, Queen María Luisa, and Godoy. That he would attack his patrons is, to say the least, boorish. One historian likened him to Byron with his penchant for the brutal and obscene, his skeptical insolence and hatred of respectability: "The stamp of scorn lies upon everything he did."

An unknown Frenchman who visited Spain about this time jotted down his impression of the *Caprichos.* These comments were discovered by a French scholar named Lefort and published in 1877. Whoever he was, he seems to have been familiar with Goya's work, and, noting a "malicious exuberance," compared it to that of Hogarth and Bunbury in England. As for plate 19, women plucking feathers from "small persons who fly up into the air only to fall back to earth," what could this be if not Queen María Luisa's succession of lovers?

Plate 36: "Would seem to recall the Queen's jollifications on frequently stormy nights."

Plate 39: "Goya has made fun of the long and absurd genealogical tree which was prepared for the Prince of the Peace, making him out to be a descendant of the ancient Gothic Kings. . . ."

Another Frenchman, that amiable serpent Gautier, may have the final word on our man from Fuendetodos: "The old Spanish art was buried with Goya. He came just in time to collect and immortalize it. He thought he was merely drawing caprices; what he drew was the portrait and the history of old Spain, though he believed he was serving the new ideas and beliefs."

11

There was a touch of Goya in that quasi-master Luis Paret, suspected of providing young women for the lecherous Infante and exiled to Puerto Rico. At his birth the planets must have been confused. Like Goya, he was born in 1746. A French painter who visited Spain introduced him to Watteau, and Paret grew so enamored of bucolic scenes featuring luxuriant gardens decorated with silk and satin beauties that he became known as the Spanish Watteau. Charles III thought highly of Paret. He was elected to the Royal Academy on the basis of a muddled magnum opus titled *The Discretion of Diogenes* that almost prefigures modern symbolists: an extraordinarily garish metaphysical goulash of bulbous ornaments, lurid canopies, antique temples, clouds scudding over the full moon, bewhiskered wise men, two dogs that for some reason share a single collar, on and on. A magician exhibits pectorals a weightlifter would envy, a snake looped around his muscular left arm. His right hand clutches an occult device with an owl perched on top. Diogenes, wearing not only the mandatory toga but an Oriental turban, ignores the madness and reads a book while seated by himself in the lower right corner. He symbolizes the master who scorns those weaknesses afflicting us: vanity, mendacity, ambition, and all the rest, who rejects our world of swarming, destructive illusions.

Paret submitted it to the Academy in 1780. Goya saw it. The *Caprichos* came out nineteen years later and the most famous plate features a dreaming man titled *El sueño de la razon produce monstruous.* The dream of reason gives birth to monsters. Owls and bats trouble this dreaming man. Paret's schizoid masterpiece has the dream of reason splashed all over it.

Not only was Paret eccentric, he was a comedian. Before his exile to Puerto Rico he painted King Charles at a dining table in an apartment wide enough and long enough for a soccer game. The title of this painting usually is translated as *Charles III at Dinner* or *The Midday Repast of Charles III.* The King dines alone because Queen María Amalia died soon after arriving from Naples. The emptiness of the apartment emphasizes how alone he is. A kneeling page offers him a plate while courtiers hang around doing nothing. Beside the table sits a mastiff hoping for a scrap; other dogs wander about the apartment. Gigantic tapestries embellish the walls. These tapestries illustrate the biblical story of Joseph. However, Paret chose to enliven them with erotic mythology, which seems not only impertinent but more than a little audacious. Onieva states that the artist signed the bizarre tour de force with Greek characters as though he were El Greco: Luis de Paret, son of his father and mother, did this.

February, 1799. Paret died and the *Caprichos* were announced.

Goya printed three hundred sets, which meant—with eighty plates—twenty-four thousand impressions, and quite a few that for one reason or another didn't satisfy him. They were displayed at a shop beneath his apartment on Calle del Desengaño that sold trinkets, perfumes, and liqueurs. According to legend, four men chased a lovely woman down this street. She wore a beautiful white gown and when they caught her they tore away the gown. What did they see? A corpse. Disenchantment Street. One historian claims that Goya lived across the street from the shop, but all agree on the price: an ounce of gold, 320 reales, little enough considering his reputation. Why weren't they sold at a book store? The Inquisition might turn its heavy face toward these etchings and booksellers wanted no part of it.

The Osunas bought four sets and played at charades based upon the work, featuring Charles, María Luisa, and Godoy. They must have felt secure.

Thirteen days after his public announcement Goya declared in the *Gaceta de Madrid* that anyone wishing to buy these etchings must do so within two days. Many years later he admitted that he cancelled the sale because he feared the Inquisition. All right, but if he was uneasy why not cancel the sale at once? Why give the Inquisition another couple of days to study them?

Ten of these etchings were published in Paris in 1825. Delacroix, among others, looked carefully. He copied plate 32 which shows a woman imprisoned, but added the head of a donkey from plate 24, nobody knows why. Maybe he was practicing, no symbolism intended.

John Ruskin certainly would appreciate the *Caprichos*. Wrong. He got hold of a set that he denounced as fit only to be burnt; and being a man of his word, that's what Ruskin did.

Perhaps not unnaturally the Inquisition mistrusted Goya. Here was a man who had beautified church ceilings in the orthodox manner, who had respectfully portrayed Joaquín Company, Archbishop of Valencia and head of the Franciscan Order. On the other hand, look at those caricatures.

Not much time had elapsed since that vigilant fraternity was burning, twisting, stretching, and crushing, and its pious membership looked forward to a resumption of the good old days. Charles couldn't live forever and his son Ferdinand might agree that heretics like all poisonous weeds ought to be uprooted. Thus, with a closet full of unsold prints—240 sets—and possibly expecting an icy hand on his shoulder, Goya offered the complete edition to His Majesty via the Royal Printing Office. He stipulated that the money should go to his son Javier. Charles and María Luisa accepted. They knew these etchings existed; María Luisa might have seen them. In any event, it would be a good idea to keep track of them. Twelve thousand reales seemed like a small price to pay.

As for Goya, he didn't make as much as he hoped, but things could have been worse. He got out of an embarrassing, inconclusive failure with his dignity more or less intact and a pension for his son.

Five years earlier he had petitioned the King for payment of salary in arrears, reminding His Majesty that he had been very sick and hadn't been able to work because he couldn't understand what people were saying. Jovellanos intervened on his behalf and he received another commission—the ceiling of a new church at the edge of Madrid, San Antonio de la Florida. He should illustrate St. Anthony's famous miracle: the resurrection of a murdered man.

The old Hermitage of San Antonio had been a shrine often visited by laundresses who washed clothes in the nearby river. Apple trees grew readily on this fertile ground; manzana means apple, hence Manzanares. It was desirable property so Charles and María Luisa bought a considerable amount, as did Prime Minister Godoy and the Duchess of Alba. By the end of the eighteenth century it had become rather exclusive.

This new church, the cupola and vaulting of the apse which he was to beautify, seems to have challenged Goya. It would be an unusual job. He ordered eighteen large earthenware pots, five dozen big paintbrushes, a dozen small brushes, four pounds of glue, and quite a lot of paint: light ochre, dark ochre, vermilion, black earth, red earth, Venetian umber. That was by no means all. Ivory black, crimson, yellow, Molina blue, London carmine, more pots, sponges, basins, lamp black, crimson lake, badger-hair brushes, and more. These items were listed on his bill to the court. And a coach for transportation, not unreasonable.

The future St. Anthony was born in Lisbon, son of a Portuguese knight. At fifteen he enrolled with the Canons Regular of St. Augustine but quit after two years and in 1220 he became a Franciscan. This order was attempting to convert the Moors. As a result, many Franciscans in North Africa were killed. The idea of becoming a martyr fascinated Anthony and he was sent to North Africa at his own request but in Morocco he got sick. He returned to Europe, landing at Messina because his ship was blown off course. From there he traveled to Assisi while the Chapter General was in session. The Church assigned him a small hermitage near Forli and here by chance—being asked to speak at an ordination—his enormous talent for preaching was recognized. He traveled around Italy and his sermons attracted so many listeners that the churches weren't big enough to hold them. At times he was obliged to speak in the market-place. On one occasion, overwhelmed by his desire to preach, he exhorted the fish in a lake.

At the Chapter General of 1226 he was elected to deliver certain vexing questions to Pope Pius XII. During this interview Anthony got what he had long wanted, permission to devote himself entirely to preaching. For the rest of his short life—dead at thirty-six—he excoriated unbelievers in and around Padua with such vigor that people called him the Hammer of Heretics. Soon after his death he was canonized. Extraordinary events took place at his shrine, but he was most celebrated for the miracle at Lisbon.

He was in Padua when he learned that his father, Don Martín Bulloes, stood accused of murder. Being granted leave to go and defend his father, Anthony flew through the air to Lisbon "in a flash," arriving at court. He said his father was innocent. The judges weren't convinced. He asked that the corpse of the victim be brought to court. When this had been done Anthony questioned the dead man, "bidding him in the name of Our Lord Jesus Christ to say in a loud voice, understandable by all, if his father was the man responsible for his death. Whereupon the corpse arose and publicly declared that the accused man was innocent; after which declaration he sank back again into his bier."

Now, when you paint a church cupola you are supposed to reward your patrons and parishioners with cherubs, angels, fluffy white clouds in a blue sky, and so forth. That was what Tiepolo did. That was what other artists did. That was the way it ought to be done. Goya disagreed.

He relied for detail upon an inspirational book, *Christian Year,* that had been translated into Spanish by Father José Francisco Isla and became hugely popular, but he made a few changes. For the Lisbon courtroom he substituted a Spanish landscape and a collection of scruffy Madrileños for the Portuguese lawyers. He painted a beatific Anthony and a greenish corpse preparing to testify. The cupola became a gigantic canvas on which he depicted his favorite subjects: urchins, vagrants, pretty girls, hags, blind beggars, ancient men with beards—flotsam of Madrid. And a stocky man wearing a buff jerkin and slouch hat who has turned away, presumably the murderer.

In the pendentives and the half dome above the altar a bevy of cherubs and angels, which should be acceptable. The nineteenth-century critic Pedro de Madrazo didn't approve; he thought Goya's angels with camellia skin and flashing eyes looked like whores.

El Conde de Viñaza also disapproved. He said he could not think of a more profane master than this Rembrandt, Velázquez, Vicelli, and Veronese rolled into one. An energetic painter, true. Goya knew how to play magical tricks with color, granted. But where was the spirituality? "The miracles of the exemplary man of Padua are familiarly treated as a spectacle of wandering rope-dancers might be!"

William Rothenstein, circa 1900: "One expects an odour of frangipane from the altar rather than incense, and I found myself looking under the seats for some neglected fan or garter ribbon. . . ."

Richard Muther thought it an artistic can-can: "The figures are as full of piquant intention as can be found in the most erotic paintings by Fragonard. . . . All that the Church paintings of the past had created is despised, forsaken; and this satire upon the Church and all its works was written in the land of Zurburán, of Murillo."

Thomas Craven thought Goya's effort more suitable to a high-class brothel than to a place of worship. Mr. Craven has only just begun. Instead of angels Goya painted strumpets, "his favorite duchess among them—insidiously rouged; he painted naked children climbing over railings, ballet dancers, recognizable beauties stretching out their legs, and alluring women ogled by dandified men."

Madrileños should have grown accustomed to Goya by the time he did San Antonio. They probably nudged one another and rolled their eyes while contemplating his newest work.

Eh! Goya! What do you expect?

No sooner did he finish San Antonio than María Luisa asked for an equestrian portrait of herself aboard Marcial, her favorite horse. Marcial had been a present from Godoy. Excepting horses in the bull ring he wasn't good at this. All his life he had seen horses trotting, galloping, rearing, snorting. They ought to be alive with personality but they look like porcelain animals. The French critic Louis Viardot, discussing an equestrian of Charles IV in *Études sur l'Espagne,* said that Goya had set His Majesty on the back of a pig. María Luisa posed in the King's apartments at El Escorial and in a series of letters to Godoy she complained: "Two and a half hours I have spent perched on a platform with my hat on, wearing a cravat. . . ."

October 8: "I have been very patient. . . ."

Hour after hour dressed in the uniform of a Colonel of the Guard, she pretended to ride Marcial's wooden surrogate. Her expression is familiar, between a smile and a smirk. Marcial's alter ego doesn't look his best; forequarters and hindquarters don't match. Infrared photos show that Goya tried again and again.

October 9: "The portrait on horseback in three sittings is finished as far as I am concerned and they say it is a better likeness than the one with a mantilla." Usually she accepted the judgment of sycophants.

October 31, 1799. He became First Painter to the Court. Primer Pintor de Camara. With this promotion a boost in salary to 50,000 reales a year. Things were going well. Aristocrats who mattered and those who didn't matter pulled up at his door. He employed an assistant named Esteve, which is to say, not every portrait by Goya came exclusively from the master's hand.

He was commissioned to embellish a chapel at Monte Torrero near Saragossa. He did three paintings—all three blown apart during the Napoleonic invasion. Jovellanos saw them, noting in his diary on April 7, 1801, that the largest depicted St. Isidore flying through the air in papal vestments to protect King James during the conquest of Valencia. On the Epistle side, St. Ermengild in prison. On the Gospel side, St. Elizabeth attended a sick woman. Admirable works, Jovellanos noted. Parishioners thought otherwise, objecting specifically to St. Elizabeth whose breasts were exposed. Goya was instructed to paint a garment over her bosom. Not until this had been done would the Vicar General of Huesca bless the chapel.

Goya by now had an international reputation. The French ambassador Ferdinand Guillemardet sat for a portrait. Like Jacques Louis David, Guillemardet had voted to guillotine Louis XVI. We are told that he knew quite a lot about organizing military hospitals. Why this qualified him for the ambassadorial post is not explained.

Guillemardet chanced to see—not long after he got to Madrid—the saucy young Marquesa de Santa Cruz, daughter of the Osunas, whom Goya painted in 1799 or thereabouts sporting a gold fan, a gold ribbon in her hair, silvery-gold pointed slippers, and what looks like a gown of black ostrich feathers. The Marquesa is rosy-cheeked and plump. She carries the exalted name of Joaquina Téllez-Giron y Alfonso Pimental and she will burst into laughter at any moment. Guillemardet was overcome with lust.

Goya painted her again in 1805, married these past four years to Don José Gabriel de Sila-Bazán y Waldstein. Now she plays the role of Euterpe lounging on a burgundy velvet couch, dressed—half-dressed—in a white muslin negligée with blue shadows, a gown so diaphanous you can make out her navel. Creamy flesh overflows the top and her auburn hair is festooned with wild grape leaves. She holds a guitar disguised as Euterpe's lyre. On the sounding box is an X-shaped Basque cross, a swastika, emblem of the House of Santa Cruz. Euterpe's lyre indicates that Joaquina worshipped music; but Joaquina in 1805 was twenty-one with more than music on her mind. She loved bullfights. So passionately did Joaquina love bullfights that she bought a seat near the matadors.

The swastika goes back to our beginning when it was most likely a symbol paying homage to the sun. Our word derives from the Sanskrit svastika, which relates to good fortune or well-being, though we don't think of it that way. During the twentieth century, because of that emblem, Goya's *Marquesa de Santa Cruz* almost went to Germany. Franco wanted to give it to Hitler. Things didn't work out and subsequently it was bought for a collection in Bilbao. Anthony Hull in his biography of Goya has traced it from there to England, via Madrid and Zurich, "having been bought in Switzerland by the Viscount Wimborne interests in 1983." However, Spain demanded its return, claiming false documentation. Interpol stepped on stage, issuing arrest warrants for those suspected of falsifying papers. Meanwhile, Christie's planned to auction the *Marquesa* in April of 1986, expecting to gross a world record of 9 million pounds. Then something extraordinary happened. Spain's Minister of Culture prevailed over greed, so the Marquesa Joaquina Téllez-Giron y Alfonso Pimental went home, where she may be seen lounging practically naked in the Prado. Her descendants refer to this picture as Grandma in a slip.

Concerning poor Guillemardet, the Marquesa was happily in love with the Marqués.

One other thing about Guillemardet. He may have obtained and concealed an edition of the *Caprichos* in the French embassy. These days he sits in the Louvre big as life. He looks raffish, quick-witted, good for a bon mot, the colors of his plumed hat red, white, and blue à la Française, naturally. Gold sword. Important gold buttons. Ringlets on his forehead in lieu of a Napoleon forelock. He gazes to his left, no doubt remembering a certain Spanish lady.

Goya's bold treatment excited French painters. Delacroix, for one, is known to have studied the Guillemardet portrait. Critics were not so impressed. M. Lachaise wrote in 1868: "Its flashy coloring, shaky modeling and undistinguished pose are hardly such as to prompt us to retract the views which we have already expressed on this artist's type of talent. It is merely an attempt at Velázquez, nothing more, and his attempts fall far short of compositions by Boilly, Vernet, Bosio. . . ."

Goya at this time seemed anxious to portray old friends, sponsors, intellectuals who had been trying to drag Spain out of the ossified past and expose it to the Enlightenment seeping across northern Europe. He had painted Jovellanos in 1798. He also painted Bernardo Yriarte, the poet Juan Antonio Meléndez Valdés, and Don Andrés del Peral.

There are a couple of strange things about Peral. According to the *Boletín* of the San Fernando Academy, a portrait of Andrés Peral by Goya was exhibited in 1798. This seems to be the *Doctor Peral* on display in London's National Gallery. Although one biographer identifies him as an eminent physician, previous owners have stated that he was Spain's financial representative to the French government and a Doctor of Laws. He is said to have owned a major art collection. Most biographers identify him not as a Spanish diplomat but an artisan, a gilder like José Goya. In other words, a semiskilled craftsman who worried about the cost of wine and sausage. If so, how did he acquire a formidable art collection?

The second thing is Peral's left arm. His right hand is thrust into his vest. We don't see much of it. His left arm is unnaturally long, the hand almost obscured by deep shadow, and close examination shows that the sleeve was repainted. Nobody knows why. Peral had a wooden arm. Goya might have lengthened the sleeve to conceal this but Peral objected, insisting that he be represented just as he was.

Critics admire this painting. Sir Charles Holmes called the revelation of personality disquieting: "The stiffness of the pose, the keen suspicious glance of the eye, the pallid face, the mouth ever so slightly awry, make up a record as complete as a description by Tolstoi. And to this liveliness and subtlety of characterization there is added an art as refined in its way as that of Gainsborough."

Goya was now more than half a century old but never forgot the craft he learned during those apprentice years in Saragossa. He could wave his brush like a magic wand, evoke an early style, play variations. Should Her Majesty wish a flattering portrait of herself astride good Marcial, certainly. Should Her Majesty wish to be represented as a maja, of course. No longer a Colonel of the Guard, she becomes a superannuated schoolgirl—ribbon in her hair, black lace mantilla, bloated face. Would you charge this travesty to Goya? He was following orders and the Queen apparently liked what she saw. His protean talent sends connoisseurs barking in various directions. One asserts that he found himself, discovered his genius, when he stopped trying to please. Another thinks he never dared to displease; throughout his life he remained sly, vindictive, endowed with genius but uneasy.

Whether he and the Duchess met again, we don't know. If they did maybe it was by accident, maybe at court. Not that a chance encounter would have made any difference because María Cayetana had found a new lover, General Antonio Cornel y Ferraz, distinguished graduate of María Luisa's boudoir. And the records do not show any commissions from the House of Alba after 1797. The birds had flown.

María Cayetana in her late thirties was shrinking, fading. The Queen observed with satisfaction that she was little more than skin and bones, albeit as crazy as when she had been young. The Condesa de Montijo saw her in June of 1802 and wrote to the poet Meléndez Valdés that she was very close to death. Irrational, barely conscious, she had been unable to receive the sacraments. Tomasita Palafox, her sister-in-law, watched beside María Cayetana's bed for several weeks. The Duchess frequently trembled and appeared to be suffering.

On July 23 she died. The family physician, Dr. Jaime Bonell, certified that she died of colic at 12:40 in the afternoon.

July 24, 1802. The *Gaceta de Madrid* published this notice:

The many and commendable aptitudes that distinguished Her Excellency, above all the gentleness and kindness of her nature, her noble generosity and the charity with which she fervently empathized with every woe as soon as it came to her ears—she sheltered widows, cared for the sick, instructed helpless children, supported honest orphans on their life's path, and distributed without abate great sums to her servants, who loved her like their mother—have caused her death to be felt very painfully by all.

To this day people speculate, mistrusting Dr. Bonell's report. Who or what killed the fabulous Duchess of Alba? An epidemic. Fevers of summer. She drank an icy beverage from the snow of the Guadarramas. She drank an almond-flavored beverage called horchata. She ate fresh lettuce. She expired of consumption like Mimi.

Her funeral took place on July 26 at the Church of the Padres Misioneros del Salvador. There she was buried and there ended the direct Alba line. Because she had no children the title passed to an eight-year-old relative, Carlos Miguel F. J. Stuart y Silva, descended from James II of England.

Rumors spread that she was poisoned. By whom? By somebody close to her, said Madrileños in the street. By her physician, who obeyed the command of powerful figures. By somebody at court—the Queen or the Prime Minister. Spanish grandees had other ideas: She was poisoned by servants who knew she would leave them a great deal of money and were anxious to line their pockets. One nineteenth-century account states that Dr. Bonell and some attendants were imprisoned and María Cayetana's estate sequestered; but who poisoned her "and for what reason the dose was administered remains as yet unknown."

King Charles, suspicious of the household staff, ordered Godoy to investigate those who were present during her illness. That Godoy found anything is doubtful because no more is heard of the inquiry. María Cayetana's will was abrogated by order of the court. Servants got nothing.

Immediately after her death Charles notified the executor, José Navarro Vidal, that he and the Queen would like to inspect her jewelry. María Luisa's obsidian eye focused on a diamond bauble valued at 300,000 reales and a strand of pearls worth 38,000 reales. Not comparable to various items belonging to the Spanish Crown but La Alba had worn them, therefore María Luisa wanted them. Supposedly she bought them at the appraised value.

And the Prime Minister? How did María Cayetana feel about that long-gone affair? Godoy received the keys to Buenavista Palace, purchased once upon a time by grandfather Alba. What remained of her estate was to be divided among the principal beneficiaries, but legal maneuvering delayed a settlement for more than thirty years. Buenavista Palace became in turn a military museum, the Turkish ambassador's residence, an artillery school, and finally was acquired by the Spanish Department of War.

Rumors of poison would not go away, just as rumors that she posed for the famous nude do not go away. In the twentieth century descendants of the Alba family ordered her remains to be exhumed so that pathologists might determine, if possible, the cause of death.

On November 17, 1945, the casket was opened. María Cayetana had mummified.

Drs. Blanco Soler, Piga Pascual, and Pérez Petinto issued a two-hundred page autopsy report: *Esbozo psicologico, enfermedades y muerte de la Duquesa . . .*

They concluded that she died of encephalitis preceded by a lymph infection that damaged the kidneys and lungs. There was no trace of poison. "The mummy's feet were found sawn off, with the ankle-stumps stuck into a pair of large, black rope-soled sandals." Her right foot lay in the coffin, about halfway up, but her left foot was missing. The feet were amputated "perhaps owing to a miscalculation as regards size, and in obedience to the law of minimum effort, to save the trouble of going back to the undertaking establishment. . . ."

In 1842 or 1843 the Church of the Padres Misioneros del Salvador had been renovated and authorities moved her to San Isidro cemetery. A new casket was ordered, perhaps because the old one had disintegrated. The Duchess was small, less than 5'4", but the new casket wasn't long enough. Eh! What to do? A solution was obvious. Who would know the difference? It looked like a safe bet and except for those nagging rumors of poison the re-burial party would have guessed right.

As to the missing foot, pathologists concluded that somebody in 1842/3 had forgotten it. Nonsense. You don't forget a foot. Somebody stole it. The female foot has excited men since Aurignacian days— perched on tiny platforms, naked, sheathed in silk. One glimpse of a lady's foot can be overwhelming. A French emissary, M. Blécourt, wrote in 1702 that a Spanish husband would rather see his wife dead than with her feet exposed in public.

She was photographed when the coffin was opened. She looks like what you might encounter at a Halloween party. She is yawning and her lower teeth are uneven.

Dr. Bonell said that after her death Goya wandered around Madrid in a kind of trance, mute, unapproachable. Maybe he was destroyed by grief, but maybe not. He might have been obsessed by the need to comprehend her death so that he might use it in his work. Certain artists are like the onion, beneath each membrane another. If you continue peeling in hopes of catching him you end up with nothing in your hand.

He made no statement except one ink sketch; three hooded figures attending the corpse of a young woman. The position of the corpse is almost identical to that of a woman in *Tantalo*, an etching for the *Caprichos* done in 1797 or 1798. The woman appears to have fainted while a distraught Tantalus clasps his hands. The commentary, probably written by Goya, states that if he had been a better lover she might have revived. Perhaps at that time he couldn't help wondering. Maybe, after all, it wasn't too late. But that etching was made five years before she died. By 1802 other things were on his mind.

The gilder's son was now a gentleman of means, entitled to live on a scale befitting Spain's preeminent artist. He bought a splendid house in a fashionable area, a house boasting solid granite walls and a courtyard. He bought books, many books, and quite a lot of jewelry. He bought expensive paintings. Tiepolo. Correggio. And in his new house was a fine studio. Here came patrons from every direction. Las Condesas de Villafranca and Lazan. La Marquesa de Santa Cruz and La Condesa de Haro, both related to the Alba family. Theatrical people. Singers. Lorenza Correa. Pedro Mocarte. Pérez de Estala, industrialist. Here they came from various directions while memories of the Duchess receded.

12

In 1799, on the eighteenth day of the second month of the Republican calendar—18 Brumaire—Napoleon ousted the Directory, proclaiming himself First Consul of the Republic.

Soon he declared himself Emperor.

And with most of Europe under his belt he peered over the mountains at Spain which controlled access to the Mediterranean by way of Gibraltar, to say nothing of exotic New World colonies bulging with Indian silver and gold.

What about the Spanish government? Historian Klingender describes the triumvirate as a half-wit king who renounced cares of state for the satisfaction of hunting, an intelligent queen unscrupulous in the exercise of unlimited control over the king, and a twenty-four-year-old playboy elevated to the dignity of Prime Minister: "These were the guardians of the divine right of kings at a time when the principle of legitimacy was challenged by an ex-corporal dethroning half the monarchs of Europe."

Napoleon suggested that Portugal might be carved up like a Chateaubriand. France would be entitled to one-third. Spain assuredly deserved one-third. And, of course, Prime Minister Godoy—that saga-cious, astute, most excellent, most perspicacious statesman—Minister Godoy without question deserved one-third of Portugal. He should be-come Prince of the Algarve. Godoy must have been ecstatic. What he didn't know was that Ferdinand, urged and abetted by conservatives, was plotting to seize the throne. Not only would Godoy be killed, Ferdinand intended to have his own parents murdered.

This unsigned note was inserted among prayer books on the King's faldstool: *Prince Ferdinand prepares a movement in the palace. The Crown is imperiled. Queen María Luisa runs great risk of death by poison. . . .*

Shakespeare would have snapped it up.

Martin Hume's early history of Spain gives a more theatrical account of this dastardly business. Charles discovered a note on his dressing table: *Haste, haste, haste!* The mysterious note went on to reveal that Ferdinand was plan-ning a coup. Her Majesty would be poisoned. Steps must be taken at once to foil the plot. What should be done? Charles consulted his wife. They went unannounced to Ferdinand's apartment and found him working on some papers. Ferdinand tried to hide them, but the King seized these doc-uments which "proved to be in the highest degree compromising."

Charles immediately wrote to Napoleon:

Monsieur mon frère, I have found with a horror, which makes me shud-der, that the most terrible spirit of intrigue had penetrated into the heart of my own palace. Alas! My dear son, the heir of my throne, has formed a horrible plot to dethrone me, and has gone to the length of attempting the life of his mother. A plan so terrible . . .

That night the Duke of Bejar, holding a candelabra to illuminate the corridors, led a procession through the Escorial. After him a platoon of the royal guard in blue and red uniforms, followed by the Prince: "a stout, well-built, fresh coloured young man of 23, of singularly sinister aspect . . ." Fer-dinand was a prisoner after his examination on the charge of treason.

According to the Treaty of Fontainebleau, thirty thousand French troops would be allowed to enter Spain whence they should proceed westward to occupy Portugal. But here came almost a hundred thousand Frenchmen and instead of proceeding westward to Portugal they set up camp at strategic locations below the Pyrenees. Could this be the vanguard of an occupying army? Certainly not. They were observers.

What next? French troops seized Pamplona and Barcelona. The royal couple panicked. They decided to board ship at Cádiz and escape to the Americas. Ferdinand's spies reported that Godoy's mistress Josefa Tudó was packing her belongings, which could only mean that she and Godoy were planning to sail away with Charles and María Luisa.

At Aranjuez, a few leagues south of Madrid, the great escape collapsed, halted by Ferdinand's supporters bellowing "Death to the Sausage Man!"

Godoy tried to hide in a rolled-up carpet. Or he hid in the palace attic for thirty-six hours and when he surrendered, desperate for water, they tore off his clothes before dragging him to Ferdinand. Hume's account is specific. As the mob broke into his bedroom Godoy threw on a dressing gown and escaped "by a secret door to the lumber-room above, where he lay hidden under a roll of matting. . . ." Another version states that he was hiding in a pile of furniture and when he crawled out a horse stepped on his face, bloodying his nose. If a horse steps on your face you get more than a bloody nose. Anyway, Ferdinand jailed him. Charles and María Luisa were not handled so roughly. Ferdinand let his parents know that he alone would be able to control the people and demanded that his father abdicate. King Charles, broken in spirit, signed a decree making Ferdinand the sovereign.

Lady Holland visited Aranjuez some time before this imperial fiasco and disliked the place, calling it "ill-calculated." Streets were excessively wide, sand drifted across the pavement, white stone houses reflected the harsh Iberian light. ". . . a healthy and pleasant residence till ye end of May, but then it becomes hot, and from the marshy ground in its neighbourhood the people suffer from agues, &c." She saw the private gardens of Their Majesties, noting a hedge behind which Charles would conceal himself in order to shoot sparrows. The King of Spain shooting sparrows. Although she didn't intend to do so, and probably never realized it, her diary exposed a degenerate and frivolous monarchy.

The uprising at Aranjuez, tumult, revolt, rebellion, opera buffa, whatever it should be called, rang down the curtain on Godoy.

Six days later Joachim Murat occupied Madrid. His arrival at the head of French troops sounds impressive. Red leather boots, green velvet waistcoat resplendent with gold braid, the white plume of his helmet swaying in a breeze. He thought the Spaniards were delighted to see him: "The joy that burst from them was nothing short of delirious. Never was a people more unhappy because of their bad government, and never was anything worthier of its fate." Murat wasn't altogether wrong. Neither did he quite understand. Spaniards were indeed dissatisfied, but the delight Murat observed had little to do with French troops. Spaniards were happy because their Prince, The Desired One, El Deseado, was returning.

And here came Ferdinand one day after Lieutenant-General Murat. Contrary to what we might expect, vainglorious Ferdinand entered the capital modestly, as though to demonstrate that he would be a different sort of king. Madrileños loved it. Women tossed flowers at him. Men threw down their capes for his horse to step upon. It is said that he advanced slowly, with dignity. The dawn of a new day after all the corruption, stupidity, and squalor.

Ferdinand tried to please Murat by giving up the sword of Francis I, captured during the battle of Pavia in 1525. He tried to please his subjects by ordering the release of various political prisoners including Jovellanos.

The Royal Academy asked Goya to paint Ferdinand. Fine, said Goya.

King Ferdinand was busy, what with one thing and another, but two sittings were arranged, forty-five minutes each. Goya asked Ferdinand to pose again, but one day after that second session Napoleon requested the honor of King Ferdinand's presence at the chateau of Marracq near Bayonne.

Whether he was frightened by the thought of defying Napoleon or too stupid to guess what lay ahead, Ferdinand set out for Bayonne. At Vitoria a crowd of citizens implored him to stop and cut the traces of his coach. One of Napoleon's agents reassured him: "I will let myself be beheaded if the Emperor has not recognized Your Majesty as King of Spain and the Indies a quarter of an hour after your arrival at Bayonne."

The military garrison at Irun, last stop, promised him an escort to safety. No, said Ferdinand.

April 20, 1808. Ferdinand crossed the Bidasoa. Nobody welcomed him. A league or so deeper into France he met three Spanish grandees whom he had sent to inform the Emperor of his arrival. They told him that Napoleon had announced in their presence that Spain never again would have a Bourbon monarch. By this time, possibly, Ferdinand understood. It didn't matter; he had ventured into Napoleon's sticky web. He seems to have realized that he couldn't escape so he continued toward Bayonne.

Luring the deposed King Charles and María Luisa to France was easy. Murat, acting on Napoleon's orders, dispatched Godoy to Bayonne. He then assured the royal couple that Napoleon would be delighted to see them. Charles wrote to his imbecilic brother Antonio that abdication had been forced upon him and he was going to visit their good friend and ally, Napoleon.

At the chateau they gathered: Charles, María Luisa, Ferdinand, Prime Minister Godoy.

And there Ferdinand learned that he must give up the throne to his father or be charged with treason. He replied that Spaniards wanted him, not his father. Charles threatened to strike his son with a riding crop, and may actually have done so. María Luisa—wearing a yellow crepe gown borrowed from Empress Josephine, a wreath of red and yellow roses on her gray head—called her son a bastard. Napoleon ordered Ferdinand out of the room.

At last, seeing French muskets everywhere, Ferdinand signed papers of abdication; whereupon the resurrected King Charles delivered the Spanish throne to France. Chabrun expressed it like this: "Napoleon could have had few scruples with regard to the royal family and precious little respect for a nation which allowed itself to be led and represented by such people. 'Spain can no longer be saved except by Napoleon,' he dictated to Charles IV, and Charles IV duly appended his royal signature."

Napoleon let it be understood that his brother Joseph, King of Naples, might consent to govern, should that be what the citizens wanted. Before long, to nobody's surprise, here came a delegation from Madrid with news that Spain would feel honored to have Joseph Bonaparte wear the crown.

Napoleon wrote to his brother on May 11, telling him what was expected. He, Joseph, was to be King of Spain:

"You will receive this letter the 19th; you will leave the 20th."

Joseph left Naples on the twentieth. By one account, the twenty-first.

Charles, his consort, their son, and Godoy were escorted to exile in France. Charles asked whether there would be plenty of game for hunting. As to María Luisa, Napoleon later said that her character was in her face "and it is incredible." Portraits of the ex-corporal Napoleon tell a similar story.

Some historians think he made a fatal mistake at Bayonne, though it would not become apparent for a while. Confronted by the vacuous flabbiness of Charles and Ferdinand, he mistook decadent Bourbon rulers for the people of Spain.

Joseph seems to have been uncommonly perceptive; he got no more than a few leagues into Spain when he wrote to his brother that the enterprise would be disastrous. From Burgos he wrote again. Indeed, he felt uneasy before catching sight of the Pyrenees. En route from Naples he had met his old tutor, Abbé Simon, at that time Bishop of Grenoble. The Bishop congratulated him. Joseph answered like a poet:

Will my brother's star shine always luminous and clear in the sky? I do not know, but sad presentiments assail me in spite of myself. They obsess me, they dominate me. I much fear that the Emperor, in giving me a crown finer than that which I lay down, has laid on my head a burden heavier than it could bear. So pity me, my dear Master, pity me, do not congratulate me.

He got to Madrid on July 20, 1808, in his pocket a crisp new constitution meant to guarantee religious and social reform. Nobody greeted him; he rode through deserted streets, seeing no Madrileños, nothing but closed doors and shuttered windows. Orders had been issued to decorate the houses but fanatic patriots threatened to kill anybody who obeyed. As a result he saw rags dangling from balconies.

Historian Robert Sencourt thought Joseph as admirable as Ferdinand was contemptible, and said Napoleon couldn't have chosen better. Joseph was forty years old, tall, handsome, "with a splendid bearing, and a high-bred courtesy of manner . . . but his eyes lacked the extraordinary power which made Napoleon's regular features so commanding." It must have been difficult to face Napoleon. Sencourt goes on to say that Joseph, although indolent and vain, was indescribably superior to any recent Spanish king, better than any regent Spain would have for a long while.

Ferdinand addressed an unctuous letter to Napoleon: "Sire, I offer Your Imperial and Royal Majesty my most heartfelt compliments on the satisfaction Your Majesty has had in the installation of Your Majesty's beloved brother on the throne of Spain. . . ."

Quite a few Spaniards felt that Joseph Bonaparte might be just what the country needed. Others did not. Some thought him a deliverer, others thought him a usurper. He had loyally served his brother as King of Naples where he proved to be reasonable and serious, although like most good Frenchmen he loved a bottle of wine, maybe two, maybe three. Madrileños named him Joe Bottles. He wandered through Madrid without an escort, loitered in gardens, and otherwise tried to communicate. There were two obstacles, or problems, neither of which was his fault. Spaniards understood that he was King by fiat, appointed by his brother, a puppet subject to removal at any moment.

The other problem began three months before he arrived.

Twenty-five thousand French troops were billeted in or near Madrid and General Murat frequently staged maneuvers and parades to dissuade restless Spaniards from considering revolt. On May I, when the general and his staff returned from Mass they entered a storm of hisses; Madrileños had learned that by order of King Charles—which is to say, by order of Napoleon—the King's two youngest children and their witless uncle Antonio Pascual would be taken to Bayonne. This would leave no member of the imperial family in Spain. Napoleon meant what he said; never again would Spain have a Bourbon monarch.

May 2. A crowd gathered in front of the palace. When three carriages arrived the mood of the people changed from anxiety to rage.

After so many years it is impossible to know just what happened. An equerry might have been dragged from his horse. The reins of a coach might have been slashed. One of Murat's aides might have been attacked by the mob. Hume thinks General Murat decided to give the Spaniards an obedience lesson so he ordered up a substantial number of troops "and without notice poured into the mass a murderous musketry and artillery fire." Whatever the provocation, Madrid exploded. Never mind the disparity: unarmed civilians confronting Napoleon's experienced troops. Madrileños snatched up anything lethal—ox-goad, butcher knife, rusty sword, blunderbuss, cudgel, bayonet, hammer, pitchfork.

On the north edge of Madrid an old artillery barracks held several cannons with ammunition. The place was guarded by seventy French soldiers and by fourteen Spaniards who had orders to obey the French. But an artillery captain named Velarde showed up leading a company of volunteers. He demanded that his countrymen join the revolt. All seventy French soldiers threw up their hands, perhaps to Velarde's amazement. The fourteen Spaniards hesitated, with good reason; if the revolt failed, as seemed likely, they would be shot. Another hero now stepped forward. The barracks commandant, Don Luis Daoiz, shredded his orders and is said to have trampled on the pieces. So, by authority of Daoiz and Velarde, ammunition was distributed. Five ancient cannons were dragged out of the yard.

Soon enough here came a French general named Lagrange with four thousand soldiers. Spaniards drove them back. Murat sent more troops, but those in the barracks continued to fight. Lagrange held up a white flag. Daoiz, although wounded, went out to discuss the situation. They began to quarrel and Lagrange somehow was injured. French grenadiers bayoneted Daoiz.

Half a century later Manuel Castellano painted *The Death of Daoiz.* Anybody who likes academic art will love this one. Ten feet by thirteen feet. A multitude of uniformed French automatons scurry forward—gesticulating, shouting, drumming, bugling, bayoneting Spaniards and vice versa. Not a drop of blood. Well, no more than a trace. Castellano meticulously orchestrated his picture; if you turn a print upside down so that it becomes almost abstract you see how balanced it is. French tricolor thoughtfully planted in the middle. Contemporary sources give a different and much less orderly picture: children throwing rocks, women with knives attacking French cavalry, hospital orderlies murdering sick Frenchmen in their beds. An unidentified Spanish officer described a prison escape after convicts heard people shouting "Mueran los Franceses!" and "Viva el Rey!"

Murat was justifiably anxious. Late at night somebody had tried to kill one of his aides, who skewered the assailant with a sword. A group of Spaniards then chased the French officer. Somebody else on Murat's staff was nearly stabbed by a Madrileño who announced after being captured that he had felt inspired to kill three Frenchmen.

Napoleon had told Murat to be cautious: Should war break out, all would be lost. What did Murat do? When the riot spread across Madrid he called up more troops, including ninety-six members of the swaggering Turkish bodyguard.

A long time afterward, in 1953, Paul Morand prefaced his account by observing that nations like to deport their rulers but object if others do it for them. He states that French cannonballs plowed through a crowd of patriots in the Plaza de Oriente and Polish lancers charged citizens who had gathered in the Calle d'Acala. Every house became a fortress: "Furniture, sacks of pepper, and boiling oil poured down from the balconies. . . ." We are told that the general of the Imperial Guard fell dead, hit by a flowerpot. Soldiers murdered inhabitants of houses from which shots were fired. Riflemen entered a monastery and the heads of decapitated monks rained down into the street. Morand was a French diplomat attached to the embassy in England during the first World War. He was also a good fiction writer. He may have been practicing his second trade when he produced that version of the Madrid riot—it's a little too picturesque—but there's no doubt that he studied the affair.

Biographer Anthony Hull speculates that Goya and his son were nearby when Murat's cavalry attacked the mob, maybe walking along San Jerónimo Avenue toward the Puerta del Sol, toward the home of a banker named Gabriel Bález. The first French soldier killed in the Puerta del Sol was hit by a bullet from a window of the Bález home and the Turkish bodyguard retaliated by killing several members of this household. Goya's daughter-in-law was related by marriage to Bález, so Goya and his son might very well have been going to visit the family.

In 1966 a Madrid weekly, *Blanco y Negro*, published an old engraving that showed Murat's troops being attacked in front of a four-storied house at the corner of Puerta del Sol and Calle del Arenal. The house was long ago demolished but appears to be the house where Goya lived in 1808. If so, he may have had a box seat, although to this day historians squabble over the possibility.

When the rioting ended Murat issued this statement from headquarters on the hill of Principe Pío: Citizens of Madrid, led astray, have succumbed to revolt and murder. French blood has been spilled. Vengeance is required.

Vengeance in the form of a tribunal authorized to execute every Spaniard caught with a weapon: pocket knife, scissors, anything resembling a weapon. Under pain of death citizens must disarm. No gathering to exceed eight persons. Every building where a Frenchman was killed shall be burnt to the ground.

Murat won. This couldn't be doubted. The children Francisco de Paula and María Isabella were en route to Bayonne. Their uncle Antonio Pascual left Madrid on the morning of May 4. Don Antonio had been president of the governing Junta, and to his fellow members he addressed a note in bad Spanish:

> For the guidance of the Junta I let it know how I have gone to Bayonne by order of the King, and I tell the Junta to go on just the same as if I were in it. God send us good quittance. Adieu, Sir, until the valley of Jehosephat.

About four hundred Spaniards were killed during the riot or shot by firing squads on May 3. Some, probably most, had been rioters. Others had nothing to do with it but were executed because Murat demanded blood. Some were executed in the French barracks. Some were bound to the stirrups of Mameluke cavalrymen, led to the Prado, and shot. Others were shot in Retiro Park, others on the hill near Murat's headquarters. Principe Pío—named for an Italian prince and soldier of fortune who married a Spanish heiress—this so-called mountain of Prince Pius seems to have been the preferred killing ground.

Juan Suárez, about whom we know very little, survived Napoleonic justice. His escape sounds like something from a Hollywood thriller. He was on his knees, hands bound, expecting a bullet at any instant when he managed to wriggle free of the rope and scramble into a ditch. He jumped up, executioners fired at him but missed. Juan Suárez "gained the wall" and found sanctuary in the Church of San Antonio de la Florida. Why Murat's troops didn't enter the church to hunt him down is not explained.

The names of quite a few Spaniards executed on this hill have been preserved:

> Antonio Mázias de Gamazo, laborer, aged sixty-six to seventy. Bernardo Morales, master locksmith. Domingo Braña, aged forty-four, tobacco porter in the Madrid customs house. Domingo Méndez, a mason working on the Church of Santiago and San Juan. Francisco Gallego Dávila, chaplain of the monastery of the Incarnation, Madrid. José Loret, shopkeeper. Juan Antonio Martínez, beggar. Julián Tejedor de la Torre, silversmith in the Calle Atocha. Lorenzo Domínguez, harness maker. Manuel Antolín, royal gardener in the Paseo de la Florida. Martín de Ruicarado, quarryman working on the Florida hillside. Rafael Canedo, of no fixed occupation . . .

One biographer notes that until Goya painted the executions on Príncipe Pío all monuments celebrated the memory of heroes; his tribute was the first altar to those anonymous millions whose deaths are irrelevant.

He represented Christ as a laborer but added the stigmata to make sure we understand. In front of the laborer another victim, face pressed to earth, arms outstretched as though nailed to a cross. Sarah Bernhardt was so impressed or depressed by this picture that she used it as mise en scène for the last act of *Tosca*. Mario, flat on the ground after being shot, wore a white shirt and yellow trousers like the Christ figure in Goya's painting. On the esplanade of Santangelo Castle stood a similar detachment of soldiers, Rome silhouetted above the castle ramparts. Goya filled the background with buildings that look more ecclesiastic than secular: an arch in front of what could be a monastery, the spire of which could be a seventeenth-century church. Hugh Thomas commented that these gloomy structures remind us of a discomfiting fact. Both groups, killers and their victims, most likely are Christian and the God worshipped beneath that belfry permits egregious atrocities. Like it or not, we pursue our dreams at the mercy of onerous and somber institutions.

Was Goya alluding to Jerusalem?

Fuendetodos? The hills near this parched village where he was born have been described as lonely, moonlike, similar to the landscape in *Tres de Mayo*.

One of his servants, a gardener named Isidro, claimed that Goya watched through a telescope as men were shot on Príncipe Pío. Not possible. From where he lived he couldn't have seen the executions with or without a telescope. In any event, about midnight he told Isidro to get the blunderbuss and come with him. Where do you think we went? Isidro asked. To the hill where the poor dead lay unburied. Although black clouds filled the sky, the moon had risen. Isidro remembered that his hair stood on end when he saw the master, portfolio in hand, turn toward the corpses. Goya sat on a hillock, opened the portfolio and waited for a shaft of moonlight. Something groaned and fluttered. At last the moon broke through. There lay bodies in pools of blood, face up, face down, one who seemed to be kissing the earth, another with hands lifted as though praying for vengeance. Dogs were eating the bodies and growling at birds circling above.

This melodramatic account may have been invented by the novelist Antonio de Trueba. When he was a young man Trueba worked for his uncle, a Madrid ironmonger, and got the facts straight from the horse's mouth—Isidro himself. So he said. Another legend has Goya prowling the streets at night, sketching murdered men by lamplight. And he began to paint with a rag soaked in Spanish blood.

Murat thought the slaughter exemplary. French losses, he declared, totaled thirty-one. Nobody familiar with events of the day believed it. Murat also said that May 3 had delivered Spain to Napoleon: "La journée d'hier donne l'Espagne à l'Empereur." But of course that's how generals talk. Some unidentified French officer shrewdly remarked that yesterday's event had placed Spain beyond Napoleon's reach forever.

Murat was obeying orders; one might say he was being a good soldier. During the last week of April he had received a communiqué from Napoleon that didn't coincide with earlier advice to be cautious. Subject: Rioters. Should the rabble stir, let it be shot down. Napoleon used the word canaille, more or less equivalent to rabble, scoundrels, blackguards, scum, riffraff, yet more contemptuous and arrogant as only French can be.

News of the Madrid revolt got to Bayonne during that ugly confrontation between the royal couple and their son. Napoleon was furious. So was King Charles who told Ferdinand: "The blood of my subjects has been shed and the blood of the soldiers of my great friend Napoleon! You are in part responsible for the slaughter." María Luisa allegedly muttered something about guillotining her son.

Those two days in Madrid shocked Napoleon. Thus his famous proclamation:

> Spaniards, your nation was perishing after a long death-agony. I have seen
> your ills; I bring you the remedy. . . . I shall set your glorious crown on the
> head of one who is another myself.

Too late. The dragon no longer slept. Crowning Joseph Bonaparte with the Spanish crown probably was destined to fail, but after Murat butchered four hundred Madrileños in the Plaza de Oriente and the Plaza del Sol and the French barracks and in Retiro Park and on the hill of Príncipe Pío—after May 2 and May 3, very few Spaniards could welcome a French king. Nationalistic anger swept up peasants, vagrants, grooms, chestnut vendors, priests, grocers, fishermen, tinsmiths, Spaniards of every degree. A few didn't join the atavistic dance. Some felt uncertain. Many had become disillusioned with an oafish King and a harlot Queen. Still, Charles was their sovereign. Ferdinand was his son. Meanwhile, foreign soldiers patrolled the streets.

Clerics denounced these heralds of Armageddon, minions of the Antichrist. Drovers equipped with branding irons attacked French troops. The mayor of Móstoles, a village just west of Madrid, declared war on

Napoleon. Spanish officers suspected of cooperating with the French were murdered by their own men. Anger spread to the Balearic Islands.

Although Napoleon underestimated the problem, his brother Joseph did not; he told General Savary that nobody in Spain was neutral. They are all against us, he said. He warned his brother that twelve million exasperated people hated the occupation. "Sire," he wrote, "your glory will be checked in Spain." He wrote to his uncle, Cardinal Fesch, that he knew what he could accomplish and what he couldn't. He wanted to return to Naples. If not that, he wished to retire on an estate a hundred leagues from Paris. He would do his best, but he had no illusions.

We might assume that Goya reached for his brushes immediately. In fact, he waited six years. Not until he saw a print titled *The Third of May* by a minor artist, Isidro González Velázquez, did he go to work. Although this seems odd it tells us something about artists. If what they create is authentic, not a calculated production, the impulse flows from an unidentifiable reservoir. The poet Lorca used a Spanish word, duende, and we will get back to this. Six years Goya waited. Not until he saw the unimaginative print of a journeyman did he know what to do with those revolutionary days.

One Spaniard appears in both paintings. He could have been imagined or he could have been somebody Goya recognized. He wears a green jacket. On May 2 he is stabbing a white horse. On May 3 he lies in the foreground, dead, mouth open.

The tonsured priest with clasped hands probably represents Father Gallego Dávila, chaplain of the monastery, who was shot.

The composition derives from an 1813 engraving by Miguel Gamborino titled *The Assassination of Five Monks from Valencia.* The posture of the central monk is almost exactly reproduced by Goya's laborer in a white shirt: arms outstretched, palms visible, Christ crucified. Gamborino thought a couple of angels drifting overhead would be appropriate; Goya skipped them. Years earlier he might have included angels. Not now.

Earlier artists had thought of war as panoramic: allegorical figures at the barricades, plumed helmets, flashing sabers, cavalry charges. Goya saw torture, starvation, rape, dismembered corpses.

If an artist wanted to depict suffering he would paint Christ or one of the saints, not some everyday locksmith, harness maker, mason, vagrant, quarryman, tobacco porter. Ribera painted St. Bartholomew being flayed alive half a dozen times—which tells us less about St. Bartholomew than about Ribera. In any event, Bartholomew isn't as terrified as these Madrileños, perhaps because the saint believed in God. These citizens have doubts.

Critics object to both paintings on technical grounds. *Dos de Mayo* is esthetically unsatisfactory, a mêlée without a center. Are those horses actually dying? The struggling men look like actors on stage. As for *Tres de Mayo*, victims and firing squad are too close together. Perspective is wrong, etc. But as Richard Schickel observed, one reason these paintings create such an impression is that Goya made no attempt to be academically correct.

Aldous Huxley said he lacked a talent Rubens conspicuously possessed, the ability to fill an entire canvas with figures or details of landscape, "and upon that plenum imposing a clear and yet exquisitely subtle three-dimensional order." Huxley thought Principe Pío more successful. Here, "the artist is speaking his native language, and he is therefore able to express what he wants to say with maximum force and clarity." It's a comment worth remembering. The early tapestry designs are pleasant, so are conventional pictures in the style of Mengs or Bayeu; but after a while something began to change. A different artist created the ruthless portraits of Charles IV and Ferdinand VII and the etchings called *Desastres de la Guerra*—naked headless bodies hanging upside down from tree limbs. And finally, that apocalyptic vision on the walls of La Quinta del Sordo. As you look at this mature work you understand what Huxley meant about Goya's native language.

Sartre thought most depictions of violence ineffective because they did no more than obligate the viewer to experience what he would have experienced if, in fact, he had been present. Therefore, Goya's pictures repel but fail to illuminate. In Picasso's *Guernica*, however, "calm plastic beauty" enhances the emotional impact. That dyspeptic critic Wyndham Lewis disagreed, sneering at Picasso's "unalterable intellectuality," "frigidity," and "desiccation."

Frederick Licht, who edited *Goya in Perspective*, wrote that although Picasso represented the bombing of Guernica, the mindlessness and brutality couldn't be conveyed in traditional terms. Picasso, rather than create a painting in the usual sense, withdrew; he could do no more than recognize the importance of this atrocity and call attention to it. Licht wonders if the artist today can be anything more than a medium who transmits recognitions of the world.

Delacroix wrote in his journal on May 14, 1824: "Men of genius are made not by new ideas, but by an idea which possesses them, namely, that what has been said has not yet been sufficiently said."

Once upon a time I sat for half an hour on a bench in front of *Guernica*. What I couldn't help looking at over and over was that screaming horse. I have no idea how long Picasso thought about it, but the message is immediate. Goya waited six years. These altogether different interpretations are, of course, identical.

Except for a growing hatred of war he may have been uncertain how he felt. He saw the result of French occupation; he knew the Spaniards retaliated with equal ferocity. In 1808 he was sixty-two years old, not an age when he would be expected to cut a Frenchman's throat. Nor did he publicly declare himself. The important thing was to go on drawing and painting. He kept no diary, nor did he confide in anyone; if he did, his thoughts and feelings weren't recorded. Good capitalist that he was, few matters concerned him so much as preserving his wealth.

Margherita Abbruzzese in a 1967 biography reflects upon Goya's character but also considers the artistic tradition of Spain, going back as far as the Middle Ages. Speaking of literature, she says that from *Lazarillo de Tormes* to Cervantes "every exponent of the Spanish soul has drawn his inspiration from the inexorability of Nature, from social conditions, from ceaseless political oppression and the whole drama of absolutism and revolt. These are the external themes of Spanish art. Spain is the country of extremes: boundless wealth and brutalizing poverty, fatalistic resignation and the bloodiest rebellions."

13

Saragossa, like other cities and towns, boiled with rage at news of those executions in Madrid. A revolutionary force coalesced around one Jorge Ibort—aka Gaffer George—and a couple of peasants, Mariano Cerézo and Tío María. And because a distinguished figurehead very often helps the cause, these insurgents recruited Don José de Palafox y Melzit, Duke of Saragossa, Captain General of Aragón. Not only was Palafox a prominent aristocrat, he had once served in the Spanish imperial bodyguard. Then, too, he was handsome, which shouldn't make a difference, but usually does.

Word of a Saragossa uprising brought the expected command from French headquarters: Surrender.

Palafox allegedly replied: "War to the knife!" This defiant challenge has been attributed to others. No matter who first said it, the people got ready.

French troops besieged Saragossa twice. During the first attack they fought their way up to the walls before Joseph called them off; he needed soldiers and too many were being killed. For several months the city was not disturbed. Thousands of hungry, anxious laborers pushed through the gates and the military garrison expanded. General Palafox invited Goya to visit. It's said that Goya accepted this invitation with pride, proud that his countrymen had refused to submit. He left Madrid in a fancy carriage. Why should His Majesty's Court Painter travel like a peasant? French troops didn't molest him because they knew he served Joseph Bonaparte. Spanish irregulars saluted him because—well, he was Goya. Besides, they had no doubt about his loyalty to Spain.

What he found in Saragossa horrified him. He sketched the devastation and he painted María Augustín, Saragossa's Joan of Arc, who brought food to cannoneers on the ramparts. When all these men, including her lover, were killed, she by herself loaded and fired a cannon. Goya in plate 7 of the *Disasters* imagines her holding a firebrand to the touchhole. One scholar perceives "innate sexuality" in this—a long, smooth weapon holding a twenty-six pound cannonball and explosive powder that María Augustín will ignite.

She became famous throughout Europe, her bravery immortalized by artists and writers. Lord Byron: "Scarce would you deem that Saragoza's tower . . ."

Goya went from Saragossa to Fuendetodos. People in the village years afterward claimed to have met him; he talked with his hands and couldn't hear a word they said.

Saragossa withstood the next assault for two months. After French troops broke through the walls fighting continued street by street. Marshal Lannes, an experienced commander, wrote to Napoleon that never before had he met such resistance: "I have seen women allowing themselves to be killed in front of a breach. We have to lay siege to every house." Fifty-four thousand Spaniards died. Saragossa resembled a gigantic plague hospital, thousands of bodies rotting among smoking ruins. According to an 1815 report, sick and wounded people who jumped out the windows of a burning infirmary were caught on French bayonets. Lunatics whose cells had been opened "sang, laughed, and declaimed with a loud voice. . . ."

Lady Holland wrote in her diary that after Joseph's men captured the city General Palafox, who had been wounded, was treated with great cruelty. Several drawings by Goya were found in his possession. These drawings "French officers cut and destroyed with their sabres, at the moment too when Palafox was dying in his bed." As a matter of fact, General Palafox recovered and spent four years conversing with roaches in a French prison.

Goya's portrait of the heroic María Augustín seems to have vanished, possibly slashed by French sabers. Lady Holland thought she was killed during the second siege "as were 3 other women who had been inspired by her courage." However, Lord Byron met her in Seville, where she was showing off her medals.

Goya would paint General Palafox after the French released him. He straddles a charger stolen from a carousel. His sword points toward a burning city on the horizon while his lumpen steed pretends to gallop. How curious that an artist who caught the gleam of satin, who exposed the touching innocence of children, and delineated some of the most expressive hands since Rembrandt—how strange that he would have trouble painting horses.

Palafox became the talk of Europe, especially in England where anti-Napoleonic forces congregated. Here came a delegation of Spaniards to London. Here came Portuguese envoys.

The British decided on Lieutenant-General Sir Arthur Wellesley. He should embark for Portugal, a good place from which to invade Napoleonic Spain. Sir Arthur accepted the challenge pensively because everybody was afraid of Napoleon: "Tis enough to make one thoughtful. . . ." He described his army as "scum of the earth." Not a good beginning. And he said, "By God, I don't know what the enemy will think of these men, but they fill me with terror."

The British haven't always chosen wisely, nor have the Americans, Germans, Swedes, nor any other nation. But this time they picked a winner. Sir Arthur had a spotted record, so there were doubts. His Iberian campaign cleared the slate. It would bring promotions, international huzzahs, more citations and ribbons than any man could handle, to say nothing of a Spanish estate and a magnificent collection of paintings. 1809: Viscount Wellington. 1812: Earl of Wellington. 1814: Duke of Wellington.

On October 25, 1808, exasperated and worried that the Spanish campaign was not proceeding as expected, Napoleon had addressed the Legislative Assembly in Paris, saying he himself would lead the armies. He would settle the business and plant French eagles on the forts of Lisbon.

November 4. As promised, the Emperor took command of two hundred thousand French troops in Spain. And he made it clear that he wouldn't tolerate any nonsense: "Messieurs Monks," he said to some Spanish clerics, "if you try to interfere with my plans, I shall have your ears cut off." A month later, he came knocking at the gates of Madrid and he made it clear that if Madrid tried to interfere with his plans he would kill every soldier he found. Madrileños hesitated. They talked it over. They wanted to resist. Saragossa and all that. However, nobody wanted to spit in Napoleon's face. Madrid gave up.

The Emperor didn't stay long, no more than a day because he thought the Spaniards had learned a lesson. He visited the royal palace and in a magisterial gesture placed one hand on a carved lion. "My brother," said he to Joseph, "you are better lodged than I."

His principal lieutenants in France, Foreign Minister Talleyrand and Police Chief Fouché, were said to be conspiring against him and news from Austria was troublesome; he bade Joseph adieu, promising to return if needed, or when he could. Later, marooned on St. Helena, he wrote that the Spanish war had been his undoing. "The circumstances of my disaster are tied to this fatal knot. It compounded my difficulties, divided my forces. . . ."

Had he listened to his brother Joseph, what then?

Cities rise and fall, emperors come and go; our man continued working at his trade.

Not long after Madrid capitulated he painted a knife grinder whetting a blade on a millstone. José Gudiol finds a certain restlessness in this picture, maybe a projection of Goya himself, an awareness of the distance now separating the artist from the social class to which he was born. The knife grinder stares at us without expression; all the same you know he would enjoy carving up a French soldier.

About this time Goya painted that mysterious city on a rock: an isolated citadel, three aerial creatures not from this world flapping around the summit. Flames engulf the base. What's going on? He started with a brush but finished with a reed, which enabled him to produce clotted irregular strokes unlike anything he could have achieved with a brush or palette knife. Today, of course, you make your own rules, but in nineteenth-century Spain you didn't paint with a reed or your thumb or anything except a brush. Neither did Victorian England like much experimentation. Turner's late painting got bad reviews. *Storm At Sea* especially irritated the public. Margaret, what's that fellow up to? It's all whitewash and soapsuds. Why doesn't he paint like everybody else?

Next, a giant allegory of Madrid meant to hang in City Hall. Goya represented Madrid as a woman gesturing toward a medallion supported by winged spirits. At her feet a placid white dog, supposedly a greyhound although this greyhound is not in a rush to go anywhere and probably couldn't. Four-footed subjects bored him, which might explain why his animals seem to have been assembled rather than created. Bulls, horses in the ring, yes, and the most malevolent cats on earth. But those are exceptions.

Now, inside the medallion Goya painted Joseph Bonaparte—based on a print borrowed from a Peruvian, Don Tadeo Bravo de Rivero, who lived in Madrid and was at this time an official of Joseph's government. Which is to say Goya collaborated, though it might be explained, excused, justified, whatever. Several years before the French arrived he had painted Rivero and later he had done some work in Rivero's mansion, so they were old acquaintances. Explanation aside, what seems obvious is that he wanted to ingratiate himself with Joseph.

The medallion didn't much please Joseph who preferred the frigid neoclassic style of Jacques-Louis David. He didn't praise Goya, nor did he commission anything.

And very soon Joseph had to leave town because here came an English-Portuguese army led by Wellington. He escaped a few hours before the Iron Duke arrived. Just about everybody was glad to see Wellington, but that allegory in City Hall was embarrassing. It implied that civic officials had been cooperating with the Bonapartes. What to do? They scraped Joseph off the medallion and substituted a liberal password: Constitución.

Wellington didn't spend much time in Madrid; he retired to Portugal for the winter. So here came Joseph, escorted by French bayonets. How about that picture in City Hall? Out went Constitución, replaced by another portrait of Joseph. This time the artist was one of Goya's pupils, Dionisio Gómez.

A few months later Joseph again was ousted. Ferdinand, beloved Ferdinand, would be returning. Joseph was scraped off, replaced by Constitución.

That should have been the final word, what with Ferdinand enthroned for good. Not so. Ferdinand hated the word Constitución. He ordered it scraped off and a portrait of himself substituted. Nobody knows who did this, but it was such a poor job that in 1826 the civic elders hired a court painter, Vicente López, to have another go at Ferdinand.

This, of course, concluded the business. Wrong. Ferdinand went to his reward, whatever it may have been, in 1833. He has been described as "uxorious and susceptible" because he married four times. Only one wife survived his embrace. María Antonia of Sicily died in 1806, María Isabel of Portugal in 1818, María Amalia of Saxony in 1829. They might have lived longer had they married Henry VIII. Anyway, we are told that after María Amalia's death Ferdinand spent hours gazing at a portrait of his niece, María Cristina of Naples. She became his last wife and survived him by forty-five years, probably amazed at her good luck.

That uxorious face on the battered medallion was scraped off after his death, replaced by Constitución. At last, the final word. No. Ferriz and Foxa—not a duo of concert pianists but historians—Ferriz and Foxa told the authorities in 1872 that Goya's original work might be exposed if the subsequent daubing and lettering could be removed. A certain Palmaroli got the job. Down he went, cautiously, through the layers. When he hit bottom very little Goya could be found. Now what? Here was an empty space that must be filled. One couldn't have the robust lady of Madrid gesture at nothing. Foxa pointed out that Spaniards always react to something or other and it would be a serious mistake to excite them. Thus, following much consultation, authorities decided to paint on the medallion three words forever associated with Goya and the spirit of Spain: Dos de Mayo.

There ought to be a moral in this twisted tale. If so, nobody knows what it is.

After all that scraping, painting, scraping, and repainting there shouldn't be enough left of the original work to attract scholars. Nevertheless they contemplate, speculate, dissect, evaluate. One rebukes Goya for having rendered space with excessive simplicity, for disposing figures in a single plane parallel to the surface, omitting oblique lines of escape, ad infinitum. Beyond such learned analysis what the Madrid allegory reveals about Goya is a determination to survive. He agreed to paint Joseph. He may have felt, as many Spaniards did, that Joseph was a decent sort. Still, anybody named Bonaparte was the enemy. Goya had traveled quite a distance from Fuendetodos but in his mind there were leagues and leagues to go. Kings succeed one another, good, bad, mediocre. It might be necessary to humor such men, which doesn't guarantee allegiance.

He painted Joseph's aide-de-camp, General Nicolas Guye, a handsome officer with russet hair and sideburns. More than once Goya complained that hands were difficult so you might expect his treatment of hands to be clumsy and ineffective. Quite the opposite, and in this opulent study General Guye's hands reveal more than his face. During the French retreat he was killed. Even now, two centuries later, it's a little sad. Goya seems to have represented the intruders without bias, however he felt about them viscerally; they were subjects for his brush. It's known that Joe Bottles sat for him several times, although these portraits have disappeared.

Goya's subjects at this time included two aristocratic young ladies, daughters of the Marquesas de Santiago and Montehermoso. When Victor Hugo was a boy he lived in Madrid where his father Léopold served as chief of staff to Marshal Jourdan. Victor managed to get acquainted—unusually well acquainted—with the future Marquesa de Montehermoso, which may be irrelevant but is rather interesting because at that time he was about ten years old. Well, you say, he was French.

And the afrancesado most bitterly hated by Spaniards, Manuel Romero, Minister of Police—Romero sat for a portrait. If Goya felt uncomfortable about this we don't know. Letters to Zapater recount his triumphs, how the nobility praised him, how much he was paid, illness, grocery orders, references to chocolate and olive oil, life in the big city. You might almost take him for a Saragossa merchant visiting Madrid. Sánchez Cantón thinks Goya loathed Romero and expressed his loathing in the portrait. The Minister's right hand is concealed in his coat, "his left fist clenched, his look is stern, his lips tightly closed. His character is exactly portrayed." It is a picture "full of astuteness and malevolence."

Canon Juan Antonio Llorente was Secretary-General to the Inquisition. This man compiled the first history of it and he wore a decoration pinned on his chest by Joseph Bonaparte: the Order of Spain, derisively known to Spaniards as the Eggplant. According to one scholar Llorente worked on the history without permission, using secret files. Others say that Joseph authorized him to examine the records. No matter. Goya painted him almost gently. Here we have an official of that terrifying institution whose features radiate humanity, intelligence, good humor. Llorente is dignified, sensitive, resolute, an exceptional man. And there on his chest the Eggplant glows like an unearthly gem. It's a full-length treatment, impressive from a distance. Seen close up, the Secretary-General looks positively benevolent. He was known as the Spanish Voltaire.

Or you might read that face differently. Apostate. Traitor. A paradoxical man, he later plunged into liberal studies while remaining Catholic. After his appointment as Secretary-General he wanted to reform the Holy Office. Godoy and Jovellanos agreed to help, but when they fell from power Llorente's authority declined. His enthusiasm for progressive French ideas made him suspect. He welcomed Joseph Bonaparte, seeing in him the regeneration of Europe, and when British troops under Wellington approached Madrid he fled with the Frenchmen. He wrote, or completed, his book on the Inquisition while living in France. There he remained until 1823 when he returned to Spain. He died that same year "of grief and sadness, discouraged by the fickleness of men and the ingratitude of nations." Whatever he was, Llorente's life registered those turbulent years.

Gudiol, analyzing this stately portrait, remarks that we may observe to what extent Goya dismissed conventional, anecdotal aspects of his subject, giving us instead "the essential human factor and the imperishable reflection of its truth."

August 20, 1809. Joe Bottles Bonaparte issued a decree suppressing religious Orders and sequestering their property. A December 20 announcement was more specific:

> Article I: A museum for pictures, containing selected examples of the different schools, will be established in Madrid. For this purpose the paintings required to complete the collection thus decreed will be removed from all public institutions, including the palaces.
>
> Article II: A comprehensive collection of works by famous artists of the Spanish school will be formed, with a view to presenting it to our august brother, Emperor of the French. We shall express to him at the same time our desire to see the collection placed in one of the halls of the Napoleon Museum. . . .

Goya served on a committee charged to select fifty Spanish paintings destined for the Napoleon Museum. And at this point we come upon Francisco Goya, saboteur. He, along with fellow conspirators Maella and Napoli, chose works of little value by secondary artists—Masters of the Rear Ranks. They could not ignore acknowledged masters such as Velázquez and Zurburán because Napoleon wasn't a fool; but they reasoned that he wouldn't consider himself an authority so they decided upon minor works along with a few replicas, in other words, fakes. Three by Velázquez, two by Murillo, four by Ribera, five by Zurburán. The committee made these choices after much deliberation, excessive deliberation, while waiting for the French to be expelled. The guerilla tactics evidently succeeded; not one of these fifty pictures left Madrid. At least, not one got to the Napoleon Museum, although some were destroyed or stolen.

What would you call Goya? He paints Joseph Bonaparte as though he sympathized with the French, yet doesn't wear the honorary Eggplant. He paints any number of Spaniards who welcomed the French, among them the despicable Minister of Police. He willingly paints General Joseph Querault of the occupational forces. But then, with nobody looking, he and his fellow judges sabotage the desire of Napoleon to stock a Paris museum with Spanish masterworks.

Quite a few illustrados at first believed the invasion would help their country. They understood how stagnant, lethargic, and provincial it had become under a decadent Bourbon monarchy. France, they knew, was dramatically changed by revolution; now, with luck, Spain could benefit from its enlightened neighbor. Respected intellectuals such as the Captain General of Barcelona, El Conde de Ezpleta, declared that only Napoleon could resurrect Spain.

Many Spaniards probably concluded that Joseph and his brother were hatched in different nests. Joseph seemed tolerant. He allowed bullfighting, which had been prohibited under Godoy. He abolished the Inquisition, good news to all but fanatic conservatives. However skeptical they might be, however resentful of a Bonaparte on the throne, Spaniards did not overlook this. It meant, among other things, fewer restrictions on reading. New books popped up in the stalls, unorthodox books. Joseph could be hated as a Frenchman, yes, Napoleon's brother, true. So they called him El Rey Intruso, the Intruder King. And Joe Bottles. And because he ordered the construction of little parks throughout Madrid they called him El Rey Plazuelas, King of Tiny Squares. Still, he didn't threaten to cut off the ears of monks. Maybe he deserved a chance.

He understood the situation. He knew that his presence in Madrid was useless and he wanted to leave. He wanted to leave before the inevitable consequence of Spanish hatred would compel him to leave. He wrote to his brother that events had betrayed his hopes: "I have accomplished nothing and can do nothing. I beg Your Majesty to permit me to relinquish to Your Majesty's hands the rights which Your Majesty has deigned to transmit to me. . . ."

Napoleon didn't answer.

Joseph was lonely in Madrid because his wife, Queen Julie, refused to join him. Once upon a time he had been an attorney in Marseilles, which is surprising because we don't expect anybody named Bonaparte to work for a living. He married the daughter of a rich merchant and they had two daughters. When Joseph was appointed King of Naples she reigned alongside him. But then, as the saying goes, he found consolation elsewhere. Queen Julie left him and retired to Paris. The prospect of becoming Her Majesty, Queen of Spain, would cause most women to swallow their pride but Julie remained in Paris. Joseph therefore looked to the multilingual and promiscuous Señora de Montehermoso, to the Countess of Jaruco, and to a certain Nancy Derrieux.

1811. El Año de hambre. Twenty thousand people in Madrid starved to death. Twice each day carts rumbled through the city collecting bodies. The memoir of a contemporary named Romanos said people lay in the streets begging for a potato, a drop of soup. "I once counted several persons dead or dying in a walk of about three hundred paces, and ran home crying to throw myself into the arms of my mother, who was so terrified that for several months she would not let me go to school anymore."

Joseph ordered bread from the palace bakery distributed among those who were ashamed to beg, forbidding his servants to let them know who sent the bread. He himself, deeply troubled, wandered through the poorest quarters. At times he would be recognized and people would exclaim: What misfortune that such a man is named Bonaparte! Stories of his compassion and generosity may be exaggerated but there seems no doubt that he did his best, knowing it wouldn't help. And apparently the citizens understood. If he went to the theater he would be applauded. Country people would visit Madrid to honor him. Scholars and poets attended his dinner parties.

Romanos said that one day while strolling through the city Joseph paused to chat with a little boy whose father had dressed him as a member of the civic guard. Joseph spoke French, Italian, and Spanish and considered them interchangeable. He spoke to the child in the patois he used: Ah! Bravo, boy! E per que tienes tu questa spada? Why do you wear this sword?

Para matar Franceses, the little boy answered. To kill Frenchmen.

Excuse him, Your Majesty, said the boy's father. He repeats what he hears from servants and people about.

14

A fugitive Spanish government existed in Seville because Madrid had been occupied for almost three years. The last Spanish army, ignoring advice from Wellington, challenged French troops at Ocaña and was routed. Córdoba and Granada fell to Napoleon's troops. What remained of the Spanish government retreated to Cádiz but the Spaniards could retreat no further without getting their boots wet. Cádiz faces the Atlantic.

Although France now controlled most of the great peninsula, French soldiers met looks of sullen hatred. Sentries were picked off, equipment stolen or destroyed. And with Joseph for a Commander in Chief the structure of the army began to disintegrate. French officers argued, grew jealous of one another. Some denied the authority of Joseph.

Guerillas tormented the French, who retaliated by murdering civilians and burning villages. Peasants were intimidated by fear, which meant uncultivated fields, less food. One French general wrote in a communiqué that Spanish obstinance was destroying his armies: "It is useless to cut off the heads of the Hydra in one place . . . it will devour the population and the wealth of France. We need more troops. . . ."

More troops.

The war had been going on long enough that soldiers digging graves for comrades would unearth the bones of men killed in previous battles. And because they were starving just about anything went into the stewpot. Frogs. Mice. Bugs. Dogs. Snails. Worms. They slaughtered the horses and oxen that were pulling carts heaped with treasure; jeweled reliquaries, silver candlestick holders, and gold crucifixes were abandoned in scorched fields or left in carts too heavy for starving men to pull. They drank from stagnant puddles and filthy streams. If they came upon a well or cistern they would drink, never mind a body floating on the surface. Leeches grew inside their mouths. They vomited, collapsed, and died.

Women, some with children, followed the armies. When a battle ended, if their men had won, they searched for husbands and fathers and brothers. If the enemy had won they could expect to be raped, possibly murdered. Blackburn reports that a soldier who approached a convent being used as a hospital saw amputated limbs along the wall, "while more arms and legs kept flying out the windows. . . ." At La Coruña, two thousand horses were shot to prevent enemy soldiers from riding them. A mule driver who stole an apple was hanged, the apple stuffed into his mouth. One Spaniard kept a bag of French ears and fingers.

Everybody knew the Iron Duke meant business and nobody knew it better than he. Still, life is meant for living wherever you happen to be, so a pack of English hounds accompanied him. Between military engagements he would go fox hunting.

At Talavera he led the English/Portuguese troops to victory. After this battle a fire sprang up in dry grass where quite a few soldiers lay dead or dying, "and men were ashamed because their pangs of hunger increased with the smell of roasting meat." It sounds like a passage from Homer.

Goya's *Colossus* is a big painting, although not enormous. The vision, though, is huge and many people think he never painted anything more terrifying. The creature looms above a desperate crowd. People look like fleas. Horses bolt, cattle lunge frantically. And who is the colossus? Gulliver in Lilliput? Napoleon? But look you, the apparition turns his back upon our world. What does it mean? Only one animal stands oblivious, indifferent—that icon of stupidity, the Ass. Margherita Abbruzzese wrote that Goya's monsters, the dwarfs of Velázquez, Picasso's *Guernica*—each tells us the same thing in the language of protest: "The truth must be seen and must be shown to others, including those who have no wish to see it. . . . And because the blind in spirit stay their eyes on the outward aspect of things, then these outward aspects must be twisted and deformed until they cry out what they are trying to say."

How much of the fighting Goya watched isn't known. He did see what was left behind: stripped torsos and bloody human limbs stuck on tree branches like fragments of marble sculpture, this and more, enough for his purpose. He kept no journal of his thoughts but he registered a prodigious flowering of rage, not hastily in a sketchbook; later, after he had time to absorb the meaning, hunched over copper plates. Vallentin called these disasters of war "the work of a memory that knew no forgiveness." How long did he scratch away at his fantastic idea? Perhaps a decade. The complete sequence wasn't published until 1863, thirty-five years after his death, and he seems to have said nothing about it during the war. Some historians think he owned a copy of Jacques Callot's album, *Les Misères et Malheurs de la guerre*, published in 1633. Callot had watched the troops of Louis XIV devastate Lorraine. Goya was a better technician than Callot, but that's not what differentiates them; Goya intuitively found the luminous detail.

Sánchez Cantón remarked that events of the 1936–39 Spanish civil war showed the terrible truth of his nervous, implacable vision. What he sketched or painted wasn't vaguely pacifistic; he recorded facts, occurrences, some of which he had seen, others related to him by witnesses. A man kneels with outstretched arms, accompanied by sixty-four illustrations of atrocities, starvation, irrational suffering. At least once before, in his painting of the executions on Principe Pío, Goya used that symbol of a kneeling man, arms outstretched, palms punctured.

During the occupation of Madrid and somewhat earlier he painted a number of things that have been called escapist. His grandson Mariano. A beautiful woman named Francisca García. The celebrated actress Antonia Zárate. The handsome bullfighter Romero José. A rustic, sturdy, healthy woman balancing a jug of water on one hip. A placid matron holding a fan, a matron who doesn't look too bright and probably didn't think about war. Bosomy nymphs on balconies, bosomy nymphs with liquid eyes. One is thought to be Leocadia Weiss who would become his mistress. The balcony scenes have been dated anywhere from 1800 to 1813 but the date isn't important; what these harmonious pictures tell us is that Goya was searching for peace.

He and his wife drew up a common will on June 3, 1811, ordering that when the time came they be shrouded in the Franciscan habit. Twenty Masses would be said for each. They made bequests to the Holy Land and for the redemption of prisoners.

June 20, 1812. Josefa died and was buried in the Church of St. Martín.

Under terms of the will, their joint inheritance would be divided. Goya with his son Javier showed up at the office of one Antonio López de Salazar in late October and put into writing—amicably and unofficially, as was noted—the inventory they had compiled of goods acquired by the artist during marriage. Altogether, properties and cash, it amounted to 357,728 copper reales. Among the items: Four corner cabinets. Sofa. One large mirror "with pier-glass." Two easy chairs. Blue cupboard. Blue-and-gold cupboard. Stove. Tin-plate bathtub. Dining table. One "iron divan." Eighteen Victoria chairs and twenty-eight chairs painted blue, which suggests that Francisco and Josefa often gave parties. And this inventory lists eight footstools covered in yellow damask. Eight yellow footstools. You can almost see them scattered about, dreadful as Easter eggs. My God, Margaret, there's another!

He loved jewelry. He owned a cravat pin with four precious stones, valued at 4,000 reales.

Silver? Trays, cruets, plates, candlesticks, candlestick snuffers, laver, marcelinas, cups, knives, on and on.

He didn't itemize what was in his studio, which seems odd. His library was valued at 1,500 reales, although not itemized. At times he would embellish a letter with a sketch so we might assume he left doodles in some of those books. Nobody knows what happened to them.

All of his paintings and prints were legally regarded as property acquired during marriage, which may not sound right, but that's how it was. By ceding these to Javier, and by giving his son the house, Goya pocketed 147,627

reales. Javier got a fraction of this amount in cash, but what he got otherwise was stupefying. Ten Rembrandt prints. Two paintings by Velázquez.
One by Correggio. Two by Tiepolo. A collection of Piranesi. And there
were Goya's own paintings: *The Duchess of Alba. Pedro Romero. Philosophy and St.
Jerome. St. Anthony. St. John. Lazarillo de Tormes. Colossus. Drunkards. Water-Carrier.*

Why did Goya want all that cash? British and patriot forces were in the
vicinity. Madrid would be liberated, though nobody could say when.
Josefa was ill and might not live much longer. He himself was old and
rich and crusty and a little short of breath, not in very good shape to join
the resistance. It appears that he gave some thought to escaping, in which
case he would need plenty of reales.

Josefa died a few weeks before Wellington entered the city, and some
biographers think that during this period he meant to slip away. His son,
for a reason not entirely clear, may have notified police. In any event, Goya
probably couldn't have eluded the French long enough to reach patriot
territory.

August 12, 1812. Here came the Iron Duke, at his back thirty thousand English and Portuguese. At his side two famous guerilla chiefs, El
Empecinado and El Médico. Bells tolled joyously throughout Madrid.
Citizens waved palm branches. Women offered fruit, wine, laurel crowns.
Some of them rushed forward to kiss Wellington's boots. They kissed his
sword and they kissed his horse. An 1816 painting by William Hilton, as
thoughtfully orchestrated as Castellano's *Death of Daoiz,* shows Wellington
talking to somebody while on the other side of the picture a woman lifts
a bare-bottomed infant to the sky. Hilton must have thought it essential
to the composition.

Major William Napier states that Madrileños crowded around the Iron
Duke, touched his uniform, flung themselves to the ground in ecstasy,
blessed him aloud:

Y viva la Nación!

Y viva la Velintón!

Only a few hours before this triumphant arrival Joseph Bonaparte had
fled. General Hugo, the author's father, supervised that ignoble departure.
He had been appointed Governor of Guadalajara by Joseph with specific

instructions to eliminate Juan Martín Diez, El Empecinado. The Indomitable One. General Hugo had done a good job in the Kingdom of Naples, crushing an elusive gang leader known as Fra Diavolo, but Spanish insurgents were slippery. His son Victor would later write that it was impossible to catch El Empecinado because people gave false information and deserted their villages before the French arrived, destroying or taking anything useful. This kind of resistance was more or less invented and just about perfected by Spaniards as the only way to fight Napoleon's powerful army. Otherwise they must submit and they knew what that would mean. As a result, teachers, peasants, clerks, bandits, servants, doctors, and monks became guerilla leaders. Victor Hugo observed that among the roster of guerilla chiefs no distinguished names could be found. They were ordinary citizens who had been abused until they cared for nothing except revenge.

Here was Lucas Raphael, a monk whose father had been executed because he would not pledge allegiance to Joseph. Here was the shepherd, El Pastor. The priest, El Cura. The grandfather, El Abuelo. The one-armed man, El Manco.

Juan Martín Diez, from a family of cobblers, gave Victor Hugo's father more headaches than he could have imagined. Diez fought as American Indians fought the United States Army at that time, retreating when overmatched, scattering, regrouping. El Empecinado thought well of his French adversary. He sent General Hugo a letter urging him, as one free man to another, to change flags and join him in fighting for the independence of Spain: "It would be more worthy of a soldier such as yourself to serve the liberty of a people than the ambition of a tyrant."

General Hugo's answer, if he did answer, has not been preserved.

Goya painted El Empecinado with thick black hair, thick eyebrows, pirate whiskers, face like a walnut. If his guerillas caught a French soldier they would cut the man in half or roast him alive.

French response to Spanish defiance was predictable: "Anyone taken with arms will be hanged, without further formality."

The guerilla chief Francisco Espoz y Mina drew up a proportionate table of reprisals. Four French officers to be killed for each Spanish officer. Twenty French soldiers for each Spanish soldier. The French

replied that five prisoners had been hanged by Mina's irregulars. Therefore five Spaniards would be hanged at the place where the French had
been murdered.

A British officer reported seeing hanged women and children, fires
burning under the bodies.

Wellington: "I have seen many persons hanging in the trees by the sides
of the road, executed for no reason that I could learn. . . ."

Napoleon's troops killed wounded Spaniards, robbed, broke into
churches to steal whatever they liked and desecrate the Host. Accordingly,
Spanish priests killed French citizens who thought they would be safe inside a church.

Several French soldiers unwisely decided it might be nice to sleep in a
garden. During the night they were murdered, their corpses dragged along
a road. General Abbé retaliated by hanging twenty Spanish hostages taken
at Pamplona. Mina therefore ordered sixteen French prisoners hurled
from a precipice.

Spaniards circulated a Civil Catechism inciting hate:

Who is the enemy of happiness?
Napoleón.
What sort of man is Napoleón?
The cause of evil, the end of all that is good.
How should Spaniards comport themselves?
In accord with the teaching of Jesus Christ.
Is it a sin to kill a Frenchman?
No, Father, one gains entrance to heaven by killing heretic dogs.

Guerillas lurked in passageways, corridors. A partisan with a knife
could be hiding in a barrel, behind a wagon. Napoleon's troops began to
lose their appetite for munching on a ragged Spanish army.

Miguel de Azanza, a Spanish afrancesado, had been one of Joseph's
ministers. His daughter married a Frenchman. The young couple tried to
leave Spain but Mina's guerillas ambushed their convoy at a pass in the
Saline Mountains, murdered the groom and carried off the bride. French

troops caught Mina's brother. Victor Hugo, at this time a child, escaped to France in a carriage with his mother. En route they passed a cross. Mina's brother had been cut in pieces and nailed to the cross: "The horrible intention had been to rearrange the pieces, and make these fragments once more into a whole corpse."

Years later Victor Hugo would write in *Les Contemplations*:

Olympus slowly turns into Calvary;
martyrdom is written everywhere;
a huge cross lies in our deep night;
and we see bleeding in the four corners of the world
the four nails of the Cross.

15

Velintón, aka Wellington, nearly annihilated Marshal Marmont at the battle of Arapiles near Salamanca. It didn't end the war, but no longer could there be much doubt. Very soon the coup de grâce would be delivered at Vitoria, and Beethoven from a safe distance would compose *Wellington's Victory.*

This engagement interests history buffs who don't care about logistics or military maneuvering but who are fascinated by human behavior. Joseph had accompanied his troops, no doubt to inspire them, but abruptly quit the field, leaving behind a good many intimate possessions including his silver pot de chambre. Silver, mind you. The Tenth Hussars captured it. And ever since, the story goes, Joseph's pot has been used as a champagne cup.

The Vitoria debacle occurred June 21, 1813. Joseph must have been uncommonly lonesome because, with the Iron Duke baying at his heels, he consoled himself in the fragrant embrace of the Señora de Montehermoso. We hear nothing further of the Countess of Jaruco, nor of Madame Nancy Derrieux. Anyway, had Joseph thought more about military business and less about the Señora he would have learned that Wellington's force outnumbered him eighty thousand to sixty-five thousand. This is not prohibitive. Clever generals throughout the centuries have beaten those odds. All the same, Joseph neglected his homework. So confident was he that he ordered grandstands built in Vitoria to accommodate spectators.

Wellington's men very nearly bagged him. Joseph had literally to hop out one side of his carriage while the Tenth Hussars—pistols blazing— charged the other side. It sounds like a low-budget film.

However implausible this may seem, Joseph escaped those pistol-packing Hussars and got to France. Napoleon was enraged. The Spanish campaign had turned to ashes. He gave orders that if Joseph showed up in Paris he should be arrested. Joseph wasn't alarmed, presumably because he understood his brother; he arrived perfectly cognito, he chose to attend a theatrical performance, and he visited who else but La Señora de Montehermoso now conveniently resident in Paris.

When the curtain rises on the next act we find Joseph costumed as a lieutenant general, charged by Napoleon to defend Paris at all costs.

March 31, 1814. France surrendered. Two weeks later Joseph fled to Switzerland. Well, it had been an exciting life. We might expect him to enjoy the golden years admiring alpine meadows. No. He returned to Paris when Napoleon escaped from Elba and more or less governed the country until Waterloo. He then purchased a brig with the idea of smuggling his brother to the Americas. Napoleon huffily rejected this plan, choosing exile on St. Helena to such undignified behavior.

August, 1815. Joseph popped up in New York under a nom de disguise, Count of Survilliers, perhaps still marveling at his narrow escape from the Hussars. He was recognized on Broadway by a former guardsman who blurted: "Your Majesty!" New Yorkers probably paid little attention, assuming that if Joseph and the guardsman weren't crackpots they must be shills for a play.

He attempted to see President Madison. The President was otherwise engaged.

He bought a town house in Philadelphia and some choice real estate at

Point Breeze in Bordentown, New Jersey. According to Berganini, Point Breeze on the Delaware was his particular delight. He brought his belongings from Europe—paintings, library, and furniture. The locals were pleased with their aristocratic neighbor who spent quite a lot on roads, bridges, and community projects. He invited neighbors to evening entertainments, shocking American ladies who never had seen a ballet. And, as usual, devoted himself to bedroom business, producing an undetermined number of illegitimate children. "He also kept in readiness a barge with sixteen rowers to convey friends from Philadelphia."

He corresponded with his brother on St. Helena. And the ex-Emperor said: "If I were in his place, I would make myself a great empire of all Spanish America, but you will see that he will become a bourgeois American and spend his fortune making gardens."

1841. He moved to Italy, joining his wife after a separation of twenty-six years. They lived together until his death three years later. Now he rests in the Invalides, very close to his brother.

The Paris *Herald Tribune* reported in 1963 that the legal status of some property Joseph owned in Bordentown had not been decided. If no descendant could be found to claim it, the land would go to a cranberry company, Ocean Spray.

Now, following intermission, we return to the Vitoria battlefield where Joseph eludes the aggressive Hussars.

Wellington's men discovered some two hundred paintings he had been exporting—stripped from Spanish convents, palaces, public buildings, churches. Titian, Velázquez, Murillo, and Correggio, among others. All were handsomely represented. Scholars think Joseph may have developed a taste for art while sacking Madrid. Later in Switzerland and still later in the United States he acquired paintings legally.

Wellington showed Joseph's collection to the president of the Royal Academy in London who exclaimed that Correggio's work and that of Giulio Romano ought to be framed with diamonds. The Academy president may have seen Goya's *Marquesa de Santa Cruz*; if so, he ignored it. Wellington seized these paintings in accordance with the rules of war, however paradoxical that may sound, though he felt uneasy. After all, they belonged to Spain and Spain was England's friend. He decided to ship them to Madrid. Ferdinand for reasons imperfectly explained told him to keep them.

Goya met Wellington the night of his triumphal entry into Madrid and did a pencil sketch. The Iron Duke was tired, his eyes large. Even his mouth suggests fatigue. A biographer of Wellington wrote that the exhausted victor looked like a drowning man restored unexpectedly to the surface, unshaven, hollow-eyed, damp hair stuck to his forehead, rather shaken by the spent bullet that had bruised his thigh.

Somewhat later Goya did a half-length portrait where he is considerably less frazzled. One critic thinks it a good likeness, nothing more, perhaps because artist and subject felt no emotional contact. Another sees a disdainful conqueror. Another sees a face cut from wood, a virile man with sensuous nostrils, expressionless, a man of prodigious self-mastery. The artist and the general nearly got into a fight over this portrait. Goya snatched some pistols from a table after Wellington criticized it. Goya broke a vase over Wellington's head. Goya threw a plaster cast at him, or maybe grabbed a sword, intending to cut out the Duke's heart. Something occurred. Wellington didn't like painters and tried to avoid them; he was an exact domineering man who thought artists should be meticulous about detail. On one occasion he felt so annoyed by the way Sir Thomas Lawrence painted a saber that he ordered the artist to try again. As for Goya, he had been around such men often enough that fits of temper didn't impress him and if he was threatened by Wellington he might indeed have retaliated.

Why should Wellington be upset by the picture? Myself, I see a handsome, decisive man, obviously intelligent. He appears to be a man who won't tolerate fools, which is a very fine trait. He could be difficult, yes, anybody can see that, but if there's trouble in the bushes you want this man on your side.

No matter what happened in the studio, when he left Madrid for a tour of northern Spain he took the canvas along. The paint hadn't dried and the frame is said to have been too small, which doesn't make sense. But then, a stupid or drunken carpenter made the Duchess of Alba's coffin too short. Anyway, the picture was damaged. Wellington sent it back.

Fix it. Also, the Iron Duke had received some additional medals which he thought Goya should paint on his jacket. Goya added a medal here, a medal there. Wellington wasn't satisfied. Goya later did an ink wash of the Iron Duke as a sparsely feathered peacock.

Although he no longer needed to count the change in his pocket he would sometimes use an old canvas for a new picture. Frugality is a persistent habit. He painted Wellington on horseback. A very large painting it is, almost ten feet high, and his approach seems more French than Spanish. During the twentieth century when it was X-rayed what do we see behind Wellington but the head of a Frenchman, possibly Joseph Bonaparte.

Despite the Iron Duke's vanity, despite a reputation as an insatiable lecher, despite this or that, his leadership forced Napoleon's troops back toward the Pyrenees. Spaniards anticipated a new day. The monarchy would return. Not Charles and María Luisa who were someplace in France; their son Ferdinand would wear the crown. Most people thought Ferdinand would be a splendid king.

After that squalid affair at Bayonne the royal couple and Godoy had been dispatched to Compiègne. However, Charles didn't like the northern climate, he suffered from gout, and he was bored. Napoleon let them migrate to Provence.

October 18, 1809. Charles, María Luisa, and their Prime Minister entered Marseilles in a gilded coach drawn by six white mules, accompanied by footmen dressed in scarlet and gold. At table they were served by kneeling lackeys and otherwise enjoyed the obeisance they felt they deserved. Napoleon gave Charles permission to go hunting in the forest near Mazargues. It was almost like the good old days. Charles, neither stingy nor unkind, would visit the poor and distribute what they wanted. Late in the afternoon, following siesta, he played cards or took a violin lesson. Godoy, less popular, might be greeted with hisses if he wandered about the city.

After a while Napoleon cut their allowance from 500,000 to 200,000 francs. A number of servants were dismissed. María Luisa sold some jewels.

Anon, they asked if they could move from Marseilles to Rome. Joseph interceded on their behalf and Napoleon said all right. They were lodged in the Palazzo Borghese, then the Palazzo Barberini. Charles enjoyed his card games and played his violin with court musicians. According to the *Mémoires* of a certain M. de Beausset, he once attempted Boccherini's famous quintet but gave up and returned to María Luisa and Godoy, the violin tucked under his arm, wiping his forehead with a red cotton handkerchief. "They can't follow me," he said. "Ah, if only I had my cellist Dupont. But these Romans can't manage it."

M. de Beausset reported that a French aristocrat came visiting and María Luisa asked whether he had seen Godoy wearing fine clothes. No, Madame, he replied, only the black suit he now wears. The uniforms were brought out and Godoy dressed up as Prime Minister.

"Walk back and forth, Manuel," said the Queen.

Godoy paraded around the room.

"Qu'il est beau!" exclaimed the Queen.

"Qu'il est beau!" said the King.

"Mon Dieu, qu'il est beau!" cried the attendants.

Godoy became Generalissimo, Grand Admiral, Captain-General, "and no one could tell which enjoyed it all most, the King, the Queen, or the Prince himself."

María Luisa began to disintegrate. On October 22, 1817, she wrote that the rain never stopped. "I live in utmost solitude. I am old, my nerves torment me, and I see that my days are to be very short." A week later: "It is so lonely, so silent, so cold. . . ."

She died of pneumonia on January 2, 1819. Godoy was at her bedside. Charles had gone to visit his brother, the King of Naples.

Four days later María Luisa's coffin, under a mantle of scarlet velvet bordered with ermine, attended by twenty-one cardinals, was placed in the Sacristy of Santa María Maggiore. By authority of the Pope it was then placed in the crypt of St. Peter's, awaiting translation to the Escorial.

Charles had planned to leave Naples on January 14 but he collapsed. He sent word to his brother, who was out shooting. Villa-Urrutia's biography of María Luisa states that when the King of Naples got this message he said: "I think these reports are exaggerated. Let's shoot first, and then we'll see." At this point another messenger arrived with news that Charles was dying. "My brother will die or he will get better," said the King of Naples. "In the first case, what can it matter to him whether or not I have amused myself shooting, and in the second, he, who is such a good shot himself, will be delighted to see me coming back with a big bag to celebrate his convalescence." Two more days the hunt continued; only then did he stop to catch up on the news. Charles was dead. Well, nothing could be done about it. The King of Naples continued hunting.

Charles is not credited by historians with much intelligence. Even his father called him an ass, publicly. But as somebody pointed out, he might have been smart enough to recognize his mediocrity and seeing no help for it resigned himself to dabbling at this or that, playing cards, wrestling with stable hands, shooting sparrows, loitering in the palace carpentry shop.

What bitterness he and María Luisa felt toward their renegade son didn't soften. If so, not much. Ferdinand must have felt just as angry because he refused to honor the stipulations of their wills and demanded that whatever they owned be returned to Spain.

After the Bayonne debacle he and his young brother and their moronic uncle, Don Antonio Pascual, spent six years in Talleyrand's chateau at Valençay. They strolled through the garden, played billiards, and Ferdinand helped his uncle embroider a robe for a statue of the Virgin in a local shrine. The chateau had an excellent library. Talleyrand was disgusted that the Spaniards didn't read. Don Antonio sometimes would turn the pages of a book looking for offensive pictures; if he found anything unpleasant he would tear it out or mutilate it. Ferdinand came upon some books by Rousseau and Voltaire which he burned, almost setting the library on fire. All three spent hours at prayer.

During the war a liberal Cortes, Parliament, had functioned in Cádiz. This government-in-exile drew up a constitution: 384 articles based not upon monarchic privilege but national sovereignty. It standardized taxes, abolished the Inquisition, established a unicameral legislature, and otherwise looked to France and America for guidance.

As for Napoleon, things hadn't gone so well, what with Joseph driven out of Spain. It might be helpful to ingratiate himself with Spaniards, let Ferdinand wear the crown. He dispatched a gracious letter to Valençay, addressing his royal prisoner as My Cousin:

> The circumstances in which my Empire and my politics find themselves at present awaken in me the desire at once to finish with the affairs of Spain. England is fomenting in anarchy and jacobinism . . . I therefore desire to give no opportunities to the English influence, but to reestablish the bonds of friendship and neighborliness. . . .

March 22, 1814. Ferdinand reached Cataluña, but instead of going directly to Madrid he went to Valencia for a meeting with conservatives. Just before he got there—fifteen miles up the road—he met his cousin, Cardinal Luis de Bourbon, head of the Council of Regency. Luis had traveled fifteen miles to welcome Ferdinand, to impress upon him the fact that times had changed. Now there was a document safeguarding ordinary citizens from imperial caprice.

Ferdinand ordered his coach to stop. He stepped down and waited in the road. Cardinal Luis therefore was obliged to stop, get out of his coach, and walk forward to greet the King. Ferdinand lifted one hand so the Cardinal might kiss it. Luis tried to press the King's hand down. Ferdinand turned white with rage. He extended his arm full length and said: "Kiss!" or "Kiss it!"

Luis obeyed. Those who accompanied the Cardinal must have known immediately what Spanish citizens should expect.

In Valencia the King received a welcoming address, signed by sixty-nine conservative members of the Madrid government.

En route to Madrid he met no hostility, quite the opposite. Spaniards could read the writing on the wall. Most towns along the way had a central Plaza de la Constitución which abruptly became Plaza Mayor while people shouted "Death to Liberty! Long live Fernando!"

Madrid prepared to greet the King, although with mistrust; like most cities, Madrid tended to be liberal. The governing Cortes had been in session on May 10, making final arrangements. The members then retired to their homes. Late that night every known liberal was arrested. Members of government, poets, intellectuals, journalists, nobles, attorneys, actors, artists, high and low, rich and poor, all were jailed.

May 12, 1814. A royal proclamation in the *Gaceta de Madrid* stated that anyone who spoke or acted in support of the Constitution would be executed. Ferdinand entered the city one day after this decree was published.

He meant to put things right toute de suite. He restored the Holy Office and otherwise let it be understood who was in charge. Spaniards had brought him back in a frenzy of patriotism, some of it feigned, much of it genuine, hoping and half believing that he would reign wisely, judiciously. Instead, as Hume wrote: "Chains, exile, and death to those who had fought hardest, and struggled most, to shake off the yoke of the foreigner."

Ferdinand guessed or suspected—advisors may have told him—that resurrecting the Inquisition might cause trouble. Conservatives would approve, while fear of torture and death would silence liberals; but progressive ideas were seeping through Madrid and beginning to affect the provinces. His decree pointed out that because of the Holy Office, Spain had not been contaminated by errors that created such turmoil in other countries.

That may be true. One usually can make such an argument. I lived in Barcelona a few years after the Spanish civil war and Barcelona was very much in order. Franco's Guardia Civil patrolled the streets wearing ludicrous black patent leather hats and carrying tommy guns. Some of those men probably grew up in Cataluña, others came from nearby provinces, and they seemed decent enough. They didn't swagger, they didn't threaten anybody, but they were visible. Once I rode the night train to San Sebastián with five or six members of the Guardia Civil. They were playing cards under a feeble yellow light bulb and drinking wine from a leather bag. The murderous guns were stacked rather nonchalantly on a vacant seat. There were some empty wine bottles on the floor of the coach and when the train creaked around a mountain curve they would go rolling back and forth. The men drank and played cards with the remarkable dignity innate to Spaniards. One of them offered me a drink from the bota and they laughed because I couldn't squirt a stream of wine into my mouth as they did, but the laughter was affectionate.

I remember the language school in Barcelona: a labyrinth of glass cubicles, one student and one teacher in each cubicle. After I had been attending school for several weeks my teacher wrote something on the blackboard as he often did, but rather than step aside to let me see how a verb should be conjugated he looked around. He then stepped aside just long enough for me to see a number which he quickly erased. I've forgotten the exact number but it was over 100,000. He said that was how many people Franco executed when Barcelona fell in January of 1939.

I lived in a pensión, a boarding house, on the top floor of a clammy stone building just off Vía Layetana. It was always cold, even at noon, smelling of damp clothes, mildew, and vinegar. From the balcony I could look across hundreds of cubistic rooftops and hear traffic horns far below and watch flocks of pigeons rising and descending in immense spirals. Two women, both named Conchita, served meals in a funereal dining room. I stayed for about six months. When I told the owner that I must leave because I wanted to visit North Africa he said he regretted that I must go. By this time, of course, everybody knew I was an American tourist. As I left the boarding house one of the Conchitas handed me a little gray folder. On the outside was a reproduction of St. George spearing the dragon. It opened up to show a map of Cataluña with a message printed in English. Several words had been misspelled. Had I been French or Italian it would have been printed in that language. This was the unpunctuated message:

> With the best wishes for all the friends of the Catalan-speaking countries once free in the past they will be free and whole again thanks to the will and strength of the Catalan people.

The Conchita who gave me that resistance folder twelve or thirteen years after the end of the civil war told me she would be killed if I told anybody where I got it.

A week or so later in Algiers I chatted with a Spanish waiter. He had fought against Franco and just managed to escape. He had been in North Africa since 1938. He told me that he had not seen his family since then and had no idea if they were alive or dead. He could not go back, he said, because the fascists would kill him.

I remember one afternoon in a Barcelona cafe talking to a Canadian who said that on a narrow street of the Gothic quarter he had been robbed. He reported this to the police and next day got his wallet back. Secret police were everywhere and just about everywhere you looked there stood the Guardia Civil with those guns. Barcelona during the early 1950s was not contaminated by error, law and order prevailed; from which you may conclude that a fascist government is best. Some people think so. It's a matter of opinion. It depends on your values. You might conclude that Ferdinand acted on behalf of Spain in the name of national security when he restored the Inquisition. The garotte, he quite rightly thought, was an effective way to stifle dissent. He announced that every heretic would have his tongue bored through with a red hot iron.

Goya did not overlook such events. Plate 79 of *Desastres* shows the fair maid of Liberty flat on her back, bosom exposed. Ghostly figures play about the corpse while monks dig her grave.

Truth has died. Murió la Verdad.

16

Malraux relates the hallucinatory experience of Count Joseph de Gobineau, known during the nineteenth century for espousing Nordic racial superiority. He was a diplomat, scholar, Orientalist, and bigot who wrote on the Italian renaissance, on various religions and philosophies, and produced a number of artistic short stories. These days he is remembered for the discredited subject nearest his heart: *Essai sur L'inégalité des races humaines*, which perhaps is not read by anybody except French doctoral candidates. En route to Persia he disembarked at the island of Malta "where golden saints have fibre on their heads instead of white hair because the sacristans grow lentils in their crowns." No more did he venture ashore than he met Harlequin strumming a guitar beneath shuttered windows. A black cat. A troupe of musketeers. The cast of an Italian play—the actors singing. Not until Count Goubineau saw confetti in the air did he understand that he had arrived on the night of carnival.

Malraux finds a similarity to those berserk revelers Goya painted in the burial of the sardine: *Entierro de la Sardina*.

This unsettling work has not yet been precisely dated. While recuperating from the illness that deafened him, according to some. Maybe a decade later. It celebrates Ash Wednesday, three days of carnival to mark the beginning of Lent. One could be what one yearned to be: Harlequin, Moor, devil, bandit, horse, witch, cat, virgin, harlot, dog. A man could wear a padded gown to become a woman with tremendous breasts; a woman could dress in male clothing and curse and spit and make obscene gestures. It ended with a procession, votaries escorting a huge papier mâché mannequin to the banks of the Manzanares for burial. Originally this offering to misty gods of the past had been a roasted pig disguised as a fish; by Goya's time, a sardine. However, mysterious transmutations occur in the alembic of the brain so Goya didn't paint a sardine but a grinning fool with lifeless eyes. Ferdinand? Napoleon? A burlesque allegory of war? In a repressive society the prudent artist resorts to symbolism.

Excepting those who see only a boisterous celebration, this macabre work makes people uncomfortable. Malraux comments that the figures are not men and women in fancy dress, they are butterflies hatched for one brief moment from a larval world, the revelation of freedom. Goya's picture therefore symbolizes not a dream fulfilled so much as a desire to be free.

You might think ironsmiths, bricklayers, stable hands, knife grinders, peasants, chambermaids, and others with little to lose would protest the heavy hand of El Deseado. Wrong. Spaniards trapped from birth at the bottom of the heap were fiercely conservative. As Klingender explains, the more these people suffered, "the more fanatical did they become in their loyalty to Church and crown, which they associated with their memories of a better life in the past." They saw in Ferdinand the restoration of Spanish values.

Goya's *Dos de Mayo* embodied the fierce independence of these people; at the same time it reiterated a Spanish belief in autonomy. Ferdinand may have sensed this. He ordered inscribed medals for widows and relatives of men killed during the revolt, medals expressing sympathy:

Fernando VII to the victims of May 2.

No contemporary account mentions Goya's two paintings. They might or might not have been exhibited. Since then, of course, they have been reproduced nobody knows how many times. They appear on postage stamps, on souvenir cards, on ceramic mugs. He probably commemorated the war with two other paintings. All four allegedly hung on a triumphal arch; but if these last two ever existed they have been lost.

Delacroix borrowed the spirit of *Dos de Mayo* for his allegory celebrating the French revolution of 1830: *Liberty Leading the People*. Manet borrowed heavily from *Tres de Mayo* for his antiseptic *Execution of Emperor Maximilian* in 1867. Manet liked it so much that he repeated the arrangement on a water color sketch titled *The Barricade*.

Courbet, Daumier, and others have imitated, emulated, helped themselves to Goya one way or another.

July 8, 1814. Members of the Royal Academy welcomed King Ferdinand. Goya was present.

Joseph had decreed in 1809 that a museum should be established in Madrid. Toward that end quite a few palaces and public institutions were looted, but Wellington upset everything. As a result, paintings had been stored in various buildings. Ferdinand ordered the Academy to retrieve them and proceed with the idea of a national gallery. This had been considered for many years, long before Joseph; allusions to a national gallery have been traced back to 1650.

Mengs wrote to an author named Vargas Ponce that he hoped the numerous paintings dispersed among royal residences could be collected in the new Palacio Real: "I could then compose, to the best of my ability, a treatise for the guidance of those interested, dealing with every artist. . . ."

Ponce wrote to Goya's friend Ceán Bermúdez, who had studied to be a painter: "Some of the best canvases of Murillo would be appropriately hung in a gallery containing the pick of our paintings. In my opinion the wing which is still to be added to the new palace should be erected with this end in view."

Academicians, even those who mistrusted Ferdinand, probably felt encouraged by his evident respect for good painting.

Ferdinand, who viscerally mistrusted Goya, continued to pay his salary but asked almost nothing in return. Symmons remarks that no other patron showed such consummate generosity. What could have been percolating in Ferdinand's not very impressive mind? And our hero, the

Fuendetodos bumpkin, what was he thinking? He must very often have reflected on the years. He was old enough to think the unthinkable, a time when he would be seventy. Innumerable days, innumerable months, he had spent at the easel. Compound this investment with a suspicious King. Well, what does a prudent man do? Not only does he inspect the horizon, he watches where he puts his feet.

What Goya might not have foreseen was Inquisitorial concern about those seductive paintings of a woman on a couch. Velázquez painted Venus admiring herself in a mirror, true, but he painted her back, not her front. And she was only a myth, not a particular Spanish woman.

The Inquisition had custody of *Maja Vestida* and *Maja Desnuda*, found in 1808 among other questionable pictures belonging to Godoy. The Tribunal didn't learn of this erotica for six years, which is unexpected because we assume that maniacal censors know everything. Don Francisco de Garivay, keeper of these works, was asked to provide information about artists who devoted themselves to creating pictures "so indecent and prejudicial to the public good."

Goya and his son Javier were summoned to the bar. The artist stood accused of two extremely serious offenses: collaborating with the French, which was treason, and painting a naked woman—moral depravity.

He asked a bookseller named Antonio Bailó and the Director General of the postal service, Fernando de la Serna, to verify his patriotism. They don't sound influential but they must have been persuasive. Goya accepted the Eggplant from Joseph Bonaparte, yes, but nobody ever saw him wear it. He didn't escape to Portugal while Frenchmen governed Spain because he feared reprisals against his wife and son. This probably was true. At one time during the occupation of Madrid he traveled almost a hundred miles in the direction of Portugal before police threats caused him to turn around. How else Bailó and Serna defended his patriotism is not entirely clear, but Goya squeezed by the political charge.

Concerning moral depravity, he was asked if he had painted this naked female. If so, why? At whose request? Toward what end?

His answer, if he answered, has been lost.

The Director of Confiscations testified that a naked Spanish woman had indeed been painted by the defendant. Still, one ought to bear in mind that the artist was emulating Titian. And who would condemn the Italian genius? Would it not then be incumbent to censure Velázquez, whose *Venus and Cupid* was much admired by the Spanish Court?

This excellent logic prevailed, although during the seventeenth century the beady eyes of Inquisitors had focused sharply on the Velázquez nude, as well they might. Never has there been a more enticing female rump. Gentlemen may argue; Boucher's Mlle. O'Murphy, for example. And not all critics appreciate the Velázquez beauty. Thomas Craven dismissed it as a studio piece meant to gratify a patron, a tour de force. At any rate, Velázquez escaped the Inquisitors because King Philip liked it.

Casanova, our supreme authority on women, observed in a chapel on the Calle San Jerónimo a painting of the Madonna with the Holy Infant at her breast. He thought the painting unremarkable except for Mary's splendid bosom. It had graced the chapel for 150 years during which time so many Spaniards wanted to pray that carriages blocked the entrance and so many alms were given that the chapel fairly gleamed with gold candlesticks. During a subsequent visit, however, he found the chapel almost deserted. Why? The old chaplain had died and the new chaplain thought the painting scandalous. A recently painted kerchief hid Mary's bosom. Casanova decided to call upon the new priest. He expected to find a stupid old man but found an active, clever young man who offered him chocolate.

Why did you ruin such a beautiful painting? Casanova demanded.

The young priest answered that the Madonna's beauty was unfit to symbolize one whose aspect should purify and purge the senses instead of exciting them. The picture diverted his mind from holy things.

Who obliged you to look at it? Casanova demanded.

I did not look at it, said the priest. The Devil, that enemy of God, made me look at it despite myself.

Casanova suggested that instead of mutilating the picture he should have mutilated himself, which angered the priest. And the longer Casanova thought about this, the more he became alarmed. The priest might notify the Inquisition. He therefore went to see the Grand Inquisitor of Madrid—an ugly old man, kindly and intelligent, who laughed all the way through his story and refused to call it confession. "The chaplain is himself blameworthy and unfit for his profession," the Grand Inquisitor said, "in that he has adjudged others to be as weak as himself. Nevertheless, my dear son, it was not wise of you to go and irritate him."

Casanova met a Frenchman named Ségur who lived in Madrid, who had an unusual fountain on his property: a child urinating into a marble basin. The child might have been Cupid or any little boy except that the sculptor had given him a halo, which meant the Frenchman was mocking God. Monsieur Ségur had just emerged from three years in prison.

Hugh Stokes reported in 1914 that he saw on Tadda's fountain in the courtyard of the Palazzo Vecchio a singing child clasping a dolphin to his breast, "no less heavenly because so frankly pagan. He has no brother in Spain, where every Holy Child has the shadow of the Cross above his brow."

Sencourt's history of the Spanish Crown appeared in 1932 and at times he wrote with the airy romanticism of an Edwardian landscape painter; but again he wrote with elegance, solidity, and perception. Here is Sencourt on religion in Goya's day:

> The Spaniards as a people were more profoundly and uncompromisingly Catholic than any other nation on earth. They believed with firm and simple faith that the voice of the Church was the voice of sacred truth, and that in obedience to her counsels, and by acceptation of her mysteries, they would rise from out of the world of nature to a celestial realm of divine powers and presences, the realm of grace, which was a direct participation in the life which was the light of men. Nothing compromised their faith that in the Host which they saw the priest consecrate at the Altar, the Lord of Heaven was with them till the end of the world. . . .

During Goya's lifetime the Church wasn't what it used to be, although Charles IV expanded its authority to prevent French heresies from contaminating the peninsula. According to some historians, Spain might not have been as dangerous for intellectuals as other countries in Europe. That peripatetic English diarist John Evelyn, for example, wrote that he felt more threatened in Milan than anywhere in Spain.

Those who hoped to reform the Church sometimes repeated unverifiable stories and manufactured statistics, although it could be argued that their intentions were good. A sixteenth-century Tribunal gliding from the sepulcher would terrify anybody.

What disturbed Spaniards as much as liberal philosophy was nakedness, female nakedness. Charles III in 1762 had almost burned various fleshy paintings in the royal collection: five Titians, three by Rubens, including *Diana At Her Bath* and *Rape of the Sabines,* one by Veronese, one by Guido Reni, at least one Dürer, and the work of many lesser artists. This is surprising because he loved pictures. He is known to have bought collections from the Marquis of Ensenada, the Marquis of Los Llanos, the Duchess of Arco, and a certain Don Juan Kelly. The Ensenada collection, particularly impressive, included work by Velázquez, Rembrandt, Tintoretto, Cano, and Murillo. Mengs, however unimaginative as an artist, realized that something must be done to stop this auto de fé; he got the seductive ladies transferred to his studio, although we don't know how he pacified or diverted Charles.

We should note that Charles kept in his bedroom a clothed Venus exhibiting a moderate amount of flesh, not much, which tells us how deprived he felt, how deeply he missed his Queen, María Amalia, who died a few months after leaving Naples to join him in Madrid. His confessor, Fray Joaquín de Eleta, was known as an irreconcilable fanatic, which might explain that urge to eliminate paintings of beautiful women. Or we might look to Charles himself. Years earlier when he was King of Naples an old Roman statuette of a satyr copulating with a goat disturbed him. Although he might have drowned the ecstatic couple in the Tyrrhenian Sea he couldn't bring himself to do that. Why not?

Three decades later his son resolved to burn the pictures Mengs had rescued. Tomlinson comments with a trace of levity that the incendiary passion must have been inherited.

This time, the Marquis of Santa Cruz risked his neck. The Marquis was Lord High Chamberlain and official adviser to the Royal Academy of Fine Art. He obtained a reprieve on condition that the women be sequestered in the Academy. Authorization was required to look at them. There they sat in cold storage from 1792 until 1827.

Lady Holland saw a collection of nudes, presumably these.

August 2, 1803: "Went with M. de Lambert to the Cabinet of Natural History and to the Academia de las 3 nobles artes. . . . By favor we were admitted into the forbidden apartment into which the pious monarch has banished all naked pictures; indeed an order was given for their destruction, but upon a promise being made that the eyes of the public should not be shocked by such sights, they were spared."

April, 1815. Five months after being alerted to Goya's scandalous woman the Inquisitorial purification committee declared him innocent. Those must have been frightening months. Just what exonerated him is not known; probably his commemoration of the revolt had something to do with it. And he may have had sympathizers on the committee. He squeezed through their fingers, not by much. Ferdinand said to him at one point: "You deserve to be garotted, but you are a great artist so we will pardon you."

He continued painting—religious scenes for the Queen's apartments, one thing or another—with little enthusiasm. He probably felt ambiguous toward Ferdinand who treated him well enough but whose policies he despised.

Francis Galton in *Hereditary Genius* devotes a chapter to what he calls "influences affecting the natural ability of nations." The Church, he says, having captured those with gentle natures and condemned them to celibacy, made another sweep of her huge nets "to catch those who were the most fearless, truth-seeking, and intelligent in their modes of thought, and therefore the most suitable parents of a high civilization, and put a strong check, if not a direct stop to their progeny. Those she reserved on these occasions to breed the generations of the future were the servile, the indifferent, and again the stupid." He goes on to say that Spain emptied itself of intellectuals at the rate of one thousand annually between 1471 and 1781. During that period, on average, 100 were executed and 900 imprisoned each year. Altogether: 32,000 burnt, 17,000 burnt in effigy, 291,000 condemned to imprisonment or otherwise punished. "It is impossible that any nation could stand a policy like this without paying a heavy penalty in deterioration of its breed."

17

Josefa died in 1812, three years before Goya's trial, otherwise the Holy Office would have interrogated her.

He was now living with Leocadia Zorilla-Weiss, a cousin of his daughter-in-law. How he met Leocadia is a matter of scholarly dispute, perhaps at Javier's wedding, maybe while strolling along the boulevard eating chestnuts. She had married a German watchmaker, Isidro Weiss, and they had two sons but the marriage broke up. It's said that he charged Leocadia with unseemly behavior. She was four decades younger than Goya, opinionated, intelligent, and talkative, unlike the placid Josefa who doesn't seem to have thought about anything more intricate than her wardrobe. Leocadia's quick tongue would have meant nothing to Goya because he was deaf as a tree stump. She kept house for him. Almost certainly she did more than dust shelves and cook paella. She had a daughter, María del Rosario, born October 2, 1814, quite a while after her separation from Isidro. According to baptismal records the child's father was Isidro Weiss. Goya was extremely fond of little Rosarito.

Charles IV celebrated his accession to the throne in 1789 with an afternoon of bullfights. Six years later he abolished the sport, ritual, drama, whatever it should be called. No more strutting toreros, no brassy corridas. However, Spaniards have been addicted to bullfighting since time began, which Joseph Bonaparte understood, and what better way to ingratiate himself—not only with Madrileños but with Spaniards throughout the peninsula—than to reinstate the bullfight?

Just when Goya began the *Tauromaquia* sequence isn't known. The first etchings were sold in 1816. They quickly became popular, adding a good many reales to his bank account, so he bought a villa for himself and Leocadia just outside the city, a box-like two-story building with a tile roof and a marble fountain in front.

During this period he got an important commission from the Seville cathedral worth 23,000 reales. His friend Ceán Bermúdez probably recommended him. Bermúdez was an art historian and occasional government functionary whose insatiable passion, as he himself put it, was art. Neoclassic principles seemed to Bermúdez the summit of artistic expression. Like Mengs, he had watery praise for Rembrandt. Talented, yes, but an artist who failed to appreciate the high beauty of antiquity. El Greco? Knowledgeable, masterful, but El Greco didn't pay close attention to Nature.

While considering the work of his friend Goya, Bermúdez balanced on one foot, then the other. A painting or an etching ought to be carefully planned, yet all too often like a fighting bull Goya lowered his head and charged. Brushes were invented for the art of painting; one shouldn't attack the canvas with thumbs, fingers, a spoon, whatever was convenient.

Having observed Goya paint with his fingers and the point of a knife, Bermúdez rebuked him: "I told him quite frankly . . . "

In a letter to Tomás de Verí, dated September 27, 1817, Bermúdez sounds apprehensive. He wrote that he was trying to instill in Goya "the requisite decorum, humility and devotion" appropriate to a large painting that the cathedral wanted. The subject would be two holy martyrs: Justa and Rufina. Bermúdez goes on to say that the tender postures and virtuous expressions of the saints should move people to worship them and pray for them. You know Goya, he continues, so you will understand the difficulty: "I gave him written instructions on how to paint the picture. . . ." He admitted that Goya had done what every artist who wishes to avoid the fatal mistake of anachronism must do: "He read accounts of the martyrdom of the two sisters. . . ."

Goya probably said something in a loud voice after getting those written instructions on how to paint.

Justa and Rufina were patron saints of Seville. According to legend, in 1504 they supported the cathedral belfry during an earthquake. Zurburán had painted St. Rufina in 1630 or thereabouts holding a couple of decorative water jars, one hand extended in a supplicatory gesture as though arguing that the earthquake isn't her fault. Murillo painted both saints in 1665. They have picked up the tower, which wasn't difficult because it's about half their size. Justa holds a palm branch, emblem of martyrdom. She looks bored. Rufina gazes upward with a melancholy expression. At their feet a selection of crockery because they were daughters of a potter.

On July 19, A.D. 303, two Christian women of Seville were martyred. They had refused to sell pottery during the festival of Adonis. This angered the pagans who smashed the merchandise. The women retaliated by kicking over images of Salabona and Venus. The Governor therefore had them stretched on a rack and torn apart with hooks, their agony perfumed by an incense-burning idol. One heretic died on the rack, the other was strangled. Or they might have been condemned to the strange torture of climbing a mountain barefoot. In any event, the names Justa and Rufina have come to represent these Christian martyrs—although Justa was at first called Justus. What further distortion of fourth-century fact contributed to the miraculous appearance of Justa and Rufina in 1504 has yet to be learned.

Goya visited the cathedral three times to measure the space. He seems to have felt intimidated because Zurburán and Murillo had been there first, which doesn't sound like the man we know.

Bermúdez in a letter to Verí praised Goya's interpretation, saying that the Chapter, indeed the entire city, had gone mad with joy "at having the best picture to be painted in Europe so far this century."

Not quite true. The picture evidently troubled the officiating priest, though we don't know why. The Count of Viñaza dismissed it as secular and profane. Goya imagined a couchant lion described by one critic as a Newfoundlander in disguise gently licking the toes of St. Rufina. Another thought the saints looked like buxom majas and a good many Sevillanos probably agreed because they knew all about his blasphemous remarks and disgusting behavior. He used prostitutes to model for religious paintings. He declared that he would cause the faithful to worship vice. And before seducing a woman in his studio he would drape a cloth over a statue of La Virgen del Pilar. Goya? Eh!

J. D. Passavant, a nineteenth-century art historian and painter of forgettable pictures, had no more doubts than Bermúdez about the right way to paint and the wrong way to paint. Meticulous draughtsmanship, lofty sentiment, these things mattered. Goya? Decadent. Not only was his style insipid, lacking character, he treated holy subjects irreverently. "It is very sad to contemplate artistic taste in Spain. . . ."

Beruete y Moret thought Goya's saints uninspired, feckless. So the drumbeat continued. But if drawing and painting is what you must do, well, after attending to your wounds you keep going.

Next came *Disparates* or *Proverbios.* Blunders. Follies. Nonsense. Epigrams. Like the disasters of war they weren't published during Goya's lifetime; the copper plates were packed in a box and lay undisturbed for at least a decade. Scholars detect literary allusions in the *Disparates.* One plate suggests that he studied *Gulliver's Travels.*

About this time, 1817/18, he decided to buy a new house. A very nice place it was, a brick and adobe villa, adjacent garden, another garden in the courtyard, and five white poplars beside a stream, just beyond the Segovia bridge. Twenty-three acres with an orchard. According to the deed: ". . . on the site where the Hermitage of the Guardian Angel formerly stood." The house of his nearest neighbor was known as La Quinta del Sordo because the owner, or previous owner, had been deaf, an odd coincidence. Gradually, over the years, Goya's house acquired that name. He was familiar with the place; La Quinta has been identified in one of his 1812 paintings.

On the walls he painted some of the most bizarre and repulsive pictures ever done with a brush. Rossetti was born the year Goya died but they could be a millennium apart. Rossetti, Alma-Tadema, Millais, Watts, John Roddam Stanhope—this sugary pre-Raphaelite world saw nothing ugly. Goya with his bucolic tapestry cartoons and pious illustrations for church alcoves started out like that.

Jean-François Guillou thinks the grotesque forms arising from the netherworld of Heironymus Bosch had their antecedents in medieval illuminations and carried a moral lesson. Bosch relied upon a bestiary shared by the people, transmuting it in the crucible of his mind until it emerged as more than collective reproduction. Goya three centuries later, not much affected by medieval thought, brought forth a series of pictures no less grotesque, no less moral. Bosch, Grünewald, Breughel, and their sixteenth-century associates if confronted by Goya's universe would have nodded wisely.

What he left on the walls of his villa are the so-called Black Paintings. Upstairs and downstairs he worked on them until 1823 and he made a technical mistake that all but guaranteed disintegration. He applied oil paint to plaster. Whatever drawing he did with chalk made things worse because oil and chalk don't mix.

Half a century later Baron Frédéric-Emil d'Erlanger bought La Quinta from a certain Luis Rodolfe Coumont who had bought the place in 1868. Erlanger was a wealthy French banker of German descent. He recognized the value of these murals and had them photographed. He also had them transferred from the walls to canvas by a process called "double transfer," which wasn't entirely successful. The walls had been deteriorating because water seeped through the adobe brick, so Baron Erlanger hired a young artist named Martínez Cubells to touch up Goya's work. Cubells had a reputation for imaginative restoration and his brothers may have helped. In other words, the umber and indigo and purplish black that we see might not have been what Goya painted.

In January of 1878 the result was shown at the Madrid Fine Arts Exhibition. A critic, Juan Riaño, described this Goya-Cubells pastiche as a series of sketches that had existed in the artist's house, "clever, but certainly among the most disagreeable specimens of his style."

Later that year they were shown at the Exposition Universelle in Paris. They were not displayed with other paintings but next to some bedspreads in a corridor leading to the Scandinavian ethnological exhibit. Few people stopped to look, nor were they formally acknowledged in the catalogue. Among those who did stop to look was an artist and author of some repute in those days, Philip Gilbert Hamerton. These pictures, according to Mr. Hamerton, were "the vilest abortions that ever came from the brain of a sinner . . . revolting." Nor is that all. The Spaniard "groveled in a hideous inferno . . . a disgusting region of horrible motives." Take that, Goya.

A more civil Englishman, Frederick Wedmore, noted that Goya did not commend himself to the ordinary Briton.

An Italian connoisseur denounced the paintings as suggestive of medieval sorceries, deviant, abnormal.

An Italian senator, Tullo Massarani, no doubt hoping to impress his constituents, recoiled from "the diseased mind of demonomaniacs."

Next we encounter three Frenchmen, which usually is instructive.

Prosper Merimée wrote to a friend: "I cannot forgive you for admiring Goya. . . . It is not so much the subjects as the technique of his paintings that disgusts me."

Baudelaire, possibly referring to himself, said Goya was an artist of the absurd who gave credible shape to the monstrous, whose apparitions were viable and harmonious.

Malraux thought Goya a brother to phantoms, the supreme interpreter of anguish: "Once his genius had hit upon the deep melody of the song of Evil it mattered little whether in the depths of the night his multitude of shades, his throng of owls and witches, returned to haunt him or not."

In 1880, Baron d'Erlanger gave the Goya-Cubells murals to the Prado.

As for La Quinta, it was demolished in the late nineteenth century to make way for a railroad siding.

Goya painted six murals downstairs, eight upstairs. A number of critics and/or psychologists are persuaded that he was out of his mind. What may be said with no argument is that how a spectator interprets this work depends upon himself. According to some, these Black Paintings are allegories of the human predicament. For instance, two Spaniards knee deep in a bog—maybe a wheat field—are pounding each other with cudgels. Cudgel-fighting used to be a sport in Salamanca. Is that what Goya had in mind? Beneath a stormy sky they beat each other to death. Are they brothers? Uccello in the fifteenth century painted a couple of horsemen battling, oblivious to an imminent flood. Goya might have seen this. Uccello was a Florentine. We know very little about Goya's Italian visit and it's no great distance from Rome to Florence.

There's a lonesome dog—nobody ever saw a lonelier dog—who could be lost in a sandstorm, possibly sinking into quicksand, bewildered by a senseless universe. Nothing but the pooch's head. What does it think? One biographer suspects there may have been a dog at La Quinta and the composition was suggested because it often sat in the yellowish light of a window. Bonnard resurrected Goya's dog for his 1910 luncheon: *The red check tablecloth.* They are by no means identical, true, but look at them side by side.

Asmodea, or *Fantastic Vision.* Two flying figures. One shouts and points at a rock resembling Gibraltar where Spanish liberals sought refuge during the worst of times. Escape? Two witches bound for the sabbat? Did Goya recall the legend of three men who appeared over Galicia on a cloud, descended to earth for a meal, and flew away? Sometimes he wove folk tales into his tapestry cartoons. Here we have two figures, not three, but like every original artist Goya stole no more than he needed.

In the dining room we have Judith getting ready to decapitate dead drunk Holofernes. She seems bemused, nostalgic, regretful. You might suppose Goya would reserve that for the kitchen, if anywhere. No. Judith will behead Holofernes in the dining room. He looks so drunk that he probably won't object. Does this represent the power of women? Might it be Leocadia decapitating ex-husband Isidro Weiss? A nineteenth-century critic wrote that Judith was a known model, Ramera Morena, perhaps a slut from some wayside inn—"one of Goya's regular models, whose name has been preserved." Not exactly. If Ramera Morena isn't capitalized the words become generic, meaning dark whore. In fact, Goya may not have used a model. If he did, nobody knows who she was.

Also in the dining room, if allegory appeals to you, the brutal nature of Mankind is exemplified by Saturn which periodically obscures its moons. Very bad luck to be born under the sign of this planet, as medieval astrologers and alchemists knew quite well. According to the *Compost of Ptholomeus:* "The children of the sayd Saturne shall be great jangeleres and chyders. . . ." We might remember from school days that Saturn fathered many sons and was terrified by a prophecy that one of them would depose him. He solved the problem by biting off their heads. In Goya's version he has swallowed the head and now, lunatic eyes bulging, munches the left arm. Francisco and Leocadia almost certainly hosted musicales and dinner parties in this room. What did Leocadia say about that bloody horror looming above her table? Did the guests comment? Did they pretend it wasn't there? Leocadia, the zarzuela is utterly divine.

Julius Meier-Graefe, high priest of art criticism in days past, looked upon the cannibalistic scene with equanimity: "As far as I am concerned his giant can devour two people at a time, but it must be in such a way that it makes my mouth water."

Wyndham Lewis: "The zest with which Saturn leans to suck his struggling offspring's blood as it spurts resembles that of a Flemish burgher stooping to a roast goose."

Not many artists have cared to illustrate this graphic moment. During the eighteenth century Saturn's lunch usually was ignored, sometimes reproduced in miniature on ivory, now and again as ornamental porcelain accompanied by a desperate attempt at humor. Rubens was one of the few artists who took it seriously. Saturn is chewing on the little boy's chest and nothing about Rubens' treatment will amuse you, from the tortured flesh to the shrieking face. According to Frederick Licht, Rubens endowed this gruesome spectacle with dignity by turning myth into drama so that we suppress our revulsion "and dwell instead on the finely observed, perfectly rendered interplay of action and expression." Now, this painting is beyond doubt the work of a great artist. However, most people who visit museums are not connoisseurs so it may be appropriate to ask what the bourgeois spectator feels or thinks. First, unsuppressed revulsion. One glance may be enough. All right, Margaret, let's go see the water lilies. Or, if he is a thoughtful merchant on vacation, he may wonder how Saturn—an ogre, yes, but no colossus—could manage to eat a child that must weigh at least twenty kilos.

Although Goya was inspired by Rubens he did more than filch the idea. Licht points out that Goya's depiction makes no allowance for anything but madness and ferocity. Here we have a bona fide image of human depravity and should your mind have a skeptical slope you might notice that although Saturn is well into his lunch, having swallowed the head and the right arm, quite a lot remains to be eaten.

Charles Yriarte, of Spanish descent, was born and raised in France. He meant to become an architect but ended up as a civil servant and sometime journalist. What he cared about most was art and he developed into a sensitive critic if not a practitioner. When he writes that the mind of Goya is unfathomably deep and extraordinarily disturbing, the phrase resonates. Then he tells us that Goya foresaw everything. Rubbish. Nigel Glendinning, whose books on Goya provide a torrent of information, says that Yriarte went to Morocco in 1859 as a journalist covering the Spanish campaign. There he met and shared a tent with the novelist Alarcón who most likely introduced him to Madrid's cultural elite. Here is Yriarte on Saturn: "He stuffs his gaping mouth with food, tears at the flesh. . . . This murderer is no god, but a fearful being with a villainous face, the piece of flesh representing the victim is ghastly. One turns away in horror. . . ." Simurghs, dragons, basilisks, mooncalfs, wiverns, ghouls, centaurs, krakens, witches, devils, ogres. What do such imaginings tell us?

Most critics facing Saturn become a trifle queasy. The subject is, one might say, distasteful. Early photographs of the wall at La Quinta show him with an erection, which suggests that Goya intended to represent not only the taker-of-life but the giver-of-life. What happened to Saturn's erection is a mystery. That creative restorer Cubells might have painted over it. Or the double-transfer process, which sounds traumatic, might have disabled it. A French artist employed by Yriarte, working from photographs, left no doubt that Saturn was excited. Untrue, according to some scholars. The painting was in bad shape, especially the lower limbs, and what has been called a penis might have been a loincloth. Another strange thing: The French copyist straightened the child's hips and legs, presenting a less feminine morsel. What was on the copyist's mind?

A door at La Quinta separated Judith from Saturn. Was that coincidental? Did it provide an entrance to the underworld?

Possibly a monster eating his child symbolizes the transition from chaos to an orderly universe. The problem is, we have no idea what Goya was thinking. He didn't say he had painted the cannibalistic Roman god and he didn't label the painting; biographers merely surmised that it must be Saturn. If so, how to explain the female legs and rump? Saturn didn't eat his daughters. Muscular shoulders imply masculinity; rounded buttocks and streaming hair suggest femininity.

Two little paintings dated 1805 feature gynandrous cannibals and may represent the end of Fathers Gabriel Lallement and Jean de Breuf, or Broboeuf, Jesuit missionaries tortured to death by Iroquois near Quebec in 1649. One reason for thinking so is a black hat on the ground near a stripped white corpse. However, Goya's cannibals don't resemble Iroquois, and if he wanted to show the murder of two priests he could have, surely would have, studied pictures of American Indians. Besides, the Iroquois weren't cannibals. Anyway, we are confronted by one of Goya's bisexual primitives holding up a severed arm and a head. The cannibal looks pleased. There he stands, legs wide apart, exhibiting an almost triangular pubic area. It brings to mind the latent, at times obvious, homosexuality in Goya's letters to Zapater.

May 24, 1780: "I cannot express enough the jubilance I have at the idea that God is permitting us to see each other . . . I am licking my fingers in advance just thinking about it."

In October of 1781 he wrote: "I like you so much and you are so attractive . . ."

February, 1784: "I fear no bodies of any sort except human bodies, and the one Goya loves most is yours."

Jacqueline Hara comments in a preface to her edition of these letters that he wanted to provoke and shock his correspondent. What do we know about Zapater? Not much. They met while attending Father Joaquín's school. Almost nothing else has been learned about this affluent, complacent, Saragossa gentleman, only what can be deduced from Goya's letters. Even the date of his birth is uncertain. Goya's portrait of him circa 1800 shows a middle-aged man who resembles George Washington around the mouth. He and Goya could have been the same age. Maybe Goya was older, implied by a form of address he uses, calling Zapater his little son, hijito. He wants to embrace his little son.

October 10, 1797. He writes just after receiving a letter that excited him. Zapater evidently lent him an earlier portrait and Goya plans to copy it: "I would never have believed that friendship would reach the peak that I am experiencing." He urges Zapater to visit, adding that he has prepared the room where they will sleep together. Still, as Hara reminds us: "There is an obvious danger of taking excerpts out of context and choosing elements that suit the purposes of a particular interpretation." During the eighteenth century it was usual for men to express friendship with declarations that would be awkward these days. Today no heterosexual man would conclude a letter as Goya did: "I am utterly yours."

Equivocation aside, this "amistad fraternal" drifts toward eroticism. Considering Goya's robust appetite for women and how many times he impregnated Josefa, it's unexpected. Zapater didn't marry, which may be suggestive yet proves nothing. Crusty heterosexual bachelors and garrulous heterosexual spinsters are common enough; or, if ambivalent, the latent hunger is buried in such a deep trench that nine psychiatrists couldn't dig it up. Also, Zapater's nephew censored quite a few letters and may have destroyed some. Goya students will interpret this as they choose. However the correspondence should be judged, solid citizens don't like these insinuating letters. Early in his career there are hints. Reva Wolf mentions that one of his tapestry designs, Winter, doesn't quite match the finished tapestry. In the cartoon a man trudges through snow wearing sandals and a skirt, which is certainly peculiar, not only because he's a man but because of the season.

Lunatics battling. Hanged criminals. Emasculated cannibals. An obscene goat preaching a sermon to fascinated rustics. A man in a skirt.

Naked bodies impaled on tree limbs like snacks for a butcher bird's pantry. Strangulation. What next? This sort of business makes John Public scowl.

Each year on May 15, before settling on the meadow to enjoy themselves, Madrileños visited the hermitage of San Isidro to drink from a fountain that miraculously appeared during the twelfth century. Isidro was a peasant whose plow had turned up a stream. Four centuries later this stream or fountain cured young Prince Philip, later King Philip II, of some dangerous illness. As a result, the peasant became a saint. Goya's house, like the hermitage, stood on the far side of the Manzanares, which meant that each year the San Isidro pilgrims approached him. In a gloomy, visionary painting they stumble toward the miraculous fountain—singing, howling, raving—led by a blind guitarist. Do they symbolize the return of El Deseado? One pilgrim with "round Italian eyes and forelock," grinning horribly, looks up at Goya in the window. Napoleon? Whoever he may be, whatever he represents, the face is smeared with madness. Could it be a parable of civilization disintegrating?

Elsewhere in this labyrinth of mirrors four hags fly over a bilious landscape; they are said to evoke the tormented people of Aeschylus or the ancient Furies. But how much did Goya know? Sixty years earlier at Father Joaquín's mausoleum of learning in Saragossa he picked up a spattering of Latin grammar and some knowledge of Virgil. What else? All we can be sure of is that he had left the visible world behind.

Mercedes Barbarossa in 1939 thought he was foretelling the future. Having written the history of an epoch, he predicted human flight: "In twenty of his canvases, he pursues the idea of flying balloons equipped with machines strongly resembling motors." Leonardo anticipated flight, as we know. So have others. Myself, I suspect our man was less mechanistic, closer in spirit to Jung.

With one possible exception it's unlikely that anyone modeled for these murals. Goya has entered the opium-drenched world of Coleridge beholding Kubla Khan. Blake closed his eyes, looked inward. Ideas uncalled for, said Beethoven, come from I know not where.

An elegant woman of Madrid, *La Manola*, belongs to the world we recognize. There are no certified portraits of Leocadia, which by itself is surprising, but she might have posed for this. Veiled, melancholy, she leans against an amorphous structure variously described as a balustraded rock or a vault. Her pose is that of the mythical tombside woman. A 1796 sketch from the Sanlúcar Album shows a woman in a similar pose leaning against something, but she appears younger than *La Manola* and she is nude. Who posed for the Sanlúcar sketch? La Alba? Did she suffuse Goya's mind years later when he painted this ghostly woman? Antonio de Brugada, who knew Goya and his housekeeper/mistress, declared that the model was Leocadia. Or could it be the actress Rita Molinas? Again we have black lace, her cheek resting on one hand. Rita Molinas observes us wearily, a bit cynically.

In 1759 when Crown Prince Charles left Naples to assume his duties as King Charles III of Spain the last thing he saw was Vesuvius lazily smoking in the distance. Herculaneum had been discovered in 1709, Pompeii in 1748, so everybody knew about Vesuvius and those buried cities. Charles himself ordered the excavation of Herculaneum and it is almost certain that Mengs, who spent a while in Italy, studied the newly exposed pavement. The stiff, academic *Parnassus*, which Goya could have seen in the Aldobranini Palace during his Italian visit, was perhaps Mengs' greatest work. Apollo with a lyre occupies center stage "like an actor-manager basking in the limelight," attendant deities all around. Mengs obviously drew upon ancient Roman mosaics for his composition. And photographs of La Quinta taken during the 1860s show decorative wallpaper quite similar to patterned walls at Pompeii. In other words, an ancient woman from the Villa of Mysteries could have been on Goya's mind when he painted *La Manola*.

His atelier of horrors has been called an attempt at self-analysis. Maybe. Or is this a projection of latter day analysts? What can't be argued is that he left more dynamic images on the walls of La Quinta than in any of his religious works. The ghoulish tableaux fascinated Wyndham Lewis who remarked that hallucinatory fumes exhaled by these paintings have inspired a wealth of academic abracadabra. In his opinion, they represented a nightmare that made Goya's earlier attempts to portray gamboling witches look like neighborhood housewives dancing.

Sánchez Cantón admitted that he wasn't fond of symbolism; he saw Goya's shocking murals as the product of berserk imagination. Greatness, yes, in the emotional depth, tormented conception, and what he called the tremendous vision of a subhuman species, but he could find no esoteric significance, still less a coherent design:

Commonplace mythological subjects—Saturn, The Fates—and Judith the well-known biblical scene, alternate with realistic ones, sometimes brutal, and sheer fantasies. The attempt to organise them into a system of transcendental thought with a preconceived plan behind them seems to me completely opposed to Goya's temperament and art. He was an artistic, not a philosophical, genius, with more feeling and imagination than ideas, and those ideas he had were neither very clear nor very deep, let alone systematic.

18

Ferdinand believed that Spaniards who had been faithful to the monarchy during the period of French occupation ought to be rewarded, traitors punished. Therefore, like a good housekeeper he decided to clean up the mess. Yellow being the Liberal color, Satanic badge of independent thought, a man wearing a yellow kerchief was apt to have his mustache shaved and be led through the city with a cowbell jangling around his neck. A woman who challenged Ferdinand by wearing a yellow ribbon might suffer the traditional punishment, tar and feathers.

Martin Hume observed in his thoughtful account that this battered country now lay subject to reactionary fever of the worst kind. At Ferdinand's right stood the military, the priesthood, and compliant citizens who never doubt a leader. During the war they had been joined by intellectuals outraged by foreign soldiers in Spain. Now the French were gone. Spain must direct itself. Thus in accord with natural law those hereditary enemies, progressives and conservatives, again staked out their positions.

Goya, a less than vociferous liberal, must have been considering various matters, not least that heap of reales in the Bank of San Carlos. He had

215

worked too long and hard to sacrifice them through some ridiculous act of defiance. He knew the Bourbon monarchs. Ferdinand might rejuvenate a moribund dynasty but the situation probably would get worse. A rank wind was blowing.

January 1, 1820. An army major, Rafael del Riego, led an uprising in the village of Las Cabezas de San Juan. He moved against Málaga and Córdoba, but his troops began to desert. With forty-five soldiers he fled to Estremadura. All seemed lost. Then, for no evident reason, one province after another approved the Constitution. Asturias. Coruña. Saragossa. Valencia. Navarre. Out went the Tribunal. Out went legal jurisdiction of the Church.

Three months after Riego's perilous move Goya swore allegiance to the Constitution at the Academy of San Fernando.

April, 1823. Here came French troops once again. But this time, with Napoleon exiled and France restored to good standing in the Holy Alliance, they came to help Ferdinand. Under the Duke of Angoulême the so-called Sons of St. Louis, aided by conservative Spanish peasants, took Cádiz in less than six months. The Holy Office therefore was able to resume its good work, sniffing out heretics, summoning, judging, condemning, proscribing such authors as Gibbon and Voltaire. Minister of Justice Francisco Calomarde ordered the execution, imprisonment, or banishment of thousands of army officers and citizens. An ecclesiastic society called The Exterminating Angel—founded by the Bishop of Osma—systematically attacked liberals.

Riego was shot or hanged. One report has him stuffed into a basket, crowned with a green liberty cap, dragged through the streets behind a donkey, and disemboweled. Another states that he was hanged and quartered as a felon in the Plaza de Cebada. He is said to have been an attractive figure, impetuously brave, erratic, conceited, enthusiastic. During the Napoleonic war he spent some time as a French prisoner and became a Freemason. According to Sencourt, he tried frantically to save himself, submitted abjectly to the Church, asked God to pardon his crimes, begged fellow citizens to pray for his soul and purge it of excess. On the scaffold he repudiated everything he had fought for.

Juan Martín, the indomitable El Empecinado, was a Castilian peasant, most famous of the irregulars who fought Napoleon. Goya painted him, robust and swarthy, wearing the tunic he almost certainly wore when he rode beside Wellington into Madrid. His valiant service on behalf of Spain had been rewarded with imprisonment until the Riego uprising set him free. Why did Ferdinand imprison a national hero? Because he was defiantly liberal.

El Empecinado understood that Ferdinand's reactionaries would be after his head. He tried to reach Portugal but was caught at the border. For ten months he was tortured by authorities at Roa, exhibited in an iron cage on market day, starved, shackled in one position, "and his prayers that he should promptly be put out of his misery only brought upon him fresh persecution." He refused to acknowledge any crime, refused to beg for mercy, refused to accept a peerage in return for abjuring the Constitution, so they hanged him—or meant to hang him. While he was being led to the scaffold a royalist officer showed him the sword he used to own, which infuriated El Empecinado. He broke loose. Popular histories credit him with grabbing the sword and killing the officer. Hume merely states that El Empecinado scattered those who held him captive, "tripped over the shroud in which he was clothed, and, fighting furiously to the last . . . was dragged by the neck until he was dead. . . ."

Ferdinand appeared, disappeared, and reappeared according to circumstances. In a scene that might have been devised by Wagner he entered Madrid on a chariot drawn by relays of young Spaniards, royalists all. Musicians played. Poets declaimed in honor of beloved Ferdinand. Citizens shouted "Death to the Constitution!"

Banishment, prison, torture, the gallows—this is what a nonconformist might expect while Ferdinand wore the crown. Certified loyalists earned titles of nobility: Marquis of Royal Appreciation, Marquis of Fidelity, Marquis of Constancy. The Duke of Angoulême, a bona fide nobleman, got so disgusted that he refused a decoration Ferdinand offered.

Goya must very often have thought about Rafael del Riego and Juan Martín as well as what he himself had witnessed. Quite a few acquaintances and friends had moved to France because it was now apparent that Ferdinand would be worse than his father.

Minister of Justice Calomarde intensified domestic surveillance, a reliable weathervane of despotism. It was illegal to possess books printed during the constitutional period. No foreign books of any sort. University students could not attend class until government inquisitors certified them untainted by liberal ideas. Soldiers in the ranks were questioned; one thoughtless word could mean the gallows. A new Minister of War, Rufino Gonzales, tightened the screws. Nobody was safe.

Goya had been cleared by the Inquisition, not by much. The government would remember. And Leocadia's son, Guillermo, had belonged to Riego's militia.

All of which brings us back to La Quinta. Recent X-rays of the paintings as they now exist in the Prado have revealed more than anybody suspected. X-rays together with stratigraphic examination have disclosed that, with one exception, what we see isn't what Goya originally painted. Riego's successful revolt liberated Spain from Bourbon tyranny; it didn't last long but that's not the point. Just about everybody, royalists excluded, felt optimistic and during this interregnum Goya started work on his murals.

Maurice and Jacqueline Guillaud note that beneath the sinister images we find another world representing an altogether different creative urge and state of mind. *La Manola* was not the melancholy veiled creature we now see leaning against a tomb; at first she was an amiable bourgeois neighbor welcoming guests, standing hospitably beside the fireplace. The pilgrimage to or from San Isidro—demented believers following a blind guitarist—Goya at first painted a triple-arched bridge spanning a river, mountains in the background. He didn't usually do that sort of thing. He must have been feeling cheerful. What about Saturn? Obscured by the cannibal was a dancing figure, arms uplifted, one foot in the air, perhaps illustrating a traditional Aragonese dance, exuberant, reminiscent of early Etruscan wall paintings. In those days, he could hope and believe. It may not be coincidence that about this time he did some religious work: *Agony in the Garden, St. Paul, St. Peter Repentant.* And the *Last Communion of St. Joseph of Calasanz,* about which one critic remarked that Goya felt "an essential and immediate need of God." Later he shared the fatalistic gloom of Flemish diabolists and the long gone muralists of declining Etruria.

One mural was not repainted. Here a goat in a friar's habit preaches to avid disciples. A young woman sits apart, wide-eyed, hands thrust into a muff for protection. With this alarmed figure he may have symbolized his last hope. Richard Schickel wrote that he lived in an era not unlike our own when citizens feel disoriented, alienated, when illusions finally have been exposed as illusions and the air seems charged by a spirit of radical change.

September, 1823. He made over the country estate to his grandson Mariano to avoid possible confiscation. This Deed of Gift listed various improvements: new drainage system, vineyards, fences, a well, a house for a resident gardener. These and other improvements naturally increased the value of La Quinta, which no doubt pleased our hero with his bright eye for money. Then, too, he enjoyed working in the garden, more often as he grew older. Three decades later his grandson would sell the house. Mariano seems finally to have understood that his grandfather was important, therefore the painted walls might be worth something. He had them appraised.

Soon after turning over La Quinta to his grandson Goya went to live with an Aragonese priest, Father José Duaso y Latre, who was a censor and editor of *La Gaceta.* In other words, a man of considerable influence who might be able to protect him. And at this time of great apprehension when any moment could bring a tapping at the door Goya painted María Martínez de Puga. Nothing in the model's face or in the structure of this portrait betrays anxiety, nothing but serenity. Goya had retreated to some inaccessible chamber of his mind.

Historians regard Ferdinand as the worst king Spain ever had, yet in 1819 he gave his blessing to the Prado. And on May I, 1824, he declared political amnesty. By this time, however, just about every Spaniard mistrusted him. The declaration might be suspended, revoked. It could be a trick. Goya saw a chance to get out. Such an idea must have tormented him because he was Spanish to the marrow, Spanish as Lorca and Picasso.

Pleading ill health he requested a six-month permit to soak his aching carcass in the waters of Plombières in the Vosges Mountains, which would mean traveling almost to the Rhine. Why Plombières? Other spas were closer. Plombières offered three types of mineral water, recommended specifically for gout, rheumatism, and paralysis. Dr. Roya Villanova in 1927 was among the first to analyze Goya's numerous complaints. Elaborating on information obtained from descendants of Dr. Arrieta—the man who saved Goya's life in 1819—Dr. Villanova concluded that he had been suffering from arteriosclerosis since 1797. The 1819 crisis probably was a result of typhoid fever. Goya also suffered from rheumatism and partial paralysis.

During the late eighteenth century Voltaire, disgusted with Frederick II, got permission to submerge his aching bones in those same mineral baths. It's been suggested that Goya knew this and was making a sardonic comment. I doubt it. I suspect the reputation of Plombières as a cure-all for aging bones was reason enough.

30 May, 1824. Success.

Our Lord the King, yielding to the request of the Painter to the Chamber Don Francisco Goya, has been pleased to accord him His Majesty's royal license to go to take the mineral waters of Plombières in France, in order to assuage his rheumatism.

Whether he traveled by diligence or on horseback has been argued. Blackburn supposes that he booked a seat on the Cataline mail coach, an awkward bright red contraption hauled by ten mules, their manes threaded with bells, bodies shaved so that they resembled giant mice—a startling image borrowed from Gautier and acknowledged. The carriage rested on a cradle of knotted rope and could accommodate a dozen passengers seated elegantly on pink satin cushions. Ahead of the diligence rode a postilion to look out for highwaymen. Drivers were armed with blunderbusses in case of attack. Gautier, who rode one of these coaches some decades after Goya, called it a saucepan hooked to the tail of a tiger.

He traveled north, crossed the Ebro and reached Bordeaux in late June, a stubborn old crank of seventy-eight. His permit must have zipped through the bureaucracy in record time because Madrid to Bordeaux was no three-day trip. Ferdinand probably wanted him out.

Refugees had to be approved by a committee of Spanish exiles. What happened if a refugee failed the examination isn't clear. Leocadia arrived ahead of him and was given the following document:

> We, the undersigned, refugee Spanish officials resident in Bordeaux, certify that Doña Leocadia Zorilla de Weiss has found herself obliged to take refuge in France, in 1823, in order to escape from persecutions and from insults of every kind which have been brought upon her by her political opinions, and by the circumstance that her son Guillermo has been a member of volunteer militia in Madrid.

Goya sailed through with no trouble. He had Spanish friends in Bordeaux and everybody knew he was a famous painter. He didn't join Leocadia as might be expected; he spent a few days with the poet-playwright Leandro Fernández de Moratín who later commented that he showed up alone, not very strong, deaf, not knowing a word of French but happy and anxious to see the world. One biographer states—probably because of Moratín—that Goya had forgotten the few words he learned "in the far-off days when he believed the language would guarantee his social reputation." Not true. He did speak some French, clumsily.

Seeing the world meant Paris. Away he went. Moratín cautioned him to return by September, otherwise the winter might finish him. Plombières? That could wait. However much his bones ached, he would see Paris.

He showed up in the fashion capital of the world wearing a huge checkered cap. Except for that square Spanish head he must have looked like a British tourist.

He stayed in a hotel at 15 Rue de Marivaux, but how he spent his days and nights is mostly speculative. He knew a liberal ex-politician named Joaquín de Ferrer and his wife, Manuela, a lawyer named González Arnao, a few others. And he had brought along his tools of the trade. Ferrer commissioned a bullfight scene, perhaps more than one. The gendarmes knew he had arrived and watched him but didn't note any subversive activities. They reported that he stayed mostly in his hotel, received no guests, sometimes visited public places and monuments. They wrongly estimated his age at seventy, correctly reported that he was extremely deaf. In their opinion he was not apt to create mischief because his French was so bad.

He may have visited museums and galleries, which would be logical, though there seems to be no proof. Gerard, Ingres, Watteau, Boucher, Greuze, and Corot were on display. Gericault's *Raft of the Medusa.* And the *Massacre of Chios* by Delacroix, heavily indebted to Goya's *Third of May.* The controversial exhibit, the main event, succès de fou or bête noir depending upon one's attitude, was the Constable show. Goya may or may not have bothered to look.

He probably had no idea of his influence. He might have been told that young artists were studying his work, particularly in France. He wouldn't live to know about Courbet, Daumier, Manet, Cezanne, or Edvard Munch in Norway. All of them recognized a singular talent. He would never know about Beckmann, Klee, Nolde, Marc, Kandinsky, and many others who studied what he had done.

Klee visited the print room of the Munich museum in 1904. He found Goya's *Proverbios, Caprichos,* and *Desastres de la Guerra* "thoroughly captivating." Somebody gave him photos of Goya paintings: "These were things I laid to good account professionally. . . ."

The Belgian novelist Joris-Karl Huysmans, disguised as a wealthy esthete in *À Rebours,* "turned to his portfolio of prints and laid out his Goyas. . . . He buried himself in them, following the painter's fantasies, totally absorbed by vertiginous scenes in which witches rode on cats, women struggled to pull out the teeth of a hanged man, and bandits, succubi, demons and dwarfs . . . "

Nigel Glendinning in a comprehensive survey points out that it was natural for elements of Goya to be reconsidered during the late nineteenth century. Freud was at work on dreams, nightmares, and the subconscious. Poets explored symbolism, implying, hinting. What had seemed irrational, therefore not worth a thought, now demanded investigation.

Glendinning catalogues a few specimens from *Incoherent Art,* an 1883 exhibit at the Galerie Vivienne in Paris:

Alphone Allais was showing a plain piece of white art paper with the title "Chlorotic Young Ladies" First Communion in Snowy Weather . . . a picture entitled Rabbit, in which a real cord emerged from a gentleman's mouth painted on the canvas, to end up round the neck of a live animal eating carrots in a cage in front of the picture; and there were paintings which substituted objects for things they resembled. Mesplès, for instance, showed a valley in which the poplars were goose feathers and the moon a piece of bread. . . .

Young ladies in a snowstorm, goose feathers, a rabbit munching carrots. Goya might have wallowed in it. He might not have cared. Mengs? The brothers Bayeu? Tiepolo? What would they have thought?

Anybody who accompanies García Lorca on his nocturnal ride through Andalusia won't be surprised that he was fascinated by Goya. Black pony, red moon, olives in my saddle-bag. La muerte me está mirando desde las torres de Córdoba. From the towers of Córdoba death looks down on me. Lorca wrote more prophetically than he knew. After a sojourn in the United States, Cuba, and South America, he returned to Spain. Fascists shot him and dumped his body in an unmarked grave.

While he was in Cuba he gave a lecture titled *Duende,* this being the tutelary god, daemon, anima, goblin, indwelling spirit. Like the problematic Stone of Alchemy, nobody can say with assurance what it is, but it made Goya "lay on terrible bitumen blacks with knee and fist. The dark spirit stripped the Catalan poet Verdaguer naked to face the ice of the Pyrenees. It drove Jorge Manrique to lie in wait for death on the desolate plains round Ocaña. It dressed the delicate body of Rimbaud in the coarse green trappings of the circus. It gave Count Lautreamont dead fishes' eyes at dawn on the boulevard." Artists translating into a private idiom the repugnance they feel.

In 1824 when Goya marched around Paris wearing that absurd checkered cap, who should be living there but the abominable Godoy. Charles and María Luisa both had died five years earlier and without them he didn't amount to much. He was nearly broke, although people thought he had smuggled a fortune out of Spain. His wife, the fragile Countess of Chinchón, now living in Toledo, hadn't spoken to him since 1808. For a long time he had wanted to marry his mistress Pepita Tudó, but a divorce was required and neither Charles nor Ferdinand would allow it. For a short time he lived on a small estate near Rome. Not much happened. Roman society ignored him. He and Pepita thought they might do better in Paris. They took rooms at 59b Boulevard Beaumarchais. Pepita tried to organize a chic salon but again not much happened. She attracted mediocrities. After a few years she left him and went back to Madrid.

Louis XVIII granted him a small allowance, perhaps because Louis remembered that Godoy once upon a time had treated French exiles kindly, or because he knew Godoy had married the Countess and shouldn't be seen as a beggar. He managed to reclaim a few of his Spanish titles, then his daughter by the Countess gave him a substantial annuity. He took a second-floor flat at 20 Rue Michaudière. So he rounded out his extravagant life writing disjointed self-serving memoirs, doing not much for thirty years, attended by two female servants.

Although he was hated by the Spanish people certain charges levied against him were distorted or blatantly false. The *Gazeta Nacional de Zaragoza* in February of 1812 declared that his corruption had pervaded all classes of society, that he was "degraded" and "vicious," that for twenty years Spain had endured his disgusting behavior, on and on. Not only did he share the Queen's bed, he shared the King's bed, a rumor now thought to have been started by French diplomats. Early in the nineteenth century Richard Ford called Godoy a beast of prey "always craving and swallowing." Napoleon didn't know quite what to think, changing his opinion more than once. At last, on St. Helena, he said: "That man was a genius."

Authors and poets meant a lot to him. Vallentin believed that this man who cared little about public opinion had the reverence of the illiterate for intellectual achievement. During his tenure as Prime Minister he was known as a patron of the arts. Poets would address verses to him; he kept them in his files. He carried the files to Paris.

He had bought quite a few paintings from Goya and through marriage to the Countess of Chinchón—daughter of the Infante—he inherited that collection. So there was a time when he could have furnished a gallery with valuable and important works. Members of the San Fernando Academy sometimes visited his palace in Madrid to study them. He was proud of his collection and of his taste, excessively perhaps; but the commissions he bestowed while Prime Minister disprove the idea that he was altogether obsessed with erotic fantasies.

During those last years in Paris he wrote about revolutionary dogma contaminating Spain, how such beliefs attracted young people from the middle class as well as certain priests and aristocrats. In Madrid one could see young men from distinguished families "impudently parading the revolutionary bonnet rouge, and ladies of the highest nobility showing themselves in public decked out with tricolore ribbons." He longed for the glorious years. Why not? There was a time when he could snap his fingers for whatever he wanted. With María Luisa's approval he had tried to establish himself as a legitimate descendant of Gothic kings, this Estremadura provincial called the Sausage Maker. And this strange outcast, detested by his own people and flogged by historians, lamented the condition of Spain where a stupid tyrant, Ferdinand, shut down universities but opened a bullfighting school in Seville.

His combined salaries in 1793 totaled more than 800,000 reales. Rental income from Crown estates brought another million. Just before he was caught hiding in a rolled-up carpet he was worth forty million reales. Nor was that the end of it; he bestowed contracts and appointments upon those gentlemen who sent the prettiest wives and daughters to plead their cases.

When the government collapsed Spain's army consisted of some fifty thousand soldiers including sixteen thousand cavalrymen with no horses. Leading the parade, of course, Generalissimo Godoy. After him, five captains-general, eighty-seven lieutenants-general, 127 field marshals, 252 brigadier generals, and on down the line. As for the navy: Grand Admiral Godoy, two admirals, twenty-nine vice-admirals, sixty-three contra-admirals . . .

So, at last, this Prince of the Peace with a heavy, sleepy, voluptuous, eye loitered day after day, year after year in the gardens of the Palais Royale. He liked to sit on a bench and watch children at play. Sometimes they asked Monsieur Manuel to referee their games. They had no idea who he was. Nor did many adult Parisians recognize the stout old gentlemen with white whiskers. Among his titles were Secretary to the Queen, General Superintendent of Roads and Postal Services, Knight of the Golden Fleece, Duke of Alcudia, Universal Minister of Spain and the Indies, President of the Botanical Garden, Count of Evoramonte, and Grand Admiral of the Fleet—the fleet that unwisely engaged Nelson at Trafalgar.

Goya might have known he was in Paris and might have known the address. Godoy could have been told that the artist was in town. Nothing indicates that they met for a glass of pernod.

Monsieur Manuel lived until 1852. He was buried at Père Lachaise. Once upon a time the Countess of Chinchón had slipped a ring on his finger. It was there when he died.

19

Goya didn't listen to many people. He listened to members of the imperial family as best he could; after all, he knew where he was and what he was. He listened to the aristocracy, or pretended to. And it appears that he listened to Moratín's cautionary advice about Parisian winters because he got back to Bordeaux ahead of the freezing rain and snow. Leocadia and her daughter Rosario joined him at 24 Cours de Tourny. Guillermo seems to have been stationed nearby at Bergerac with other Spanish militiamen and moved into the household later.

Goya's eyes by now were so bad that he hooked together three pairs of wire-framed spectacles neatly described by one historian as a tangle of long-legged insects. Nevertheless he kept working. With a lithographic pencil he turned out miniatures on ivory and marble: ducks, flying dogs, giants, weddings, bow-legged old people, majas, light-hearted fantasies, some not so light-hearted.

At a cafe on Rue de la Petite Taupe, now Rue de la Huguerie, he dawdled with other expatriates. There in majestic deafness he would sip chocolate and observe, perhaps reading lips well enough to understand what they were talking about. It's said that he dressed as usual—Bolivar hat, russet frock coat, ruffled shirt with broad cravat, monocle dangling from a ribbon. These exiles had little to fear in Bordeaux, either from the French government or the Holy Office.

Braulio Poc: proprietor of the chocolate shop, veteran of the battle for Saragossa.

Manuel Silvela: headmaster of a boarding school, at one time mayor of Madrid. He never returned to Spain.

Don Juan Bautista: Navarese banker.

José Pío de Molina: Alcalde-Major during the Bonaparte regime. He would become Goya's landlord.

Don José Miguel de Azanza: afrancesado, viceroy of Mexico under Charles IV, whose daughter was kidnapped and whose son-in-law was murdered by the guerilla chief Mina.

José de Carnerero: man of letters.

Antonio de Brugada: marine painter.

Marqués de San Adrián: aristocrat.

Spaniards all. At Braulio Poc's emporium they gathered to argue, to read newspapers, speculate, exhume the past, justify, condemn, hunt for meaning in meaningless independence.

Goya painted several of these chocolate-shop friends. Bautista, the Navarese banker who was also Count of Muguiro y Iribarren, fleshy red underlip, forehead round as an egg, reputed to be capable and decisive. Silvela, a powerful man with brutish features. An unidentified young woman who may have belonged to the Silvela family.

Moratín, dramatist whose plays were strongly influenced by Molière. His comedy about an old man and a young girl had made him famous. During the reign of Charles IV he had accepted Godoy's patronage, which included a subsidy for travel. He went to France, stopping first at Bordeaux where he attended the theater every night. After one performance he met a parade of citizens in the street who were carrying two freshly severed heads on pikes. He wrote in his journal: "Decapitation of two priests. Têtes por las calles." He had arrived during the Reign of Terror. Later in Paris he attended the Comédie Française as might be expected, and noted without comment that he had seen bleeding heads on the boulevards and watched Louis XVI being escorted to the Temple.

Moratín is said to have been good looking when he was young, with the remote air of an esthete, his agreeable features somewhat disfigured by smallpox. Now, twenty-five years after Goya first painted him, he has coarsened. He was writing a book on the origin of Spanish drama but an author must wait for inspiration so he attended plays, promenaded, inspected old prints in musty shops, enjoyed his chocolate and those bittersweet arguments, meanwhile complaining that he had no time to work. He boasted that Goya followed him everywhere, didn't leave him a free moment. He told a friend that Goya was anxious to paint him again. "I concluded that I must be very handsome, to have such skillful brushes aspire to multiply my effigies."

Gautier, passing through Bordeaux years later, noticed the Spanish influence. Bookshops carried at least as many books in Spanish as in French. Elderly refugees strutted and swaggered à la Don Quixote.

When Goya's six-month permit was about to expire he requested another so that he might take the healing waters at Bagnères in the Pyrenees, although he had not yet gotten around to Plombières. He was granted another six months, six more months to enjoy the excellent cuisine and wines of Bordeaux.

Again he fell sick and became restless. A letter by Moratín to Juan Antonio Melón, dated April 14, 1825, states that Goya decided he had a great many things to do in Madrid and should be on his way—cap, cloak, wineskin, saddlebags. He was almost eighty but he meant to ride alone through the Pyrenees "astride a dark chestnut mule." Whether his friends could have convinced him otherwise is doubtful. Then the Spanish government extended his leave of absence for a year. Ferdinand probably was sick of hearing Goya's name.

In the fall of 1825 he rented a house on Rue de la Croix-Blanche. It had the sort of light he wanted and there was a garden. Leocadia's daughter Rosario loved the garden and Goya loved the child, calling her Mariquita, his lady-bird. Apparently she was a cheerful, intelligent little girl who enjoyed games and was learning to play the piano. Moratín, whose correspondence with Melón gives the best account of Goya's life at this time, remarked that Rosario chattered in French like a skylark, parrot, or little bird, depending upon the translator, and raced around happily with neighborhood children. The old man gave her some drawing lessons.

Critics who have studied Rosario's adolescent work don't agree. One said she responded to these lessons with an aptitude she also displayed for the piano. Another said she exhibited astonishing facility, but went on to note that children often have the ability to pick out essential features and isolate decorative elements, an ability that can be mistaken for talent. Another sourly observed that Rosario's efforts never exceeded the limits of earnest mediocrity.

Goya himself lost all critical sense. Rosario, he declared, was perhaps the greatest phenomenon of her age in the world. Javier had disappointed him, which might explain why he persuaded himself that Rosario was miraculous. He neglected whatever he was doing in order to help the child. He wrote to Joaquín de Ferrer that she had great potential. Every professor in Madrid has marveled, he said—which doesn't sound likely unless they were afraid of irritating the old man. He wanted her to study in Paris. He was sending along a sample of her work. Would Ferrer be good enough to help? "I will repay you with my own works. . . ." With some of his own drawings or paintings he would reimburse Ferrer. You begin to wonder if he was senile.

Rosario later studied at the Prado and would be appointed drawing mistress to the future Queen of Spain, Princess Isabel. If she might have been more than a competent instructor will never be known. In 1840 at the age of twenty-six she was caught is a street riot. When she got home she was trembling with fright, developed a fever and soon died. Her stepfather's extravagant praise may have affected her otherwise than he hoped; she might have felt unworthy, intimidated, knowing that she—like Javier—was commonplace.

Goya worried about the condition of his estate in Madrid and wanted to talk with his son. He thought they should discuss family business. Aragonese are by repute opinionated, dogged, tough, capable of driving nails into stone with their heads, so it might be expected that he would cross the Pyrenees at the age of eighty to visit his son and to find out how he stood with King Ferdinand. Moratín at last gave up trying to dissuade him, notifying Melón that Goya would be traveling by himself and if he made it to Madrid he should be congratulated. If he doesn't get there, said Moratín, don't be surprised because the least accident might leave him stiff and dead in a corner of some rustic posada.

It took Goya a month to reach Madrid. He visited La Quinta to see the murals. He visited San Antonio de la Florida for another look at the frescoes he had done in 1798.

He sat for a portrait by Vicente López who had succeeded him as First Painter to the King. Most likely the sitting was uneventful, though popular biographies would have it otherwise. Goya leaped to his feet and demonstrated how he had fought bulls, using a brush for a sword. He stopped López before the portrait was finished, saying further touches would ruin it. He took up the palette in order to paint López but couldn't because his fingers were twisted by arthritis. Contemporary critics don't give López very high marks, although he was expressive and careful, a proficient journeyman at the very least. The truculent and stubborn old man whose features he preserved could not be mistaken for a bourgeois gentilhomme or a doddering boulevardier. Goya looks every bit as fierce and drenched in duende as Beethoven.

While in Madrid he learned that his request for a pension of 50,000 reales had been granted and that he might stay in France permanently. Ferdinand, however he felt about Goya, couldn't overlook the fact that the great artist had served his father Charles IV and his grandfather Charles III. Besides, it wouldn't cost much. Goya wasn't apt to live much longer.

In good spirits, therefore, the old curmudgeon saddled up and headed north.

His Bordeaux friends were glad to see him but his energy seems to have frayed them around the edges. He's quite well, Moratín wrote to Melón. He amuses himself by sketching, wanders about, sleeps in the afternoon.

Early in 1828 he and Leocadia and Rosario and Guillermo took a large apartment being rented by his friend Don José Pío de Molina at 39 Fosses de l'Intendance, now Cours de l'Intendance. The ground floor was occupied by a jewelry shop and a bookshop. One flight up, the landlord with his two sons. Above them, a Mexican heiress with her husband and baby. Above them, Goya & Co. with Don José Pío de Molina. Above them in the attic somebody whose name is not known.

Milkmaids on donkeys rode past the apartment every day and Goya liked to watch them. *Milkmaid of Bordeaux* might be one of them. Onieva halfway identifies her as a popular Bordeaux woman who delivered milk to the Goya household. Onieva suspected that she was riding a donkey, not visible in the picture, which would explain why the artist is looking up at the model. However, the model could have been Rosario—at that time an art student—seated on a platform. Anyway, Goya thought it was a pretty good painting; he told Leocadia not to sell it for less than an ounce of gold.

His eyes became so weak that he needed a magnifying glass but he never stopped. Carnival freaks. Performing animals. The head of an old man who might be St. Peter. A sleepwalker. Guillotine. Whatever caught his attention. There seems to be no pattern.

Once again over the Pyrenees. He painted his grandson Mariano, now twenty-one, fashionably dressed. Years later because of a fault in the canvas a dimple appeared in Mariano's cheek.

Bordeaux again. He wandered about the streets if he felt like it, enjoyed the afternoon siesta, looked forward to letters from his son. He learned that Javier and some friends were planning to visit Gibraltar, then up the Mediterranean coast and north to Paris. He urged Javier to come through Bordeaux, advised him about a certain bank, asked to be remembered to various people in Madrid, spoke of his shock at the murder of "Gallardo"—presumably the liberal poet Bartolomé Gallardo. He suggested that Javier send his wife María Gumersinda and their son Marianito to Bordeaux for a visit.

Javier replied that Gumersinda and Mariano would be there soon. He himself would arrive when affairs permitted.

On March 26, 1828, Goya wrote to Javier: "I am very impatient, awaiting my beloved travelers. . . . I am now feeling much better, and hope to be healthier than before my illness. . . ." He mentioned that his landlord, José Pío de Molina, advised drinking Baleriana, valerian, a stimulant derived from the pink or white flowers of that herb. He had suffered a stroke. He was found unconscious on the floor of his studio, brush in hand. The brush in hand makes one suspicious. It sounds like a final arabesque, one last flourish, as though the actuality of his life needed embellishment. Nevertheless he had been working. An unfinished portrait of Molina stood on the easel.

María Gumersinda and her son Mariano arrived on March 28. Goya became so excited that he collapsed.

Leocadia wrote to Moratín, who was in Paris, that on April I the family breakfasted together. The rich food troubled Goya. Next morning about dawn he awoke, unable to speak. Later that morning he could talk but his right side was paralyzed. For thirteen days he lay almost helpless, the body weakening, paralysis spreading.

Leocadia wrote to Moratín: "He would look at his hand as if stupefied. . . ." He said he wanted to make a will. His daughter-in-law told him it had been done.

April 16, 1828. A little before two in the morning he died. Four days later Javier showed up.

If he received the final sacraments has been questioned, and if he was vested for burial according to Spanish usage in the Franciscan tertiary habit. Antonio de Brugada's widow was alive in 1888. She had been present when his body was laid out. She recalled that the leather cap Goya usually wore was placed on his head and he wore a cloak, "remains of which were still there when the coffin was exhumed."

In 1811 he and Josefa had registered their joint will:

In the name of God the All-Powerful, Amen. We, Don Francisco Goya, by profession painter, and Doña Josefa Bayeu . . . Being in good health and sound in mind, judgment, memory, and understanding, as accorded us by the Divine Majesty, we firmly believe and confess the mystery of the Holy Trinity, Father, Son, three Persons and one God; likewise all mysteries and sacraments which our holy Mother the Catholic, Apostolic, and Roman Church believes . . .

He provided for Javier, who was further enriched by the Duchess of

Alba's bequest and by the fact that he held copyright to *Los Caprichos.*
Then, too, Javier got all the art work listed in the 1812 inventory; he had
marked each painting with an X to identify it as his property—Javier
being Xavier in Aragonese.

For Leocadia, not one peseta. Mistresses often are left outside but she
was no door mat. She must have known, at least suspected, that he
wouldn't leave her anything and it would be uncharacteristic of her to accept such indignity. There may have been a moralistic streak in Goya.
Maybe he disliked thinking about the will, evidence of his own mortality.
Maybe he assumed that Javier would take care of Leocadia. As he lay
dying he said he wanted to make a will; maybe at the last hour he decided
to include Leocadia. It's been suggested that his daughter-in-law, guessing
what he had in mind, deliberately confused the old man by reminding
him that the will had been made.

Javier gave Leocadia 1,000 francs and let her keep some of the furniture. That was it. She may have been a garrulous shrew, an intrusive step-
mother; he was the legal heir, yes, but he sounds insufferable. Tight-fisted,
churlish, vain. His father was about to die and he knew it, yet he loitered
in Madrid, promising to visit Bordeaux when affairs permitted—a week,
two months, six months—meanwhile hoping for news that it was over.

Leocadia wrote to Moratín that Javier had taken the silver dinner service and Goya's pistols. She asked for help. Whether Moratín replied isn't
known; he himself was sick and died a few weeks later. She appealed to
others. Pierre Lacour, who had given Rosario some drawing lessons, did
what he could. Nobody else bothered. She moved into a cheap apartment
near Braulio Poc's chocolatería. Probably in gratitude she gave Lacour her
copy of the *Caprichos* with the titles in French.

She decided to sell the milkmaid painting. Don Juan Bautista, Count
of Muguiro, had been pressing her to let go of it and wanted to know the
price. She said Goya had told her to accept no less than one ounce of
gold. The Count of Muguiro bought it, although we don't know what he
paid. Because of his affection for Goya he might have paid more than she
asked. One of his descendants bequeathed it to the Prado.

On October 14, 1831, Leocadia requested a pension from the French government. Granted: I franc, 50 centimes per diem. For reasons best understood by government bureaucrats, Leocadia's pension subsequently was canceled. A couple of years later she returned to Madrid where she lived until 1856, living among shadows and memories by chance or by choice on Disenchantment Street.

At one time she had owned a series of Goya's drawings. How or when she disposed of these isn't clear. They were auctioned in 1869, bound in red silk. The album brought less than two francs.

What about Mariano? An early historian remarked that his father, Javier, was less Goya than Bayeu, prudent, calculating, less concerned with art than with Don Dinero and the quotidian business of life. Mariano at least in temperament was all Goya, no Bayeu, his body scarred by duels he provoked. Like his father and grandfather, he enjoyed counting those reales, but he was a gambler. Bonds insured by the Bank of Spain didn't excite Mariano. He tossed the dice and at first did very well. Then the speculative investments soured. Goya once painted him in a curiously inappropriate setting, next to a sheet of music. The arts held as much appeal for Mariano as a plate of sauerkraut and his grandfather's genius meant nothing. Eventually he bought a title: Marquis of Espinar. He bought it from an obscure nobleman worse off than himself but was never able to have the rank certified. In 1868 he recalled that a certain Father Bavi had supplied a model for the famous maja paintings. This priest, said Mariano, worked among the lower classes in Madrid, comforted them when they were sick and helped them to die in the arms of Christ, for which reason he was called El Agonizante. While making the rounds of his district, El Agonizante met a voluptuous young woman and brought his protégée—that delicate euphemism—to Goya. El Agonizante subsequently was hanged for murdering the protégée. Now, after so many years, it might be difficult to disprove Mariano's horror story.

Mariano died almost unnoticed in 1874 in the village of Bustarviejo, a bankrupt ersatz marquis who thought very little of the name he inherited.

Funeral rites for Goya took place April 17 at the church of Notre Dame in Bordeaux. Poc, Brugada, and Molina among the palbearers. Goya had no burial plot because he didn't expect to die in Bordeaux.

Martín Goicoechea had been one of his oldest friends and was the father of his daughter-in-law María Gumersinda. Patron of the arts, affluent merchant from Saragossa, a man with liberal concepts, Goicoechea understood quite well what was happening in Spain under Ferdinand and decided he would be better off elsewhere. He moved to Bordeaux. There he died and was entombed in the Muguiro family vault. Three years later Goya was buried alongside Goicoechea.

Lafuente Ferrari's 1955 book on San Antonio de la Florida states that the limestone monument which had marked Goya's tomb in Bordeaux was embedded in a granite block marking his tomb in Madrid. This monument—"a sort of cylindrical cippus"—bore the following text:

HIC JACET
FRANCISCUS A GOYA ET LUCIENTES
HISPANIENSUS PERITISSIMUS PICTOR
MAGNAQUE SUI NOMINIS
CELEBRITATE NOTUS
DECURSO PROBE LUMINE VITAE
OBIIT XVI KALENDAS MAII
ANNO DOMINI
M.DCCC.XXVIII
AETATIS SUAE
LXXXV
R.I.P.

Molina registered Goya's death at the Bordeaux town hall and said that he had been eighty-five years old rather than eighty-two, which probably explains one mistake on the memorial tablet, although we should ask how Molina got it wrong. Goya at times lamented the fact that he was getting old. He might jokingly have told Molina that he was eighty-five. But he died on April 16, not May 16.

Charles Poore visited Spain twice just before the 1936–39 civil war and went on pilgrimage to Bordeaux. Even then, by his account, not much of Goya remained. He found a plaque in the Cours de l'Intendance "with a ferocious profile by Benlliure," and in the cemetery a dreadful monument he likened to a British mailbox.

Beruete y Moret, Director of the Prado in the early twentieth century, refers to this plaque as a modest tablet "placed at a fair height upon a house of the Cours de l'Intendance."

Né a Fuendetodos (Espagne)
>   Le 30 Mars 1746
>   Est Mort dans cette Maison
>   Le 16 Avril 1828

Goya and Martín Goicoechea lay side by side in the cemetery of La Grande Chartreuse for six decades. Relatives of Goicoechea may have come to visit. If anyone related to Goya stopped by we know nothing about it. Years ago a white plaster statue of the Virgin, shaggy with moss, stood on the vault.

In 1833 the worst of all Spanish kings died and some of the Bordeaux exiles decided to go home. Had it not been for them Goya might be as neglected as Paret, Mengs, and the Bayeu brothers. The Spanish government evidently didn't care and only three Goya paintings were displayed at the Prado. The museum thought so little of his work that *Dos de Mayo, Tres de Mayo,* and the great portrait of Charles IV with his family had been stacked in the reserve collection.

Delacroix, Merimée, Victor Hugo, Daumier, Millet—these and other French artists-writers-intellectuals seem to have been among the first to appreciate Goya. Maybe because of them King Louis-Philippe handed Baron Isidore Taylor a bag of gold and dispatched him to Spain. Baron Taylor returned with quite a few choice items, several bought from Goya's descendants.

In 1838 the Louvre opened a Spanish gallery to show Goya along with El Greco, Velázquez, and less exalted masters. Not everybody applauded.

Why? asked a satirical magazine, *Le Charivari,* have this man's paintings been acquired? A caricaturist? Oui! The fellow is droll. Serious artist? Non!

Glendinning quotes the 1849 judgment of Gustave Deville who

thought an artist ought to play a cohesive role in society. Goya, alas, degraded his work because of a preoccupation with squalid emotions—"hardly the proper role for an artist of undoubted ability, who, had he made the effort, might have become a leading figure in European art."

Thirty-five years after his death the Royal Academy of San Fernando published the complete *Desastres de la Guerra* and a year later the *Disparates.* Until then only a few isolated proofs had been circulating. Flutters of interest, yes, but no realization that, M. Deville notwithstanding, Goya was enormously influential.

Not until the fiftieth anniversary of his death, 1878, did anybody think about bringing his body home. Alfonso XII approved—it may have been his idea—but Alfonso died while the project was being discussed or negotiated.

In 1885 the Spanish ambassador and the Spanish consul at Bordeaux obtained permission to convey Goya's body to Spain.

Whoever opened the tomb must have gotten a terrific shock. Side by side lay two cadavers, intermingled because the wood had rotted. One skull, thought to be that of Goya, was missing. The Spanish consul, Don Joaquín Pereyra, had noticed ten years earlier that the tomb was disintegrating. Also, La Grande Chartreuse is a large cemetery and the Muguiro vault stood in a remote sector flanked by an alley called Rue Coupe-Gorge—Cut-Throat Street—suggesting that in times past the neighborhood seldom was visited at night. Grave robbers could go about their business undisturbed.

What to do with a couple of intermingled cadavers? Instructions from Spain were not forthcoming. After a year Goya and his friend returned to the tomb.

Vasari wrote in 1568 that men of genius could expect to be honored by their contemporaries as well as by posterity. Chabrun, less romantic, wrote in 1965 that an artist's reputation usually depends upon criteria different from those that enable his work to survive after his death: "Thus, a certain length of time must elapse before we can forget his immediate fame and rediscover a creative personality which his contemporaries would be surprised to find us appreciating for qualities which they themselves discounted."

20

In 1849 a young artist from Navarre, Dionisio Fierros, painted Goya's skull. On the back of the frame in handwriting identified as that of the fifth Marqués de San Adrián by one scholar, by another as that of the sixth Marqués, was this attribution:

Skull of Goya
painted by Fierros

This painting hung on a wall of the San Adrián mansion at Tudela for some years. A Saragossa junk dealer bought it at auction in 1928. Saragossa civic authorities then obtained it for the regional museum. From there it moved to the Ateneo in Madrid. Historians continue to debate its authenticity. They point to the cranium, traditional abode of sensibility and intellect. The Fierros cranium suggests a rather undeveloped man.

In 1966 the Madrid weekly *Semana* covered an exhibition of Fierros' paintings, which renewed public interest in Goya's skull. The San Adrián mansion, long vacant, was searched for clues. And it was learned that Fierros owned the skull and that it was to be enshrined under glass in his studio. Quite obviously he thought it was the real McCoy. His son and heir, Nicolás, who became an anatomist at the University of Salamanca, is known to have inspected the skull, "from which he extracted at least one of the parietal bones." Nicolás might have known how his father got the skull, but in 1894 he died unexpectedly.

Another of the painter's descendants, Dionisio Gamallo Fierros, was interviewed for an article in the Madrid newspaper *El Español,* February 20, 1943. He stated that the skull remained in his grandmother's possession until 1910 or thereabouts when it was broken up by some anatomy student who didn't realize what he was destroying. "All the fragments were dispersed, except two, which he still possesses."

Who stole it from La Grande Chartreuse? If not the painter Fierros, if not the fifth or sixth Marqués, who should be suspected? Disciples of Gall and Spurzheim, according to one theory. Gall and Spurzheim, gurus of phrenology, a pseudoscience that entranced millions of eighteenth-century Europeans and Americans. The mind consists of separate, localized faculties, each being seated in a particular enclave of the brain. To what extent each has developed may be judged by the shape of the skull. Hence, by applying calipers to lumps and depressions, the puzzles of human behavior may be solved.

Or it may be that Alcalophiles made off with Goya's skull—those lovers of ugliness he met in 1797 while at work on the *Caprichos.* Now we have a theory reeking of decadent worship. Candles at midnight in secluded temples. Reliquaries. Incense. Death often has been called the patron saint of Spain and Wyndham Lewis wrote with mordant wit: "Misadventure to illustrious corpses seems likewise peculiar to hispanity."

After the church of San Francisco el Grande was declared a national pantheon in the 1860s archaeologists went looking for whatever remained of Cervantes, Velázquez, Murillo, Lope de Vega, Herrera, Tirso de Molina, Mariana, and other notables from the Golden Age. Heaps of bones were examined. Not much could be verified, only the skeletons of Garcilaso de la Vega, Quevedo, and Calderón de la Barca.

No matter who stole Goya's head, or why, how did it get from La

Grande Chartreuse in Bordeaux to Saragossa or Tudela or wherever it first appeared in Spain?

The Goicoechea tomb was opened again in 1899. At last Goya would return. But now the skeletons were hopelessly mingled. Those in charge decided that if all the remains were sent to Spain nobody could argue that the great artist was left behind. Therefore, Goya and his friend were dispatched to Madrid for burial in the cemetery of San Isidro. According to one scholar they arrived on June 6, 1899. We might assume that in a day or so, surely no more than a week, Goya and Goicoechea would be reinterred, the long journey complete. Wrong. Not until May 11, 1900, were the remains placed in a mausoleum at San Isidro alongside Menéndez Valdés and Leandro Moratín.

Now, certainly, Goya and his friend could rest in peace.

Wrong. Spanish authorities felt that the church of San Antonio de la Florida would be more appropriate, considering that he had painted the ceiling. However, there was a problem. Tourists crowded San Antonio. Besides, it was a parish church which meant incense and burning tapers, which meant the frescoes little by little were being damaged. How to proceed? First, San Antonio must be classified as an historic structure—which might not seem necessary, but that's how it was. This took a while. Quite a while. Five years. What next?

Four years drifted by while government functionaries meditated, but in 1909 a committee of academicians was appointed to study and evaluate the circumstances under which services were conducted, to inspect the frescoes, and to submit a report. This report, titled *Estado de las pinturas de la iglesia de San Antonio* . . . was published with amazing speed in 1910 in the Bulletin of the Royal Academy.

One year later the Bulletin emphasized the necessity of constructing another church for parishioners. This, naturally, would reduce the number of people squeezing into Goya's church.

So far, so good.

In 1915, authorities called for a report on the state of the frescoes, whereupon the committee of academicians prepared a statement: *Informe acerca del procedimiento empleado por Don Francisco Goya en las pinturas decorativas* . . .

By 1918 the project was dashing ahead. Funds were raised through public subscription to erect a new church, identical in every respect, alongside Goya's church. The municipality of Madrid contributed. The federal government contributed.

Eight years later the Municipality, which owned the land in question, made this property available.

May 14, 1928. By authority of the King, ownership of Goya's church was transferred to the Royal Academy with a proviso that henceforth it should be known as the Hermitage of San Antonio de la Florida and Panthéon of Goya. And should you wish a better understanding of what was required to accomplish this, consult *Proceedings of the Royal Academy of San Fernando of 1927–8*.

Sometime during the 1920s civic officials commissioned a granite head of Goya by the prominent sculptor Juan Cristóbal. It stood on a pedestal outside the old church, facing the Moncloa road, but during the 1936–39 civil war it was damaged. Then it disappeared.

Scholars continue to argue about the date on which he was moved from San Isidro to San Antonio. November 29, 1919? November 19? Who cares? Most visitors want to know whose bones rest beneath the cupola. Goya? Yes, although not entirely. Martín Goicoechea? He may be represented. Whatever the fact, it seems unlikely the tomb will be reopened. Still, who could guess that in 1945 pathologists would examine the mummified Duchess of Alba?

Just north of the royal palace stands the Hermitage of San Antonio, close to the Manzanares. Goya experimented with several ideas for the miraculous resurrection and Madrileños believe the Duchess very often stopped her carriage to watch the paint-spattered artist at work. They see her as one of the figures around Saint Anthony. That one in a red skirt, they say, that's Goya's maja.

Under a blue and gold and scarlet canopy rests a decapitated skeleton. Goya waits for her, Madrileños tell you. The Duchess is late, so Goya waits for her.

Baudelaire said he painted the black magic of our civilization.

SELECT BIBLIOGRAPHY

Abbruzzese, Margherita. *Goya*. Translated by Caroline Beamish. London, 1967.

Adhemar, Jean. *Goya*. Translated by Denys Sutton and David Weston. Paris, 1948.

Anderson, Janice. *Life and Works of Goya*. Avenmouth, Bristol, 1996.

Barbarrosa, Mercedes. *The Living Goya*. Boston, 1939.

Baticle, Jeannine. *Goya: Painter of Terrible Splendor*. Translated by Alexandra Campbell. New York, 1994.

Berganini, John D. *The Spanish Bourbons*. New York, 1974.

Beruete y Moret, Aúreliano de. *Goya As Portrait Painter*. Translated by Selwyn Brinton. London, 1922.

Bihalji-Merín, Oto. *Goya Then and Now*. Translated by John E. Woods. New York, 1981.

Blackburn, Julia. *Old Man Goya*. New York, 2002.

Bucholz, Elks Linda. *Goya*. Translated by Phil Greenhead. Cologne, 1999.

Calvert, Albert F. *Francisco Goya: Painter of Kings and Demons*. New York, 1974.

Cary, Joyce. *Art and Reality*. Garden City, New York, 1961.

Casanova, Jacques. *Memoirs*. Edited by Madeleine Boyd. New York, 1929.

_____. *Memoirs*. Translated by Arthur Machen. New York, 1961.

Chabrun, Jean-François. *Goya*. New York, 1965.

Ciofalo, John J. *Self-Portraits of Francisco Goya.* Cambridge, 2001.

Crastre, François. *Goya.* Translated by Frederic Taber Cooper. New York, 1914.

Craven, Thomas. *Men of Art.* New York, 1940.

Derwent, Lord George. *Goya: An Impression of Spain.* London, 1931.

De Salas, Xavier. *Goya.* Translated by G. T. Culverwell. Milan, 1978.

Descargues, Pierre. *Goya.* New York, 1979.

Edwards, Samuel. *The Double Lives of Francisco de Goya.* New York, 1973.

Formaggio, Dino. *Goya.* New York, 1961.

Gassier, Pierre. *Goya.* Translated by James Emmons. Cleveland, 1955.

Gassier, Pierre, and Juliet Wilson. *Francisco Goya: Life and Complete Works.* New York, 1971.

Gautier, Théophile. *Travels in Spain.* Translated by F. C. DeSumichrast. New York, 1910.

Glendinning, Nigel. *The Interpretation of Goya's Black Paintings.* London, 1975.

_____. *Goya and His Critics.* London, 1977.

Gudiol, José. *Goya.* Translated by Patricia Muller. New York, 1965.

Guillaud, Jacqueline, and Maurice Guillaud. *Goya: The Phantasmal Vision.* New York, 1987.

Guillou, Jean-François. *Great Paintings of the World.* Godalming, England, 1999.

Hara, Jacqueline, trans. *Francisco Goya: Letters of Love and Friendship.* Lampeter, Wales, 1997.

Harris, Enriqueta. *Goya.* London, 1971.

Herr, Richard. *The Eighteenth-Century Revolution in Spain.* Princeton, 1958.

Holland, Lady Elizabeth. *The Spanish Journal.* London, 1910.

Holland, Vyvyan. *Goya.* New York, 1961.

Hull, Anthony. *Goya: Man Among Kings.* London, 1987.

Hume, Martin. *Modern Spain.* London, 1900.

Huxley, Aldous. *On Art and Artists.* New York, 1960.

Klingender, F. D. *Goya in the Democratic Tradition.* New York, 1968.

Lafuente Ferrari, Enrique. *Goya: The Frescos in San Antonio de la Florida.* Translated by Stuart Gilbert. Geneva, 1955.

Las Casas, Bartolomé de. *Devastation of the Indies.* Translated by Herma Briffault. Introduction by Hans Magnus Enzenberger. Translated by Michael Roloff. New York, 1974.

Lassaigne, Jacques. *Goya.* Translated by Rosamund Frost. New York, 1948.

LePore, Mario. *The Life & Times of Goya.* Translated by C. J. Richards. New York, 1967.

Lewis, D. B. Wyndham. *The World of Goya.* New York, 1968.

Licht, Fred, ed. *Goya in Perspective.* Englewood Cliffs, New Jersey, 1973.

————. *Origins of the Modern Temper.* New York, 1979.

Malraux, André. *Saturn: An Essay on Goya.* Translated by C. W. Chilton. New York, 1957.

————. *Goya.* Translated by Edward Sackville-West. London, 1947.

Muller, Priscilla E. *Goya's "Black" Paintings.* New York, 1984.

Myers, Bernard. *Goya.* London, 1968.

Nordström, Folke. *Goya, Saturn and Melancholy.* Stockholm, 1962.

Onieva, Antonio J. *Spanish Painting in the Prado Gallery.* Translated by John MacNab Calder. Madrid, 1957.

Petrie, Sir Charles. *King Charles III of Spain.* New York, 1971.

Poore, Charles. *Goya.* London, 1938.

Rapelli, Paola. *Goya.* Translated by Emma Foa. New York, 1999.

Rothenstein, Sir William. *Goya.* London, 1901.

Sánchez, Alfonso Pérez. *Goya.* Translation by Alexandra Campbell. New York, 1990.

Sánchez Cantón, Francisco J. *The Prado.* New York, 1959.

————. *Life and Works of Goya.* Translated by Paul Burns. Madrid, 1964.

Schickel, Richard. *The World of Goya.* New York, 1968.

Sencourt, Robert. *The Spanish Crown 1808–1931.* New York, 1932

Starkweather, William E. B. *Paintings and Drawings By Francisco Goya.* New York, 1916.

Stearns, Monroe. *Goya and His Times.* New York, 1966.

Stoichita, Victor, and Coderch, Anna. *Goya: The Last Carnival.* Translated by Anne Glasheen. London, 1999.

Stokes, Hugh. *Francisco Goya.* London, 1914.

Sullivan, Edward J. *Goya and the Arts of His Time.* Dallas, 1983.

Symmons, Sarah. *Goya: In Pursuit of Patronage.* London, 1988.

————. *Goya.* London, 1998.

Thomas, Hugh. *Goya: The Third of May 1808.* New York, 1972.

Tomlinson, Janis. *The Tapestry Cartoons and Early Career At the Court Of Madrid.* New York, 1989.

————. *Goya in the Twilight of Enlightenment.* New Haven, 1992.

_____, ed. *Images of Women.* Washington, D.C., 2002.

Trapier, Elizabeth du Gué. *Goya: A Study of His Portraits.* New York, 1955.

Vallentin, Antonina. *This I Saw: the Life and Times of Goya.* Translated by Katherine Woods. Westport, Connecticut, 1949.

Vasari, Giorgio. *Lives of the Artists.* Translated by George Bull. New York, 1965.

Virch, Claus. *Goya.* New York, 1967.

Waldmann, Susann. *Goya and the Duchess of Alba.* Translated by John Gabriel. Munich, 1998.

Wilson-Bareau, Juliet, and Mena Marqués, Manuela B. *Goya: Truth and Fantasy.* New Haven, 1994.

Wolf, Reva. *Goya and the Satirical Print in England and on the Continent, 1730–1850.* Boston, 1991.